As a child **Sarah Morgan** dreamed of being a writer and, although she took a few interesting detours on the way, she is now living that dream. With her writing career she has successfully combined business with pleasure, and she firmly believes that reading romance is one of the most satisfying and fat-free escapist pleasures available. Her stories are unashamedly optimistic, and she is always pleased when she receives letters from readers saying that her books have helped them through hard times.

Sarah lives near London with her husband and two children, who innocently provide an endless supply of authentic dialogue. When she isn't writing or reading Sarah enjoys music, movies, and any activity that takes her outdoors.

Readers can find out more about Sarah and her books from her website: www.sarahmorgan.com. She can also be found on Facebook and Twitter.

For my parents, with love.

And thanks to my children for providing endless authentic dialogue and for proving that any bed can be broken if you bounce hard enough.

To Julia, for her friendship, brainstorming skills and staying power.

Wish Upon a Star

Sarah Morgan

All the characters in this book have no existence outside the imagination
of the author, and have no relation whatsoever to anyone bearing the same
name or names. They are not even distantly inspired by any individual
known or unknown to the author, and all the incidents are pure invention.

Mills & Boon, an imprint of Harlequin (UK) Limited,
Eton House, 18-24 Paradise Road, Richmond, Surrey TW9 1SR

Wish Upon a Star © Harlequin Enterprises II B.V./S.à.r.l. 2011

Originally published as *The Christmas Marriage Rescue* © Sarah Morgan
2006 and *The Midwife's Christmas Miracle* © Sarah Morgan 2006

ISBN: 978 0 263 88999 4

024-1011

Printed and bound by
CPI Group (UK) Ltd, Croydon, CR0 4YY

CHRISTY

PROLOGUE

'MUM, where are we spending Christmas?'

Christy glanced up from the letter she was reading. 'I don't know. Here, I suppose, with Uncle Pete and your cousins. Why do you ask? Christmas is ages away.' And she was trying not to think about it. Christmas was a time for families and hers appeared to be disintegrating.

And it was all her fault. She'd done a *really* stupid thing and now they were all paying the price.

'Christmas is a month away. Not ages.' Katy leaned across the table and snatched the cereal packet from her little brother. 'And I don't want to stay here. I love Uncle Pete, but I hate London. I want to spend Christmas with Dad in the Lake District. I want to go home.'

Christy felt her insides knot with anguish. They wanted to spend Christmas with their father? She just couldn't begin to imagine spending Christmas without the children. 'All right.' Her voice was husky and she cleared her throat. 'Of course, that's fine, if you're sure that's what you want.' *Oh, dear God, how would she survive?* What would Christmas morning be without the children? 'I'll write to your father and tell him that you're both coming up to stay. You might need to spend some time at Grandma's because Daddy will be working at the hospital, of course, and it's always a busy time for the mountain rescue team and—'

'Not just us.' Katy reached for the sugar. 'I didn't mean that we go without you. That would be hideous. I meant that we all go.'

'What do you mean, all? And that's enough sugar, Katy. You'll rot your teeth.'

'They go into *holes*,' Ben breathed, with the gruesome delight of a seven-year-old. He picked up the milk jug and tried to pour milk into his cup but succeeded in slopping most of it over the table. 'I learned about it in school last week. You eat sugar, you get *holes*. Then the dentist has to drill a bigger hole and fill it with cement.'

'You are so lame! What do you know about anything, anyway?' Katy threw her brother a disdainful look and doubled the amount of sugar she was putting on her cereal. 'Stupid, idiot baby.'

'I'm not a baby! I'm seven!' Ben shot out of his chair and made a grab at his sister, who immediately put her hands round his throat.

'*Why* did I have to be lumbered with a brother?'

'Stop it, you two! Not his throat, Katy,' Christy admonished, her head starting to thump as she reached for a cloth and mopped up the milk on the table. 'You know that you don't put anything round each other's throats. You might strangle him.'

'That was the general idea,' Katy muttered, glaring at Ben before picking up her spoon and digging into her cereal. 'Anyway, as I was saying. I don't want Ben and I to go home for Christmas, I want all three of us to go.'

The throb in Christy's head grew worse and she rose to

her feet in search of paracetamol. 'This is home now, sweet-heart.' Thanks to her stupidity. 'London is home now.'

As if to remind herself of that depressing fact, she stared out of the window of their tiny flat, through the sheeting rain and down into the road below. There was a steady hiss as the traffic crawled along the wet, cheerless street. Brick buildings, old, tired and in need of repainting, rose up high, blocking out what there was of the restrained winter light. People shouted abuse and leaned on their horns and all the time the rain fell steadily, dampening streets and spirits with equal effectiveness. On the pavement people jostled and dodged, ears glued to mobile phones, walking and talking, eyes straight ahead, no contact with each other.

And then, just for a moment, the reality disappeared and Christy had a vision of the Lake District. Her real home. The sharp edges of the fells rising up against a perfectly blue sky on a crisp winter morning. The clank of metal and the sound of laughter as the mountain rescue team prepared for another callout. Friendship.

Oh, dear God, she didn't want to be here. *This wasn't how it was supposed to have turned out.*

As if picking up her mood, Ben's face crumpled as he flopped back into his chair. 'It isn't home. It'll never be home, it's horrid and I hate it. I hate London, I hate school and most of all I hate you.' And with that he scraped his chair away from the table and belted out of the door, sobbing noisily, leaving his cereal untouched.

Feeling sick with misery, Christy watched him go, sup-pressing a desperate urge to follow and give him a cuddle but knowing from experience that it was best to let him calm down in his own time. She sat back down at the table and tried to revive her flagging spirits. It was seven-thirty in the morning, she had to get two children to a school that they hated and she had to go on to a job that she hated, too. What on earth was she doing?

She topped up her coffee-cup and tried to retrieve the situation. 'London at Christmas will be pretty cool.'

Katy shot her a pitying look. 'Mum, *don't* try and communicate on my level. It's tragic when grown-ups do that. *I* can say cool, but it sounds ridiculous coming from anyone over the age of sixteen. Use grown-up words like "interesting" or "exciting". Leave "cool" and "wicked" to those of us who appreciate the true meaning.' With all the vast superiority of her eleven years, she pushed her bowl to one side and reached for a piece of toast. 'And, anyway, it won't be cool. The shopping's good, but you can only do so much of that.'

Christy wondered whether she ought to point out that so far her daughter hadn't shown any signs of tiring of that particular occupation but decided that the atmosphere around the breakfast table was already taut enough. 'I can't go back to the Lake District this Christmas,' she said finally, and Katy lifted the toast to her lips.

'Why not? Because you and Dad have had a row?' She shrugged. 'What's new?'

Christy bit her lip and reflected on the challenges of having a daughter who was growing up and saw too much. She picked up her coffee-cup, determined to be mature about the whole thing. 'Katy, we didn't—'

'Yes, you did, but it's hardly surprising, is it? He's Spanish and you're half-Irish with red hair. Uncle Pete says that makes for about as explosive combination as it's possible to get. I suppose things might have been different if you'd been born a blonde.' Katy chewed thoughtfully. 'Amazing, really, that the two of you managed to get it together for long enough to produce us.'

Christy choked on her coffee and made a mental note to have a sharp talk with her brother. 'Katy, that's enough.'

'I'm just pointing out that the fact that you two can't be in a room without trying to kill each other is no reason to keep us down here in London. We hate it, Mum. It's great seeing Uncle Pete but a short visit is plenty. You hate it, too, I know you do.'

Was it that obvious? 'I have a job here.' In the practice where her brother worked as a GP. And it was fine, she told herself firmly. Fine. Perfectly adequate. She was lucky to have it.

'You're a nurse, Mum. You can get a job anywhere.'

Oh, to be a child again, when everything seemed so simple and straightforward. 'Katy—'

'Just for Christmas. Please? Don't you miss Dad?'

The knot was back in her stomach. Christy closed her eyes and saw dark, handsome features. An arrogant, possessive smile and a mouth that could bring her close to madness. *Oh, yes.* Oh, yes, she missed him dreadfully. And, at this distance, some of her anger had faded. But the hurt was still there. All right, so she'd been stupid but she wouldn't have done it if he hadn't been so—so *aggravating.* 'I can't discuss my relationship with your father with you.'

'I'm eleven,' Katy reminded her. 'I know about relationships. And I know that the two of you are stubborn.'

He hadn't contacted her. Pride mingled with pain and Christy pressed her lips together to stop a sob escaping. He was *supposed* to have followed her. Dragged her back. He was supposed to have fought for what they had. But he hadn't even been in touch except when they made arrangements about the children. *He didn't care that she'd gone.* The knowledge sat like a heavy weight in her heart and stomach. Suddenly she felt a ridiculous urge to confide in her child but she knew that she couldn't do that, no matter how grown-up Katy seemed. 'I can't spend Christmas with your father.'

She'd started this but she didn't know how to finish it. He was supposed to have finished it. He was supposed to have come after her. That was why she'd left. To try and make him listen. 'A wake-up call', a marriage counsellor would probably call it.

'If I have a row with one of my friends you always say, "Sit down, Katy, and discuss it like a grown-up."' Katy rolled her eyes, her imitation next to perfect. 'And what do you do? You move to opposite ends of the country. Hardly a good example to set, is it?'

Christy stiffened and decided that some discipline was called for. 'I'm not sure I like your tone.'

'And I'm not sure I like being the product of a broken home.' Katy finished her toast and took a sip from her glass of milk. 'Goodness knows what it will do to me. You read about it every day in the papers. There's a strong chance I'm going to go off the rails. Theft. Pregnancy—'

Christy banged her cup down onto the table. 'What do you know about pregnancy?'

Katy shot her a pitying look. 'Oh, get a life, Mum. I know plenty.'

'You do?' She just wasn't ready to handle this stage of child development on her own, Christy thought weakly. She needed Alessandro. She needed—

Oh, help…

'And don't write to him. Ring him up.' Katy glanced at the clock and stood up, ponytail swinging. 'We'd better go or we'll be late. The traffic never moves in this awful place. I've never spent so many hours standing still in my whole life and I don't think I can stand it any more. I'll ring him if you're too cowardly.'

'I'm not cowardly.' Or maybe she was. He hadn't rung her. Gorgeous, sexy Alessandro, who was always wrapped up in his job or his role on the mountain rescue team, always the object of a million women's fantasies. Once she'd been wrapped up in the same things but then the children had come and somehow she'd been left behind...

And he didn't notice her any more. He didn't have time for their relationship. *For her.*

'Ben's upstairs, crying. I'm here eating far too much sugar and you're ingesting a lethal dose of caffeine,' Katy said dramatically as she walked to the door, her performance worthy of the London stage. 'We're a family in crisis. We need our father or *goodness knows* what might happen to us.'

Christy didn't know whether to laugh or cry. 'You haven't finished your milk,' she said wearily. 'All right, I'll talk to him. See what he says.'

It would be just for the festive season, she told herself. The children shouldn't suffer because of her stupidity and Alessandro's arrogant, stubborn nature.

'Really?'

'Really.'

'Yay!' Katy punched the air, her ponytail swinging. 'We're going back to the Lake District for Christmas. Snow. Rain. Howling winds. I'll see my old friends. My phone bill will plummet. Thanks Mum, you're the best.'

As she danced out of the room, no doubt *en route* to pass the joyful news on to her brother, Christy felt her stomach sink down to her ankles. Now all she had to do was summon the courage to phone Alessandro and tell him that they were planning to return home for Christmas.

How on earth was she going to do that?

CHAPTER ONE

'EMERGENCY on its way in, Mr Garcia.' The pretty nurse stuck her head round the office door. 'You're needed in Resus.'

Alessandro dropped the report on staffing that he was reading and wondered how many times a day he heard that statement. He was always needed in Resus. Sometimes he felt as though he lived in Resus. Particularly at the moment when almost forty per cent of the staff were off with flu.

He strode out of his office, nodded to one of the A and E sisters who hurried past him, looking harassed, and shouldered his way through the double doors into Resus.

Chaos reigned.

'She's bleeding from somewhere, we need to find out where.' Billy, one of the casualty officers, was trying to direct operations and he looked up with a sigh of relief as Alessandro appeared by the side of the trolley. 'Oh, Mr Garcia. Thank goodness. Dr Nicholson is already tied up with that climbing accident and—'

'What's the story?' Alessandro cut him off and Billy sucked in a breath.

'Her husband brought her in by car. She was complaining of abdominal pain all night and he was driving quickly in an attempt to get her here and took the car into the ditch.' Clearly out of his comfort zone, he dragged a hand through his hair, leaving it more untidy than ever. 'She's had a bang on her head and her obs suggests that she's bleeding but we don't know where from.'

Alessandro took the gloves that a nurse was holding out to him and made a mental note to speak to Billy about the quality of his handover skills at some point in the near future.

'Does "she" have a name?' he enquired softly and Billy coloured.

'Megan. Megan Yates.'

Alessandro swiftly dragged on the gloves and turned to the woman who was lying on the trolley, noted her pale, blood-streaked cheeks and the fear in her eyes. 'Megan, this must be very frightening for you, but you're in hospital now and we're going to make you comfortable as quickly as we can.' He lifted his gaze to Billy. 'Bleep the on-call gynae team,' he instructed calmly, donning the rest of the necessary protective clothing and glancing at the monitor. 'We need to keep an eye on her pulse and blood pressure.'

Her pulse was up, her blood pressure was dropping and she was showing all the signs of haemorrhage. But, unlike his less experienced colleague, he had no intention of sharing his concerns with an already worried patient.

Billy followed his gaze. 'The gynae team?' His tone was level but his expression was confused. 'I thought after an RTA and trauma, she'd need—'

'And she's of childbearing age, and before her husband landed the car in the ditch she was suffering from abdominal pain,' Alessandro reminded him, 'so that is not to be forgotten. I want two lines in her straight away, wide-bore cannulae.'

Responding immediately to his decisive tone, Nicky, one of the A and E sisters, pushed a trolley across Resus and Billy put a tourniquet on the woman's arm and ripped open the first cannula. 'You think she might have a ruptured ectopic?'

'I don't know yet, but let's just say I have a low threshold of suspicion so I'm treating it as that until I have reason to think otherwise.' Alessandro continued to deliver a steady stream of instructions while the staff around him bobbed and moved in perfect unison. They were so used to working together that they often anticipated each other's needs. He turned back to his patient. 'Megan, is there any chance that you could be pregnant?'

'No—well, I mean...' The woman closed her eyes briefly. 'It's so unlikely it's virtually impossible.'

'In this department we deal with the unlikely and the impossible on a fairly regular basis,' Alessandro replied with a wry smile. 'When was your last period?'

'Months ago,' she whispered. 'I have endometriosis.'

He heard the catch in her voice and put a hand on her shoulder. 'That must be hard for you,' he said gently. 'But right now we need to find out what injuries you suffered in the accident and try and get to the bottom of your abdominal pain. We need to undress you so that we can do a proper examination, head to toe, and find out exactly what is going on. Nicky?'

Nicky was already removing clothes, fingers and scissors moving swiftly as Alessandro started his examination.

'Where's her husband?' He was checking the body methodically, on the alert for anything life-threatening. 'Was he injured?'

'He's fine,' Billy muttered as he successfully put the second line in and taped it in place. 'Waiting in the relatives' room. Nicky put him there.'

'She has a nasty laceration of her shoulder.' Nicky reached for a sterile pad while Alessandro examined it swiftly.

'That's going to need stitching but it can wait,' he murmured, his gaze sliding to the monitor again. 'Her pressure is still dropping. I want to know why. And I want to know now. Did someone bleep the gynae team?'

'On their way,' a staff nurse reported and Alessandro's eyes narrowed.

He didn't like the look of his patient.

'Oh...' Nicky finished cutting off the woman's clothes and her face reflected shock before she quickly masked it. 'We have some blood loss here, Alessandro.'

One glance was all it took for him to measure the degree of the understatement. 'Fast-bleep Jake Blackwell,' he ordered in a calm voice. 'Cross-match six units of blood and get her rhesus status. We may need to give her anti-D. And someone get a blanket on her before she gets hypothermia.'

Jake Blackwell, the consultant obstetrician, strode into the room minutes later. 'You need my advice, Garcia? Struggling?' His eyes mocked but Alessandro was too worried about his patient to take the bait.

'I need you to do some work for a change,' he drawled, but although his tone was casual and relaxed, his eyes were sharp and alert and his handover to his colleague was so succinct that Billy threw him a look of admiration.

Jake listened, examined the woman swiftly and then nodded, all traces of humour gone. 'Megan, it looks as though you might have an ectopic pregnancy—that means that the egg has implanted somewhere other than your uterus and, in your case, it seems that it may have done some damage that we need to put right with an operation.' He lifted his eyes to Alessandro. 'She's going to need surgery. We'll take her straight to Theatre. Damn. I'm supposed to be somewhere else. I need to make a couple of calls—speak to the anaesthetist, juggle my list.'

Alessandro leaned across and increased the flow of both the oxygen and the IV himself. 'Just so long as you juggle it quickly. We'll transfer her to Theatre while you do what you need to do. Her husband is in our relatives' room if you want to tackle the issue of consent.'

'Great.' Jake walked to the phone and punched in a number while Alessandro monitored his patient.

'Phone down and get that blood sent up to Theatre as soon as it's available,' he ordered, and Nicky hurried to the nearest phone to do as he'd instructed.

Minutes later the woman was on her way to Theatre and Jake disappeared to talk to her husband.

He reappeared in the department hours later, after Alessandro had dealt with what felt like a million road accidents, intermingled with a significant number of people with flu.

'Why don't people stay in bed when they have flu?' he grumbled as Jake appeared in the doorway of his office. 'For a start, if they can get out of bed then it isn't flu and it certainly isn't an accident or an emergency. Why come to a hospital and spread it around?'

'Because they're generous?' Jake strolled into the office and dropped onto the nearest chair without even bothering to move the pile of files that were covering it. 'Hell, I'm knackered. I've spent the whole day in Theatre saving lives. One drama after another. You don't know you're born, working down here.'

Alessandro thought of the two major RTAs, the heart attack and the sickle-cell crisis he'd dealt with since lunchtime. And the only way he'd known it had been lunchtime had been because he'd looked at the clock on the wall. He hadn't eaten for hours. 'That's right. I spend my life sitting on my backside.'

'Backside?' Jake grinned. 'That doesn't sound like a particularly Spanish word, *amigo*.'

Feeling tired and bad-tempered, Alessandro scowled at him. 'Haven't you got anything better to do with your time than sit in my office, moaning?'

'Actually, I came down to see if you fancy grabbing a couple of beers after work. I have a feeling that our problems are nothing that alcohol can't fix.'

Alessandro pulled a face. 'Not tonight.'

Jake yawned. 'You working late?'

'I'm cleaning up the house.' Alessandro felt the tension rise inside him. 'Christy and the kids are arriving tomorrow for Christmas. I need to throw out four months' worth of take-away cartons and fill the fridge with broccoli or she'll hit the roof. You know Christy and her obsession with nutrition.'

Jake stared, his blue eyes suddenly keen and interested. 'You guys are back together?'

'No. We're not back together.' Alessandro all but snapped the words out, his anger suddenly so close to the surface that his fingers tightened on the pencil he was holding and broke it in two. 'We're spending Christmas in the same house for the sake of the kids.'

'I see.' Jake's eyes rested on the broken pencil, his expression thoughtful. 'Well, that promises to be a peaceful Christmas, then. Better warn Santa to wear his flak jacket when he flies over your barn. Wouldn't want him to be caught in flying shrapnel as you two tear bits off each other.'

Alessandro thought about all the occasions he'd seen

Christy in the last six weeks. Brief occasions when they'd handed over the children. They'd barely spoken, let alone rowed. 'It isn't like that any more.' Christmas promised to be as icy cold as the weather and Alessandro was suddenly struck by inspiration. 'Why don't you join us? You're their godfather.'

Jake nodded. 'I might do that if I can drag myself away from the irresistible lure of this place. You know how I am with cold hospital turkey and lumpy gravy. I've been trying to break myself of the addiction for years.' He stretched his legs out in front of him. 'You know, about this thing that's going on with you and Christy—'

'There's nothing going on. We're separated and that's all there is to it. And I don't want to talk about it.' Alessandro's gaze was shuttered and Jake sighed.

'I just hate to see the two of you like this. You're my best friends and if anyone was ever meant to be together, it's you two. You should hang onto what you've got. It's hard enough finding anyone you get on vaguely well with in this world. Christy was crazy about you, right from day one. And you were crazy about her. I remember the day you guys met—'

'I said, I don't want to talk about it,' Alessandro said coldly, his dark eyes stormy and threatening as he rose to his feet and paced over to the window, angry with Jake for stirring up memories that he'd spent ages trying to bury. *How could he ever forget the day he'd first met Christy?*

He stared out of the window. Outside, snow lay thick on the ground, disguising the usually familiar landscape. In the distance the fells rose. He studied their familiar jagged lines and then turned, his volatile Mediterranean temper bubbling to the surface. 'She left me.'

'I know.' Jake's voice was soft. 'I wonder why she felt she had to do that?'

Alessandro's jaw tensed. 'If you're implying that any of this is my fault, you're wrong.'

'Christy adores you. She's crazy about you and always has been. If she left you, she must have been desperate,' Jake said quietly. 'She must have felt there was no other way to get through to you.'

'That's ridiculous. She could have talked to me.'

Jake's expression was inscrutable. 'Could she? Did you make yourself available?'

Alessandro sucked in a frustrated breath. 'How could we talk when she left me?' He sounded impossibly Spanish and Jake gave a wry smile.

'So is that what this is all about?' His eyes narrowed. 'Pride? She was the one to walk away from you so you're not going to go after her? Why did she leave you, Al?' Jake's voice was calm as he rose to his feet. 'Try asking yourself that question while you're binning take-away cartons.'

And with that parting shot he left the room and closed the door quietly behind him.

Christy had changed her clothes a dozen times and in the end settled on a pencil skirt, a pair of heels and a blue jumper in the softest cashmere, which she'd bought in a small shop on the King's Road to cheer herself up. It hadn't worked, but she knew she looked good in it. And she wanted to remind Alessandro what he was missing. Not that she wanted them to get back together again, she told herself hastily, because she didn't. Oh, no. She wasn't that stupid.

Obviously he wasn't interested in her any more. Their marriage had worn itself out. He was an arrogant, selfish, macho workaholic who suited himself in life and clearly he didn't love her any more. If he'd loved her, he *never* would have let her leave.

As they drove deeper into Cumbria she saw the fells rise under a crown of snow and felt the tension leave her. The winter winds had dragged the last of the leaves from the trees and the sky was grey and menacing but it was wild and familiar. *It was home.*

Why, she wondered, had she thought that she could be happy in London? She'd never been a city girl. For her, life had always been about being outdoors. Being active and close to nature. When Christmas was over, she'd move back up here and find a job in the Lake District. There must be some other department she could work in that didn't have links with Alessandro. She didn't have to throw away everything she loved just because their relationship was on the rocks.

She needed to build a new life.

A life that didn't include Alessandro.

'Mum?' Ben's little voice whined from the back of the car, disturbing her thoughts. 'Are we there yet?'

'Nearly. Don't you recognise those trees?' Christy changed down a gear and took the sharp turning that led down the lane to the barn.

They'd discovered it during the second year of their marriage. Katy had been a baby and they'd both fallen in love with the potential of the old, tumble-down building bordered by fields and a fast-flowing river. They'd spent the next few years living on a building site while they'd lovingly turned it into their dream home.

And there it was, smoke rising from the chimney like a welcome beacon.

Christy swallowed and slowed the car. Except it wasn't a welcome, was it? Alessandro didn't want her any more. He'd made that perfectly clear. For him, their marriage was over. And the fact that they were about to spend three weeks together was everything to do with the children and nothing to do with them.

It was going to be something akin to torture.

She was going to be dignified, she reminded herself as she pulled the car up outside the front of the barn and switched off the engine. They were both civilised human beings. They could spend time together for the sake of their children.

She wasn't going to lose her temper. She wasn't going to show him how upset she was. She wasn't going to reveal that she wished she'd never left. She wasn't going to cry and most of all she wasn't going to let him know that she thought about him day and night.

But then the front door was pulled open and all her resolutions flew out of her head.

Alessandro stood there, his powerful, athletic body almost filling the doorway. He looked dark and dangerous and Christy caught her breath, just as she had on that very first day they'd met. One glance at those brooding dark eyes was enough to make her forget her own name. Wasn't time supposed to put a dent in sexual attraction? she thought helplessly. Wasn't she supposed to have become bored and indifferent over time? Well, it certainly hadn't happened in her case. But that was probably because Alessandro was no ordinary guy, she thought miserably as she switched off the engine and tried to slow the rhythmic thump of her heart. He was strong, unashamedly masculine, hotly sexual and almost indecently handsome. The combination was a killer and no woman would ever pass him by without giving a second and third look.

He stood now in his usual arrogant, self-confident pose, legs planted slightly apart, his hair gleaming glossy black in the fading winter sunlight, his shoulders broad and muscular under the thick, ribbed jumper. He wore scuffed walking boots and ancient jeans and she thought, with a lurch of her heart and a sick feeling in the pit of her stomach, that he'd never looked more attractive. And she had absolutely no doubt that other women felt the same way.

He was a red-blooded male with a high sex drive and they hadn't shared a bed for almost two months.

Had he taken a lover?

The thought flew into her head from nowhere and she pushed it away again, too sick at the thought to even dwell on the possibility.

'Dad!' Katy and Ben were out of the car before Christy had a chance to get herself together and suddenly she realised that they were doing what she wanted to do. She wanted to run and hug him. She wanted him to tell her that this was all a ridiculous misunderstanding and hear him tell her that everything was going to be all right.

And then she wanted him to take her to bed and fix everything.

But he didn't even glance towards the car. He just hugged the children and fussed over them, which meant that it was up to her to make the first move.

Thank goodness for the children, she thought miserably as she opened her car door. Because of them, they wouldn't have to spend time as a couple and clearly Alessandro didn't consider them to be a couple any more.

She strolled over to him, glad of the cashmere jumper. It was cold. Significantly colder than London.

He was still hugging the children but their eyes met over the top of two dark little heads.

'Christianne.' His voice was cool, his handsome face blank of expression, and suddenly she wanted to leap at him and claw him just to get a reaction.

How could he seem so indifferent?

How could he call her Christianne in that smooth, formal tone when he only ever called her Christy?

After everything they'd shared—*a fierce, perfect passion*—how could he be so cold towards her?

'Alessandro.' Rat. Snake, she thought to herself. How could you do this to me? *To us?*

'Good journey?' He had a trace of a Spanish accent that he'd never lost despite the fact he'd lived in England for the past twelve years. She'd always loved his accent but suddenly it just seemed like a reminder of the differences between them.

'Fine, thanks. Traffic was pretty heavy coming out of London, but I suppose that's to be expected at this time of year. First day of the Christmas holidays.' She almost winced as she heard herself talking. She sounded so formal. As if they were strangers rather than two people who had shared everything there had been to share for the last twelve years. Any moment now, they'd be shaking hands.

Fortunately Katy grabbed Ben and started to dance a jig. 'No more school,' she sang in a delighted voice. 'No more vile, horrid school with demented, stinky, bullying teachers.'

But Alessandro wasn't looking at the children. He was looking at her, with those hot, dark eyes that were a symbol of his Mediterranean heritage.

She saw his gaze slide down her body and rest on the high-heeled shoes; the shoes that had seemed so pretty in London and now felt utterly ridiculous with snow on the ground and the cold bite of winter in the air. In London, it hadn't felt like winter. It had just felt wet and miserable. The shoes had cheered her up. Given her confidence. *Reminded her that she was a woman.*

Noting his disdainful glance, her confidence evaporated

and she knew instinctively that he was thinking about all the people he'd had to rescue from the mountains because they'd been wearing ridiculous footwear. Suddenly she wanted to defend herself. To tell him that she wasn't walking anywhere but that the shoes made her legs look good and she'd wanted him to notice.

Suddenly nervous and not understanding why, she waved a hand at the fells. 'When did it snow?'

'A week ago.' His wry tone said it all and she looked back at him, noting the dark shadows under his eyes with a flash of surprise.

She knew that Alessandro had endless stamina. Why would he look tired?

'I suppose you've been really busy, then.' She almost laughed as she listened to herself. What a stupid thing to say. When was Alessandro ever not busy? Work was his life. As she'd discovered to her cost.

'The weather isn't helping.' He strode over to her car and retrieved the cases from the boot. 'I'm afraid I have to go back to the hospital after you've settled in.'

Katy groaned an instant protest. 'Daddy, no!'

'Sorry, *niña*.' Alessandro stooped and dropped a kiss on his daughter's head. 'There are lots of staff off sick, but I'm sure they'll be better soon. I'll have more time next week and we'll go climbing, that's a promise.'

Christy frowned as she followed him into the barn. 'You're not taking her climbing in this weather, Alessandro.'

'You used to climb in this weather.' His sardonic gaze made her heart tumble.

They'd argued about it so many times. When they'd first met, she'd been young and reckless. He'd been fiercely protective. Possessive. Hadn't wanted her out there in the mountains where danger might exist. And she'd teased him and gone anyway, loving the fact that he cared enough to want to stop her from doing anything remotely dangerous. Provoking him. *Pushing him to the edges of patience.*

'Well, I don't climb now.' Her life was so safe and boring that it was enough to make her scream. She frowned at the thought. It was funny, she mused, how your lifestyle could change so gradually that you didn't even notice it happening. One day you were hanging from a cliff by your fingernails and the next you were wading through a pile of ironing, listening to the radio.

How had it happened?

There'd been a time when she would have tugged on her walking boots and her weatherproof jacket and headed out into the hills without a backward glance. But all that had changed once the children had arrived.

Pushing aside the uncomfortable thought that her life was posing some questions she didn't want to answer, she walked past him into the house. 'Perhaps we'll talk about it later.' She tossed her hair out of her eyes. 'When you eventually come back from the hospital.'

The atmosphere snapped tight between them and Christy cursed herself. She hadn't intended to irritate or aggravate him. She'd wanted to be super-cool and indifferent in the same way that he was clearly indifferent to her.

If he wasn't indifferent, he would have followed her to London and talked about their problems.

He would have dragged her home where she belonged.

But he seemed to hurt her at every turn. Even now, by going straight back to the hospital, *by not wanting to be with her*, he was hurting her.

His eyes narrowed, his mouth tightened and his shoulders tensed. 'I'll take the cases up to your room.'

He sounded like a hotel concierge, Christy thought miserably as they trailed their way upstairs. Showing her around. Any minute now he'd be wishing her a pleasant stay. She'd expected anger and hostility, but what she hadn't expected was his coldness. She didn't know how to deal with coldness.

The children ran ahead, whooping and shrieking, excited about seeing their rooms again, oblivious of the rising tension between the two adults.

Envious of their carefree, uncomplicated approach to life, Christy watched them go. 'They're so pleased to be here,' she said softly, and Alessandro turned to her with something that was almost a growl.

'Of course they are pleased to be here. It's their home. They *never* should have left. And you never should have taken them!'

She inhaled sharply, shocked by the sharp stab of pain that lanced through her. He'd said that 'they' never should have left. He hadn't said anything about her. He didn't care about her. The only reason that he cared that she'd moved out was because he missed his children.

It was all about the children.

She felt a lump building in her throat and swallowed it down with an effort, reminding herself that she had to behave like an adult even though she wanted to break down and cry like a child.

'You're blaming me for this situation, Alessandro?'

'You're the one who decided to move out of the family home.'

It was only supposed to be temporary, she wanted to shout. *You were supposed to come after me.* But pride stopped her saying what she wanted to say. Pride and the knowledge that he hadn't cared enough to come after her.

Her eyes blazed into his. 'And that makes this my fault?'

'I missed one lousy anniversary.' His eyes flashed dark with frustration and he ran both hands through his hair. 'And you walked out.'

Christy bit her lip. He just didn't get it. He couldn't even understand why she was so upset. How had they come to this?

She swallowed hard. 'It wasn't about the anniversary, Alessandro.' Although that had hurt badly. 'It was so much more than that. And we can't talk about this now. The children will hear us.'

'You didn't talk about it at any time,' he said roughly, his eyes dark and dangerous, his accent thicker than ever. 'You just left, ripping all the important things in my life away from me.'

She winced at his description and forgot her resolutions not to argue with him. 'I *tried* to talk to you but you were always at the hospital or out on a rescue!'

'It's my job, Christy.'

And he'd been avoiding the issue. 'We never communicate any more, Alessandro. When did you last spend time with me?'

'You were in my bed every single night.' His arrogant declaration brought a flush of colour to her pale cheeks.

'That was just sex,' she muttered. 'The only place we ever spent time together was in bed.'

Right from the first moment they'd met, they'd been unable to keep their hands off each other—to exercise anything even remotely resembling self-control.

Awareness throbbed between them and as she caught the passion and fire in his eyes, only partially concealed by thick, dark lashes. Painfully aware of his vibrant masculinity, she turned away, trying desperately to ignore the agony of need that flared inside her body.

It didn't mean anything, she told herself miserably. Alessandro was a red-blooded Mediterranean man and sex had always been important to him. It didn't mean that he loved her. Sex was not a way to solve problems.

But maybe it would be a start, she thought to herself.

If they shared a bed tonight, perhaps they'd feel closer and could start talking.

'When did we last spend time together, Alessandro?' she said in a choked voice. 'Wasn't I important? Do strangers in trouble matter more than your own wife?'

A muscle worked in his jaw and he let out a long breath, but before he could speak, the children came barrelling out of their bedrooms. 'We're going outside to play in the snow,' Katy yelled, ponytail flying as she took the stairs two at a time with Ben close behind her.

'Don't forget your coats,' Christy called after them, suddenly desperate for them to stay, to breathe life and fun into the place. She didn't want to be on her own with Alessandro. Didn't have the energy for the confrontation that was brewing.

Reading her mind, he took a step towards her. 'So—I'm here now. If you want to talk, then talk.' He looked remote and unapproachable and she felt everything sink inside her.

She knew that some of the nurses and junior doctors found Alessandro intimidating, but she'd only ever loved the fact that he had no tolerance for anything less than perfection. It was what made him such an excellent doctor. So why did she suddenly find him so formidable?

'We can't talk about this in five minutes with you due back at the hospital. It's too important for that.'

'If you've got something to say, say it.' His mouth was grim as he moved towards her. 'You're trembling. Do I make you nervous, Christy?'

If he kissed her, she was lost.

She backed away and hated herself for it. 'Don't be ridiculous. Of course you don't make me nervous.'

'Feeling guilty about leaving?' He kept on coming, his eyes locked on hers. 'Conscience pricking you?'

'I don't have anything to feel guilty about.'

'Yes, you do.'

'You're seeing everything from one side as usual, which is totally unreasonable.'

'You talk to me about unreasonable when you were the one who walked out?'

There was a long silence while the atmosphere throbbed and hummed. His dark eyes slid down to her mouth and she thought she saw a sudden flare of hunger. But then it was gone and he bent to pick up her case.

'You're right. This isn't the right time to talk about it. You've been gone for almost two months so waiting a few days longer for a cosy chat isn't going to kill either of us. I'll take this through to your room.' His tone was flat, emotionless and she watched him as he walked.

Her room? What did he mean, 'her room'?

Her knees still shaking, she followed him, her heart diving south as she saw that he'd put in her in the guest room. He stood for a moment, one dark eyebrow raised in challenge, and she bit her lip, hiding the pain.

So much for using sex as a problem-solver.

Was he expecting her to beg? Clearly he didn't want her sleeping in the same room as him, the same bed as him, but she wasn't going to let him know how much that hurt her. She had too much pride.

'Great. This is excellent.' She swept into the room as though the sleeping arrangements had been her choice. 'We did this up nicely, didn't we? I always liked the throw on the bed.'

His gaze was steady on her face. 'You should be comfortable enough.'

Oh, no, she wouldn't, she thought miserably. She wouldn't sleep a wink, knowing that he was just down the corridor. Sleeping naked... Alessandro always slept naked and she felt a sudden rush of heat at the thought. *She missed him so much.* 'I'll be fine. This is perfect.'

Something flamed in his dark eyes and she wondered what she'd said to anger him. After all, he'd been the one to put her in the spare room. If anyone had a right to be angry, surely it should be her? But he'd drawn the battle lines and made his position clear.

He didn't even want her in his bedroom. Didn't want their relationship to be mended.

And why did that come as a surprise? If he'd wanted to mend it, he would have followed her to London and dragged her back.

Which was what she'd thought he'd do.

She felt tears prick her eyes but fortunately Katy chose that moment to race back into the room, her hair and brightly coloured jumper dusted with snow. 'Oh, Mum, this is wicked. There's so much snow and—' She broke off and glanced around her. 'What are you doing in here?'

'This is where I'm sleeping, sweetheart.' Christy kept her tone bright, as if it were the most normal thing in the world for she and Alessandro to be sleeping apart, but Katy's expression changed from happy to stubborn.

'In the *spare room*?'

Christy suppressed a groan. Katy definitely saw too much. 'Your father and I need some space,' she said quietly, and Katy glowered at both of them.

'This is Christmas. Goodwill and all that. If you argue, you'll upset Ben.'

'We're not arguing,' Christy said weakly, and Alessandro gave a disapproving frown.

'Our sleeping arrangements are none of your business, Katherine.' He spoke quietly, but there was a warning note in his voice that made Katy's narrow shoulders tense.

'No.' Her expression was mutinous. 'You're not sleeping in here. I want you to sleep in the same bed, like everyone else's parents.'

'Sweetheart, plenty of your friends' parents don't sleep together. Look at Rosie's mum and dad. They—'

'That's different. They're divorced.' Katy glared at her fiercely. 'You and Dad are *not* getting divorced. That isn't going to happen.'

Christy heard Alessandro drag in a long breath and bit her lip hard. Just hearing the word said aloud made her feel sick but at that moment all her thoughts were channelled towards alleviating her daughter's distress.

'Look, sweetheart, you're too young to understand at the moment.' She kept her tone modulated and reasonable. 'But you have to leave this to Daddy and I. We'll sort it out together in our own way.'

Katy put her hands on her hips and gave an innocent smile. 'You think so?' And she turned on her heel and left the room.

Alessandro swore softly in Spanish. 'I will speak to her—'

'No.' Christy shook her head. 'She's upset. I'll talk to her later, when she's had time to calm down.'

'And what are you going to tell her? That this was your choice? I need to get back to the hospital.' He gave her a long, burning look loaded with accusation and then strode out of the room. Christy stared after him, feeling numb. It was clear that he blamed her for the entire situation and the knowledge that he'd absolved himself of all responsibility should have stoked her anger. Instead, it left her feeling exhausted. She'd known Alessandro angry, she'd known him passionate but she'd never known him cold before now.

There was no hope for them. None at all.

And it promised to be anything but a happy and peaceful Christmas.

CHAPTER TWO

ALESSANDRO drove too fast, eyes narrowed, hands gripping the steering-wheel of his sports car.

He'd put her in the spare room, expecting to get a re-action, expecting her to throw herself into his arms. She hadn't even blinked.

Until she'd walked out three months earlier, they'd never even slept apart. Now she was behaving as though separate beds were an everyday occurrence.

Clearly it was what she wanted.

He parked in his space, still thinking about Christy, oblivious to the biting cold or the wail of approaching sirens.

She'd looked more beautiful than ever. She was the only woman he'd ever met who could appear so impossibly slender and yet still manage to have curves in all the right places. The gorgeous blue jumper had brought out the amazing colour of her eyes and her silky soft hair had tumbled past her shoulders like a blatant taunt. Had she done that on purpose? She knew how much he adored her hair. And then there were her legs, long, slim and tempting in those ridiculously high heels. She looked sexy and alluring and nothing like the way that a respectably married mother of two children was supposed to look.

Had she already taken another lover?

Discovering the meaning of insecurity for the first time in his life, Alessandro climbed out of the car, battling against a burning desire to put his fist through something. An ominous expression on his handsome face, he slammed his way through the doors that led from the ambulance bay into the department and almost crashed into his colleague.

'What are you doing here? We weren't expecting you back.' Sean Nicholson, the senior consultant in the A and E department and the leader of the mountain rescue team, took a step back, eyebrows raised in question.

Alessandro dragged in a breath and bottled up his temper. 'We're short-staffed,' he said tightly. 'And this seems as good a place to be as any.'

Sean's eyes narrowed. 'That bad, eh?'

'Don't ask.'

'Doesn't do to run away from women,' Sean drawled. 'They catch up with you in the end.'

Only if they want to, Alessandro mused, his temper still stewing and simmering. Clearly Christy wanted no more to do with him. She'd moved out, come home only because she wanted the children to have a family Christmas, and she had no qualms about sleeping in the spare room.

Sean thrust a set on notes into his hand. 'Well, I'm not sorry you're here. This place is starting to resemble a war zone.'

A bit like home, then, Alessandro thought bitterly, walking through to a cubicle to see the patient that Sean had given him, but before he could open his mouth to speak, Sean caught his arm.

'Alessandro?' Sean's eyes were suddenly intent and

thoughtful. 'I don't suppose Christy wants to come back to work, does she? Just for the two weeks leading up to Christmas? We've got six nurses off sick at the moment. The numbers just aren't adding up.'

'Christy?' Alessandro frowned. 'She's a practice nurse...'

Sean raised his eyebrows. 'Only for the last few years,' he said, his tone mild. 'Before that she was an A and E nurse, and a damn good one. I know it's a long shot, but...' He caught the dubious look on Alessandro's face and gave a shrug. 'Give it some thought.' He walked off and Alessandro stared after him.

It had been years since Christy had worked in A and E. She'd carried on working in the department part time after Katy's birth, but once Ben had arrived she'd given up completely for a few years and then taken a part-time job in the local GP practice.

Why would Sean think she could fill the gap in A and E? She'd be out of her depth, out of touch, unable to cope with the pressure—it was a ridiculous suggestion. Christy was a mother now. The children were her priority. There was no way she'd be able to cope with the demands of A and E.

He dismissed the thought instantly and buried himself in work. He worked through a long and busy night without taking a break and eventually arrived home at five in the morning.

The house was in darkness as he showered and crawled into his cold, empty bed. Sleep should have swallowed him whole but instead he stayed on the edges of wakefulness, unable to find the rest he craved.

His mind was full of Christy, at that moment probably sleeping peacefully in their spare bedroom.

The thought of her warm, perfect body sent his tension levels soaring and he eventually gave up on sleep just as the weak, winter light was filtering through the curtains. Cursing softly, his body thrumming with frustration, he pulled on a pair of fleecy tracksuit bottoms and a sweatshirt and went out for a run.

The snow was crisp and fresh on the ground, unmarked, and his breath clouded the air as he pounded silently along the track that led from his house to the river. Today the boulders were tipped with snow and the water was ice cold and as clear as glass. He ran until the breath tore at his lungs and his muscles ached and eventually arrived home to find the children sprawled on the sofas, watching Christmas cartoons on television. Christy was in the kitchen, making pancakes.

She glanced up as he walked into the room and for a moment they just stared at each other. Then she cleared her throat and turned back to the frying-pan, jiggling it with one hand to stop the pancake burning.

'Do you want some breakfast?' She was wearing a pair of jeans that fitted her snugly and the same blue jumper that he'd admired the day before. Her hair was loose, her cheeks were flushed and she looked pretty and far too young to be the mother of the two children watching television in the next room. Alessandro felt a vicious tug of lust that had him backing out of the room. It was just because he hadn't seen her for two months, he told himself firmly. As soon as he got used to having her around, he'd be able to control himself. Until then, he needed to keep some distance.

'No, thanks. No breakfast.' His stomach was growling, the pancakes smelt delicious, but he couldn't trust himself to be in the same room as her and not grab her. Later, he promised himself, when he had his feelings well and truly under control, they'd talk. 'I need to get back to the hospital.'

'Alessandro.' Her voice was exasperated and she tilted

her head to one side, her amazing, fiery hair sliding over her shoulder. 'You didn't come in until five and you were out running two hours after that. Even you need to rest some time!'

The only way she could possibly know the detail of his movements with such accuracy was if she hadn't been able to sleep either.

Registering that fact, he studied her face, saw the colour seep into her cheeks as she realised just how much she'd betrayed. Felt a flash of satisfaction that she wasn't as indifferent as she appeared to be. *Maybe there was hope for them.*

'Just for a few hours this morning,' he said huskily. 'We're ridiculously short-staffed. Everyone is off sick. I'll be back after lunch.' Suddenly he wished the children were at school so that he could just grab her and do what he wanted to do. He'd have her on the kitchen table in five seconds flat, naked in ten.

And he had a feeling that she wouldn't resist.

When had either of them ever been able to hold back in the bedroom? Their mutual passion had always been a driving force in their marriage. It was how they'd solved most of their problems.

'So short-staffed you're not even allowed to sleep?'

'There's a flu bug going around,' he muttered, dragging his eyes away from the smooth skin of her neck and trying to kill the erotic images dancing around his brain. 'Half the nurses are off sick.'

'You'll be joining them if you carry on pushing yourself like this,' she said tightly, and he sighed.

'You know what A and E is like.'

'Yes.' She grabbed some plates and slammed them down on the table with more force than was necessary. 'I should do. I used to work there and I was married to you for long enough.'

'Was?' He repeated the word, a jealous, possessive anger springing to life inside him. She must have detected something ominous in his tone because she looked up at him and he saw the misery in her eyes.

His insides twisted and he ran a hand over the back of his neck to relieve the growing tension. In all their years of marriage, he'd never seen Christy cry. He'd seen her helpless with laughter and wild with temper, but he'd never seen her cry and the shimmering mist of tears in her green eyes brought a sick feeling to the pit of his stomach.

'Christy—'

The phone rang and Christy leaned across to answer it, clearly relieved at the interruption.

Knowing her as he did, he guessed that such a display of weakness would have horrified her.

Alessandro watched as she pulled herself together. He heard her clear her throat and speak, saw a smile touch her wide, generous mouth and watched her glorious hair slide over her shoulder as she tilted her head and listened. He'd always loved her hair. The colour of autumn leaves, it fell past her shoulders in soft, wild curls. He was so absorbed by the soft, feminine curve of her jaw that he didn't even realise she'd replaced the receiver.

'That was Sean.'

'Nicholson?' Alessandro struggled to concentrate. 'Did he want to talk to me?'

'No.' Her voice was calm as she reached into the oven for the stack of pancakes she was keeping warm. 'He wanted to talk to me.'

'What about?'

Christy put the pancakes in the middle of the table.

'Working in A and E. He wants me to do bank work for the two weeks leading up to Christmas to cover all the nurses you have off sick.'

Alessandro watched while she reached into the fridge for maple syrup. 'And you said no.'

'Actually, I said yes.' She added a plate of lemon slices and a bowl of sugar to the table.

Alessandro stared at her in blatant astonishment. 'Why would you say yes?'

Her gaze lifted to his, her green eyes cool. 'Why wouldn't I?'

'Well, because…' He dragged a hand through his dark hair and frowned, suspecting that he was about to get himself into hot water. 'Because it's a long time since you've worked in A and E. You've been at home with the children for years now and—'

'And you think my brain has gone to mush?' Her tone had an edge to it as she reached into the cutlery drawer and withdrew a knife. 'Why don't you just say it, Alessandro? You don't think I'm up to it, do you?' She slammed the drawer shut with a decisive flick of her hand and Alessandro closed his eyes briefly and wished he'd stayed at the hospital.

'I'm just thinking of you. You've no idea what A and E is like now.' He spread lean, strong hands to emphasise his point. 'Every day there's a new piece of high-tech equipment to master and the work is full on and relentless. Every single day we're stretched to the limit. And then there's the violent drunks—'

She put the knife on the table next to the syrup. 'You don't think I can cope with a violent drunk?'

Alessandro eyed the dangerous glint in her eye and felt the hot burn of lust spread through his body. He'd always loved her passion and her strength. The fact that she was afraid of nothing. 'You're a strong woman, that's true, *querida*,' he drawled, 'but—'

'But nothing! Believe it or not, I still have a brain, Alessandro, and giving birth to your children hasn't changed that fact.' Passion and fire burned in her eyes and he was suddenly relieved that she'd put the knife down.

'You're overreacting.'

'Well, excuse me, but when I'm patronised I do have a tendency to overreact,' she said in a dangerously sweet tone. 'And let's be honest here for a moment, shall we? You're not thinking of me. You're thinking of yourself. You're afraid I'll embarrass you. Or that when you get home, your dinner won't be cooked. Or that I'll be too tired for sex—'

'Enough!' He said the word sharply, his eyes sliding to the door, but there was no sign of the children.

'Yes, Alessandro. I've had enough.' She glared at him. 'But you're not thinking of me, are you? You just don't want anything to upset the perfect order of your life.'

He inhaled sharply. 'A and E is busy and challenging and—'

'And you don't think I'm up to it,' Christy repeated, her jaw lifting in a stubborn expression that he knew so well. 'Well, I'm going to prove you wrong. I was a good nurse, Alessandro. You seem to have forgotten that.'

'I haven't forgotten that and you don't have to prove anything to me,' Alessandro said stiffly. 'You've been looking after the children and that's important. It's enough.'

'For you, yes. But what if it isn't enough for me?' Her voice was strangely flat. 'You carry on building your career, moving forwards and upwards, and you've never once stopped to wonder whether I'm happy standing still.'

Alessandro stared at her. 'I thought you were happy being at home with the children. Being a practice nurse.'

'Ben has been in full-time education for three years,' she replied shortly. 'And being a practice nurse was a forced decision based on the hours. You know that.'

Did he? *Did he know that?* Had he ever stopped to think about the choices she'd made? Feeling trapped in a corner, Alessandro ran a hand over the back of his neck.

'If you weren't happy, you should have talked to me.'

'When? The only way to guarantee an audience with you over the past year would have been to break something vital and arrive at your place of work in an ambulance.' She slammed a pan down on the side. 'I *tried* talking to you, Alessandro. You weren't listening.'

'I'm listening now.' He refrained from saying that he couldn't hear much above the banging and clattering that she was making as she worked her way around the kitchen.

She paused, the rapid rise and fall of her chest an indication of the depth of emotion bottled up inside her. 'And now isn't the time. Isn't that typical?' Rubbing a hand over her forehead, she gave a humourless laugh and took a breath. 'Children! Breakfast!'

Alessandro didn't budge from the doorway. 'We're going to talk about this, Christy.'

'Some time, yes, but the pancakes are getting cold so it can't be now.' She slid a pancake onto Ben's plate. 'But I'm starting at the hospital this afternoon. Late shift. You're looking after the children.'

Alessandro opened his mouth to suggest that she delay it a few days to give him time to run through the essentials with her, but the children pushed past him and he decided that Christy was right. This wasn't the right time. She had no idea what A and E was like now, he thought fiercely, and made a mental note to ask Sean and Nicky to keep a discreet eye on her.

'You're working at the hospital, Mum?' Katy poured maple syrup over her pancakes. 'What's going to happen to us?'

'When Daddy isn't around, you'll go to Grandma's,' Christy said immediately, and Katy's face brightened.

'Cool. Shopping.'

Alessandro frowned. 'You don't mind spending most of the week at your grandmother's?'

'Why would I?' Katy gave a wide smile. 'She always says that the great thing about being a grandma is having someone to spoil. I'm more than happy to be that someone.'

'Her chocolate cake is awesome,' Ben added, heaping sugar in the middle of a pancake. 'It's all gooey and she cuts *really* big pieces. And she never worries about it spoiling your appetite.'

'You see?' Christy looked at Alessandro and gave a shrug. 'And, anyway, it will only be for part of the day. I'll still have plenty of time to spend with the children. Everyone's happy.'

Were they? Alessandro poured himself a strong cup of coffee and wondered what it would be like having Christy working in the department.

He was finding it hard enough being around her for the short period of time he was at home without contemplating falling over her at work, too.

'Look at it this way.' She gave him a smile loaded with subtle messages. 'You're always at the hospital. At least this way I get to see you.'

And that, Alessandro decided, was going to be the biggest problem. He wouldn't be able to use work to take his mind off Christy because she was going to be right there, under his nose.

* * *

'I can't believe you said yes to this.' Nicky, the A and E sister, grabbed Christy and gave her a hug. 'We are *so* pleased to see you back.'

'It's been years and I'm a bit nervous,' Christy confessed, stroking a hand down the blue scrub suit that the nurses wore in A and E. It felt unfamiliar. 'I'm afraid I'm going to make a mistake.'

'No way.' Nicky shook her head and waved a hand dismissively. 'You're an experienced nurse. And, anyway, if in doubt just shout.'

'Alessandro doesn't think I can do it,' Christy said softly, and Nicky gave her a searching look.

'Well, he's a traditional Mediterranean man but I guess you knew that when you married him. I suppose he sees you as his wife and the mother of his children. But that'll change after you've been in Resus together.'

Unless she messed it up. Christy felt a stab of insecurity. It was obvious that Alessandro thought she'd been away from A and E nursing for too long to be much use.

Would she be able to prove him wrong?

She, of all people, knew how exacting he was. He was noted for his absence of tolerance when it came to mistakes.

'Anyway, you've picked a good shift to start on,' Nicky said cheerfully, leading her round to the main area of the department. 'Your handsome husband isn't working this afternoon, so you can find your feet without him watching you with those brooding dark eyes. And it's Sunday afternoon. Lots of rugby injuries. Yummy men dressed in virtually nothing and covered in mud. My idea of heaven. Bring 'em on!'

Christy laughed, suddenly realising just how much she'd missed the camaraderie that was so much a part of working in the A and E department.

'Where do you want me to work this afternoon?'

'Out here at the sharp end,' Nicky said immediately. 'You can help me. It will be like old times. If it's quiet, we can warm our bottoms on the radiator and catch up on the gossip.'

Almost immediately the phone rang. Remembering that it was the hotline to Ambulance Control, Christy picked it up without hesitation, listening carefully while the person on the other end outlined the injuries of the patient they were bringing in.

When she'd replaced the receiver, she repeated the information to Nicky, her tone brisk and professional. 'Sounds bad. Shall I get Sean?'

'We need to assemble the trauma team,' Nicky agreed. 'Shame your Alessandro isn't on, it's right up his street. Still, never mind, we'll bleep the on-call orthopaedic reg.' Her eyes gleamed with humour. 'He'll have to do.'

The children were already asleep when she arrived home and Christy fell into bed, exhausted but elated. *She'd done it.* She'd worked a shift in A and E and she hadn't killed anyone or even slightly injured them. And she'd had fun. It had been exciting and unpredictable and the time had passed so fast that she'd been astonished when Nicky had pointed out that it was time to go home. Astonished and disappointed because she'd been enjoying herself. Really, really enjoying herself.

And now she was back in the spare bedroom. For a short time she'd forgotten about her problems. But there was no forgetting them now, with the cold, empty stretch of bed next to her.

He didn't want her, she reminded herself miserably.

He didn't want her in his bed and he didn't want her in his A and E department.

Leaving home and going to London had just brought to a head something that would have happened anyway.

Their marriage was on a slow downhill slide and she didn't seem able to stop it.

The next morning, Christy scraped a thick layer of ice from her windscreen, dropped the children with her mother and arrived at A and E to find the department in chaos. The waiting room was full to bursting and the triage nurse looked unusually stressed as she tried to calm everyone and maintain order, filtering the urgent from the non-urgent.

'A bus carrying Father Christmas and a bunch of elves hit a patch of black ice at the head of the Kirkstone pass,' Nicky told her as she hurried past, carrying an armful of equipment. 'Mostly walking wounded but they've just brought the driver in and he's badly injured. Can you go into Resus and help? Alessandro is in there and they're short of a circulation nurse. Donna is there but she's newly qualified and I'm worried that your husband might take her head off if she's less than perfect. I need you to give her some help. I'm helping to stave off a riot out here. Apparently even elves don't respond well to four-hour waiting times.'

Without arguing or asking any further questions, Christy pushed open the doors of Resus and felt her heart hammer hard against her chest.

She hated to admit it, but the prospect of working with Alessandro made her nervous. She didn't need Nicky's reminder that he was capable of removing someone's head if he wasn't happy. It was one of the things she'd always respected about him. He cared deeply about each patient and wasn't willing to settle for anything other than best practice.

She knew him to be an exacting taskmaster with a zero tolerance for anything other than perfection.

It was all very well for Nicky to tell her to keep an eye on Donna, but who was going to keep an eye on her?

What if she couldn't remember what to do?

A blood-stained Father Christmas outfit lay in a pile and the patient was groaning with pain. Alessandro stood at the head of the trolley, co-ordinating the medical team as he assessed the patient. 'There's some bruising over the anterior chest wall,' he murmured as his eyes slid over the patient, conducting a visual examination. 'No evidence of open wounds or penetrating trauma.'

Christy walked towards the trolley, momentarily distracted by the sight of him in action. She'd forgotten what an exceptionally gifted doctor he was. Slick, competent and a natural leader. Nothing ever fazed him.

He lifted his eyes from the patient and saw her. His expression didn't change. 'You need protective clothing before you handle the patient,' he said coldly. 'At the very least, latex gloves and an apron.' He turned his attention back to his patient and Christy felt the colour flood into her cheeks. Of course she knew that the first thing she should have done was to reach for protective clothing. All blood and body fluids had to be assumed to carry HIV and the hepatitis virus. She knew that. It was just that seeing him had rattled her. Affected her confidence.

Determined not to let him get to her, she quickly donned the clothing that she needed and walked back to the trolley.

Her hands were shaking and her heart was banging against her ribs. She'd done this before, she reminded herself firmly. Many times.

Alessandro was listening to the patient's chest, his face blank of expression as he concentrated. When he was satisfied, he looped the stethoscope round his neck and turned to the circulation doctor, a pretty blonde girl who was examining the patient's femur. 'Blood loss?'

'I'm keeping pressure on that wound and it's under control.'

'OK, I want two peripheral lines in and take some blood for cross-matching, full blood count, U and Es, and let's get an arterial sample. I want blood gas and pH analysis. What's his blood pressure doing? I need an ECG here.' His instructions were smooth and seamless and swiftly Christy took over from one of the other nurses, who was clearly struggling and whom she presumed to be Donna.

Instinctively her eyes flicked to the monitor as she reached for the adhesive electrode pads and attached the patient to the ECG monitor. 'It's dropping. Ninety over fifty.'

Suddenly her hands weren't shaking any more. Her movements were smooth, confident and almost automatic. She knew what she was doing and it was as if she'd never been away.

'We'll start with a litre of Hartmann's,' Alessandro said immediately, and Christy busied herself with her patient while he made a rapid assessment of brain and spinal-cord function.

'Put your tongue out for me,' he instructed the patient. 'Wiggle your toes.'

'His blood pressure is still dropping,' Christy said quietly, and Alessandro's gaze flickered to hers.

'Increase the flow rate and let's give him some analgesia.'

'First line is in,' the blonde doctor said as she slid a wide-bore cannula into a vein and Christy pulled the IV stand towards her so that she could attach the giving set and start the infusion.

'Get that second line in straight away, Katya,' Alessandro instructed, and the blonde doctor reached for the second cannula and moved round the trolley to the other side of the patient.

The man gave a groan of pain and Alessandro immediately switched his attention back to his patient. 'We're going to give you something for the pain now, Derek,' he said calmly and Christy reached for the drugs that she knew would be on the trolley. 'Morphine and cyclizine?'

With speed and efficiency she drew up the drug and handed it to Alessandro, along with the ampoule to check. Then she moved closer to the trolley and closed her hand over the patient's, offering comfort.

'We'll soon have you more comfortable, Derek,' she said quietly, and felt the man's fingers tighten over hers.

This was the bit that the doctors often forgot or ignored, she thought to herself as she felt the man's grip. They forgot the importance of touch. They forgot that as well as being injured, the patient was anxious and scared.

It was another thing that she'd always admired about Alessandro. No matter how tense the situation, he never forgot his patient. He wasn't a touchy-feely doctor, but he understood the importance of communication in lowering stress levels.

Her eyes flickered to the machines next to her. 'His blood pressure is stable,' she said quietly, and Alessandro gave a nod.

'Good. He's still in pain so I'm going to give him a femoral nerve block before we splint and X-ray.'

Immediately Christy reached for the needle she knew he was going to need and an ampoule of lignocaine.

Alessandro felt for the femoral artery and cleaned the skin. Then he held out his hand for the local anaesthetic that Christy had prepared.

She watched while he inserted the needle perpendicular to the skin and then aspirated to check for blood. 'That's fine,' he murmured, moving the needle up and down as he injected the local anaesthetic.

Katya moved forward, standing close to Alessandro. 'What happens if you puncture the artery?'

'I resign.' Sounding impossibly Spanish, Alessandro dropped the syringe back on the tray that Christy was holding and gave a brief smile. 'But before I resign, I compress it for five to ten minutes or until the bleeding stops. Then I carry on with the femoral nerve block.' He turned his attention back to his patient. 'That should give you some relief very quickly, Derek.'

Katya turned away but not before Christy had seen the flirtatious glance.

She wanted Alessandro.

Christy's stomach lurched and she swallowed hard.

She was used to women staring at Alessandro. It had always happened and perhaps it always would because he was a man who inevitably attracted the attention of the female sex. But this was the first time she'd seen it happen when their marriage was in trouble.

Had he done something about it?

She bit her lip. Katya was very pretty. Alessandro was a hot-blooded Spaniard with a high sex drive, she knew that better than anyone. With their marriage in its current state, it was hard not to worry.

Had something happened between them?

The man closed his eyes and shook his head. 'We were on our way to a school—delivering presents.'

'Don't worry about that now.' Pushing aside disturbing thoughts of Katya with her arms wrapped around Alessandro,

Christy gave a reassuring smile as the man gripped her hand tightly.

'Will you get someone to phone the school and explain? These kids believe in Father Christmas. What will they think if I don't turn up?'

Alessandro looked taken aback but Christy squeezed the man's hand. 'I'll talk to one of the nurses outside see if one of your elves can make a call.'

Alessandro looked at her blankly and she just smiled and turned to Donna, who was hovering nervously. 'Can you speak to Nicky?' she said quietly. 'Ask her to talk to one of the elves and call the school.'

Visibly relieved to be given an excuse to leave, Donna backed out of the room.

Alessandro watched her go with an ominous frown in his dark eyes. 'She's nervous.'

'She's learning and you can be scary,' Christy said calmly. 'Do you want to immobilise the limb now?'

He looked at her. 'I'm scary?'

'Not everyone is born with your confidence. Derek, we're going to splint this leg of yours and for that I need to take some measurements on your uninjured leg.' Having offered an explanation, Christy moved the blanket and measured the uppermost part of the patient's thigh.

Donna slipped back by her side. 'It's done,' she said breathlessly. 'They've phoned the school and everyone is fine.'

'Good. Well done.' Christy smiled at her patient. 'You can stop worrying. Even Father Christmas is allowed to be held up when he's delivering presents.'

He smiled weakly. 'You probably think I'm mad, worrying about that while I'm lying here with a broken leg, but I don't want to disappoint the children. I think the pain is getting easier.'

'The splint will help the pain, too,' Christy explained, and then turned to Donna and handed her the measurements she'd taken. 'We're going to use a Thomas splint. Can you go and fetch me one, please? You'd better get the size above and below, just in case. It will save you making another journey.'

Working as a team, they prepared to fit the splint and Christy applied the adhesive tape and then wrapped the leg from ankle to mid-thigh with gauze bandage, talking Donna through what she was doing.

The girl lost her nervous appearance and moved closer to the trolley, her expression keen and interested.

Alessandro applied traction to the leg, gently pulling the ankle with one hand and supporting the knee with the other.

Katya stood closer to him than was strictly necessary and Christy tried not to mind and concentrated instead on helping Donna.

'You can see that he's correcting the abduction and the external rotation,' she explained as she helped manoeuvre the splint onto the leg until it was in the right position.

She and Alessandro worked together smoothly, closely observed by both Katya and Donna.

Once the cords were tied and twisted, Christy put wool roll padding under the thigh. 'Now we just need to bandage the whole splint from thigh to lower calf,' she said to Donna, 'lift and support the leg on a pillow and check the distal pulses.'

'Great.' Alessandro turned to Katya. 'Can you arrange for X-rays and then we'll refer him to the orthopaedic team? I want X-rays of the pelvis, hip and knee.'

Katya gave a feline smile. 'Of course, Alessandro.'

Donna shot a questioning glance at Christy, who dragged

her gaze away from her scrutiny of Katya and volunteered the information she knew was needed.

'For the femoral shaft to fracture, there must have been a violent high-energy impact and that is associated with other injures.' *He wouldn't be sleeping with Katya*, she told herself firmly. *Alessandro wouldn't do that.* He might be the archetypal alpha male, but he was an honourable man with strong principles. 'So when we're X-raying, it's important to check pelvis, hip and knee.'

But if he considered their marriage to be over, would he do that?

CHAPTER THREE

CHRISTY started to clear up some of the debris that had accumulated while Katya and Donna arranged the X-rays. She knew how important it was to keep Resus tidy and well stocked, and she thought that the comfort of routine might relieve the sick feeling building in her stomach.

Forcing herself to be rational and mature, she hung a fresh bag of IV fluid from the drip stand and then started to replenish the drugs that they'd used.

Eventually the patient was transferred to Theatre and she was left alone in the room. She picked up a laryngoscope from the intubation tray and snapped it open, testing that the bulb worked. She stared down at the curved, silver blade in her hand and didn't hear the door open behind her.

'So—working in A and E is obviously like riding a bike.' Alessandro's deep, masculine drawl came from directly behind her and she turned, her stomach jumping. There was no reason to feel nervous, she told herself firmly. They'd worked together as a smooth, efficient team. She hadn't done anything wrong.

'It came back to me.'

'Obviously.' His dark eyes lingered on her face. 'You've missed it, haven't you?'

She caught her breath. It had been years since she'd stopped working in A and E and yet that was the first time he'd ever asked her that question. 'Yes,' she breathed. 'I missed it terribly.'

Something flickered in his eyes. 'You never said.'

'You never asked.'

Their eyes met and held and Christy felt the heat flicker and stir in her pelvis.

Why did she have to find him so completely irresistible? The attraction between them was so powerful that it blinded her to every other aspect of their relationship, which was probably the reason they hadn't sorted their problems out earlier.

'We should talk more,' he said roughly, and she gave a wan smile.

'You're not always that easy to talk to, Alessandro.'

'Am I really scary?' There was a frown in his eyes and she realised that her earlier comment had genuinely bothered him.

'You can be intimidating,' she said honestly. 'But that's partly because of your skills and experience. You can't expect a newly qualified nurse to respond to an emergency situation with your confidence.'

'If she can't cope with the situation, she shouldn't be in Resus,' Alessandro growled, and Christy sighed.

'You're so hard on people. In an ideal world, I suppose you're right. But we don't live or work in an ideal world. And the best way to learn is by the patient's bedside, gaining hands-on experience with the appropriate supervision.' She scanned the trolley, checking that she'd replaced all the drugs they'd used. 'All the studying in the world doesn't prepare you for the pressure and demands of Resus when a patient is bleeding before your eyes.'

Alessandro looked at her thoughtfully. 'You were good with her,' he conceded. 'The nurse, I mean.'

It was so unlike him to offer praise that she blinked in astonishment and then felt the warmth spread inside her.

'Thank you.'

'Do I scare *you*?' His direct question made her catch her breath.

She wondered whether she ought to admit that the only thing that scared her was the thought of losing him.

She opened her mouth to tell him, but pride trapped the words in her throat before she could utter them. *She was sleeping in the spare room*, she reminded herself. *He hadn't come after her.*

It was the wrong time to be honest about her feelings when she was so unsure about his.

'No,' she said finally, her voice quiet. 'You don't scare me, but you can be difficult to reach and sometimes I just give up rather than keep trying.'

He muttered something in Spanish and ran a hand over his jaw, a jaw that was already showing signs of stubble. Then he reached out and slid a hand behind her head and pulled her face to within inches of his in a gesture that was both male and possessive. 'I *don't* want a divorce, Christy. Be clear about that.'

She stared up at him, hypnotised by the look in his dark, brooding eyes. They were the words she'd waited to hear for two long months and he'd chosen to say them in Resus under harsh, fluorescent lights with the likelihood that they'd be disturbed at any moment. She wanted to ask why he'd let her go. She wanted to ask about Katya. Suddenly, she wanted to know how he'd spent the last six weeks. 'And what if I want a divorce?'

She said the words to goad him and remembered too late that goading Alessandro, with his volatile, Latin temperament, was not a good idea.

'You don't.' He slid his other arm and around her and jerked her against him in a decisive gesture that was so much a part of him.

She felt the strength and power of his body and the breath trapped in her throat. 'Alessandro…' she couldn't concentrate on anything when he was this close. Couldn't think…

'Need me to prove it to you?' He breathed the words against her mouth, his tone silky smooth and dangerous, and she gave a whimper, knowing what was coming and willing herself to reject him. 'Need me to prove that you still want me?'

'No, I don't, I—'

His mouth came down on hers with seductive intent and immediately she sank against him because no one kissed like Alessandro and resisting him was impossible. His hand was buried in her hair, the skilful slide of his tongue erotic and demanding as he took her to the edge of sanity with a speed that shocked her.

His kiss was hungry and primitive and she clutched at him, pressing against him, her need so intense that she forgot everything except her desire for him.

Kissing him gave her the reassurance she needed and then he released her and stepped back, his expression cold. 'The children need both their parents. We're a family, Christy, and that isn't going to change.'

The tiny flicker of hope died inside her. 'Alessandro—'

'We won't ever speak of divorce again, Christy. And don't pretend you don't want me.'

Oh, she wanted him. How could she pretend otherwise when her nipples were pressing hard against the soft fabric of her scrub suit and her mouth was still swollen from the ravages of his kiss?

She wanted him. But how did she explain that she needed more than the physical when his solution to every problem was sex? He was a red-blooded, Mediterranean male with a high sex drive. She'd known that right from the first. *Had loved the fact that he couldn't get enough of her.*

And the fact that he'd made it clear that his thoughts were only for the children caused her intense pain. The kiss hadn't been about her, she thought miserably. It had been about the children. Alessandro was Spanish, through and through. He believed utterly in the sanctity of the family.

He would stay married to her for the sake of the children.

Could she do the same? Could she stay with him, knowing that he didn't love her any more?

'We can't talk about this here, Alessandro,' she croaked. 'Not now.'

His eyes dropped to her mouth and the tension rose between them.

'When, then?'

'I don't know.' She felt so shaky and miserable that she didn't feel up to another confrontation. Didn't feel up to listening to more evidence that he was determined to save their marriage for the sake of the children.

'Well, it has to be soon.' He was standing close to her. So close that her heart rate increased alarmingly.

Was it normal? she wondered. Was it normal to be married to someone for twelve years and yet still want to rip their clothes off at every opportunity?

'I need to go home and prepare dinner,' she said huskily as she dragged off her gloves and washed her hands, seeking any excuse to turn away from him. 'Mum's dropping the children in an hour. Are you joining us?'

She expected him to tell her that he was staying at the hospital but as she risked a glance at him she collided with his hard, unyielding gaze.

'*Sí.*' His Spanish accent was more pronounced than usual. 'I'm joining you, *querida*. I want to eat dinner with my children. Why wouldn't I?'

The children.

It was all about the children, she thought dully as she washed her hands and walked out of the room.

As a couple, they didn't exist any more.

Checking that her parents were still seated at the dining table, Katy grabbed her brother's hand and dragged him upstairs and into the spare bedroom. 'It's time to interfere.'

'What's interfere?' Ben started playing with his toy aeroplane and Katy snatched it away from him and held it out of reach.

'Interfere is when you try and help someone do something they should be doing for themselves.' She threw the aeroplane onto a chair and grabbed his hand. 'Come on. We're going to bounce on the bed.'

Ben tried to jerk his hand away from hers. 'I was playing with my acroplane.'

Katy rolled her eyes. 'You can play with it again in a minute, but for now we're going to bounce.'

Ben eyed the bed doubtfully. 'We're not supposed to jump on the beds.'

'And when has that ever stopped you?'

'I'll get into trouble with Mum.'

'And if you don't do it, you'll get into trouble with me,' Katy informed him sweetly. 'Take your pick.'

'I do like bouncing.' Ben looked at the wide bed with something close to yearning. 'Come on, then. Just a quick one. How hard do you want me to bounce?'

'Just hard enough to break it,' Katy muttered under her breath, slipping off her shoes. 'I'll help you. Come on.' And she leapt into the middle of the bed and started jumping, her dark ponytail flying around her shoulders as she leaped higher and higher.

Ben gave a delighted giggled and climbed up next to her.

'Come on.' She grabbed his hands and encouraged him to bounce, too.

Downstairs in the kitchen, Christy and Alessandro were finishing their meal in tense silence when there was an enormous crash above them, followed by a plaintive yell.

'Oh, no.' Driven by her maternal instincts, Christy was out of her seat and up the stairs in record time, Alessandro right behind her.

In the bedroom they found Ben sobbing noisily on the carpet and Katy with her arms around him. She looked up when her parents entered. 'Poor Ben. He bounced on the bed and...' she gave a baffled shrug, her expression both innocent and mystified '...it must have broken or something. Unbelievable, the rubbish they sell you these days.'

'The bed broke?' Christy looked at the collapsed bed in horror and disbelief. 'Oh, my goodness. It looks as though the frame has snapped right through. How did you—?' And then she saw the blood on Ben's cheek and dropped to her knees. All the training in the world didn't prepare you properly for coping when your own child was injured, she thought frantically. 'You're bleeding. Alessandro, he's bleeding.'

'I see it.' Calm and steady, Alessandro scooped his son into his arms and swept the aeroplane and Christy's clothes off the chair so that he could sit down. 'What's happened to you?'

'Katy told me to bounce,' Ben hiccoughed, his face blotched with crying, 'so I bounced, but when the bed broke I fell off and banged myself. It hurts.'

'Where did you bang yourself?' Alessandro ran strong fingers over the little boy's arms and legs, hunting for damage—trying to find the source of the bleeding. He found it on the boy's palm. 'It's fine. Just a scratch. He must have run his hand over his cheek. That's why he has blood on his face.'

Christy stood there, heart thumping, relieved that Alessandro was there. She'd always been a wreck inside when either of the children had been ill or injured. She suddenly realised how much she'd missed his strength.

Still cuddling Ben, Alessandro threw a frowning glance at the bed. 'That's well and truly broken. You won't be sleeping there tonight.'

Christy gave a tiny frown and turned to Katy. 'I'll have Ben's room. Your brother can share with you.'

'No way!' Katy shrank back, her face a picture of exaggerated sibling horror. 'He snores, fidgets and talks in his sleep. No way am I sleeping with a monster baby like him.'

Ben clutched at the front of Alessandro's shirt and scowled at his sister. 'I'm *not* a baby!'

Christy sighed. 'Katy, there's no other option.'

'Yes, there is. If there's sharing to be done, you can jolly well share with Dad. At least you're married. I'm *not* sharing with my brother! That's totally gross.' And she stomped out of the room, ponytail swishing like a statement.

Alessandro stared after her with an expression of blatant masculine incomprehension. 'Is she hormonal?'

Christy rubbed her aching forehead. 'Hardly. She's eleven years old.'

'She's acting like a teenager.'

'She's going through a difficult phase. She's...' Her eyes met his and the words tailed off. They both knew that if Katy was going through a difficult stage, it was probably their fault. Christy's hand fell to her side. 'On top of everything else, I suppose it isn't exactly fair for her to have to share with her brother. She is getting to an age where privacy is important,' she murmured, and Alessandro nodded agreement.

'You can use our bedroom. I'll take the sofa downstairs.'

Christy felt the heavy punch of disappointment deep inside her but smiled. 'That's very decent of you. Thanks.'

She didn't care, she told herself. She didn't care that he obviously couldn't face the thought of sharing a room with her, let alone a bed. *She didn't care that he'd rather sleep on the sofa than be with her.*

Once, they hadn't been able to keep their hands off each other. They'd been like greedy, naughty teenagers seizing every opportunity to rip each other's clothes off and feast. Now it seemed as if they couldn't create enough distance.

'How will Father Christmas come if Daddy's sleeping downstairs?' Ben's anxious voice interrupted her thoughts. 'We all know that he can't come if anyone is there to see him.' The sweet innocence of his question made her heart twist.

'I...er... He...' Christy fumbled for an answer that might work, casting a desperate look at Alessandro.

'I'll keep my eyes tightly shut for the whole night?'

Ben shook his head, his expression solemn. 'That won't work. If you're awake, he knows.'

'Well, Daddy's under a lot of strain at the moment,' Alessandro growled, 'so I'm sure I'll be asleep.'

Was he under strain? He always looked infuriatingly cool and relaxed, Christy mused as she studied his handsome face for clues. Perhaps those dark, brooding eyes were a little more shadowed than usual and the sexy mouth a little more grimly set.

The strain of having her to stay, she thought miserably.

He was only tolerating her because of the children. Everything he did was because of the children.

'That's settled, then,' Christy said brightly. 'Daddy will sleep on the sofa. Now, let's get you into bed. It's getting late.'

She woke early to the sound of clattering and thumping in the kitchen, accompanied by harsh masculine curses. Trying to ignore the fact that she'd had less than four hours' sleep, she slipped on her dressing-gown and went downstairs to investigate.

Bare-chested and wearing only a pair of old jeans, Alessandro was muttering to himself in Spanish as he smashed his way around the kitchen.

Her Spanish was by no means fluent, but she'd lived with him for long enough to understand that he was in a foul temper.

'What's the matter with you?'

Alessandro shot her a stormy look as he made himself a large espresso. 'It's morning. I hate mornings. Especially after a night spent in the equivalent of a shoebox.'

She tried not to look at that tempting expanse of muscular chest. He had an incredible physique. Hard. Strong. Male. 'That sofa was expensive.'

He made a sound that was close to a snarl. 'Believe me,

you'd never guess by sleeping on it. I'm aching in parts of my body that I never even knew I had before now.'

He looked so cross that she felt a smile coming and lifted a hand to her mouth to cover it.

He paused with the cup halfway to his lips, his smouldering gaze hooded. 'Are you laughing at me?' He rolled the 'r', sounding more and more Spanish as he always did when he was angry.

'I'm not laughing at you.'

Slowly, he placed the cup back on the work surface, his eyes glittering dark and dangerous as he moved purposefully towards her. 'Because if you're laughing at me, *querida*, *you* can spend the night on the sofa tonight.'

Her heart started to thump hard against her ribs and she found herself backing away. 'Alessandro, I wasn't laughing.' It was ridiculous that he could still have this effect on her, she told herself firmly. They'd been together for twelve years. It wasn't possible for a man to make a woman weak at the knees after twelve years. It didn't happen that way. People became bored with each other. Sex was supposed to become routine and infrequent.

'You would fit better on the sofa.' He was right up against her now, and she was right up against the wall. Breathing heavily. 'You are smaller. More delicate.'

At that particular point in time she didn't need him to point out their differences. Her eyes were in line with sleek, male muscle and dark body hair. He was pumped up and hard and breathtakingly sexy. There was certainly no missing the differences between them.

'I'll sleep on the sofa if that's what you want.' Why did he persist in standing so close to her? What was he thinking?

And then she made the mistake of lifting her eyes to his and instantly knew exactly what he was thinking. He was thinking of sex. She recognised the sudden darkening of his eyes, saw the tiny pulse flicker in his rough jaw. He hadn't shaved yet and he looked more like a bandit than a senior doctor loaded with responsibilities.

Her tongue flickered out in what was actually a nervous gesture, but his eyes dropped to her mouth and she sensed the change in him.

He lifted a hand and brushed her cheek gently, his breathing unsteady. 'Christy...'

He was going to kiss her.

She closed her eyes, her blood thundering round her body in excited anticipation, and then there was a clatter and laughter as the two children surged into the room.

Alessandro cursed softly and backed away from her, retreating to his abandoned coffee-cup and leaving Christy ready to sob with frustration.

'Hi, Mum.' Katy dragged a chair away from the table and sat down with one leg curled underneath her. 'Dad. Good night?'

'Marvellous. Perhaps you would like to bounce on the sofa as well as the bed,' Alessandro suggested with sarcastic bite, 'and then I wouldn't have to sleep on it.'

Ben frowned, puzzled as he poured milk into his cup, slopping it everywhere. 'But you don't like us bouncing on the furniture.'

'Dad was joking,' Katy said calmly, reaching for a cloth to mop up the mess her brother had made. 'He's obviously in a bad mood because he slept badly. Tonight he'd better sleep in the bed.'

Alessandro threw his daughter an exasperated look and then turned to Christy. 'How does she suddenly know so much?'

Christy gave a weak smile. 'She's growing up. Don't worry. I'll sleep on the sofa tonight. We'll take turns.'

She poured herself another cup of coffee and missed the thoughtful smile on her daughter's face.

The first person she saw when she arrived at work was Jake Blackwell, the obstetrician.

'Babe! I heard you were back.' He strolled towards her and dragged her into his arms for a hug.

Christy closed her eyes and held onto him. He was their oldest friend and suddenly she wondered exactly what Alessandro had told him. 'It's good to see you.'

Jake gently disengaged himself and looked down at her with a searching gaze. 'That bad, huh?'

'Oh, no, everything is fine,' she lied with a forced smile, and Jake gave a soft laugh.

'If everything is fine, my angel, then why is Alessandro taking everyone's heads off and walking round like a volcano on the brink of eruption?'

'He's angry with me because I took the children away,' Christy muttered, and Jake looked at her thoughtfully.

'You think so?'

Christy stepped back and ran a hand through her hair to check it was still in place. 'What other reason would there be?'

Jake's eyes narrowed. 'Well, I can think of another one but this probably isn't the time or the place to go into that. Are you going to offer to cook me dinner some time? Don't forget I'm just a poor, starving bachelor and I haven't had one of your meals for weeks.'

Christy smiled. It was so good to have friends, she reflected. 'Of course.' It would make eating with Alessandro less tense. 'Are you dating someone special at the moment?'

Jake gave her a wicked smile. 'You know me, still auditioning for Miss Right.'

Christy sighed. She did know him. Knew his fearsome reputation with women. 'You should settle down, Jake.'

'When I find the love of my life, I'll settle down,' he drawled, 'and not a moment before. I have you and Alessandro as an example.'

'Us?' She looked at him, startled. 'What sort of an example are we?'

'The very best,' Jake said softly, lifting a hand to her cheek. 'And don't you forget that. You're crazy about each other.'

'We're separated.'

'So?' Jake gave a dismissive shrug. 'You're both passionate, fiery people. You've lost your way for a while but you'll find it again.'

No, they wouldn't.

She'd lost hope.

Suddenly Christy wanted to blurt everything out. She wanted to tell Jake that Alessandro had put her in the spare room and that he wasn't interested in her any more, but she couldn't do that standing in a draughty, hospital corridor.

As if to confirm that point, Jake's bleeper suddenly sounded and he lifted it from his pocket and read the number with a rueful smile. 'Here we go again. Women just can't do without me.'

Christy couldn't help the smile. 'You haven't changed.'

'And neither have you and Alessandro.' He put the bleeper back in his pocket and gave her a thoughtful look. 'Remember that, Christy. I'll see you later.'

She watched him go, knowing that he was wrong. She *had* changed. Probably more than she'd realised.

'Christy?' Nicky appeared in the corridor. 'I've got a woman coming in by ambulance who collapsed on the tennis court. Can you deal with her?'

Christy hurried towards her. 'Tennis? There's snow on the ground.'

'Indoor court.' Nicky grinned and pushed her into Resus. 'She's on her way now. Billy can help you to start with and he can call Alessandro if he needs to. We don't really know how serious it is. Her sister is following by car. I'll put her in the relatives' room with a cup of tea but don't forget to update her when you have some news.'

The woman arrived still dressed in her white tennis gear and clutching a vomit bowl.

'This is Susan Wilde. She was very sick in the ambulance,' the paramedic said as they lifted her from their stretcher onto the trolley. 'She was playing tennis when she suddenly complained of a headache and collapsed.'

Christy covered the woman with a blanket while she listened to the handover and then Billy arrived and started his examination.

'Mrs Wilde? Can you remember what happened?'

The woman turned her head slowly and looked at him blankly, as if she was having trouble focusing and concentrating. 'Don't know… Pain…' She groaned. 'Neck, head.' Her eyes drifted shut again and Christy checked her observations quickly.

'Her pulse is down and her BP is up,' she said quietly. 'I'll get you a venflon so that you can put a line in and we'll give her some oxygen straight away.'

Billy stared at her and then nodded. 'OK. Yes. Good idea.' He ran a hand through his hair and let out a breath. 'I might just give Mr Garcia a call. Ask him to take a look at her.'

'You get a line in and I'll call him for you,' Christy advised, handing him the necessary gear and then attaching ECG electrodes to the patient's chest. 'He's going to want you to have obtained venous access. It looks as though she might have had a subarachnoid haemorrhage.'

'Right.' Taking the tourniquet from the tray she'd handed him, Billy slid it onto the patient's arm and pulled it tight. As he searched for a vein and slid the venflon into place, Alessandro walked into the room.

'Everything all right in here?'

'I was just going to come and ask your advice,' Billy confessed, releasing the tourniquet and raising his eyebrows as Christy handed him a selection of bottles. 'What are those for?'

'BMG, FBC, clotting screen and U and Es,' Christy said calmly, reaching for the forms to go with the bottles and filling out all of them except the doctor's signature. 'I'll just go and arrange for a chest X-ray because it's obvious that you're going to need one of those.'

She thought she saw a flicker of amusement and admiration in Alessandro's eyes as she walked towards the phone.

By the time she'd finished, Alessandro was examining the patient, who by now was so drowsy she could barely answer and was making little sense at all.

Christy was just wondering whether the woman had actually lapsed into unconsciousness when she gave another groan, rolled onto her side and vomited weakly.

Christy got the bowl there in time and Alessandro frowned.

'We need to give her some morphine and an anti-emetic. Christy, I want you to arrange an urgent CT scan and contact the neurosurgeons.'

'I've already arranged the scan and the neurosurgeons are on their way down.' Christy drew up the drugs that he'd requested and gave them to him to check while Billy stared in amazement.

'You called the scanning department already? When did you arrange that?'

'At the same time that I arranged the chest X-ray. It seemed sensible.' Christy checked the woman's observations on the monitor. 'She's showing signs of raised intracranial pressure, do you want to give her some IV mannitol?'

'We'll do the scan straight away and discuss it with the neurosurgeons,' Alessandro said, a strange light in his eyes as he looked at her. 'I'd forgotten what it was like to work with you.'

She gave him a cool look. 'Had you?' He thought of her as the mother of his children, she realised suddenly. He didn't really see her as an individual any more.

Didn't think she was a capable nurse.

'Is there anything else you need?' she asked. 'Because her sister is in the waiting room and she needs an update. I can send Donna through to help you here and go with her to the scanner.'

'Go and talk to the sister,' Alessandro said immediately, 'and tell her I'll be able to tell her more once we've done the scan and talked to the neurosurgeons.'

Christy pulled off her apron, washed her hands and then walked towards the relatives' room.

CHAPTER FOUR

'SO WHAT'S it like having your wife under your nose in the department,' Jake asked cheerfully as he piled butter onto a baked potato and dropped two bars of chocolate on his tray.

'Surprisingly good. At least she knows what she's doing, which is more than can be said for half the people I'm expected to work with at the moment.' Alessandro eyed Jake's tray with disbelief as they stood in the queue, waiting to pay. 'Blackwell, you do realise that the contents of your tray are likely to give you a heart attack before morning?'

Jake shrugged. 'Chocolate and baked potatoes are the only edible objects in this restaurant. And I don't see why you're surprised about Christy. She was always a brilliant nurse. The brightest I ever worked with.'

'I forgot you worked with her.'

'She did an obstetrics module. All the doctors were crazy about her.'

Alessandro scowled. 'I didn't need to hear that.'

'Why not? It's the truth.' Jake studied a cake loaded with cream. 'Christy is gorgeous.'

'You're talking about the mother of my children,' Alessandro said coldly, and Jake shrugged and walked past the cake.

'So? That doesn't stop her being gorgeous. And, anyway, I thought you didn't want her any more.'

Alessandro inhaled sharply. 'Who said I didn't want her any more?'

'You didn't follow her to London.'

'She left to get away from me,' Alessandro said grittily. 'I assumed that following her would inflame the situation.'

'Did you?' Jake shot him a curious look. 'You really don't understand women at all, do you?'

Alessandro stared at his friend with mounting irritation. 'And you do?'

'Of course. I'm an obstetrician. I'm paid to understand women.' They arrived at the till and Jake beamed at the plump, smiling woman who looked at his tray and clucked with disapproval.

'Where's the nutrition in that lunch, Dr Blackwell?'

'I need energy, not nutrition, Delia,' Jake said cheerfully. 'We're busy on the labour ward and I'm going to need more than carrots to see me through until midnight. That's a nice jumper. The colour suits you. Is it new?'

'You always notice the little things.' Delia beamed and handed him his change. 'Early Christmas present from my daughter who lives in Canada.'

'Is that Gillian? The one with the two-year-old?'

Delia blushed with delight. 'Is there anything you don't remember, Jake?'

'I'm programmed to remember the details of everyone's labour and delivery,' Jake responded with a cheerful wink as he pocketed the change and lifted his tray.

Alessandro rolled his eyes as they walked to the nearest vacant table. 'Do you have to flirt with every woman you meet?'

'Yes, I think I probably do.' Jake sat down and picked up his fork. 'Believe it or not, Garcia, women like it when you notice them. You ought to drop your intimidating Mediterranean macho act and try it some time. Having a guy who behaves like a caveman might be a woman's fantasy, but when it comes to reality they want a man to talk to them.'

Alessandro bit into his sandwich with more savagery than was strictly necessary. 'What are you implying?'

'Nothing.'

Alessandro put the sandwich down on his plate. 'You're suggesting that I don't talk to Christy, but she was in London before I realised anything was wrong and now she's back I can't seem to reach her.'

'No.' Jake dug his fork into the potato and gave him a bland smile. 'Of course you can't.'

'Did you think Christy was happy being a practice nurse?'

Jake chewed thoughtfully. 'Well, she liked the hours, of course, because it meant that she could always be there for the children.' He waved his fork. 'But she missed the pace of A and E. Hardly surprising, really. I think she quite liked things like the asthma clinic because she could make quite a difference to the patients' lives, but syringing ears and doing dressings drove her nuts.'

Alessandro stared at him. 'When did she tell you all that?'

'I don't know.' Jake pushed his plate away and reached for his first bar of chocolate. 'We've chatted about it over the years. Christy was quite a high-powered nurse. She invariably knew more than the doctors when she worked in A and E. It's hardly surprising that she was frustrated, working in a village practice. A bit like putting a racehorse in a riding school, I suppose.'

Had she been frustrated? Alessandro abandoned the sandwich and ran a hand over the back of his neck, suddenly realising that it hadn't ever occurred to him that she was anything less than happy in her work. And he didn't like the fact that she'd confided in Jake. *Since when had Christy confided in Jake?* They were friends, that was true, but he didn't like the idea that his friend knew more about his wife than he did.

Checking that her mother was safely occupied in the kitchen, Katy slunk into the living room where her brother was orchestrating a battle between dinosaurs and toy soldiers.

'Ben, here's a really, really large glass of blackcurrant squash.'

Ben stared at it. 'I'm not thirsty.'

'Good,' Katy said sweetly, 'because I don't want you to drink it. I want you to spill it on the sofa.'

Ben's eyes widened. 'No way! You spill it on the sofa.'

'Don't be ridiculous.' Katy's tone was condescending. 'I'm eleven. I'm *way* past spilling drinks on the sofa. You'll have to do it.'

'But that will make the sofa wet and purple.'

'That's the general idea.'

'Why?'

'Because despite our efforts, our parents are still not sharing a bed,' Katy said with an impatient sigh. 'And they're never going to get back together if they don't share a bed. Everyone knows that adults should share a bed if they're married. It's how they mate.'

Ben picked up another dinosaur. 'What's mate?'

'You're far too young to understand,' Katy said disdainfully. 'You're just going to have to trust me.'

'I don't see how spilling blackcurrant squash will help,' Ben muttered, and Katy rolled her eyes.

'Because it will make the sofa sticky and wet you stupid, idiot baby.'

'I'm not a stupid, idiot baby!!'

'Then trust me and spill the squash!'

'Mum will be mad.'

Katy glared. 'Do you want to go back and live in smelly old London? Do you want Mum and Dad to live together again or not?'

Ben's face crumpled. 'Of course, I do, but—'

'Then spill it, Ben! Just spill it and stop asking questions!'

'But—'

'Ben, you spill things all the time.' Her tone was exasperated. 'You spilt your milk at breakfast. You dropped your pasta at supper. *Spill the blackcurrant before I strangle you!'*

'Mum says you're not allowed to put things round my neck. And if I spill blackcurrant, it will ruin the sofa.'

'That's the idea. Don't worry about that. It won't cost them anything because they can put in an insurance claim, but that will take weeks to come through,' Katy said airily, and Ben looked at her doubtfully.

Katy ground her teeth. 'Ben…'

'All right, I'll spill it.' Ben snatched the squash from her, sprinted across the living room, tripped over a toy he'd left there and spilt the entire contents of the glass over the sofa.

'Even better than I could have predicted,' Katy breathed, staring at the spreading, deep purple stain on the sofa with admiration and satisfaction. 'Well done, baby brother.'

Ben's lip wobbled as he stared at the mess. 'Mummy's going to be mad.'

'Very possibly,' Katy agreed, 'but she isn't going to be sleeping here tonight, and that's the only thing that matters. Don't worry, I'll protect you.'

'You shouldn't have had a drink in the living room.' Christy kept her voice level, reminding herself that it wasn't good to shout at one's children, especially when they were so clearly remorseful. Ben stood in front of her with his head down and his lip wobbling.

'Katy told me to do it!' He burst into sobs just as Alessandro walked in through the front door.

'What's going on here?'

Christy sighed, wondering whether everyone's family was as noisy and complicated as hers. 'I haven't had time to cook any dinner yet. Ben spilt blackcurrant all over the sofa. It's ruined.'

'Good thing,' Alessandro drawled, shrugging his broad shoulders out of his jacket and loosening his tie. 'It was ugly and uncomfortable and sleeping on it was having a detrimental effect on my spine. You've done me a favour, Ben.'

Katy appeared in the doorway, a yoghurt in one hand and a spoon in the other. 'That's decided, then. You'll just have to sleep in the bed with Mum.'

Alessandro turned to look at his daughter, a gleam of suspicion lighting his dark eyes. 'Are you behind this, Katherine?'

Katy took a few steps backwards. 'Don't look at me like that. It isn't good to intimidate your children. And you can't blame me for the fact that Ben spills everything. You *know* he spills everything.'

'Intimidate?' An ebony brow rose as Alessandro surveyed his daughter. 'Since when did I ever intimidate you?'

Ben's sobs grew noisier. 'It's all her fault. She made me do it and she—'

'Hush.' Christy pulled him into her arms and cuddled him close. 'I'm not mad with you, sweetie, honestly. Don't cry. Please, don't cry. It isn't important. It's only a sofa.'

'My house is turning into a war zone,' Alessandro muttered, dragging a hand through his dark hair and letting out a long breath. 'Seeing that you haven't cooked any dinner yet, let's go out.'

Katy's face brightened. 'Great idea. You'll need to get us a babysitter. I nominate Uncle Jake.'

Christy blinked. 'I think Daddy meant all of us.'

'Oh, no, we're much too tired to go out.' Katy gave an exaggerated yawn to prove her point. 'I've got holiday homework to finish and Ben needs his beauty sleep. Not that all the sleep in the world is going to make him half-decent to look at,' she added as an afterthought, and Ben sat up and poked his tongue out.

Alessandro gave a shrug and looked at Christy. 'So—you and I can go out.'

'But...' How could she say that she didn't really want to go out on a date that had been engineered by the children? If he'd asked her, that would have been different. 'Jake won't be free.'

'He's free—I saw him at lunchtime.' Alessandro was already on the phone, and Christy sighed.

'All right. I'll go and change.'

'Wear the black dress, Mummy,' Katy hissed, and Christy frowned.

'What black dress?'

'The little one that makes Daddy grab you from behind.'

Christy blushed and wondered at exactly what point her

daughter had started noticing so much. 'That's a party dress, sweetheart.'

'So? You look pretty in it.'

Christy bit her lip. But did she want to look pretty? Yes, of course she did. But wearing a party dress to go out to dinner in the middle of the week would look desperate, and she had too much pride to show Alessandro just how desperate she was.

Crazy, she thought as she rummaged through her wardrobe. She was having an informal supper with her husband and she had absolutely no idea what to wear.

She wanted to look attractive, but not obvious.

She wanted him to want her.

Wanted him to kiss her. Would that fix things? she wondered. If he kissed her and took her to bed, would they be able to heal their wounds?

In the end she settled for a slinky velvet skirt in a shade of heather and teamed it with a slinky black top that dipped temptingly at the front.

Jake walked through the door as she reached for her coat. He immediately strode over and kissed her. 'You look stunning and beautiful,' he breathed, his eyes lingering on the neckline of her top.

Glancing at Alessandro, Christy wondered why he was glaring. Presumably he was still annoyed at having their evening manipulated by the children.

Clearly he had no real wish to spend time with her. Unlike Jake, he hadn't even commented on what she was wearing.

Jake swept Ben into his arms and stooped to hug an excited Katy.

'Uncle Jake!'

'Did you bring me a present?' Ben wrapped his legs and

arms around Jake like a monkey, and Christy gasped in horror and embarrassment at his question.

'You don't ask people that, Ben,' she admonished, but Jake just grinned.

'Why not? Honesty gets you a long way in life, I always think. If only women were as uncomplicated as children, life would run much more smoothly.' He whipped a bag out from behind his back. 'Sweets and a DVD and maybe a small toy because I haven't seen you for so long.'

'Finally, a grown-up who understands us.' Katy grinned, reaching into the bag to check out the DVD. 'I'm allowed to watch 12s now. This is a PG.'

'That's right. My psyche is sadly underdeveloped and I don't want to risk nightmares. I thought I'd be all right if you held my hand all the way through.' Jake winked at her, his smile placid. 'Lead me to your father's whisky cabinet, angel. I've had a long day.'

'We won't be late,' Christy began, but Katy frowned and pushed them towards the door.

'Don't come back before the end of the DVD or you'll spoil it.'

Christy sighed. 'Don't keep them up late, Jake.'

'Go and enjoy yourselves,' Jake said, delving into the bag he'd brought and producing a new dinosaur for Ben. 'We'll be fine.'

But would she? Christy wondered.

It had been so long since she'd spent an evening with Alessandro that she didn't quite know what they were going to talk about.

Alessandro took her to a noisy, Spanish tapas bar in the middle of town.

Disappointed that he hadn't chosen somewhere quiet and romantic, Christy slid into her chair and reached for a menu.

'We used to come here a lot when we first met—do you remember?'

'The service was quick and what with the hospital and the mountain rescue team, we never had enough time.' Alessandro turned to the hovering waiter and ordered in Spanish.

Christy closed the menu and tried not to mind that he hadn't asked what she wanted.

It was just the way Alessandro was, she thought with weary resignation. The dominant male. Always strong and controlling. At times, it was wonderful. In A and E, with a desperately sick patient, his astonishing leadership qualities saved lives. At home, just occasionally, it would be nice if he showed an interest in her views.

'So...' He lounged back in his chair and surveyed her across the table, his eyes glittering dark in the dim light of the restaurant, 'how are you enjoying being back in A and E?'

Given her thoughts of a few moments earlier, Christy was surprised he'd asked. 'I... Well, I really like it.'

'You're good.'

'And that surprises you?'

He gave a slow smile. 'No. What surprises me is that you seem to have forgotten nothing in the time that you've been away.'

Should she confess that it had surprised her, too? 'I suppose I worked there for so long that some of it is second nature.' She took a deep breath. 'Do you hate having me there?'

'It is impossible to hate someone who makes your working life easier,' he drawled, lifting his glass of wine. 'With so many people off sick and others inexperienced, it becomes difficult to deliver your best performance.'

'And that's so important, isn't it?'

'Of course.' He gave a shrug. 'The patient deserves no less.'

'That's true. But the patients are not your whole life. What about me?' Her voice was soft. 'Didn't our marriage deserve the same attention?'

His broad shoulders tensed. 'We're going to talk about this now? All right, let's talk about this now.' His eyes narrowed and his fingers tightened around the glass. 'We both had busy lives—'

'With no time for each other.' She folded her hands in her lap and looked him in the eye, determined to have her say. *Determined not to let him intimidate her.* 'Do you know how many times I scraped your dinner into the bin during the twelve years of our marriage, Alessandro?'

'My working hours are unpredictable, it's true, but—'

'How many times did we sit down together and talk during the week?'

'At the dinner table, rarely,' he admitted, 'but always we were in the same bed at night.'

The remark was so typical of him that she gave a wry smile. 'That's just sex, Alessandro.'

One ebony brow swooped upwards in silent mockery. *'Just* sex, *querida*?'

Her stomach rolled and fire licked through her veins. She wasn't going to think about sex now, she told herself frantically. She wasn't going to remember what it was like to be in bed with Alessandro. He was a spectacular lover.

'A relationship takes more than an encounter in the bedroom to keep it alive,' she said huskily, and he studied her in brooding silence.

'And that's why you left? You felt neglected? I didn't ask you about your day often enough?'

'I don't think you *ever* asked me about my day. You're

a great father, a skilled and talented doctor, a fantastic climber...' She swallowed. 'But—'

'But I've been a lousy husband,' Alessandro drawled softly, and she shook her head quickly.

'Not lousy, no.' She gripped her glass. 'But you're so driven, so focused on what you do and...I suppose I feel as though you don't notice me any more.'

She wanted to ask about Katya. Wanted to know whether he'd had an affair during the weeks that they'd been apart. But something held her back. He wouldn't do that, she told herself. Alessandro wouldn't do that.

'How long have you hated being a practice nurse?'

She looked at him, surprised by the question. 'I don't hate it.' She hesitated. 'But I suppose part of me is always frustrated. I miss the pace and unpredictability of A and E. You know what it's like—sort of an addiction.'

He gave a wry smile. 'You get high on the adrenaline rush of not knowing what's coming through the door next?'

She returned the smile. 'Yes, in a way. In general practice it's all so much more predictable and routine. And a bit lonely. I was shut in a room all day, seeing an endless stream of patients. We have practice meetings, of course, and I speak to the GPs about various patients, but I miss the teamwork of A and E.'

Alessandro sat back in his chair as the waiter delivered plates of food to their table. 'So why have you stuck at it for so long?'

'Because it fits with school hours,' Christy said slowly, leaning forward to examine the various dishes he'd ordered. 'It's convenient for family life. But the children are older now...'

Should she tell him that she didn't think that she could go

back? Should she tell him that, after experiencing the buzz of A and E again, she was starting to rethink her whole life?

'Why did you never tell me any of this before?'

She shrugged. 'What was the point? One of us had to be there for the children and that wasn't going to be you—you're not that sort of man. I knew that when I married you and that was fine. And, anyway, you had a great career. And I suppose I've never told you any of this before because...' She broke off, suddenly hesitant. 'Well, because you've never asked.'

'Perhaps because I assumed that if there was a problem you would tell me.' He frowned. 'I'm not great at guessing games and reading minds. That's more Jake's forte.'

'Jake. He's such a good person, isn't he?' Christy smiled to herself and missed the dangerous flash in Alessandro's eyes. 'I can't believe we've been friends for such a long time. And I can't understand why he hasn't settled down with some very lucky woman long before now.' She heard Alessandro's sharp intake of breath and glanced up.

'Perhaps he wants someone who is unavailable,' he snapped. His tone was icy cold and she looked at him, surprised by the comment.

'Oh, no! Jake isn't like that. He'd never go after a married woman.'

'But if she wasn't married any more, she'd be fair game,' Alessandro said tightly. 'Isn't that right?'

'Well, I suppose so. Maybe.' Christy stared at him, wondering why he suddenly seemed so tense and moody. Had she said something? 'Anyway, why are we talking about Jake?'

There was a long, pulsing silence while Alessandro studied her and drummed his fingers on the table. 'He just seemed to come up in conversation,' he said silkily, and she gave a puzzled smile.

'Well, we've all known each other and been friends for the same length of time, so I suppose that's natural.' She helped herself to a spoonful of another dish and tried not to mind that Alessandro suddenly seemed tense and uncommunicative.

He didn't enjoy her company any more, she thought miserably as she chewed her way through a mouthful of food that she didn't even want. And he still hadn't said anything about what she was wearing or made a single move in her direction.

It was so unlike him. In the past, whenever they'd had a problem, he'd just grabbed her and that had been that. Now he didn't seem to want to touch her.

Was it because he didn't find her attractive any more?

Or was it because he was seeing someone else?

Back in the barn, the DVD had just finished and Ben was changing into his pyjamas in front of the fire.

'Uncle Jake, what's mating?'

Jake choked on his whisky. 'Well, I...' He cleared his throat and vowed never to babysit again. 'Ben, you've had seven years to ask that question. Why do you have to ask it now, while Mummy is out?'

'Because Katy said it earlier,' Ben said solemnly, wriggling his arms and head into his pyjama top. 'She said that we have to get Mummy and Daddy back into the same bedroom so that they can mate. It's why I broke the bed and spilled my drink.'

Jake gave up on the whisky. 'You did *what*?'

'I broke the bed,' Ben said patiently, 'by bouncing hard.

Katy did it, too. So Mummy couldn't sleep there any more. But it didn't work.'

Jake put his glass down on the nearest table. 'It didn't?'

Ben shook his head. 'Daddy went and slept on the sofa, so I spilt my blackcurrant on it.'

Jake's gaze slid to the sofa on the far side of the room, now covered in towels. 'So you did.'

'Now Daddy *has* to sleep with Mummy in the bed,' Ben said proudly, and Jake looked at him thoughtfully before shifting his gaze to Katy.

'It appears that you've been rather busy, young lady.'

'You can't tell me off. You're my godfather. You're only responsible for my religious education.'

He lifted a brow. 'No more presents, then.'

She grinned. 'Presents are acceptable.'

'I just bet they are.' Jake studied her face and thought how much she resembled her father. 'Have you been interfering?'

'Maybe. Just a little.' Her expression was wary, as if she was unsure of his response. 'Never underestimate a child.'

'I don't,' Jake said dryly, rising to his feet and reaching for his glass. He had a strong feeling he was going to need a large refill. 'Let's get your brother to bed and then you and I need to have a talk, Katherine Isabel Luisa Garcia. You have some *serious* explaining to do.'

CHAPTER FIVE

'You look knackered.' Nicky juggled an armful of dressings and frowned as Christy walked onto the unit. 'Heavy night?' She gave a saucy wink and Christy gave a wan smile.

What would Nicky say, she wondered, if she confessed that she'd spent the night lying next to Alessandro and he hadn't laid a finger on her? Not only that, but he'd clearly had no trouble sleeping, whereas she'd lain there, tense and breathless, waiting for him to touch her. His steady, rhythmic breathing had done nothing for her ego or her hopes for the survival of their marriage.

Oh, damn, damn, damn.

He obviously didn't even find her attractive any more. It was the only possible explanation for not touching her.

And just to bolster her insecurities still further, Katya chose that moment to stroll up to them. 'Hi, there.' Her voice was smoky and seductive and her blonde hair fell down her back in a perfect, smooth sheet. She wore a pale pink roll-neck jumper and a tight navy skirt that ended just above the knee, and could have walked straight out of the pages of a glossy magazine.

'Have either of you seen Alessandro? He promised to spend some time talking me through some interesting X-rays.'

Christy gritted her teeth and swallowed hard. She wasn't going to be jealous, she told herself. She wasn't going to be paranoid or childish. So, the girl was beautiful. That didn't mean anything...

'Alessandro is with a head injury patient in Resus,' Nicky said in a cool tone, 'and I need you to tie your hair back in this department, please. It's unhygienic worn loose.'

Katya frowned slightly and then shrugged. 'No problem. I have some grips in my bag.'

'Good.' Nicky gave a brisk nod, very much the sister-in-charge. 'I'd appreciate it if you'd use them.'

Katya strolled off and Nicky stared after her, still clutching the dressing packs to her chest. 'I don't like that girl. Where does she think she is? On a catwalk?'

'She looks great.' Christy said with a forced smile, and Nicky grinned.

'Oh, yeah—and how great is she going to look when a drunk has vomited down her pink cashmere? Are you OK? You look pale.'

'Just a bit tired.'

'Look...' Nicky put a hand on her arm, her gaze sympathetic, 'I know things are rough for you and Alessandro at the moment, but I know you'll work it out. The two of you were meant to be together.'

Were they?

She was starting to wonder.

'There you are!' Sean strode down the corridor towards them, interrupting them in mid-conversation. 'Christy, the mountain rescue team have had a call about a man who has fallen some distance. Might have chest and head injuries.

The details are a bit hazy but we're trying to send an advance party of five out, with the rest of the team following.'

Christy stared at him blankly. 'And?' What did it have to do with her? She hadn't been out with the MRT for several years.

'We're a bit thin on the ground in the team at the moment,' Sean said wearily. 'Everyone is either in bed with this flu bug or they're snowed in or all sorts of other feeble excuses. Alessandro is going and I wondered if you'd join him in the advance party.'

'Me?' Christy's voice was an astonished squeak and Sean gave her a keen look.

'Why not you? You're fit and you know these mountains. You were the best climber we had at one time.'

Christy licked her lips. 'Yes, but I had the kids and—'

'I wasn't aware that childbirth affected your mountaineering abilities,' Sean drawled, glancing round as Alessandro approached. 'Garcia, just the man. I'm trying to persuade your wife to join you on this callout while I scrabble around and try and get some other people together.'

Alessandro's brows met in a frown. 'Christy?'

'Why does everyone think it's such a strange idea?' Sean wondered aloud, and Alessandro's mouth tightened.

'Because the weather is foul and I don't want her risking—'

'I'll go,' Christy said immediately, turning to Nicky. 'If that's all right with you?'

Alessandro didn't think she could do it, and she was determined to prove him wrong, just as she had by working in A and E. What was the matter with the man?

'I'm used to it.' Nicky gave a resigned smile. 'I'll just run the department on fresh air as usual.'

'My walking boots are in the car but all my other gear is at home.'

'You can use Ally's gear,' Sean was already walking towards the door. 'You're about the same size. My dear wife never gets round to removing it from my boot. Come on.'

As they walked towards the car Christy's anger at Alessandro mingled with excitement. Ahead of them the fells loomed, covered in snow and ice and potentially lethal. Who had gone walking in this weather? she wondered. How had they got themselves into trouble?

'You stick right by me,' Alessandro growled as they slid into his car, and she turned and glared at him.

'Why? In case I fall down a hole? For crying out loud, Alessandro, when I was twenty I could outclimb you any day!'

It wasn't strictly true and she saw by the lift of his eyebrow that he was aware of that fact, but he didn't contradict her.

'You're not twenty any more.'

'No, I'm thirty-two. Ancient.' She stared at him in disbelief. 'Is this what this is all about? You think I'm suddenly too old to do these things?'

'It has nothing to do with age.' Alessandro crunched the gears viciously. 'You're the mother of my children.'

'And what? That means I should stay at home and knit?' Her voice rose and she took a deep breath and forced herself to calm down. 'Giving birth to children doesn't come with a personality transplant. Believe it or not, I'm still the same person I was twelve years ago when you first met me!'

'You can't just swan up a mountain when you haven't been near one for years.'

'That's rubbish! I may not have been on the team, but I've done plenty of climbing and walking and I'm every bit as fit as you are!'

The atmosphere in the car was simmering with mounting tension and she looked away, so angry that she wanted to hit something. Or someone.

'Fine.' His voice was tight as he concentrated on keeping the car on the road in the lethal conditions. 'Just no heroics.'

'Heroics?' She turned and glared at him as she tugged a hat onto her head. 'Since when have I suffered from a hero complex?'

'You always took risks when you were climbing.'

'That's *not* true.'

'As you said yourself, you haven't been with the team for a long time.' Alessandro changed gear with a vicious thrust of his hand. 'What you've forgotten could prove dangerous. I just don't want your ego to get in the way. If you don't know something, say so.'

'What I know is that I'm not the one with the ego around here,' she spat angrily, jamming her feet into her boots and yanking so hard at the laces that she almost snapped them. 'There's only room in this car for one ego and yours is taking up all the space!'

He had no confidence in her whatsoever, she thought, her temper building to dangerous levels. 'I hadn't been in A and E for years either,' she pointed out angrily, 'but so far I haven't killed anyone! This used to be my life, Alessandro! This was what I did, but somewhere along the way I've lost it all. I've lost A and E, I've lost Mountain Rescue and now I've lost—' She had been about to say 'you' but she stopped herself just in time. Instead, she clamped her teeth down on her bottom lip and blinked back the hot sting of tears.

His opinion of her was obviously at rock bottom, she thought miserably as she turned her head and stared out of the window while she struggled for control.

He slowed down to take an icy corner. 'You make it

sound as though your entire married life has been one big sacrifice.'

'No.' Confident that she was back in control again, she turned her head and studied his hard, handsome profile. *She loved him so much.* Despite everything, she completely adored him and always would. 'That isn't how it is. The children are everything. But there are parts of me that I put to one side while they were small and you can't blame me for wanting them back now.'

Alessandro was silent, his strong hands gripping the steering-wheel. 'I had no idea that you missed it so badly.' His voice was a low growl and she swallowed hard, her anger dissolving to nothing, suddenly desperate to make him understand.

'Wouldn't you miss it? If you were the one who had to give it all up, wouldn't you miss it?'

'That's different.'

'How is it different, Alessandro? Because you're a man and I'm a woman?' Her temper boiled up again and she resisted the temptation to thump him hard. 'Well, I've got news for you, my Neanderthal, chauvinistic male, it isn't different at all! Which marriage rule book says that it's the woman who has to make all the changes in her life?'

He inhaled sharply. 'You knew when you married me that I wasn't the sort of man who could stay at home and change nappies, but if you'd wanted a nanny you could have said so.'

'I didn't want a nanny! I wanted to be the one to raise our children.' She was shouting now, shouting as she zipped up her jacket and reached for her gloves. 'But I'm allowed to be honest about missing some bits of my old life. And I'm also allowed to see if I want some of those bits back now that the children are older. Is that really asking too much?'

Alessandro flicked the indicator and pulled into the car

park at the mountain rescue base. Then he switched off the engine and sat staring into the freezing cold December day, his handsome face blank of expression. 'No,' he said finally. 'It isn't asking too much.'

'When we first met, we were doing the same things,' she said, suddenly desperate to say the things that had been building inside her for months. 'We were on the same path. But somehow that's all changed. You've gone on ahead and I've been left behind.'

He turned towards her. 'Is that how you see it?'

'No,' she said quietly. 'It's just how it is.'

She wanted to ask where that left their relationship but he seemed so distant and icily remote that she didn't know what to say and was relieved to see Jake and two other members of the MRT striding across the car park towards them.

'Oh, great—there's Jake.' Grateful for a reason to escape from the chill inside the car, she opened the door and slid out.

Alessandro sat for a moment, simmering with mounting tension, the expression in his dark eyes approaching dangerous as he watched her greet Jake with a warm hug.

Had she always been so demonstrative with Jake?

Why had he never noticed how physical they were before now?

He knew that Jake found Christy attractive but never before this moment had he had reason to ask questions about where Christy's affections lay because he'd always known that she adored *him*. He'd been utterly secure in their love.

From the first day they'd met, he'd taken her adoration and devotion for granted. They had been so crazy about each other, *so hot for each other*, that it had never entered his head that she would ever look at another man.

But something had obviously changed over the years and now it seemed that Jake knew things about Christy that he didn't. Private, intimate things. Like the fact that she'd never really been happy as a practice nurse. And the fact that she missed bits of her old life.

Alessandro stared out of the window and his mouth tightened.

He should have known those things about his wife.

Why hadn't she told him? Why had Jake been easier to talk to? Experiencing self-doubt for one of the few times in his adult life, Alessandro cursed softly and reached into the back seat for the rest of his gear.

He'd get this rescue out of the way and then he was going to sort this out.

He loved her. He loved her desperately and keeping his distance from her was turning him into a crazy man. But if she was in love with Jake then he'd give her the freedom she wanted. Wasn't that what you were supposed to do with someone you loved? Set them free?

Christy lifted the pack onto her back, careful not to look at Alessandro.

He didn't think that she could do this, but she was going to prove him wrong. Prove that she was more that just the mother of his children.

'According to the call we had, he was one of four walkers taking a path just below the summit,' Alessandro said as he assembled the advance party. 'They called the police on a mobile and one of them had a global positioning instrument so we've got a good idea where they are.'

'Weather's looking unfriendly,' Jake observed as he lifted his pack onto his back and settled it comfortably.

'Might need to carry him off the hill if the helicopter can't fly in this.'

Alessandro nodded. 'That's a distinct possibility. One of his group reported that he had breathing difficulties so we're carrying an oxygen cylinder just in case. All right, let's go.'

He strode out in front and Christy walked behind him, hoping that she wasn't going to fall down gasping for breath because that would be too humiliating for words. She was fit, she reminded herself. And she knew these mountains as well as she knew her own back garden. The fact that she hadn't been part of a proper rescue for a few years really didn't signify. Once it had been a huge part of her life. The regular training sessions, callouts, social events—she'd done it all and she'd loved every minute of it. And all that knowledge was still there, she reminded herself.

All the same, she was quite relieved to be sandwiched between Alessandro and Jake. Having someone in front and behind made it easier to resist the temptation to slow the pace.

They walked steadily for two hours in decreasing visibility and deteriorating weather conditions and then heard shouts from up ahead.

'Bingo,' Jake murmured, as they pushed on through the swirling snow and mist and finally saw torches and bright jackets on the path ahead.

By now Christy's cheeks were stinging with cold and her eyelashes were wet and clumped together. But she loved being outdoors in the mountains. The wind had picked up, the weather was wild and unforgiving and it all seemed as far from the rain-washed streets of London as it was possible to be.

The injured man was sitting propped against a rock, covered in several coats. There was blood on his forehead and he had a hand on his chest, his face crumpled in pain. Hope lit his eyes as he saw them trudge towards him through the mist and snow.

Crouching next to him, offering moral support, was one of his fellow walkers, and he stood up as they arrived, his relief plainly visible on his tired features. 'Boy, am I glad to see you! My first aid isn't up to the challenge, I'm afraid. He fell about twenty feet,' he told them, 'and since then he's had real trouble with his breathing. It's really noisy. He was really struggling so I sat him up—I hope I did the right thing. I know you're not supposed to move an injured person, but—'

'You've done well,' Christy assured him quickly, heaving her rucksack off her back.

Alessandro was already reaching for the oxygen, his movements as decisive as ever.

That was one of the things she loved and admired about him, Christy thought to herself. Some doctors were fine as long as they were in a hospital, surrounded by high-tech equipment and a phone to give them access to doctors from different specialities. Alessandro was equally cool and self-assured when he was halfway up a mountain in a blizzard with a potentially seriously injured patient.

He was a man who thrived on challenge and she'd always found his inner strength and bold self-confidence incredibly seductive. There was no situation that Alessandro wouldn't be able to handle.

Ignoring her aching shoulders, she dropped to her knees beside him, trying to ignore the angry howl of the icy wind that threatened to obliterate her vision.

'His name is Simon Duke,' the friend volunteered, 'and he's fifty-two.'

'Did you see what happened?' She knew that an account

of the accident might give clues as to the injuries they were potentially dealing with.

'We've been out since early this morning. We'd just started our descent when Simon slipped.' He pulled a face. 'I've been climbing and walking in the mountains for most of my life. I never thought I'd be calling on the services of the mountain rescue team. To say that I'm finding this highly embarrassing would be a major understatement.'

'It happens to the best of us,' Jake said cheerfully, squinting through the blizzard as he heaved the pack off his back and removed the oxygen cylinder he'd been carrying. The snow was now blowing horizontally and their packs had started to freeze. 'I must say, you chose fabulous weather for your walk.'

'Ignore him, he's deranged,' Christy said dryly, then glanced towards Alessandro for guidance. 'If he fell twenty feet then he should probably be wearing a collar?'

'Definitely. But we also need to get him into a shelter while I check him over.' Alessandro reached into his rucksack and pulled out the necessary equipment. 'Jake, get that oxygen going and let's get him into a bivvy tent so that I can examine him properly. We're going to have to carry him off because there's no way they can fly a helicopter in this.'

Simon gasped and closed his eyes briefly. 'So sorry to be such a nuisance,' he panted. 'Can't believe I need oxygen.'

'I'm glad you do,' Jake drawled as he removed his gloves so that he could adjust the flow rate. 'If I'd lugged this canister all the way up this hill for nothing, I would have been steaming mad.' He handed the mask to Christy and she fixed the mask over the man's mouth and nose.

'There.' She spoke gently. 'That should help. We're just going to get you some shelter before you get too cold.'

Jake moved across to help Alessandro with the shelter. 'Has anyone placed a bet on a white Christmas?'

'We always have a white Christmas up here.' Noticing how pale Simon looked, Christy checked his pulse while her team members erected a tent. She glanced up at the patient's walking companion. 'So was this a pre-Christmas holiday?'

'Supposed to be.' He gave a rueful smile. 'We were making the most of a few days' peace and quiet before we go down to London for Christmas.'

'And he slipped?'

'Just seemed to lose his footing. I suppose there must have been a patch of ice on the rock,' the man shrugged. 'One minute he was walking along happily, in front of me, the next he was slithering downwards. Gave me a bad moment, I can tell you. I think he managed to grab hold of a rock or something, otherwise goodness knows how far he would have fallen.'

The injured man tried to say something and Christy put a hand on his shoulder and shook her head. 'Don't talk, Simon,' she said quickly. 'We'll soon have you inside the bivvy tent and then the doctor can look at you.'

His companion looked at her in surprise. 'He's a doctor?'

'You've got half the A and E department up here,' Jake said cheerfully, walking back across to them, 'and just to cap it, if you want a baby delivered then I'm your man.'

Christy giggled and then caught something black in Alessandro's gaze and her laughter faded. What was the matter with him? Normally he found Jake as amusing as she did.

Soon Simon was safely inside the protective covering of the tent and Christy saw more lights flashing through the snow. 'Looks like the rest of the team are arriving.'

'More? Obviously we've bothered a great number of people.'

'It takes a lot of people to stretcher someone off a mountain,' Christy explained. She stuck her head inside the bivvy tent and Alessandro looked up from his examination.

'He has broken ribs and a broken ankle. He's not showing any signs of a pneumothorax,' he said swiftly, 'so I'm going to splint the ankle and give him some analgesia and get him off this hill before he gets hypothermia.'

Christy helped him stabilise the injured walker and get him into a fleece-lined casualty bag.

The rest of the team joined them and Christy helped them put together the two halves of a stretcher that would be used to carry the casualty down off the mountain. It was a task that they'd practised over and over again during training evenings, assembling the stretcher as fast as possible. Once, she recalled, they'd even done it in the dark to try and mimic the conditions they might face on the mountain. Now, with Alessandro's gaze resting on her all too frequently, she was glad of that training. Glad that she knew exactly what to do and wasn't letting herself down.

Only when they were ready did they remove the shelter that was protecting their casualty.

By now, a team of twenty-five had assembled and one of the other MRT members stood at the head of the stretcher and acted as an anchor to prevent the stretcher moving downhill while it was being prepared for evacuation.

Alessandro made another check on his patient and then tied a rope to the stretcher with a bowline knot.

'We're going to have to do this very carefully,' he instructed, 'because he's already suffering from chest injuries.'

'How do I know you're not going to drop me?' Simon said weakly, and Christy smiled.

'Because you've got ten bulky guys holding onto the stretcher and a rope as back-up. And if we drop you, we're fired.'

The man managed a smile. 'You're all volunteers.'

'You think we do this for nothing?' Jake's blue eyes gleamed with wicked humour as he tightened the straps. 'That would make me certifiably insane, don't you think?'

Christy heaved her pack onto her back. 'Well, now that you mention it...'

How had she survived without this? she wondered. The comradeship and the banter. The physical challenge of extracting someone from a perilous situation.

Eventually everyone was satisfied, the safety checks had been made and the team started their descent, picking their way over boulders made treacherous by ice and snow. Whenever possible, they sledged the stretcher down the mountain and finally the mist and snow cleared and the road came into sight.

As Christy slithered and slipped, she noticed Alessandro constantly glancing in her direction.

Checking up on her?

The MRT vehicle that doubled as an ambulance was waiting.

'You're only a ten-minute drive from the hospital,' Christy told Simon as they carried him the final few metres. 'They'll soon have you comfortable.'

He shook his head. 'My wife is going to kill me. She's always telling me I'm too old to be walking in the hills.'

'Ignore her,' Jake advised cheerfully as he yanked open the back of the vehicle and prepared to lift the stretcher inside. 'What do women know about anything?' He winked at Christy and she gave a wan smile.

Thanks to Alessandro, she was starting to feel as though she knew nothing.

Leaving the rest of the work to their colleagues, Jake pulled her gently to one side and gave her a searching look. 'You all right, babe?'

'Of course.' Behind her, they were loading the injured man into the ambulance. 'Why wouldn't I be?'

'Hey.' Jake frowned. 'This is me you're talking to. Not some stranger. I can tell you're not all right. I don't suppose the look on your face has anything to do with the broken bed and the ruined sofa?'

Her eyes widened. 'You know about that?'

'I talk to my goddaughter.' For once, Jake's expression was serious. 'Obviously things aren't going that well between the two of you. I assumed that once you were under the same roof, you'd be able to sort your problems out.'

'I thought so, too.' Her voice was husky and suddenly she had a wild impulse to throw herself against Jake's broad shoulders and cry her eyes out. *She badly needed a hug.* 'But I was wrong.' She glanced across to where Alessandro was standing, his glossy dark hair touched by the snow, his manner autocratic and confident as he talked to one of his fellow team members. 'He doesn't want me any more, Jake. He doesn't love me.'

Her voice broke on the words and Jake swore under his breath and pulled her into his arms. 'Don't cry,' he said softly, his hands gently smoothing her back. 'You're wrong, Christy. He does love you.'

She pulled away from him, embarrassed at her sudden loss of control. Ashamed to have revealed something so private, even to their oldest and dearest friend. 'No.' She shook her head. 'I hoped he did, but I was just deluding myself.'

'What makes you say that?'

'When I went down to London, he didn't come after me.'

'You wanted him to?'

'Of course I did, you stupid oaf! What sort of a question is that?' She gave him a watery smile. 'I thought you were supposed to understand women?'

'Me?' Jake pretended to look baffled. 'Oh, that's just an act I put on to help me pull. It never fails. What else makes you think he doesn't love you?'

She bit her lip. 'We haven't…been close since I came home and that's not like him. Normally he's very…' She blushed slightly, embarrassed that she was revealing so much. 'Very physical.'

Jake's gaze was steady on her face. 'Perhaps he's giving you space.'

She shook her head. 'Alessandro is much too selfish for that,' she muttered. 'If he wants something, he goes after it and he gets it. You know what he's like.'

'I think he's just taken his eye off the ball.' Jake stretched out a hand to remove some snow from her hair. 'It's good to have you back on the team.'

'Alessandro doesn't think so,' she said, unable to keep the hurt out of her voice. 'He thinks that all I'm capable of is picking up after the children. He doesn't see me as a woman any more.'

'Doesn't he?' For a moment, Jake's expression was thoughtful. Then he smiled. 'Hang in there, babe. Everything is going to be fine.'

She rolled her eyes, touched by his comment but lacking his optimism. 'It's sweet of you to say so, but how can everything possibly be fine, you great dope?'

He treated her to the smile that had women lusting after him in droves. 'Because this is Christmas, my angel. Peace on earth and goodwill to all men. The time for miracles and forgiveness. Why don't you just be patient and see what special gift Santa brings you this year?'

'I don't think Santa does marriage rescue, does he?' She still didn't see how any of it could be fine, but she appreciated his efforts to make her feel better, so she smiled. 'Thank you,' she said softly, touching his arm with her hand, 'for being a good friend.'

He stared down at her thoughtfully. 'You're a beautiful, sexy woman, Christy,' he said quietly. 'If I'd seen you first, you would have been mine. But Alessandro fell in love with you on sight and there was no contest. You never even noticed me.'

She stood in stunned silence, her eyes wide. She'd never realised that he felt that way. She didn't know what to say. How was she supposed to respond? 'Jake, I—'

'Fight for him, Christianna,' Jake said quietly, a lopsided smile on his face. 'I stepped aside because I could see the strength of what you shared. I've always seen it. Always envied it. Why do you think I haven't married before now? Because I've seen what love can be and I won't settle for anything less. Fight for it, babe.'

She stared up at him. 'But if I'm right that Alessandro doesn't love me any more then...'

Jake shrugged. 'Then all you'll be left with is damaged pride, and what's pride when the love of your life is at stake? Live up to the promise of your furious, angry hair, sweetheart, and fight.'

She stood in silence with the snow falling all around her and the temperature dropping to well below freezing. There was a shriek of a siren as the ambulance took off towards the hospital and the slamming of car doors as the various members of the mountain rescue team sorted out their equipment.

He was right, of course, she thought, feeling the snow

flutter past her cheeks. Instead of playing these silly games, she should be fighting for her man. Trying to win him back. She'd never been one to give up when things got tough. That wasn't how she was.

Alessandro was the only man she'd ever loved. *The only man she ever could love.*

A smile spread across her face and, on impulse, she stood on tiptoe and kissed Jake on the cheek.

'Thank you,' she whispered. 'For being the very best friend to both of us.'

Then she turned and walked back to the car and didn't notice Alessandro staring after her, the expression in his dark eyes bordering on the dangerous.

CHAPTER SIX

'MUM, can we go to the forest to choose our tree tomorrow?'

Christy looked up from injecting brandy into the Christmas cake. 'I— Yes, why not? We usually get it the week before Christmas.'

'And is Dad coming, too?'

Christy inhaled sharply. *How was she supposed to know?* Alessandro had hardly spoken to her since they'd returned from the mountain rescue the day before. At work he'd been cold and distant and he'd arrived home late and come to bed long after her.

'Well…'

'Of course I'm coming.' Alessandro strolled into the room, still bare-chested after his shower, his jaw dark with stubble. 'Family ritual—choosing the biggest tree in the forest.'

Christy felt her insides drop with longing. She wanted to slide her hands over his bronzed, muscular body—wanted to feel his hands on her. Suddenly she had a disturbingly vivid mental picture of his hard body coming down on hers and—

'Christy?'

She snapped out of her erotic daydream and realised that he was watching her with a slumberous expression on his handsome face. *Did he know?* she wondered. *Did he know that she'd been imagining the two of them together?*

'Sorry.' The croak in her voice betrayed her. 'Did you say something?'

'I said that we are both going to the Snow Ball tomorrow night,' he said in that slightly accented drawl that always sent her pulse racing. 'Your mother has offered to babysit.'

'Oh...' Her heart fluttered. She couldn't remember the last time they'd gone out together, let alone to the Snow Ball. It was held every Christmas for all the hospital staff but usually Alessandro was working.

Her heart lifted at the prospect of a proper evening out.

It would be her chance to dress up.

To remind him that the mother of his children was also a living, breathing sexual woman.

If she was going to follow Jake's advice and fight, then what better place to start than at a party?

Ben frowned. 'But if you go out then it means you can't read my story.'

'I'll read your story.' Katy elbowed her brother hard and beamed at both of them. 'Sounds great! A lovely, family day. Christmas tree followed by Snow Ball. Can't wait.'

Alessandro's dark gaze slid towards his daughter. 'You don't mind having a babysitter again?'

'Mind? Why would we mind?'

Ben opened his mouth but closed it again in response to his sister's quelling look.

Why was he suggesting the party? Christy wondered. Was Alessandro suddenly keen to mend fences, too?

But then she remembered that, apart from that one passionate kiss at the hospital, he hadn't once laid a finger on her. It was so unlike him that the only possible explanation was that he just didn't find her attractive any more.

But Jake was right and she wasn't going to give up without a fight.

She bit her lip and mentally ran through the contents of her wardrobe.

The situation merited something new. Something sexy and feminine. There was a little boutique not far from the hospital. If she spoke to Nicky and skipped food, she should just about have time at lunchtime.

Alessandro poured himself a coffee and ran a hand over his rough jaw. 'I need to go and shave,' he said gruffly, 'I'll see you at work.'

The heavy snow had played havoc with the roads and pavements and A and E was crowded with people who had slipped on the ice.

'Show me another Colles' fracture and I'm resigning,' Nicky groaned as she carried a pile of X-rays towards fracture clinic. 'I wish people would just stay at home and watch television. I can't remember when I last ate and I am *starving*.'

At that moment the ambulance hotline rang and Nicky scooped up the phone, tucking the X-rays under her arm as she listened and asked questions.

'Child swallowed mother's iron tablets,' she called out as she replaced the phone, 'ETA five minutes. Will you and Alessandro take this one because I must get round to fracture clinic.'

Christy nodded and Alessandro came striding down the corridor in a dark suit that emphasised the width of his shoulders.

'He's been upstairs with the powers that be, arguing for

more staff,' Nicky muttered as he strode towards them, 'and judging from the black look on his face, he didn't win. Can't imagine why. He always intimidates me when he's in one of his cold moods.'

'Two sides to a coin,' Christy muttered, and Nicky frowned.

'Sorry?'

Christy shook her head. 'Nothing.' But she knew that underneath his sometimes remote, chilly exterior was a boiling, red-hot passion capable of erupting with volcanic force.

'Despite having lived in this country for the past twelve years, sometimes I still think there is a language barrier,' Alessandro growled, and then switched into a flow of rapid Spanish that was incomprehensible to all except Christy.

Nicky blinked and turned to Christy. 'All right, you're married to the guy—translation, please.'

Christy smiled. She knew enough Spanish to have picked up the gist of his tirade and most of it wasn't polite. 'He's basically saying that they weren't that sympathetic but he told them that we need more staff or the unit will have to close,' she said smoothly, choosing to leave out the blunter aspects of Alessandro's invective.

Alessandro lifted an eyebrow in mockery. 'Selective translation, *querida*?'

'My Spanish isn't good enough,' Christy lied, but her eyes twinkled. 'There were several words that I didn't recognise.'

Alessandro stared at her for a long moment and her heart rate started to increase.

Nicky cleared her throat. 'I hate to interrupt this little multi-cultural interlude but if you'd stop gibbering in a foreign language for a moment, I might be able to hand over the details of this child and get to X-Ray before some sad patient complains about the level of service in this place. I don't want to be tomorrow's headlines in the tabloids, if it's all the same to you. Call me fussy, but "Patients Abandoned by Killer Nurse" wouldn't make my mum's day.'

Alessandro dragged his gaze away from Christy's. 'What child?'

'They're bringing in a child who has ingested iron,' Christy said, and Alessandro's eyes narrowed.

'How much?'

'Don't know that,' Nicky muttered, checking her notes, 'just that he's six years old and he's swallowed his mother's tablets. Big panic. On their way in as we speak. Off you go, guys. Save lives. But do it in English or no one will have a clue what you're talking about.'

And with that she stalked down the corridor, still juggling the X-rays and muttering about her grumbling stomach as the sound of an ambulance siren grew louder.

'I'll bleep the paediatricians and an anaesthetist,' Christy said, and Alessandro gave a nod.

'I'll meet the ambulance and see you in Paediatric Resus.'

The child was crying miserably and Christy felt her heart twist. He reminded her so much of Ben. Instinctively she stepped towards the little boy but Alessandro was there before her.

'There, now,' he said softly, squatting down so that he was at the same level as the boy. 'Today is my lucky day because you have come to visit me in my special wizard's laboratory.'

The little boy's lip continued to wobble but he stared at Alessandro with wide eyes. 'Wizard?'

'Of course.' He waved a hand around the room. 'This is where I do all my experiments.' He reached into the pocket of his trousers, removed a coin and promptly made it disappear. The boy gasped in delight when it was 'retrieved' from his ear.

Christy grinned. That was Ben's favourite trick, too.

'Hide something else,' the little boy said in a small voice, and the mother gave a wobbly smile.

'Luke's always hiding things. You should see what I find in his pockets.' She bit her lip and looked at Christy, her expression full of guilt. 'I can't believe this has happened. I didn't even know those tablets were dangerous,' she whispered as she moved closer to the trolley. 'You can buy iron over the counter so I didn't really think it was too bad, but I had a friend with me and she said that iron can be lethal.' She covered her hand with her mouth and Alessandro gave Christy a sharp frown.

Interpreting his look, Christy took the mother to one side. Alessandro was successfully calming the child down—he didn't need the mother upsetting him again. 'The important thing right now is to find out how much he has taken and treat him,' she said gently. 'Did you bring the bottle?'

'Oh, yes...' The woman stuck her hand into her coat pocket and pulled out a bottle. 'It's supposed to have a child-proof cap.'

'Some children are born dexterous and inquisitive,' Christy said dryly, thinking of Ben's antics.

The mother reached for a tissue and blew her nose. 'I can't believe he took them,' she whispered, her face blotched with tears. 'Or that I was stupid enough to leave them on the kitchen table. He said they looked like sweets. I only turned my back for a moment—'

'All drugs, even vitamins, should be kept well out of reach of children, but the important thing now is to assess how many he's taken,' Christy said. 'Let's just concentrate on sorting him out. Try not to be upset because your distress will make him worse.'

Alessandro took the bottle and examined it. 'Do you know how many were in here?'

The mother shook her head. 'It was a full bottle last week and I haven't missed a dose, so quite a few.'

'And has he been sick?'

Again the mother shook her head and Christy held out her hand. 'I'll count the tablets,' she suggested, 'and that will give us an idea how many he's swallowed.'

At that moment, Billy hurried into the room to help, closely followed by the paediatric registrar.

'The important thing is the amount of elemental iron that has been ingested,' Alessandro told Billy in response to his question about iron poisoning.

Christy counted the tablets. 'Eight missing.' It was a lot, but Alessandro's expression didn't change.

'All right,' he said calmly, removing his jacket. 'We need to check his serum iron, glucose, do a full blood count. And let's get a plain, abdominal X-ray.'

Billy looked at him. 'X-ray?'

'Iron is radio-opaque,' Christy said quickly, 'the iron will show up on X-ray.' But as she studied the child, a thought flickered to life in the back of her mind. 'Luke, what did the tablets taste like?'

Alessandro frowned at her, clearly anxious to progress, but she lifted a hand and waited for Luke to answer.

'Sweets.' But he didn't quite meet her eyes and an instinct made her step closer to the trolley.

'Luke.' She kept her voice gentle. 'Did you swallow the sweets or did you hide them?' She saw something in his eyes and her conviction grew. 'No one is going to be angry with you, sweetheart,' she said softly. 'But we need to know the truth. Are they in your pockets?'

There was a long silence and then Luke nodded, his eyes huge. 'I was keeping them for later.'

Ignoring the gasp that came from his mother, Christy held out her hand to the little boy. 'Show me.'

After a moment's hesitation, Luke dug a hand into his pocket and pulled out a handful of tablets, now covered in fluff and bits of sweet paper. He dropped them into Christy's palm and she counted them quickly.

'Eight,' she said in a calm voice. 'They're all here, Alessandro. If Mrs Kennet hasn't missed a single tablet, that makes this a full bottle.'

The paediatrician breathed a sigh of relief and backed out of the room and the mother started to scold Luke, but Christy interrupted her quickly.

'Good boy, Luke,' she said firmly. 'Good boy for telling the truth.'

'But why didn't he tell us sooner?' Mrs Kennet asked, a baffled expression on her face, and Luke dipped his head.

'You were yelling and screaming and then the ambulance came and that was really cool with the light and the bell thing…'

Christy glanced at Alessandro and saw the gleam of amusement in his eyes. And relief. He was thinking of Ben, too, she thought, and her stomach twisted with love. He was a wonderful father.

They discharged Luke with a sharp lecture about the danger of swallowing things that weren't meant for him and Christy gave the mother a leaflet on preventing accidents in the home.

'Wow!' Billy's eyes were filled with admiration as he looked at her. 'I was just about to try and take blood from that child and I wasn't looking forward to it. What made you suspect that he hadn't swallowed them? It would never even have occurred to me.'

'Mother's instinct,' Christy said dryly, as she briskly tidied up the room ready for the next patient. 'Children often do unexpected things and his mother made that comment about hiding things.' She turned to Alessandro as Billy left the room. 'Do you remember Ben going through a phase of hiding everything?'

'Only too well.' Alessandro reached for the jacket that he'd abandoned. 'I seem to remember that he took my bleeper for twenty-four hours once.'

Christy grinned. 'I found it at the bottom of the laundry basket underneath a week's worth of dirty washing.'

Alessandro gave a nod and his eyes were warm. 'You did well,' he said softly. 'Extremely well. Were it not for you, that child would now be undergoing some very unpleasant tests.'

'Well, they certainly would have put him off swallowing tablets that didn't belong to him.'

'You're an excellent A and E nurse,' Alessandro said quietly. 'I'd forgotten just how good and for that I apologise. It is where you are at your best and you should certainly not be wasting your talents anywhere else. You should come back.'

She stared at him for a long moment, her breath trapped in her lungs. What exactly was he saying? Come back to A and E or come back to him?

Their eyes locked and Christy felt warmth spread inside her. It was still there, she told herself. That special bond that had always existed between them. It hadn't died.

'Alessandro?' Katya's slender frame appeared round the door. Her hair was fastened on top of her head but several strands fell softly over her eyes, giving her a sleepy, sexy appearance. 'I'm going home now, but I'll see you at the Snow Ball tomorrow night. You owe me a dance.'

Christy felt the special warmth inside her evaporate, to be replaced by a block of ice.

Was that why he wanted to go to the Christmas party? Because Katya was going?

Telling herself that she was being paranoid, Christy turned her attention back to the state of the room, trying not to listen to Alessandro's response.

It didn't matter what he thought of Katya, she reminded herself, because she was going to buy a killer dress and remind him exactly what it was that he was missing.

CHAPTER SEVEN

'I⊤'s freezing today,' Christy turned round and looked at the children who were safely strapped into the back of the car as Alessandro drove the short distance to the forest. 'Did you two remember gloves and hats?'

'Stop fussing, Mum.' Katy yawned and Ben carried on playing with his space shuttle, lifting it into the air and making it swoop downwards.

'Yeeow-w-w…' he whined, flying it dangerously close to his sister's head.

Anticipating fireworks, Christy pointed out of the window. 'Oh, look, we're here.'

They climbed out of the car and the children hurried off to take a closer look at the trees.

'I like this one,' Ben yelled, and Katy rolled her eyes in derision.

'It's completely lopsided. This one is a much better shape.'

Ben frowned. 'Isn't.'

Alessandro strolled across to them and selected an entirely different tree. 'This one,' he said in his usual decisive fashion, and Christy smothered a smile.

Even with Christmas trees, he had to be the one in charge, but the children didn't seem to mind and jumped up and down with excitement as Alessandro paid and loaded it into the car.

Back home, Christy put mince pies in the oven to heat and dug out the boxes of decorations they'd used for years.

The children had put Christmas songs on the CD player and were dancing round the room, giggling and playing together.

Like any normal family, Christy thought as she handed another wooden reindeer to Ben to hang on the lower branches. Except they weren't a normal family. Did Alessandro love her? Did he want to fix their marriage or was this show of togetherness purely for the children? She didn't know and she was afraid to ask in case she heard something she didn't want to hear.

'Please, lift me so that I can do the fairy,' Katy demanded, and Christy gave a wan smile.

Like daughter, like father. Katy knew exactly what she wanted and was prepared to fight to get it.

She thought of the dress safely hidden at the back of her wardrobe.

It had cost a fortune, but if it helped remind Alessandro that she was more than the mother of his two children then it would have been worth the investment.

Alessandro scooped Katy up easily and held her while she carefully placed the sparkling fairy on top of the tree. Then he lowered her and dropped a kiss on her forehead.

He'd save their marriage for the sake of the children, Christy thought numbly, because he was an excellent father and adored them. But she wanted so much more than that. She wanted a return to the greedy, hungry passion that they'd always shared. Their relationship had been so unbelievably intense and special that it was hard to imagine settling for less.

Did he still love her?

Because she didn't want her children growing up witness-ing a dead relationship.

She couldn't do it, she decided. She'd make one last at-tempt to fight for him and if it didn't work, they'd have to part.

She slipped away while Alessandro was reading to Ben, anxious to give herself plenty of time to get ready.

Remembering Katya's flawless appearance, she took extra time over her make-up and hair and finally slid into the dress.

Glancing in the mirror, she gave a soft, womanly smile. It was fabulous.

The dress was silver and the luxurious, unusual fabric shimmered and slid over her smooth curves.

'Not bad for someone of your age,' Katy murmured, walking into the room, sucking a lolly which she'd stolen from the Christmas tree. 'You need some diamonds to go with it. Something round your neck.'

Christy blinked. 'I haven't got anything suitable.'

Alessandro never bought her jewellery. It wasn't his style. She glanced down at the simple gold band on the ring finger of her left hand. They'd got married in such a hurry that they'd never even bothered with an engagement ring.

'Wait there.' Katy sprinted out of the room and came back carrying a silver necklace. 'Try that.'

'Where did you get it?'

Katy grinned and jumped onto the middle of the bed where she proceeded to sit, cross-legged. 'The front of a magazine, but don't worry about that. Fake is cool. Go for it, Mum.'

Laughing, Christy fastened the necklace around her throat and stood back to judge the effect. It was perfect. With a conspiratorial smile at her daughter, she slipped her feet into the extravagant strappy shoes she'd purchased and picked up her bag.

'Well? What's the verdict?'

'You look like something from the Christmas tree,' Ben breathed from the doorway. 'Like a real live princess.'

'Which has to be better than a dead princess,' Katy said dryly, rolling her eyes and sliding off the bed. 'Come on. We'd better make sure Dad isn't planning on wearing that ribbed jumper he's been in all day.'

'I'm not wearing a jumper.' His voice deep and disturbingly masculine, Alessandro appeared in the doorway, dressed in a black dinner jacket that emphasised the width of his powerful shoulders.

He looked startlingly handsome and Christy caught her breath.

After all these years, she thought to herself, he still made her stare.

And he was staring, too.

His gaze slid from her eyes to her mouth, then lingered on the swell of her breasts revealed by the cut of the fabric and then finally rested on the hemline, which stopped a long way short of her knees.

'You're not going out like that.'

Poised for a compliment, Christy felt her happiness shatter. 'Sorry?'

'It isn't the sort of dress you should be wearing. It's revealing and it's—' Alessandro broke off, the expression in his eyes dark and dangerous as he struggled to find the right words. 'It's just not suitable.'

Christy felt her own temper rise.

The dress was perfect and she *knew* she looked fabulous. All day she'd been cocooned in the delicious anticipation of the moment when he saw her in the dress. And he'd spoiled it.

'Why isn't it suitable?'

Alessandro prowled around the room, his expression dark and ominous. 'You are a wife and a mother, and that dress makes you look like…' He inhaled sharply and stabbed long fingers through his hair, 'it makes you look like…'

'A woman?' Christy slotted in helpfully. 'You didn't think I could still work in A and E, but I've proved you wrong. You didn't think I could still be a useful member of the mountain rescue team, but I proved you wrong there, too. To you, I've ceased to be an individual. To you, I'm just a wife and a mother.' Her voice cracked as she said the words. 'But I've got news for you. Yes, I'm a wife and a mother, but I'm also a woman, Alessandro Garcia, and it's time you remembered that fact and stopped behaving like a caveman.'

Having delivered that speech, she walked from the room with as much dignity as she could muster, given the ridiculous height of the heels she'd chosen.

Alessandro stood in the centre of the room, his powerful shoulders rigid with tension as he struggled to control his simmering temper.

'Well…' His daughter's voice came from directly behind him. 'I'd say that you *really* messed that one up!'

Disturbed from his contemplation of that exact same fact, Alessandro rounded on his daughter with a growl. 'I did not ask for your opinion.'

'Maybe not, but I'm in this family, too!' Katy put her hands on her hips, her temper flaring as quickly as his. 'I don't see why I should have to sit around and watch the two of you ruin everything. Mum bought a new dress and she looks nice—for an older person,' she added quickly as an afterthought, and Alessandro frowned.

'Your mother is only thirty-two.'

'Is she *that* old?' Katy shuddered and pulled a face. 'Hard to imagine.'

At any other time Alessandro would have laughed but he was too busy contemplating the facts to respond to the horror in his daughter's expression.

Thirty-two. Many women weren't even married at that age, he mused. Christy was still young. He'd met her young and made her pregnant almost immediately.

And his daughter was right. She had looked nice in the dress. More than nice. Gorgeous. Sexy. Stunning.

Closing his eyes to clear the image of long slender legs and tempting feminine curves, he realised that Christy had been spot on in her accusation. He was behaving like a cave-man. The truth was that he didn't want any other man admiring what was his. Especially at the moment, when their relationship was so precarious.

She'd given no indication as to what was going to happen when Christmas was over. Hadn't mentioned whether she was staying or going, and he was afraid to ask in case his question provoked her into leaving.

He felt as though he was totally out of step with her thinking.

She confided in Jake, it seemed, but not him.

He inhaled sharply. Jake. He knew only too well that Jake had been crazy about Christy for a short time. Given the complexity and number of Jake's subsequent relationships, he'd assumed that the connection had long since died. Now he was starting to wonder...

But no matter what, she was right about his behaviour, he reflected with grim self-awareness. He'd behaved that way from the first moment he'd met her. She'd been twenty and a virgin, and he'd fallen for her so hard that, given the choice, he would have locked her inside a room and never let her out.

She'd been with him for almost all of her adult life.

Could he blame her if she now wanted to dress up and party?

He ran a hand over the back of his neck and cursed fluently in Spanish.

Katy cleared her throat. 'Thanks to those boring Spanish lessons I endure every Saturday morning, I understood that,' she said calmly, and Alessandro threw her a quelling look.

'I don't need your comments at this time,' he said in Spanish, and she gave a smile and responded in the same language.

'Oh, I rather think you do.'

So much for expecting Alessandro to sweep her into his arms, Christy thought miserably as she reached for her coat. He hadn't seen her as an attractive woman. Just as his wife, inappropriately dressed.

Part of her wanted to strip off the dress and have an early night in the spare room, regardless of the broken bed, but part of her was still determined to show him what he was missing, so she picked up the phone and called a taxi.

Alessandro strode into the hall moments later. 'Christy—'

'We need to leave,' she said coldly, not giving him the chance to say what she would undoubtedly consider to be the wrong thing. 'I ordered a taxi so that we can both have a drink. It should be here any minute.'

Alessandro inhaled sharply. *'Por Dios*, we need to talk.'

'About what?' She swept towards the door, her head held high, her hair streaming down her back like flames. 'The fact that you don't see me as anything other than the mother of your children? You've made that perfectly clear, Alessandro. I don't need you to labour the point.'

She yanked open the front door, relieved to see the taxi arrive.

They made the journey to the manor house that was the venue for the Snow Ball in tense, brooding silence, and Christy turned her head to stare out of the window, afraid to look at him.

Afraid that she'd break down.

Merry Christmas, Christy, she thought bitterly as the taxi swept up the wide, snowy drive that led to the stately home. Christmas trees festooned with tiny lights adorned the entrance but she decided that it was impossible to be enchanted when your marriage was on the rocks.

Determined not to show Alessandro how much his casual indifference had hurt her, Christy handed her coat to the uniformed attendant and walked into the ballroom.

The party was already in full swing, the dance floor was crowded and the buffet table was loaded with festive food.

Huge boughs of holly and mistletoe decorated the room and the air was filled with the scent of pine cones and fir trees.

Christmas.

Christy blinked back tears. It should have been a happy time.

The first person she saw was Nicky, wearing a slinky green dress and clinging to her husband's arm. 'Christy!' Waving a champagne glass, she sprinted over and embraced her. 'You look amazing!'

At least someone thought so, Christy thought sadly, forcing a smile. 'Thanks.'

Nicky grinned at Alessandro. 'She looks unbelievably sexy, doesn't she?'

Alessandro's already black expression darkened still further and Christy quickly made conversation to cover his lack of response.

Clearly he didn't find her sexy.

'Come and dance,' Nicky urged, and Christy nodded.

'Great idea.' Anything was better than standing with Alessandro. He obviously didn't want her to go out. Didn't want her to have a good time and enjoy herself.

She walked towards the dance floor with Nicky and let herself go.

For a short time she blocked out everything except the rhythm of the music and the feel of her own body.

Eventually heat and thirst got the better of her and she helped herself to a drink and walked outside into the grounds for some fresh air.

The snow was thick on the ground and she suddenly wished she'd asked for her coat.

Turning to go back inside, she bumped straight into Jake. 'Well, well, Cinderella, I assume,' he drawled in a soft voice, and she smiled.

'Hi, there. Where's your date?'

'Not sure.' Jake glanced back at the house and frowned. 'In there somewhere. Last seen throwing herself around the dance floor in a most embarrassing fashion. Time to move on to the next candidate, I think.'

Christy rolled her eyes. 'You're irrepressible.'

'No, I'm just fussy,' Jake said calmly, his eyes on her pale face. Without commenting, he shrugged out of his jacket and slipped it around her shoulders. 'OK, what's happening with you?'

The jacket was warm and comforting but she frowned. 'You'll freeze.'

'Me? You're forgetting that I'm big, tough and manly.' Jake lifted her chin and forced her to look at him. 'Come one. What's happened?'

She shouldn't say anything, she thought miserably. She ought to keep her problems to herself. 'Nothing.'

'Christy, we need to get to the point fast, before we both catch pneumonia,' Jake said patiently, 'so let's put this another way. Why are you out here on your own, leaving your husband inside and fair game for that Russian doctor with the long claws and the evil eyes.'

'Katya?' Christy swallowed hard. So Jake had noticed, too. 'I can't compete with her.'

'That's rubbish,' Jake drawled, finishing his drink and putting his glass down on the wall that led towards the maze. 'I thought you were going to fight.'

'I was.' Christy looked down at herself. 'This was my weapon, but it didn't work. He was supposed to be bowled over by how stunning I am. Instead, he just went off the deep end and said that I couldn't go out looking like this.'

Jake's eyes narrowed. 'Is that right?'

'I'm the mother of his children,' Christy said wearily, and Jake grinned.

'In that silver dress? Believe me, you look more like a walking fantasy than the mother of anyone's children. I'm not surprised he didn't want you to go out looking like that. He has a possessive nature, angel. And that's your fault for marrying a brooding Spaniard. You should have picked someone safe and English, like me.'

'You're wrong. If it was about feeling possessive, he

would have grabbed me and we never would have made it to the party,' Christy said miserably. 'But he doesn't want me.'

'No?' Jake lifted his eyes from hers and looked over her shoulder, his attention caught by something directly behind her. She saw his expression change but before she could turn and see what he was looking at, he muttered something that sounded like, 'Oh, what the hell', dragged her against him and brought his mouth down hard on hers.

The kiss lasted less than a few seconds because suddenly Jake was yanked away from her so violently that she almost lost her balance.

'Get your hands *off* my wife,' Alessandro growled fiercely, his powerful body pulsing with vibrant energy and barely contained tension.

Christy swallowed. 'Alessandro—'

He didn't glance in her direction. 'Do not speak to me at the moment,' he said thickly, his voice raw with aggression. 'This is not your fault. You're inexperienced when it comes to men, but Jake is—'

'Yes?' Jake looked at him calmly, his hands in his pockets. 'What am I?'

'You've always wanted her,' Alessandro breathed with icy fury, and Jake gave a curious smile.

'Yes. I did.'

'*Por Dios*, you admit it?' Like a tiger suddenly unleashed, Alessandro stepped forward and let out a punch that sent Jake flying into the snow.

'Jake!' Christy gave a scream of horror and ran towards him. 'Alessandro, no! Stop it. Stop it now! I can't believe you just did that! What do you think you're *doing*?'

'Protecting what's mine.' Alessandro was nursing his hand, his eyes still glittering with fury as he watched Jake struggle to his feet and lift a hand to his split lip.

Christy was forgotten as the two men faced each other.

'I guess I deserved that,' Jake said softly, 'but you're only allowed the one, Garcia. And now you'd better let me finish my sentence. It's true that I wanted Christy when I thought she was available. Unfortunately that lasted all of twenty-four hours. Then she saw you and I didn't get a look-in. You were the only man for her. You still are, but you're too pig-headed to see it.'

Seeing blood on his chin, Christy took a step towards him but Jake lifted a hand to stop her. 'I'm fine. I'm going inside now to find my date. There's nothing like the sight of blood to bring out a woman's nurturing instincts.' Despite the bruise on his face, he gave her a saucy wink. 'I'll have the jacket back next time I see you, angel.'

She watched as he sauntered away, tears in her eyes. Then she turned to Alessandro in a state of appalled frustration. 'I can't *believe* you just did that. He's our oldest friend!'

'He was kissing you.'

'Well, at least he noticed me,' she yelled, 'which is more than you ever do.'

'I notice you.' Strong fingers closed around her wrist and he dragged her towards the entrance of the maze.

'Alessandro, this is ridiculous.' She tugged at her hand but he kept on walking until they reached the walled garden in the centre of the maze. A fountain bubbled and the moon shed just enough light for her to be able to make out the hard, unyielding expression on his handsome face. Soft flakes of snow swirled around them but both were oblivious to everything except each other and the steadily mounting tension.

'You think I don't notice you, *querida?'* *He backed her against the wall, his powerful body hard against hers, his hand on her waist. 'You think I'm not aware of you lying next to me in bed at night? You think I don't notice the silver dress?'*

Hunger exploded inside her and she clung to the front of his jacket, the intimate thrust of his body sending her pulse rate skyward.

He jerked the hem of her dress upwards and she gave a soft gasp of shock and excitement as she felt the strength of his hands on her bottom. 'Well, I've got news for you, *gatita*, I notice.' He brought his mouth down on hers in a hard, possessive kiss and she melted under the skilled seduction of his mouth.

No one kissed like Alessandro, she thought dizzily as she felt herself go under, sucked down into a sensual world where everything was suddenly hazy.

Her heart thumped, hot tongues of fire licked deep inside her and she slid her arms round his strong neck and held onto his head just in case he had any intention of ending the kiss before she was ready.

But clearly he didn't.

Without lifting his mouth, he slid his hands inside the silk of her panties and the warmth of his palms was such a contrast to the freezing night air that she gasped against his lips and then cried out his name as his fingers slid inside her, exploring the most intimate place of all.

He was the only man who had ever touched her that way and she felt her body explode with an excitement so intense that it was close to unbearable.

'I want you,' he groaned huskily, lifting her with a powerful movement and anchoring her between the wall and his body, *'Por Dios*, I have to have you now. I can't wait any longer.'

Exulting in the effect she was having on him, Christy wrapped her legs around him, desperate for him to finish what he'd started, desperate to ease the agonising ache that built deep inside her body. And still they kissed, as if they were never going to stop.

As if this were the last time they would ever touch.

In a swift movement that said a great deal about his physical strength, Alessandro held her secure with one arm and then reached down to deal with the zip of his trousers. Breathless with anticipation, she felt him hard and ready against her and shifted her hips with a whimper of need as the white-hot burning low in her pelvis reached almost intolerable levels.

He held her firm and entered her with a powerful thrust and she gasped against his mouth as she felt the slick, velvety thickness of his arousal deep inside her.

She forgot everything except the ferocious needs of her own body and his. She forgot that they were outdoors. She forgot the freezing cold air and the sharp, uneven surface of the bricks pressing into her back. *She forgot that their marriage was in crisis.*

Her entire focus was the building, throbbing ache that grew and grew deep inside her.

He was hard and demanding, his mouth never leaving hers, each rhythmic thrust creating erotic sensations that bordered on the painful. She tried desperately to move her hips, to alleviate the frantic ache deep in her body but he controlled her utterly and she gave a sob of relief as she felt him change the angle and drive her towards the edge.

She toppled with a force that shocked her and she clung to his broad shoulders, feeling his body tense as he drove still deeper into her and fell with her.

And finally, when their breathing had calmed and their pulses had slowed, he lifted his head and lowered her gently to the ground.

For a moment they both stared at each other, connected by the unique intensity of the experience that they'd shared.

No other man would ever make her feel like this, she thought dreamily as she stared up at him, still holding his arms for support. *No other man.*

And then he reached forward, straightened her dress and rescued Jake's jacket, which had fallen to the ground.

He placed it gently round her shoulders, his dark gaze lingering on her face with brooding intensity.

And she waited.

Waited to hear him say the words she was longing to hear. *I love you.*

Surely he was going to say it any moment now. After what they'd just shared, how could he say anything else? What other words would possibly be appropriate in this situation?

Everything was going to be all right.

This was going to be a new beginning for them.

He grasped the lapels of the jacket and hauled her against him, moulding her against his lean, powerful frame with a strength that made her gasp.

'You're mine,' he groaned, burying his face in her neck and trailing burning kisses over her bare skin. 'Mine and no other man's.'

Rigid with pent-up emotions and expecting an entirely different declaration, Christy froze. 'I'm sorry?' Her voice croaky, she pulled away from him, a warning flash in her eyes. Had she heard him correctly? 'Say that again?'

'We belong together—and I *won't* give you a divorce.'

Deciding that this wasn't the time to point out that she'd never actually asked him for a divorce, Christy felt all the soft feelings melt away. 'Is that was this was all about? You make love to me for the first time in more than two months and you do it as a gesture of *possession*?'

Immediately on the defensive, Alessandro's dark eyes narrowed warily. 'Of course not…'

But suddenly Christy was able to see the whole picture with an uncomfortable degree of clarity. 'Until Jake kissed me, you didn't lay a finger on me. You did it because he kissed me.'

He tensed. 'I'm allowed to make love to my wife.'

'I've been lying half-naked next to you in bed for the past week,' she said through gritted teeth, 'and you haven't laid a finger on me. It doesn't take a genius to understand that Jake was the reason you just ripped my clothes off in a public place in below freezing weather conditions. Permit me to tell you that I find your romantic streak less than impressive.'

'I just made love to you.'

'No, Alessandro,' she snapped, her delicate chin jerking upwards and her eyes flashing with anger. 'You just had sex with me. Sex, designed to stake your claim and wipe all thoughts of other men from my mind.'

A muscle worked in his lean jaw and his eyes gleamed dark as he lifted his head in an arrogant gesture. 'And it worked—tell me you can feel that with any other man and I will know you're lying.'

Goaded beyond reason, she lifted a hand and slapped him hard.

'You may be a brilliant doctor, Alessandro Garcia,' she choked, 'but you're a tactless, thoughtless, possessive ba—' She stopped herself before she could say the word she wanted to say, her upbringing preventing her from giving voice to a word that she'd never before had reason to use.

It was bad enough that she'd hit him when she'd never before struck anyone or anything.

If she'd needed the evidence that he didn't love her, she

had it now, she thought miserably as she turned and stumbled down the path that led out of the maze

He didn't love her but he didn't want any other man to have her.

And she couldn't see a future for their marriage.

Simmering with barely contained frustration, and cursing the inconsistencies of the female sex, Alessandro strode out of the maze after Christy, only to see her long, gorgeous legs folding into the back of a taxi, which promptly disappeared down the snowy drive.

He cursed in Spanish and then turned to find Jake watching him. His eyes narrowed with accusation. 'Did *you* put her in a cab?'

'Why?' Jake's tone was cool. 'Are you going to punch me again?'

'No.' Alessandro ran a hand over the back of his neck. 'Providing you don't kiss her again. Ever.'

'I thought it might wake you up.' Jake rubbed a hand over his bruised jaw. 'I think it worked.'

Alessandro shot him an incredulous look. 'I think you like to live dangerously. I wanted to kill you with my bare hands.'

'I hoped it would be enough to galvanise you into action and show her what you felt about her, but, judging from the tears on her face when I got her the taxi, didn't succeed.'

'Tears?' Alessandro digested that unwelcome piece of news and inhaled sharply. 'Christy *never* cries.'

'Well, she was crying just now,' Jake said flatly, his gaze steady as he looked at his friend. 'What did you do to her?'

A tinge of colour touched Alessandro's hard cheekbones. 'I made love to her,' he growled finally, 'which seemed like the right thing to do at the time.'

Jake studied him. 'Judging from the mark on your cheek, I'm guessing it wasn't.'

'Women are *totally* incomprehensible.'

'Are they?' Jake met his gaze head on, ignoring the snow settling on his white shirt. 'Christy doesn't believe you love her any more, Al.'

'She doesn't think I love her?' Alessandro's voice rang with exasperation. 'She's the one who left the family home, taking the children with her.'

'She expected you to follow her.'

Alessandro stared at him blankly. 'You're wrong. If she'd wanted me to follow her, why did she leave in the first place? And if that was true, why didn't she just come back straight away? It doesn't make sense.'

'That's because you're looking at it from a man's point of view. She was waiting for a sign that you still cared. She didn't think you loved her any more.'

Alessandro gritted his teeth. 'If that's true, making love to her should have proved otherwise. But she's just hit me and left in a taxi.'

Jake sighed. 'I think your timing might have been a bit out. If you'd made your move at any point before I'd kissed her, you'd probably be snuggled up together now, with this whole nightmarish episode behind you.'

Alessandro's eyes darkened ominously. 'I do *not* want to be reminded that you kissed my wife, Blackwell.'

'You're the one she wants,' Jake said calmly, 'but you're making such a mess of it you're going to lose her if you're not careful.'

Lose her?

Lose Christy?

Faced with that unthinkable possibility, Alessandro felt helpless for the first time in his life. 'What do I do?' His voice was hoarse. 'What do I do to convince her that I love her?'

'Try telling her.'

'She won't believe me after tonight.'

'Then show her,' Jake said quietly. 'Show her that you love her, Al, but do it fast.'

CHAPTER EIGHT

INSUFFERABLE, arrogant, miserable, vile, arrogant rat. Christy flung clothes into the suitcase, her face streaked with tears as she lengthened her list of possible adjectives to apply to Alessandro.

And as for herself—she gave a growl of exasperation and flung a skirt violently into the case. Then she sat on the edge of the bed and buried her face in her hands with a groan of humiliation and self-disgust.

Did she have no self-control?

When she thought about the way she'd behaved she just wanted to curl up and die on the spot.

He didn't love her at all and yet she'd thrown herself at him like a desperate, sex-starved groupie. She'd virtually *begged*, for goodness' sake, and all in a place where anyone could have come past and seen them at any point.

How embarrassing was *that*?

What had possessed her to behave like that?

It was true that she and Alessandro had always been very physically compatible, but they'd always kept their passion for each other behind closed doors.

Tonight she'd thought about nothing except the desperate need to have him make love to her. And for her it had all been about love.

Whereas he'd thought about nothing but possession.

With a sniff and a determined lift of her chin, she stood up and turned back to the case and then froze when she saw Alessandro standing in the doorway.

His glossy hair was dusted with snow and his dark jaw shadowed by stubble. At some point—had it been before or after they'd had sex?—he'd undone his bow-tie and it was now draped carelessly around his neck, the open collar of his shirt revealing a tantalising hint of bronzed skin and curling dark body hair. 'You're *not* leaving.'

She closed her eyes to block out the vision of perfect masculinity. 'This is never going to work, Alessandro. I'm going to sleep at my mother's tonight.'

She didn't trust herself to behave normally in front of the children.

He didn't love her. He saw her as a possession and the mother of his children. Not as a woman.

'It's worked for the past twelve years.' He kicked the door shut behind him and she opened her eyes, startled by the raw pain she saw in his dark eyes.

'Alessandro—'

'I told myself that if you loved Jake then I'd let you go, but now I find that I can't do that.'

She gaped at him. 'I *don't* love Jake.'

'You were kissing him. You're always confiding in him.'

'He was kissing me,' she corrected swiftly, 'and I confide in him because he listens.'

Alessandro's eyes darkened. 'And I don't?'

'Well, no.' She refused to be intimidated by the black expression on his face. 'No, you don't. You never show any interest in me as a woman any more.'

He sucked in a long breath. 'I admit that I may have made mistakes in our relationship.' He jerked his bow-tie from his neck and flung it onto the bed. 'But I think I at least deserve another chance.'

She stared at him. 'Was that an apology?' In twelve years she'd never known Alessandro apologise for anything. 'Are you actually admitting that you might be in the wrong?'

He took a deep breath. 'You should *not* have left and taken the children,' he growled, 'but, yes, I'm willing to admit that my behaviour may have fallen short of perfect.'

She wanted to laugh. As far as apologies went it was pretty pathetic, but for Alessandro it was a major step forward.

She dropped the suitcase on the floor of the bedroom. 'So what are you suggesting?'

His jacket joined the bow tie on the bed. 'Christmas is a week away. I want us to try again—we owe it to the children.'

Was that why he was doing this? Was it all about the children?

'All right.' Her heart was thudding. 'But there are rules.'

'Rules?'

'I carry on working in A and E and I go out with the mountain rescue team and you stop frowning and glaring at me—'

'I don't frown and glare.'

'You frown and glare.'

'All right.' His voice was rough. 'I'll try not to. You're an excellent A and E nurse. I don't know how I could have forgotten that. This last week has been easier for everyone because you've been in the department. I'm certainly not going to suggest that you give it up.'

'Oh.' A delicious warmth spread through her and she stared at him, stunned by the praise.

He lifted a dark eyebrow in question. 'Anything else?'

'Yes. If I'm staying, then we're going to spend time together, Alessandro. No more ships in the night. No more living at the hospital while I live my own life here. And a few romantic gestures would be nice.'

'Romantic gestures?' He stared at her blankly for a moment and she resisted the temptation to roll her eyes.

'Never mind. Let's just settle for spending time together,' she said wearily, lacking the motivation to explain. Romantic gestures just weren't in his nature, she reminded herself. She'd known that when she'd married him and it hadn't bothered her. She'd been in love with the man and she was still in love with him. If they could just rediscover what they'd once shared, she could live without romantic gestures.

There was a brief silence while he studied her and then he gave a brief nod. 'All right. Agreed. I have only one rule.'

Christy looked at him, her eyes wide. 'You do?'

'No more kissing,' Alessandro delivered softly, strolling towards her with a strange gleam in his eyes. 'Unless it's me.'

He was close to her now, so close that she could almost feel the heat of his powerful body, and the breath was suddenly trapped in her throat. 'I didn't kiss him.'

'Good.' Alessandro's voice was a low, lethal purr. 'Because I don't share. *Ever.*'

The sexual tension between them was stifling. 'You're behaving like a caveman again.'

'A very restrained caveman,' Alessandro pointed out in silky tones, his mouth hovering dangerously close to hers.

'So far I haven't locked the door, thrown you on the bed or done any of the things I'm burning to do. In fact, *gatita*, I'm showing remarkable self-control.'

She waited for him to kiss her but instead he studied her for a long, lingering moment, the expression in his eyes partially screened by thick, dark lashes. Then he stepped back and walked towards the shower.

'Don't wait up for me,' he drawled as he ripped off the white shirt and dropped it in the vague vicinity of the laundry basket. 'I'm sure you're tired.'

Don't wait up for him?

Christy stared at him in disbelief and mounting frustration as he strolled into the *en suite* bathroom and casually pushed the door shut behind him.

He'd had wild, abandoned sex with her just because another man had kissed her but now, when he'd declared his intention of making their marriage work, he strolled into the bathroom without laying a single finger on her.

What was the matter with the man?

Romantic gestures?

What did she mean, he never made romantic gestures?

Alessandro hit the buttons on the shower and brooded on the mysteries of the female sex. He'd just made love to her. *How much more romantic than that could a man get?* And yet she'd accused him of being possessive.

Only a desire to avoid similar confrontation had prevented him from stripping her naked and taking her to bed to finish what they'd started at the Snow Ball.

But he wasn't going to touch her, he reminded himself, turning the shower to cold to help his resolve.

She'd said that they didn't spend enough time together so he'd correct that. And he'd make so many romantic gestures that she wouldn't be able to turn around without falling over one.

Once he found out what they were…

The following day Christy found herself working alongside Jake, who had been called down to look at a young woman who was bleeding.

'Ouch.' Her voice was soft as her eyes rested on his bruised mouth. 'That looks sore.'

'It's more embarrassing than sore,' Jake drawled, touching his fingers to his lips with a wry smile. 'The entire hospital seem to be laying bets on whose wife I seduced last night.'

Christy blushed. 'Did you tell them the truth?'

Jake lifted an eyebrow. 'What do you think?'

'I think you're much too good a friend to gossip,' she said quietly, 'and I'm really grateful for that. And for lots of other things.'

He studied her for a moment and then smiled and held out his hand for the notes she was holding. 'So—where's this woman you want me to see?'

'In cubicle one. I'll act as chaperone.'

The day passed swiftly and Christy was just wondering how she'd managed to miss yet another lunch-break when the ambulance hotline rang.

She picked up the phone just as Alessandro strolled up to her. 'Tonight,' he said in a decisive tone. 'We're going out to dinner. I've booked a table for eight o'clock.'

In no position to argue, Christy spoke into the phone and listened while the ambulance gave the details of a casualty they were bringing in.

She scribbled a few notes, replaced the phone and discovered that he was still standing there. 'They're bringing in a fifty-five-year-old man with an upper GI bleed. Apparently he vomited up fresh blood about half an hour ago.'

Alessandro's gaze lingered on her face. 'Then we'd better call the physicians and warn them. You're thinking that I won't make that date of ours tonight, aren't you?'

'Well, I…' The words died in her mouth as she caught his slow, sexy smile.

'Be ready, Christy,' he said softly, 'because I'm going to be there.'

Her stomach turned over and she cursed herself for being so weak-willed. It was going to take more than one evening where he happened to show up to fix their marriage.

The patient arrived accompanied by sirens and clutching a vomit bowl filled with frank blood.

Christy snapped on a pair of gloves and an apron and helped the paramedics transfer him to the trolley.

'This is Duncan Finn.' The paramedic removed the red blanket covering his patient and Christy substituted one of the department's own. 'Suddenly started vomiting and noticed the blood.'

Katya slid into the room just as Alessandro moved round the trolley to talk to his patient.

'Any history of abdominal pain, Mr Finn?' he asked smoothly, as he swiftly examined the contents of the bowl and then picked up the patient's wrist to check his pulse and capillary refill.

The patient shook his head and Alessandro methodically ran through a list of questions as he continued his examination.

'Shall I put a line in?' Katya asked, and Alessandro gave a nod.

'Two. Christy will show you which cannula.'

Christy pushed forward the trolley that she'd already prepared and handed the other doctor a tourniquet.

'I want a full blood count, a clotting screen, U and Es, blood glucose and group and cross-match. Christy...' he lifted his head from his examination '...what are his sats?'

'Ninety-six per cent,' she said immediately, and he gave a nod.

'Did you bleep the physicians?'

'As the ambulance arrived.' Seeing that Katya had successfully cannulated the patient, Christy handed her the right bottles for the various tests and labelled the necessary forms. 'They said that they were on their way.'

'I want him to have 50 grams ranitidine, diluted in saline.' Alessandro's eyes rested on the monitor. 'Let's give him some oxygen, Christy.'

Murmuring words of reassurance to her patient, Christy slipped a mask over his face and adjusted the flow.

'I'm so thirsty,' he mumbled. 'Can I have a drink?'

'Nothing at the moment,' Christy said, and at that moment the physicians arrived.

Having made their examination and listened to Alessandro's handover, they decided that the patient needed an endoscopy and made arrangements to take him to Theatre.

Christy arranged the transfer, accompanied the patient and then returned to Resus to tidy up the mess she'd left.

Pushing open the door, she was surprised to find Alessandro and Katya still in there, talking.

Katya was standing quite close to him, closer than was strictly necessary, her eyes fixed on Alessandro's face.

'So you're saying that the differential diagnosis could have been a Mallory-Weiss tear, oesophageal varices, some sort of mucosal inflammation, gastric carcinoma or a coagulation disorder.'

'It could also have been a simple peptic ulcer,' Alessandro said dryly, dropping his gloves into the nearest bin. 'Not everything we see in this department is rare or out of the ordinary. Remember that.'

'Of course,' Katya breathed. 'I hope you don't mind me taking the opportunity to ask questions.'

'Not at all.' Watching Alessandro's encouraging smile, Christy ground her teeth.

He was *so* patient with her. Why was that? Patience wasn't one of his virtues.

'Do you fancy a drink tonight, Alessandro? I could really do with your help on a few issues,' Katya murmured, and Christy watched as her husband gave the younger girl a thoughtful look.

'Unfortunately tonight isn't possible,' he said, his Spanish accent very pronounced as he reached for a pen to sign a request form that one of the nurses was holding out to him. 'Some other time maybe.'

Some other time?

The hairs on the back of Christy's neck prickled with outrage. What did he mean by that? Why some other time? And exactly what sort of help was Katya looking for?

Ready to hit him for the second time in twenty-four hours, Christy cleared the trolley noisily and slammed her foot on the bar that opened the bin. It gaped open and she stuffed in the rubbish and let it slam shut with a crash.

Not very mature, she thought to herself, but at least it made her feel better and it reminded the pair of them that she was in the room.

He had such a nerve!

First he had hit Jake for kissing her and now he was flirting with Katya.

Aware that Alessandro was looking at her with astonishment, she gave him an innocent smile. 'Well, that's just about finished with the clearing up. I'll be off, then, and leave you to it.'

His eyes narrowed. 'Leave us to what?'

Despite her clenched jaw, she managed to beam at him. 'To whatever it is you have to do, Alessandro,' she replied in perfect Spanish, and then turned and left the room.

By the time she arrived home, she'd made up her mind that Alessandro was going to be staying at the hospital so what was the point of changing for dinner? Still seething about the sheer front of the feline Katya, she stepped into the shower, wondering how Alessandro had dealt with her.

Were they together at this precise moment?

Was he giving her personal instruction?

Still simmering, Christy wrapped herself in a large towel and padded into the bedroom, only to find him standing there holding a huge bunch of red roses.

She stared. 'What are those for?'

'They're for you.'

'Me?' He was giving her flowers? Alessandro never gave her flowers. It just wasn't something he thought to do. So why was he thinking of it now?

Her heart plummeted and she wondered again just what sort of help he'd been giving the seductive Katya. 'Feeling guilty about something, Alessandro?' Her frosty tone brought a wary look to his eyes.

He muttered something under his breath in Spanish and she glared at him.

'You *never* bring me flowers.'

'An omission which I'm trying to rectify,' he announced in a tone that reflected no small degree of exasperation and bemusement. 'You wanted me to be more romantic, *gatita*.'

She clutched at the towel, her hair trailing over her shoulders like flames. 'You think it's romantic to see my husband flirting under my nose?'

His eyes narrowed. *'When* was I flirting?'

'You really need to ask?' She flung her head back and her eyes sparked. 'She's all over you like a rash.'

'Who is?'

'Katya.' Christy hated her waspish tone and Alessandro lifted an eyebrow.

'Are you accusing me of having an affair with Katya?' His slow, masculine drawl was laced with amusement and she glared at the flowers and then at him, furious that he dared to laugh at her!

'Why is that funny?'

'She works for me, it is my job to train her,' Alessandro said smoothly, and Christy clenched her fists.

'And you have to be in close physical contact to achieve that objective?' She knew she was behaving childishly but she just couldn't help it.

'You are being ridiculous.'

'Am I?' Christy tilted her head in challenge. 'Last night you punched Jake.'

'That was entirely different,' Alessandro growled, the amusement in his eyes vanishing in a flash. 'He was kissing you.'

'And Katya was rubbing herself against you like a cat.' She broke off and Alessandro sucked in a breath, his gaze suddenly thoughtful.

'And you minded about that,' he said softly, 'so that's good, is it not?'

'Why would that *possibly* be good?'

'Jealousy shows that feeling exists.'

Did it? Did he still have feelings for her? Or were his

feelings all linked with his traditional, Mediterranean man's view of family?

'You didn't think it was such a good thing last night when you split Jake's lip,' she pointed out, and Alessandro gave a wry smile.

'Good point. OK.' He gave a shrug of his broad shoulders that reflected his Latin heritage. 'So we both admit we are hot-tempered and foolish and then you put my flowers in water and we go out to dinner.' His sudden unexpected smile was so sexy and charismatic that she felt her stomach flip.

It had always been the same, she reflected weakly. One moment he was all seething, masculine volatility and the next all indolent, simmering sexuality.

'Are you trying to talk me round?'

'Perhaps.' His voice was a lazy drawl as he slipped a firm hand round the back of her neck and trailed his fingers slowly through her hair. 'Or perhaps we have done enough talking for one evening, *querida*. What do you think?'

She couldn't think at all with him looking down at her with that slightly teasing, sexy gleam in his dark eyes.

'I— We—' She didn't finish her sentence because he brought his mouth down on hers with passionate force, drugging her with the intensity of his kiss. She felt the strength in her knees dissolve and clutched at his broad shoulders for support.

And then he lifted his head, his gaze slumberous as he studied her face. 'On second thoughts, let's go out to dinner.'

She stared at him dizzily, her vision slightly hazy. 'Sorry?'

'If we stay here, I will seduce you,' he declared without a trace of apology, 'and then you might accuse me of being possessive or not being interested in you as a person. I hate the thought that Jake knows more about you than I do so I'm going to take you out and you are going to tell me everything.'

She almost laughed. It was typical of Alessandro to try and command a conversation. But at least he was trying. 'All right,' she said softly, basking in the masculine appreciation she saw in his eyes. 'Let's go out and I'll tell you everything.'

He took her to a tiny restaurant by the side of the lake and they sat at a secluded table festively decorated with bunches of holly.

Alessandro picked up a menu and ordered and then looked at her with a wary expression on his handsome face. 'Why are you looking at me like that?'

'Do you realise that you never let me order my own food?'

'All right.' He leaned back in his chair and gave a shrug. 'What would you have ordered?'

'Smoked salmon and duck.'

He gave an arrogant smile. 'So— I ordered you smoked salmon and duck. That makes me a genius, no?'

'It makes you controlling, Alessandro.'

He frowned. 'It means I know you well.'

'It means you don't even give me the choice.'

He let out a long breath and reached for his wine. 'OK.' Suddenly his Spanish accent sounded very pronounced. 'So from now on, you want to order your own food. No problem.'

She hesitated. 'It's not just my food, Alessandro, it's everything. I want to know that you care about my opinion. About me as a person.'

'Of course I care about you as a person.'

'And yet you didn't want me to work in A and E.'

'I was wrong in that,' he conceded. 'You have proved

that you are still an excellent A and E nurse. Obviously you should be working in that area, not wasting your talents as a practice nurse. We will sort out a contract that allows you to be home for the children and work in the department.'

'You're doing it again!' She stared at him in exasperation. 'You're telling me what I should do. Try *asking* me, Alessandro. Try *asking* me what I want. Believe it or not, I have an opinion, too.'

He muttered something in Spanish and sat back as their first course arrived. 'All right.' He paused while the waiter placed the plates in front of him and then gave her a smile. 'I am asking you what you want. Tell me.'

'I want to make my own choices,' she said softly. 'I want to decide what's right for me as well as for the family. Yes, I want to be there for the children, of course I do. If anything, it's even more important now they're getting older and they have homework to do and friends to play with, but I can easily combine that with work and the mountain rescue team.'

Alessandro picked up his fork. 'I want to know why you find Jake easy to talk to and not me.' A strange expression flickered in his dark eyes. 'Am I that intimidating?'

'Not to me,' she said quietly, 'but you're very self-confident and sure of yourself. And sometimes your confidence drives everything else along in its path. You're very strong and you make decisions for people.'

He studied her through narrowed eyes. 'But I have always been the same, I think.'

She gave a soft smile. 'Yes, you have.'

'You remember the first time we met?'

Colour flooded into her cheeks. 'I'm not likely to forget.'

'You were talking to Jake in the students' bar,' Alessandro said softly, 'and I took one look at you and knew then that you were going to be mine.'

'You grabbed me by the hand and dragged me across the road to that little restaurant—'

'And then you came back to my place,' Alessandro said in a deep, sexy drawl. 'And we didn't get out of bed for three days.'

Her colour deepened. 'I got pregnant that weekend.'

'And I was so pleased,' Alessandro confessed with a complete lack of remorse. 'It gave me a reason to marry you without having to suffer a long engagement.'

She stared down at the simple gold band on the finger of her left hand. At the time, getting engaged hadn't seemed to matter. She'd been swept away by the force of his passion and the intensity of her love for him.

And that love had deepened over the years as she'd discovered what an amazing man he was.

But how had he felt about her? Had the novelty worn off? 'All the women were after you.'

'But I wanted only you.'

And how about now? she wanted to ask. *How about now?* Had he grown bored with the person she was? But she didn't want to risk spoiling a nice evening by hearing something she didn't want to hear and he was so obviously trying hard to listen to and understand her that she didn't want to threaten the atmosphere.

'It is true I am a strong person and that characteristic isn't helped by the job I do,' Alessandro confessed, disarmingly honest. 'In A and E, I don't operate by consensus. I am not going to stand there with an injured patient and ask everyone for an opinion on the correct treatment protocol. I am used to making snap decisions.'

And those snap decisions saved lives on a daily basis,

Christy knew that. He was an incredibly skilled and talented doctor and his decisiveness and confidence was an important contributing factor in his success.

'When people have a tricky patient, they always want you there,' she said quietly, knowing that it was true. 'You never panic.'

'Panicking helps no one.' Alessandro reached for a bread roll. 'And confidence is important to everyone.'

Christy knew that to be true also. It was important to have someone competent in control. 'If I had an accident, there's no one I'd rather leading the trauma team,' she said quietly, and he frowned.

'You are *not* going to have an accident, but thank you for the compliment. But I have to learn to be less controlling with you, I can see that, and I will try.'

And he did.

Over the next few days he asked her opinion on everything and listened carefully, and Christy saw a whole new side to him.

Surely he couldn't be making this much effort just for the children, she thought to herself. Surely his behaviour was an indication that he still had feelings for her?

The only physical contact they'd had had been the passionate sex they'd shared the night of the Snow Ball. And that hadn't counted, she told herself miserably, because he'd been provoked.

Why was he still not touching her?

Alessandro had such a high sex drive that never before in their marriage had she found herself in the position of having to initiate sex, but now she was starting to wonder whether she should go down that route.

But what if he rejected her?

She bit back a hysterical giggle as she prepared the children's lunch and got ready to take them to her mother's for an afternoon of Christmas shopping. It must be awful being a man, she decided. They faced rejection every time they went near a woman.

She was just pouring coffee into mugs when Alessandro strode into the room, talking into his phone.

She could tell from his responses that he was talking to Sean about a rescue, and when he snapped the phone shut she looked at him expectantly.

'Trouble?'

'A party of teenagers were climbing in the gully and it avalanched.'

Christy winced. She knew how dangerous that climb could be because she'd done it herself plenty of times when she'd been younger.

'How much do we know?'

Alessandro was already hauling equipment out of the utility room where it had been drying. 'Two of them were above it and managed to get to the top and raise the alarm. The third is stuck on a ledge.'

'So we'd do best to approach from the south-east ridge and then we'll be above him. It's just the *best* abseil,' Christy breathed, and Alessandro scowled at her.

'I always hated you doing that climb.'

She grinned. 'It was fun.'

'It was dangerous. And you have two children to think of now.'

Her smile faded. It was true, of course, and she would never take unnecessary risks. But at the same time she wished that sometimes he could think about *her*, rather than the children.

'So are we the advance party?'

Alessandro nodded. 'Yes, but it's going to take a large team to get him down if he's badly injured.'

Christy glanced out of the window. 'At least the weather looks pretty good. Should be able to fly a helicopter in this.'

Katy danced into the room. 'When are we going to Grandma's?'

'Right now.' Alessandro grabbed the rest of the equipment and strode out of the kitchen, with Christy and the children hurrying close behind.

They dropped the children and then Alessandro drove out of town towards the road that would allow them to take the fastest route to the gully.

The sun glistened on the snow and Christy frowned. 'Not a great day to climb that particular route,' she murmured, casting her mind back to her own experiences. 'The snow gets very soft if the sun is out.'

'They're fortunate that only one of them is injured,' Alessandro growled as he swung the car into the lay-by and switched off the engine. Jake and Sean walked towards them.

'We've got four hours before dark,' Sean said, his expression grim as he stared up the path they needed to take. 'Let's shift.'

They walked fast and reached the top of the gully within an hour and half.

Alessandro immediately abseiled down the gully to assess the state of the injured boy, careful not to dislodge rocks as he went.

Below them, at the foot of the gully, Christy could see the deep, tumbled snow that had avalanched off the steep face.

'They were lucky,' she said to Jake, who was now beside her and delving into his pack for the ropes he was carrying. 'They could have been buried under that.'

She watched as Alessandro attached the boy to his rope and saw him reach for his radio. Then he spoke to Sean, passing on details of his injuries.

'We're going to need to lower him to the bottom of the gully on a stretcher.'

Jake rolled his eyes and Christy grinned.

It was the most equipment-intensive rescue that they performed and immediately she started to identify safe anchor points that could be used to secure ropes.

While Alessandro gave first aid to the casualty and tried to ward off hypothermia, Christy and Jake set up the lowering belay for the stretcher and handlers.

'This is going to be fun,' Jake muttered, as he found another anchor point and then rigged the stretcher for a vertical lower. 'Which mad fools are going to volunteer to act as barrow boys?'

The stretcher would be held by a static rope at both ends and helped down by two 'barrow boys' who were responsible for abseiling down alongside the stretcher to control the descent.

Each rope was secured to the crag by five equalised anchor points, and by the time the team had finished preparing, ropes were criss-crossing the crag.

It took another hour of intensive teamwork to lower the casualty safely to the bottom and move him out of reach of further avalanches.

While all three teenagers were protected in a bivvy tent, Alessandro did a more detailed survey of the injured boy and Sean communicated with the helicopter.

Fifteen minutes later they heard the familiar clack-clack and the helicopter came up the valley towards them. The helicopter dropped an orange smoke bomb to give an indication of wind speed and direction and everyone made sure that everything was securely anchored down.

First Alessandro was winched into the helicopter, ready to receive the patient. Then the winch man was lifted with the stretcher across his waist, a high line preventing the stretcher from spinning round in the wind. Christy watched from the ground as the stretcher drew level with the open door and the winch operator helped ease the stretcher into the helicopter.

Then they jettisoned the high line and soared down the valley towards the hospital.

'Which leaves us to get ourselves off this hill in darkness and freezing cold,' Jake muttered. 'Why does Alessandro always manage to hitch a lift?'

'Because he's a brilliant A and E doctor,' Christy said as she started collecting equipment and preparing for their descent.

Jake looked at her. 'Hero-worship?'

She gave a wry smile as she pushed a rope into her rucksack. 'Possibly. But I think it's love, unfortunately.'

'Why unfortunately?'

'I don't know.' Christy heaved her pack onto her back. 'I suppose because I still don't really know where I stand with him.'

'Have you tried blunt conversation?'

She looked at him. 'I suppose I'm afraid to do that,' she said honestly. 'Afraid I might push him into saying something I don't want to hear.'

Like 'I don't really love you any more but I'm willing to make an effort because of the children'.

Jake glanced up at the lethal gully. 'You just went up there without batting an eyelid and now you're expecting me to believe that you're afraid of having a conversation with your husband?'

'That's me.' Christy scuffed at the snow with the toe of her boot. 'Miss Coward.'

'Hardly.' Jake waited as the team picked up the last of the equipment and then they all started their descent into the valley.

CHAPTER NINE

CHRISTY collected the children from her mother's and they were sparkly eyed, thoroughly over-excited and weighed down with various bags and rolls of wrapping paper.

'When Santa came down the chim*ney*,' Ben sang loudly, and Katy grimaced.

'*Don't* sing. I'll give you all my pocket money if you stop singing. It's gross. If Father Christmas hears you he'll take a detour because the noise is so terrible.'

Christy glanced in her rear view mirror. 'Did you guys buy anything with Grandma?'

'Loads,' Katy said happily, and Ben beamed.

'We bought you a—'

'Shut up!' Katy glared at him furiously. 'You don't tell people what their presents are, stupid.'

Christy sighed as she took the turning that led to the barn. 'Don't say "shut up", Katy, it isn't nice, and don't call your brother stupid.'

'Well, having all your secrets blown by your baby brother isn't nice, and he is stupid,' Katy muttered. Christy parked the car and switched off the engine. She wondered what time Alessandro would be back. Hopefully not too late. She wanted to spend the evening with him. *And the night.*

Maybe it was time for her to take the initiative, she thought to herself as she undid her seat belt and turned off the headlights.

After all, she'd been the one to stalk away after their passionate encounter in the maze at the Snow Ball. She could hardly blame him for keeping his distance.

'Tomorrow is Christmas Eve,' Ben announced as he wriggled out of his seat belt and opened the car door. 'We can hang up our stockings. Do you think he's set off yet?'

'Who?' Christy dragged her mind back to the practicalities of life, rescued her wet gear from the boot and trudged towards the barn.

'Father Christmas, of course.' Ben frowned up at her, his sweet face innocent and puzzled. 'I don't see how he can get round the whole world in one night, do you? If he doesn't set off until tomorrow, he's never going to make it. You say there's no such thing as magic, so what will he do?'

'I…er…' Christy struggled for a suitable reply as she found her keys and opened the front door. 'Well, we can't understand everything that happens in the world,' she hedged, 'and I think Father Christmas leaves the exact amount of time he needs to do his job,' she said finally. Katy rolled her eyes.

'He won't need long for you, anyway,' she told her brother loftily. 'You haven't been that good this year.'

Ben's face crumpled. 'That's *not* true.'

'You've both been good,' said Christy, keen to hurry them inside and avoid a row. 'Who fancies some mince pies? I made them earlier.'

'Me!' both children shrieked simultaneously and they

piled into the kitchen, dropping bags, hats and gloves onto the table and dragging chairs across the floor.

'Grandma was telling us about her nativity play,' Katy said, biting into a mince pie. 'Mary had nits and the two halves of the donkey started fighting halfway through.'

Christy smiled as she reached into the cupboard for a large casserole pot. 'Your grandma always has good stories at Christmas.'

Her mother taught the reception class at the local primary school and the highlight of the year was the nativity play.

'Then the innkeeper said, "We're totally empty, how many rooms would you like?"' Katy continued, curling her leg under her as she helped herself to another mince pie. 'And Joseph and Mary were so confused they completely forgot their lines and then one of the shepherds tripped and fell on the baby Jesus and—listen to this because it's the best one—one of the three kings said, "I bring Frankenstein."'

Christy laughed and Ben frowned. 'What's wrong with that?'

'Because the King brings frankincense. Franken*stein* was a monster.' Katy yawned. 'A bit like you, really.' She reached an arm across the table and Christy removed the plate quickly.

'Enough, or you'll be too full to eat your tea. Go and play a game while I get supper ready.'

'Let's play squash the present.' Katy slipped off the chair and grabbed Ben's hand. 'We'll squeeze and prod and shake and see if we can guess what's in the parcels. Then we'll see if we're right on Christmas Day.'

'If you haven't broken it,' Christy pointed out dryly, dropping onion into melted butter and frying it gently. She was wondering if she had time to take a shower before Alessandro arrived home.

Quickly she browned meat, added stock, wine and herbs and slid the casserole dish into the oven.

The children were sprawled on the living-room rug, bickering over a game of Monopoly that they'd started the day before.

Christy smiled as she watched them. They argued but there was no denying the love between them. Her children were gorgeous, she thought to herself.

Deciding that she could safely take a shower without war breaking out, she sped upstairs, stripped off quickly and padded into the bathroom.

She showered quickly, washed her hair and then padded into the bedroom and stared into her wardrobe, hoping for inspiration.

What was she going to wear? Something that would ensure that Alessandro would notice her.

But nothing too obvious or she'd look ridiculous.

Katy wandered into the room, wearing jeans, a baggy jumper and stripy socks. 'Are you going to dress up for Dad?'

Christy felt the colour rush into her cheeks. 'Why do you say that?'

'Because you've got a funny look on your face and you're staring into your wardrobe instead of grabbing a pair of jeans.'

Was that what she usually did? Christy frowned. She wore a uniform for work and it was true that when she arrived home she often just pulled on the nearest thing, which was invariably jeans and a jumper.

'Wear red,' Katy advised, springing onto the bed and sitting cross-legged. 'Dad always looks at you in a funny way when you wear red.'

Wondering just when her daughter had become so observant, Christy reached into her wardrobe and pulled out the red dress. It was made of the softest jersey fabric and skimmed over her curves. She'd always loved it but she hardly had occasion to wear it any more.

She'd been wearing it the night of their anniversary. The night he hadn't turned up. The night she'd decided to leave in order to shake him up.

What exactly was happening to their relationship now?

Certainly things between them had improved dramatically. They were working together and in many ways their relationship felt the way it had before they'd had children.

But did he really care for her or was he making an effort because he valued the institution of the family so much?

She wriggled into the dress, slipped her feet into a pair of high-heeled shoes that she loved and frowned at her hair.

Should she try and straighten it?

It tumbled in crazy, dizzying waves down her back, gold and russet mingling with rich copper. Occasionally she had it blow-dried straight, but left to its own devices it curled and twisted.

Wild, passionate hair, Alessandro had always called it.

Remembering his preference, she left the straighteners in her drawer.

'Mum?' Katy slid off the bed and hesitated, suddenly looking less confident than usual. 'Are we going back to London after Christmas?'

Christy froze. Were they? She honestly didn't know. She wanted Alessandro to ask her to stay. She wanted him to give her some indication that he wanted her. Yes, he was angry that she'd left and taken the children, but that wasn't the same as missing her, was it?

'I don't know,' she said quietly, knowing that Katy was

old enough to deserve at least part of the truth. 'I don't know, sweetheart, but we're trying to work everything out.'

Katy chewed her lip. 'If I could only have one thing this Christmas, it would be you and Dad back together and living here like we always did.'

Christy felt her stomach turn. She'd stay, she told herself. Whatever happened, she'd stay for the sake of the children. How could she do anything else? Her own needs really didn't matter, she told herself as she fixed a reassuring smile on her face and pulled her daughter into her arms.

'You don't have to worry,' she whispered soothingly. 'Everything is going to be fine for you.'

But would it be fine for her?

Only time could tell.

The casserole was cooked and she was mashing potatoes when she finally heard Alessandro's key in the door.

'Daddy!' The children hurtled towards him and he lifted them both into a hug.

Watching from the kitchen door, Christy felt her heart turn over. Whatever happened, she wouldn't be leaving, she told herself. She couldn't deprive the children of their right to live with their father. But where did that leave her?

He lifted Ben into his arms, swung him round and then laid him on the rug and tickled him mercilessly while Christy laughed.

'You're getting him all wound up,' she scolded, 'and just before bedtime.'

'Isn't that what fathers are supposed to do?' He straightened in a lithe, athletic movement and looked at her properly for the first time. His gaze slid slowly down her slender frame and then his eyes returned to hers.

'I'm very tired,' he drawled in a soft voice, stepping over

Ben and walking towards her. 'I was thinking of an early night. Does that suit you?'

There was a wicked gleam in his eyes that made her heart miss a beat. 'I'm pretty tired, too,' she croaked, and Katy cleared her throat.

'Well, before you both fall asleep, could you possibly feed us? We're both starving.'

Christy dragged her eyes away from Alessandro's burning gaze. 'Oh, yes—dinner's ready.' Suddenly flustered, aware of his eyes on her, she hurried back into the kitchen and lifted the warmed plates from the oven. 'Come on, then. Sit up.'

Suddenly she just wanted dinner to be over.

She wanted to be with Alessandro.

'Daddy, will you read me a story?'

'Of course.' Alessandro smiled at Katy and then glanced at Christy. 'Is that OK with you? Do you need help clearing up the kitchen?'

He hoped she'd say no. Clearing up the kitchen was his least favourite task and perhaps she knew that because she gave a smile and shook her head.

'You go and read to the children. I'll finish off here and meet you upstairs.'

Suddenly in the grip of a serious attack of lust, Alessandro had to force himself to follow his daughter into her pink, girly bedroom.

'Just a quick story tonight,' he muttered, as he scanned her bookshelves for something that had few pages. He wanted to be with Katy's mother.

Katy reached for a huge fat book. 'I'm reading this, but you don't have to finish it so you can relax.'

Alessandro stared at the book and decided that if it fell on someone's foot, he'd be taking them to the operating theatre. 'Well, that's a relief.'

Katy snuggled into bed. 'Have you bought Mum something for Christmas?'

Disturbed from his contemplation of how little he could get away with, Alessandro looked up. 'Of course.'

'Well, what is it?'

Alessandro frowned. 'It's a surprise. I can't—'

'Dad.' Katy sat up and wrapped her arms round her knees. 'You need to tell me what it is. Presents are important to women.'

'Which is why I chose your mother something that I know she's going to love,' Alessandro said smugly, thinking of the box in his boot.

'So?' Katy looked at him expectantly, and Alessandro sighed.

'All right, I'll tell you but you're not to tell your mother.'

Katy rolled her eyes. 'I'm eleven, Dad. I know about secrets. It's Ben that's the blabbermouth around here, not me.'

Alessandro smiled. 'All right—I've bought her a food processor.'

Katy stared at him in shocked silence. 'You bought her *what*?'

'A food processor.' Alessandro shrugged. 'You know— she uses it all the time and hers broke and—'

'I know what a food processor is,' Katy hissed, glancing towards the door to check that no one was listening, 'but, Dad, that *isn't a good present*.'

'I bought the most expensive model in the shop.'

Katy shook her head frantically. 'You have to get her something else, something that girls like.'

Wondering how he came to be sitting on a pink bedcover,

taking advice from his eleven-year-old daughter, Alessandro lifted an eyebrow. 'Such as?'

'Something more personal. Jewellery.'

'I've never bought your mother jewellery. She doesn't wear jewellery.'

'Well, she can't wear what you've never bought her,' Katy pointed out logically, and Alessandro gritted his teeth.

'It's a waste of money.'

'Dad, you're totally loaded,' Katy said scornfully. 'What's the point of having money if you don't spend it?'

'She doesn't like jewellery.'

'All right.' Katy lay back on the pillow with a weary look on her face. 'Give her the food processor and let's see what happens.'

Alessandro hesitated and then leaned forward to kiss her. 'Don't worry,' he said softly, 'everything is going to turn out fine.'

'Not if you give her a blender, it isn't,' Katy muttered, rolling onto her side and yanking the duvet up over her shoulders. 'Our Christmas is going to be well and truly puréed. You might want to think about that before you wrap it up. When I grow up I'm going to write a book called *The Inner Workings of a Woman's Mind*, and you're going to be my first customer.'

It was a novelty, Alessandro mused as he strolled along to the master bedroom suite, to be told by his eleven-year-old daughter that he didn't understand women.

Should he be amused or insulted?

Christy didn't care about things that glittered, he told himself as he swiftly undressed and strolled towards the shower.

She cared about the things that mattered, like their relationship and the children. *Por Dios*—he hit the buttons on the shower and closed his eyes as hot water streamed over his body—he'd married her so quickly that they hadn't even bothered with an engagement.

And he spent money on the things that mattered. She had a beautiful house, a reliable car...

By the time he'd wrapped a towel round his waist and walked back into the bedroom, he'd convinced himself that he'd shown his love in any number of ways that truly mattered.

And then he saw Christy standing by the bed, lost in thought as she twisted the wedding band on her finger.

What was she thinking? he wondered.

Suddenly his stomach gave a lurch. Was she thinking of taking it off? They still hadn't had a conversation about their future and he was afraid to bring the subject up in case he precipitated the unthinkable.

Christy returning to London.

'I bought you that ring in a tiny shop in the East End of London where we were working,' he said quietly, and she glanced up quickly and smiled.

'That's right. We were in such a hurry, weren't we?'

He studied her face for a long moment. Tried to read her mind. 'Too much of a hurry, *querida*?'

For a moment she didn't answer and then she gave a tiny shrug. 'Maybe. We were young. We didn't really think things through.'

Was she implying that, had she had time to think things through, she wouldn't have married him?

Driven by an intense need to protect what was his and prove his love, Alessandro moved towards her and saw her eyes narrow and darken.

He recognised the look.

She wanted him as much as he wanted her.

With a rough oath, he crossed the room and brought his

mouth down on hers in a fierce kiss, forgetting that he'd vowed to give her space. He didn't want to give her space. She was his. And he wanted her.

Now.

And she wanted him. He could tell from the way she responded to his kiss.

She was as hungry and desperate as he was.

With a tiny murmur she slid her hands down his back and he felt her fingers jerk on the towel that he'd hooked around his waist.

His mouth still on hers, he undressed her swiftly and then lifted her and lowered her onto the centre of the bed.

She was all silken flesh and warm woman, the subtle scent of her perfume casting a sensual spell that threatened his ability to operate on any level other than the most basic.

With a groan of pure, masculine possession, he covered her body with his, feeling soft curves meet hard muscle and relishing the differences between them. She looked delicate but he knew her to be strong and passionate. Knew that he wouldn't hurt her. That she was as eager as he was.

His mouth feasted on hers and his hand slid down to the top of her thighs and lingered.

He trapped her sob with his mouth, felt her body writhe under his and used his fingers to touch her intimately.

Reminding himself that he'd planned to make love to her slowly, Alessandro tried to pull away and gain some semblance of control over his reactions, but she wrapped one leg over his and drew it upwards, urging him towards her.

Wondering why he suddenly had the restraint of a teenager, Alessandro slid a hand under her hips, lifted her and thrust deep. He felt her fingers dig hard into his waist, and he thrust again, muffling her sob with his kiss.

'*Por Dios*, you feel incredible,' he said hoarsely, lifting his mouth just enough to enable him to see her face. Her cheeks were flushed, her eyes were bright and fevered and her mouth was bruised from the pressure of his. And she'd never looked more beautiful.

He shifted his position and moved, knowing exactly how to drive her upwards towards the ultimate pleasure. Her eyes drifted shut and he slid a hand into her soft, silken hair.

'Look at me, *querida*.' He gave a soft groan and brought his mouth down on hers again. *Never had he had to work so hard to find the control he needed.* 'I want you to look at me.'

He didn't know why it suddenly felt so important but it was, and perhaps she felt it too because her eyes opened and stared into his. And he saw everything there. Love. Passion.

Her fingers curled into his back and he saw her cheeks flush and her breath quicken and knew that she was close, but he held back, refusing to allow her the release she craved until he was ready.

So he slowed the rhythm and she groaned in protest and tried to shift her hips, tried to force the pace.

'Alessandro.' Her voice was a breathless whisper of desperation. 'Please, oh, please…'

Deciding that they had the whole night ahead of them so control didn't really matter that much, Alessandro drove deeper inside her and felt the sudden clench of lust as she gripped him.

And then he felt her body tighten around his and he ceased to think altogether as they reached the peak together in one long shower of erotic sensation that left them both breathless and unable to speak.

Christy lay with her eyes closed, feeling blissfully happy and content for the first time in months.

Alessandro loved her.

She knew he loved her.

The night hadn't been about the children or staying together for the family. It had been about them as a couple. About expressing their love.

He still hadn't told her that he wasn't going to let her leave, but he would. She knew he would.

He was probably just being sensitive about bringing the subject up.

Tomorrow he'd tell her that she was staying in that arrogant, autocratic manner of his. She'd say yes.

And Christmas would be perfect.

Christy was making breakfast when the phone rang.

Before she could answer it, Alessandro strolled into the kitchen and picked up the handset. His eyes lingered on her flushed cheeks for a moment and then he gave a slow smile of masculine satisfaction and she blushed deeply.

Help, she thought as she turned back to the hob to stir the porridge. She was behaving like a teenager.

She was so lost in her own dreamy thoughts that she didn't even listen to Alessandro's conversation—didn't even register that he was off the phone until he walked across the kitchen and poured himself a large mug of coffee.

'That was your brother,' he said, and his voice was so cold that she looked at him in alarm.

'Is everything all right? Has something happened?' A moment ago Alessandro had been looking at her as if he had every intention of skipping work and taking her back to bed. Now he looked remote and unapproachable and nothing like the man who'd made love to her all night.

'Nothing's wrong,' he said smoothly, 'except that his other practice nurse has slipped on the ice and broken her wrist.

So he wonders if you'd consider coming back immediately after Christmas.'

Her heart flipped. Surely this was the moment when he was going to tell her that she had to stay, *that he wasn't going to let her leave.*

'Well, I hadn't thought about going that quickly...' She hesitated, waited for him to interrupt her and tell her that she wasn't going at all, but he stood still, studying her face with brooding intensity.

What was he thinking?

'I'll ring Peter back,' she said quickly, 'and chat about it.'

'Fine.' His mouth set in a grim line, Alessandro slammed his mug down on the table so hard that most of the liquid sloshed over the wood. Then he strode from the room, narrowly avoiding a collision with Katy, who was on her way to find breakfast.

She watched her father go with a look of surprise and then saw the pool of liquid on the table. 'Now I know where Ben gets it from,' she said wearily as she walked round the table and reached for a cloth. 'Spilling drinks is obviously a genetic defect. Remind me to screen any man I marry—I don't want to spend my life mopping up puddles.'

Christy was too miserable even to raise a smile.

Now what?

She thought back to the conversation they'd had when he'd walked out of the shower the night before. He'd been talking about the time they'd met. Hadn't he implied last night that they'd married in too much of a hurry?

Obviously he was the one who was regretting their whirlwind courtship.

Perhaps, after all, he wanted to be free to date women like Katya but was much too traditional to make that decision himself.

So he was expecting her to make it.

Why hadn't he told her that she couldn't leave? She felt tears prick her eyes as she turned off the heat and poured porridge into bowls for the children.

'Mum, this isn't the story of Goldilocks, you know.' Katy stared at the meagre contents of her bowl. 'And I'm not baby bear. That's never going to keep me warm on a cold day.'

Realising that she'd only put a spoonful in the bowl, Christy gave a wan smile and filled the bowl to the top.

'Are you all right, Mum?'

No, Christy thought, suppressing a hysterical giggle. She was far from all right.

It appeared that her marriage was well and truly over and that wasn't what she wanted. It wasn't what she'd ever wanted.

Everything had gone utterly, miserably wrong and it was mostly her fault for leaving in the first place.

It didn't matter that she'd intended him to follow her the same day and make up.

All that mattered was that she adored him and that he didn't seem to want her with him any more.

And every time she tried to remind herself that last night he'd been loving and caring, that over the past days he'd listened to her and treated her like a woman, nothing changed the fact that he hadn't told her that she couldn't leave.

And Alessandro had never, *ever* had problems saying what he wanted.

So if he hadn't asked her then there was only one possible explanation.

He was hoping that she'd go back to London.

CHAPTER TEN

SHE spent Christmas Eve with the children and they went for a walk in the forest, stamping footprints into virgin snow and piercing the muffled silence with their excited squeals.

After the inevitable snowball fight, they returned to the barn wet and happy and Christy set about drying clothes and making dinner.

Would this be the last time she did this?

Would this be their last ever Christmas as a family?

She stood for a moment and looked around the kitchen, the kitchen she'd chosen so carefully. Three more days. In three more days she'd be leaving this and she'd probably never cook in this room again.

Tears stung her eyes.

'Mum, I want to leave a chocolate roll for Santa.' Ben was beside her, his eyes huge and shining, a pair of furry brown antlers jammed onto his head. 'Everyone leaves mince pies and he must be really bored with it, don't you think? I mean mince pies are great, but if you think of the population of the world, that's a lot of pastry, isn't it?'

Blinking back the tears, Christy smiled and reached into

the cupboard for a little chocolate roll. 'Good idea,' she said huskily. 'Leave him this with a little note. I'm sure he'll be really pleased.'

'And carrots for the reindeer.' Ben squinted up at her, the bells on his antlers jangling. 'Why are you crying?'

'Me? Crying? Never.' Her smile widened and she wondered if her face would crack with the effort. 'I've been chopping onions for tea.'

'I hate onions.'

'They're for Daddy's tea,' Christy said quickly, turning her back on him and washing her hands. 'Go and put that cake out now, before you forget.'

'I can't wait for Daddy to come home so we can hang up our stockings like we always do.'

Family tradition. Routine.

Thinking of Ben's innocent face, Christy thought her heart might break.

Why did life have to go so very wrong? Wasn't there something she could have done to have fixed it?

Was this all her fault?

Katy wandered into the room. 'I love Christmas Eve even more than I love Christmas.'

Pulling herself together, Christy turned round, the smile still in place. 'Why's that?'

'Because you have all the excitement and anticipation. It's all still to come.' Katy danced round the kitchen, her ponytail swinging. 'And Christmas Eve feels so Christmassy. More Christmassy than Christmas Day. Tomorrow's going to be brilliant, isn't it, Mum?'

'Yes.'

Katy stopped dancing and looked at her. 'Everything's going to be OK, Mum.'

How did you explain to an eleven-year-old girl who still

thought that life was perfect that everything was going to be anything but OK?

Keeping up a brave front was proving exhausting and she was almost relieved when Alessandro arrived home. At least the children might stop noticing her.

They ate dinner as a family and Christy was glad of the excited chatter of the children. It meant that she didn't have to speak, which was a relief because she honestly didn't know what to say with Alessandro looking so icily remote across the table.

Not only did he not want her to stay but, judging from the look on his face, he couldn't wait for Christmas to be over so that she would leave.

After dinner, she watched with a lump in her throat as Alessandro helped Ben fasten his huge red sock to the fireplace and write his letter to Father Christmas.

Finally the children were tucked up in bed and the house was silent.

When she was sure that the children were asleep, Christy tiptoed back downstairs and stuffed the stockings. It was a ritual that she and Alessandro normally performed together with the help of chilled champagne and smoked salmon. Memories filled her brain. *How many years had they ended the evening by making love on the huge rug in front of the fire?*

But not tonight.

Tonight, Christmas Eve had lost its magic.

She went to bed, but her mind was too full of thoughts to allow her to sleep, so eventually she padded back downstairs to the living room. Staring out of the huge windows into the darkness, she watched the soft swirl of snowflakes.

'Aren't you coming to bed?' Alessandro's voice came

from directly behind her and she tensed, afraid to turn in case she gave herself away.

'Don't you ever wish you were still small and believed in Father Christmas?' she breathed softly, watching the snow hit the pane and slide downwards leaving a watery trail. 'It's one of the most magical things about childhood. Believing in the impossible.'

'So what would you want him to bring you?'

She was silent for a moment. 'Love,' she said softly, without turning to look at him. 'It's the only thing that really matters in the end. Everything else is nothing without love.'

He didn't answer and the still silence of the room seemed to close them in and wrap itself around them.

'Then I hope you find it,' he said hoarsely, and she heard the firm tread of his step as he turned and walked away, leaving her with only her sadness for company.

'Mummy, can we get up now?' Ben's excited voice was the first thing she heard when she finally woke the following morning after about two hours' sleep.

'He's been prising my eyelids open for the past three hours,' Katy complained as she bounced onto her parents' bed. 'He keeps saying, "Is it time yet?" like a parrot.'

'That phrase is probably first cousin to "Are we there yet?"' Alessandro muttered, sitting up in bed and stifling a yawn.

Christy risked a glance at him and saw that he looked exhausted, too.

And tense.

Was being with her really that much of a strain?

Oh, for crying out loud. It was Christmas Day and nothing, not even her crumbling, disintegrating marriage, was going to spoil it!

'Come on, then.' Pushing away the heavy bands of stress and tiredness that threatened to crush her skull, she slid out of bed and pulled on her silk robe.

The children careered downstairs, shrieking with excitement, and she followed more slowly, watching their pleasure with an indulgent smile.

'He's been, *he's been*,' Ben shouted, dancing up to his stocking and lifting it. 'And look—he's eaten the chocolate roll and left a footprint.'

Sure enough, a large, dusty footprint lay in front of the fireplace and Christy gave a smile. Alessandro must have come back downstairs during the night to make that, she thought to herself. He'd always done it, even when the children had been too young to notice. *He was a brilliant father.*

He walked into the room moments later, his dark eyes heavy with sleep, his jeans half-undone and his T-shirt rumpled. He'd obviously reached for the first thing in his wardrobe and still he managed to look impossibly sexy, she thought with something close to exasperation.

Why couldn't she look at him and feel nothing?

How did you stifle a love as powerful as hers?

How did you carry on with life?

'Has Father Christmas been coming down my chimney without wiping his feet again?' Alessandro glowered at the footprint and Ben giggled.

'Do you think he brought the reindeer?'

Alessandro raised an eyebrow. 'Into my living room? I hope not.'

'Come on, Ben.' Determined not to dwell on Alessandro, she turned back to the children. 'What has he brought you?'

Christmas Day had begun. They opened the presents in their stockings, ate breakfast together and then went to the carol service at the local church.

Wrapped up warmly in a long coat, Christy listened to the pure voices of the choirboys and felt a lump in her throat.

It was normally her favourite part of Christmas but today it just seemed to make her feel even sadder.

'Hey.' A masculine voice came from behind her. 'I hope my lunch isn't burning while you're here.'

It was Jake.

Having him for the day would be a welcome distraction, she thought to herself as she turned to acknowledge his presence with a quick smile.

'Come on, Mum.' Katy grabbed her hand as they arrived back at the barn to the delicious smells of turkey. 'Time for all the other presents now.'

Her parents arrived moments later and suddenly the house took on the chaotic, crazy feel that only ever happened at Christmas.

'I have to go and spend some time in the kitchen,' Christy began, but Katy shook her head.

'It can wait. It doesn't matter if lunch is late. We can always eat crisps to keep us going.'

'You cannot eat crisps!'

Katy grinned. 'Just winding you up, Mum.'

Christy gave a weak smile and followed her daughter through to the living room.

Jake and Alessandro were talking by the fireplace and Katy dropped to her knees and dragged the presents out from under the tree.

'This one is for Daddy, from Grandma…'

Christy watched as everyone opened presents and tried not to mind that Alessandro didn't seem to have bought her anything.

Why would he? She was only here under sufferance. Because he wanted Christmas with his children, and she came as part of the package.

Eventually the pressure grew too much and she retired to the kitchen.

It was all right, she told herself firmly as she checked the roast potatoes and stirred the cranberry sauce. She'd cope. Whatever happened, she'd cope.

She was concentrating so hard on not breaking down that she didn't hear the kitchen door open and close. She wasn't aware of another person in the room until she heard Alessandro's deep, dark drawl from directly behind her.

'There are things that I have to say,' he said tightly, 'and you're not going to like them. But I'm going to say them anyway.'

Oh, dear God, not now, she thought. She had to produce Christmas dinner for seven people and she couldn't do that if he'd just told her that he didn't love her any more and that he wanted her to go back to London. Knowing that it was the truth was quite different from hearing it.

'We can talk later, Alessandro,' she said quickly, sticking her face in the oven to check the turkey and resisting the temptation to leave it there. 'This probably isn't the best time.'

'I don't care about that. You have to listen.' He strode across the kitchen and pulled her away from the oven. Strong hands closed over her shoulders, forcing her to look at him.

'All right, then.' She said the words with weary resignation. 'This is about me going back to London, isn't it? It's fine, Alessandro. I'll leave the day after tomorrow.'

'You're not going anywhere.' His voice was a threatening growl and then he cursed softly and released her, taking a step backwards. 'I'm doing this all wrong but— I've got you a present—let's start with that.'

He seemed to be fumbling for words and she considered it a point in his favour that he appeared to have lost his usually fluent English. Obviously he wasn't finding it easy and perversely she was glad about that. She didn't want him to find it easy.

'A present?' She stared at him with a lack of comprehension. Given the gravity of their conversation, mention of a Christmas present suddenly jarred. Material gifts were so unimportant, she thought dully, but she forced herself to smile and look interested. 'For me?'

'Of course, for you.'

He would have bought her something because of the children, she reasoned. Because Katy would have asked questions if there'd been nothing for her. 'Why didn't you give it to me when we were all round the tree?'

'Because this is a special gift from me to you and I don't want to share it.'

Not because of the children, then.

What sort of special gift was he buying her? she wondered with wry humour. A one-way train ticket south? Frosted divorce papers?

He reached into his pocket and withdrew a small box wrapped in glittering paper.

'Oh, it's pretty…' And so unlike Alessandro, she thought as she took the box, feeling the sudden uneven thump of her heart. *Don't be ridiculous, Christy*, she told herself firmly. *This can't be anything special. It can't be.*

'Open it,' he urged in a husky voice. 'Open it, *querida*.'

A lump sprang into her throat. Why was he calling her darling when they were two days away from ending their marriage for ever?

Wanting to get the moment over as quickly as possible, she ripped off the paper and saw a small velvet box.

Jewellery.

It had to be jewellery.

Suddenly she wanted to laugh and cry at the same time. She'd spent twelve Christmases with Alessandro and he'd never bought her jewellery and he decided to do it on their last one.

Why?

Trying to find the answer to that question, she looked up at him and saw an unusual degree of tension in his handsome face.

'Aren't you going to look?' His voice bordered on the impatient and he stretched out a lean, bronzed hand and flipped the box open. 'Do you like it?'

He sounded nervous and she'd never known Alessandro to be nervous of anything before. He never questioned himself but tackled life with an enviable degree of self-confidence. But today that confidence appeared to be lacking.

She glanced down at the box in her hand and felt the floor shift. Nestled in a bed of rich, deep blue silk lay a huge, sparkling diamond. It twinkled and sparkled under the kitchen lights and she stared at it stupidly.

Finally she found her voice. 'What is it?'

'It's the ring I should have given you twelve years ago,' Alessandro said gruffly. 'But I'm giving it to you now. If you'll wear it.'

'But—'

'I'm not great at speeches, so let me just say what I have to say.' He jabbed long fingers through his glossy hair and took a deep breath. 'I fell in love with you the day I saw you. Impossible, I know, but that's how it was. You were so beautiful, so warm and kind and yet so fiery and passionate. I'd never met a woman like you before and after I saw you I never looked again. And I've never stopped loving you. And if you love someone you're supposed to be able to set them free—let them go. I told myself that I'd let you go if that was what you wanted—'

'Alessandro—'

'I promised not to order or command so I can't force you to stay,' Alessandro said hoarsely, 'but I'm willing to beg. Will you stay, Christy? Will you stay if I beg?'

Beg?

She stared at him. None of it made sense. 'But you don't love me—'

'How can you say that?' He stared at her a look of stunned incredulity in his dark eyes. 'When have I ever led you to believe that I don't love you?'

She chewed her lip. 'Loads of reasons,' she said finally. 'You didn't follow me to London, you put me in the spare room and we've been lying in the same bed and you haven't made love to me—'

'Because when I *did* make love to you,' he exploded, the natural volatility of his Mediterranean temperament bubbling to the surface, 'you slapped me!'

'It was sex.'

'It was *love*, *querida*,' he said hoarsely, and she shook her head slowly.

'You never once said you loved me.'

'I did.'

'No,' she said patiently. 'You didn't.'

'So…' He spread his hands in a supremely Latin gesture. 'I had other things on my mind at the time, like the fact that you looked so incredibly sexy and we hadn't been together for weeks and—' He broke off and gave an apologetic smile. 'And I am a man and verbal communication isn't my forte. I'm working on it.'

'I thought you'd stopped loving me.'

He stared at her in shocked silence. 'I've never stopped loving you.'

Hope flared and she squashed it down ruthlessly. 'You've never stopped loving me?'

'Of course not. I know I'm not perfect.' He frowned slightly as he said the words, as if admitting such a fact was difficult, 'and I realise that I've done many things wrong. Seeing you in A and E and in the mountain rescue team made me realise how many skills you have that you're not using. You have made so many sacrifices for the family.'

'They weren't sacrifices,' Christy murmured, but he shook his head.

'You made this family work. You made it possible for me to live the life I wanted to lead. And I neglected you as a woman. I can see that now.'

She sucked in a breath. 'Alessandro—'

'You have to let me finish,' he breathed, taking the box and removing the ring. 'Over the past two weeks I have tried so hard not to be controlling and bossy and I promise to work on that but even so, I can't let you leave again. I know I drive you crazy but you love me, Christy. Over the last two weeks I've become more and more sure about that.'

She swallowed hard. 'Of course I love you. And I didn't mean to leave—at least, not in the way that you mean. You weren't listening to me and I thought it was the only way to get through to you. I thought you'd come after me—'

'You didn't mean to leave? What do you mean, you didn't mean to leave?'

'It was only ever supposed to be for the weekend,' she confessed, pushing aside the last vestiges of her pride in an effort to save their relationship. 'I thought you'd come after me and drag me back.'

He ran a hand over his roughened jaw. 'Am I really that controlling?'

'Yes. But not on that occasion, obviously. Ironic, really. The one time I wanted you to come and drag me back, you didn't do it.'

'It seems that I'm not the only one who is hopeless at communicating. When I realised you'd left I was totally and utterly devastated,' he groaned, sliding a hand into her hair and tilting her head so that he could look into her eyes. 'I thought you didn't love me any more and I could hardly blame you, because I missed our anniversary—'

'It wasn't about our anniversary,' she interrupted him in a soft voice, needing to explain. 'We just didn't feel like a couple any more.'

'I suppose I was suffering from that old cliché of taking you for granted.' He gave a shrug and a self-deprecating smile. 'I came home and you were always here. And then one day you weren't and I had the shock of my life.'

'So why didn't you come after me?'

'I genuinely didn't realise that was what you wanted, although I should have done, of course. I've lived with you long enough to understand your temper.' His voice was soft and he dragged his thumb over her cheek in a gentle caress. 'For once in my life I was trying to think of you. I wanted you back but you were obviously so fed up with me that I thought you needed time and space so I left you alone.'

'And I thought you didn't want me.'

'Then you arrived back here looking stunningly gorgeous and promptly slept in the spare room.'

'You *put* me in the spare room,' she reminded him, and he gave a wry smile,

'Another major error of judgement on my part. I was expecting you to refuse to sleep there. *Always* you sleep in my bed.'

He sounded so much like the old Alessandro that she gave a soft smile. 'Thank goodness we had some help from the children or I'd still be in there,'

'*Sí*—because we are both so stubborn and hot-tempered, *gatita*.' He gave a groan and lowered his mouth to hers, dropping a lingering kiss on her mouth. 'Perhaps if I was a cool Englishman, none of this would have happened.'

'If you were a cool Englishman,' she muttered against his mouth, 'I never would have married you.'

He lifted his head a fraction. 'Is that true? I'm always very aware that I didn't give you a chance to date other men and I confess I was worried about Jake.'

'Jake has only ever been the very best friend to both of us. And I didn't want to date other men. But what about you?' She forced herself to ask the question she'd dreaded asking. 'I was worried about Katya. I thought you might be interested in her...' She left the statement hanging and his eyes narrowed, one ebony brow lifted in question.

'Have I *ever* given you reason not to trust me?'

'No.' She shook her head. 'But our marriage was on the rocks and—'

He placed his fingers over his lips. 'Don't say it,' he breathed, 'because it isn't the truth and it never was. We are both stormy, passionate people and our journey through life is never going to be in calm waters.'

'I thought you only wanted me to stay because of the children.' Dizzy from his kiss and the hard press of his body against hers, she stared up at him and he shook his head.

'Never,' he said hoarsely, reaching for her hand and sliding the ring on her finger. 'I married you in haste and I've loved you deeply ever since. I wanted you to stay because I love you and I can't live without you. And this is the engagement ring I should have given you twelve years ago.'

Her heart thumped hard against her chest as she stared at the ring in delighted fascination. It shone and sparkled on her finger. 'I've never seen anything more beautiful in my life,' she murmured, 'but I still don't understand one thing…'

His mouth was close to hers. 'What's that?'

'If you love me and you want me to stay, why didn't you say so when Pete rang, asking me to go back early?'

'Because you'd accused me of being controlling! I was giving you a choice, *querida*.' He gave a wry smile. 'But you weren't making the choice I wanted you to make. I assumed you'd only come home because of the children and with Christmas over you had no reason to stay.'

'And I thought you didn't want me. Alessandro, I came home for Christmas for me, not for the children. The children just gave me the excuse I'd been looking for.'

'And you say we kids are complicated.' A voice came from the doorway behind them, and they both turned.

Katy was standing in the doorway, arms folded and tinsel in her hair. Her eyes were on the ring that Christy was wearing. 'Nice present, Dad,' she said softly, and Alessandro gave her a slow smile, his arms still around his wife.

'I'm glad you think so,' he drawled, and Katy smiled.

'So, are we finally a happy family?'

Jake strolled into the kitchen and looped an arm round his goddaughter's shoulders. 'You shouldn't be watching this, angel. It's probably age restricted.'

Katy rolled her eyes. 'I'm almost twelve. I know *everything*. The next thing is they'll probably go and mate or something. Pretty gross at their age, but there you are.'

Alessandro stared in stunned amazement, Christy

blushed and Jake threw back his head and laughed. 'Well, my friends?' He stared at them quizzically. 'Have you sorted things out?'

Ben dashed into the kitchen with an armful of toys. 'Grandma says, is there a cloth? I spilled my drink.'

'Oh, what's new?' Katy gave a long-suffering sigh. 'Father Christmas should have stuck a jumbo box of kitchen roll in your stocking. Don't worry, Mum. You stay talking to Dad. I'll sort it out.' She hustled her brother out of the room and Jake watched them go, a smile playing around his firm mouth.

'She's growing up,' he said quietly, and Alessandro frowned.

'Don't say that. I'm not prepared for hormones or boyfriends.'

Jake rubbed his jaw, his blue eyes bright with humour. 'I'd say you're pretty good at defending what's yours.' The smile faded and he looked at both of them. 'You two were meant to be together. Always. Remember that.'

And with that he turned and left the room, closing the door quietly behind him.

Christy turned to Alessandro. 'The turkey is cooked and the roast potatoes are on the point of burning. We ought to serve dinner.'

He gave her a wicked smile. 'When are we going to mate?'

'Later.' She couldn't remember ever feeling so happy and she flung her arms round him and held him tight. 'Oh, Alessandro, this is the best present. All I wanted was for you to love me. For us to be a family.'

'And all I wanted was you, *querida*.' His voice was husky as he lifted her hand to his lips and kissed it, his eyes holding hers. 'Always. Merry Christmas.'

* * * * *

MIRANDA

CHAPTER ONE

SHE'D MADE SUCH A MESS of her life.

Sodden with misery, Miranda sat on the rock, staring at the frozen lake, oblivious to the fact that she was slowly losing the feeling in her fingers and toes.

Around her the mountains rose, wrapped in their lethal covering of snow and ice, but she was as indifferent to their beauty as she was eager for their sanctuary. They offered refuge from glittering tinsel and other symbols of festive cheer.

It was Christmas Day, but up here in the icy wilderness of the Lake District, Christmas Day was just another span of daylight hours without meaning or significance.

And she really shouldn't be crying.

It had been six months. *Six long months.* Time enough to accept the situation and move on. Time enough to forgive herself for being *unforgivably* stupid and naive.

She was supposed to be streetwise. Independent. She was supposed to know everything there was to know about the dark side of human nature. Well, apparently she didn't. She gave a cynical laugh. Apparently even she could be duped.

She'd been stupid and gullible and she just *hated* herself for having been taken in so completely.

With a sniff, she rubbed her numb cheeks with equally frozen fingers. Crying was pointless and was something she rarely indulged in. Struggling to hold back the tears, Miranda searched inside herself for the fierce strength that she knew she possessed, but all that happened was that more tears welled up in her eyes and spilled down her frozen cheeks. Oh, for goodness' sake! She brushed them away with an impatient hand and wondered what was happening to her. She was *never* usually this pathetic! It was just because it was Christmas. Christmas made everything feel different. At Christmas, everything was focused on the image of the perfect family, but for her to be seduced by that image was completely laughable because she knew better than anyone that families were entirely imperfect.

She didn't want one!

She was better off on her own.

But she'd managed to forget that fact. Briefly, she'd lost all sense of judgment. She, of all people, who had learned long ago that the only person you could truly depend on was yourself. She *never* leaned on people. Never. And yet she'd—

Gritting her teeth, she pushed the thought away. That was in the past now. Whether she liked it or not, it was over and the past didn't matter. All that mattered was the future. And remembering not to make the same mistake again.

She straightened her spine and lifted her chin.

It was time to grow up. That was going to be her New Year's resolution. She was going to stop being such a romantic dreamer and get to grips with the realities of life. Princes didn't ride up on white chargers or horses of any other colour, come to that. Ordinary people didn't win the lottery and families were entirely dysfunctional and not to be envied in the slightest. And Christmas was just one day out of three hundred and sixty-five and it would pass soon enough.

There was absolutely no point in sitting on a rock in the middle of nowhere, feeling sorry for herself for not having something that just didn't exist.

She needed to pick herself up and make the best of the situation.

Feeling something cold brush her hand, she glanced up and realised with a flash of surprise that it was snowing. Suddenly aware of just how cold she was, she turned her head and noticed with a stab of alarm that she could no longer see the top of the mountains.

The weather had been perfect when she'd left her miserable, cramped, rented flat.

What had happened to the blue sky and the sunshine?

With a flash of panic, she realised that she actually had absolutely no idea where she was. She'd been so desperate to get away from the rows of houses with Christmas trees and fairy-lights—so desperate to escape from the glaring taunt of happy family gatherings—that she'd just climbed onto her rusty, secondhand bike and ridden out of town until the houses had been far behind her and all that had lain ahead had been the mountains. She didn't even know the area because she'd only moved here a week ago.

She'd abandoned the bike in a deserted car park and started to walk, lured by the promise of fresh air, blue sky and the absence of festivities.

Up here on the fells it hadn't seemed like Christmas. Up here, she hadn't felt like the only person on the planet who was surviving Christmas Day on her own. Up here it had just seemed like any other normal day.

Except that her life had reached crisis point.

But the time for reflection had passed and more immediate problems were now pressing in on her. Like finding the car park again. If she were to stand any chance of finding her way down the mountain, she was going to have to leave immediately.

She stood up and stamped the snow off her trainers, realising how totally inadequate they were.

How could she have been so irresponsible?

The answer, of course, was that she hadn't been thinking about anything except her problems, but problems had a way of shifting around and she knew that her immediate problem was one of basic survival.

Trying to identify the way she'd come, she walked for a few minutes and then realised that she could no longer see the ground directly in front of her. She couldn't work out which way was up and which was down. The path had vanished and beneath her feet lay a lethal, snowy carpet. A treacherous covering that concealed the way home.

The temperature was dropping, she was lost and she had no means of contacting anyone. *No one knew where she was.*

Suddenly understanding the seriousness of her situation, her heart lurched with fear and her mouth dried. Panic gripped her with tight, merciless fingers and for a moment she found it hard to think.

The weather was deteriorating by the minute and she knew absolutely nothing about surviving in freezing, wilderness conditions.

If she walked without knowing where she was going, there was every chance she could walk over a precipice, to her death.

But staying still wasn't an option either. She had no equipment, nothing with which to create warmth or shelter.

Part of her just wanted to sit down and give up. But something stirred inside her. Something that reminded her that giving up wasn't an option. Dying wasn't an option. She *had* to live.

She'd just have to find a way down. Somehow.

She was going to survive.

And once she'd done that, she was going to totally rethink her life.

Jake Blackwell trudged steadily up the path, noting the change in the weather with a faint smile of amusement. Mountains. A bit like women, he thought to himself as he shifted the pack on his back—unpredictable of mood and always to be treated with respect.

In many ways he preferred unpredictable, wild weather to sunshine and blue skies. Walking and climbing became more of a challenge, a guessing game, a battle of wits between him and the mountain.

The deep snow crunched under his boots, the air was cold enough to numb the face and in the distance he could hear the peal of bells from the village church.

It was Christmas Day.

He should have felt happy.

When he'd set out, the sun had been shining in a perfect blue sky, he'd just enjoyed a traditional turkey dinner with his oldest and dearest friends and watched their children opening presents and playing happily round a twinkling Christmas tree.

The house had been filled with warmth and joy, not least because Alessandro and Christy had finally patched up the holes in their marriage.

He was pleased for them. Relieved. But as he'd closed the door behind him, leaving them to their happiness, a hollow, empty feeling had gnawed at his insides. There was nothing like Christmas to remind you that you were on your own.

It wasn't that he was short of prospective candidates. With a total absence of vanity, he was more than aware that there were no end of midwives and female doctors who were interested in ending his bachelor lifestyle. But none of them interested him. At least, not in the long term.

He dated, of course. He was a healthy, single male so no one expected him to live like a monk. But no matter what happened during the twelve months leading up to Christmas, he always seemed to end the year on his own. No woman had ever held his attention for the long term.

Except Christy, and she'd married his best friend and he'd long since trained himself to put thoughts of her out of his head.

Alessandro was an incredibly lucky guy, he mused. Christy was an amazing woman, the children were beautiful—

With a soft curse he lengthened his stride and talked sense into himself.

What was wrong with being single? Nothing. It was just that it was Christmas Day and all the emphasis seemed to be on families.

That was why he'd chosen to go for a walk instead of returning home to his big, empty house. He could have driven to the hospital and spent the day at work, but why would he want to do that when he'd already spent too much of the year working? In fact, work was probably one of the reasons he was on his own. It was hard to get out and meet people when you were trapped in a hospital day in, day out.

His spirits lifting as he walked, he forced himself to count his blessings. He was healthy, he had a great job at the hospital and he loved his work with the mountain rescue team. He had nothing to complain about.

And if his life sometimes felt a little empty—well, he'd never had trouble filling the void before now.

He walked upwards, enjoying the snow-muffled silence and the cold sting of the air in his lungs.

The visibility was reducing by the moment and he knew he probably ought to turn back. He was familiar with the path and he was well equipped, but he also had a healthy respect for mountains and didn't want to be the one responsible for dragging his colleagues in the mountain rescue team away from their Christmas gatherings.

He was just about to turn back when he caught a flash of colour through the thickening snow. With a quick frown he narrowed his eyes and looked again but it was gone.

It had been so brief that it would have been all too easy to have dismissed the vision as nothing more than a figment of his imagination, but twelve years on the mountain rescue team had honed his instincts and sharpened his brain. So he didn't turn. Instead, he walked forward a few more steps and the stopped dead.

A small figure, half covered in snow, was huddled against a rocky outcrop. A child?

And then the snow-covered figure lifted her head and he saw that it wasn't a child. It was a woman.

And a very beautiful woman.

He couldn't remember ever seeing eyes so exotic. Dark as sloes and framed by thick, lush lashes, they simply accentuated the pallor of her skin. Wisps of damp, ebony hair framed an almost perfect bone structure and the only colour in her face was her mouth—a rich, generous curve of soft pink that might have been designed with the sole purpose of driving a man to distraction.

She looked delicate and feminine and just about the last person he would have expected, or wanted, to find in the mountains in a blizzard.

Snow clung to her hair and her whole body was shivering, and it took just that one glance for him to realise that the situation was serious. This wasn't a seasoned walker, prepared for a hike in the mountains. She looked like a woman who should have been somewhere else entirely.

The shivering was a good sign, he reminded himself grimly as he swung the rucksack off his broad shoulders and delved inside for the equipment he knew he was going to need. When the shivering stopped it meant that the human body was no longer able to produce heat. Still, he didn't need his medical degree or his mountain rescue skills to know that the girl was seriously cold.

He needed to warm her up, check her over and then decide whether he could get her down by himself or whether he was going to need the assistance of his colleagues in the mountain rescue team.

He hoped they'd all enjoyed their Christmas dinner because he had a feeling that he was going to be calling on their services very shortly.

'What are you doing here on your own? Where are your friends?' Dispensing with pleasantries, he selected various items from his rucksack, his movements swift and purposeful as he spoke to the girl, assessing her level of consciousness, knowing that her answers would give clues as to just how cold she was. 'Where are the rest of your party?'

Had the others left her and gone for help? Didn't they have the sense to know that someone should have stayed with her? Or were they in trouble, too?

For a long moment she didn't answer him and he wondered with a flash of concern whether she was too cold to speak. Had his first judgment of the situation been wrong?

'What's your name?' His tone was urgent now and he crouched down to her level and took her face in his hands, forcing her to look at him. 'Tell me your name.'

Speak to me. Say something.

Drowsiness and confusion were signs of the onset of hypothermia and he didn't like what he was seeing.

Her dark eyes slid to his and he saw something in her gaze that twisted his insides. An empty hopelessness.

'Miranda.' Finally she spoke and her voice seemed tiny in the huge emptiness of snow and ice. 'No friends. No party.' Her arms were huddled round her waist for warmth. 'Just m-me.'

'Here, sit on this.' Jake pushed a thick pad underneath her, reminding himself that there would be time enough later to talk to her about the dangers of walking alone in winter weather conditions. 'It's insulated and it will stop the snow seeping through your clothes. Then we need to get you something to eat.'

Mentally he ran through the various stages of hypothermia.

He knew that the most effective warming of the casualty came from the inside. She needed glucose and fluid and he needed to stop her losing any more heat.

He handed her a chocolate bar and then pulled a fleece hat onto her damp hair to try and prevent further heat loss from her head.

The chocolate bar slipped through her fingers and her eyes drifted closed. 'Not really hungry. Tired now...' she murmured, and he cursed softly under his breath as he rescued the chocolate.

'You need to eat, Miranda. It will warm you up.' He

pulled the wrapper off the chocolate, pushed the bar into her hands again and closed her fingers around it. 'Eat!'

Her eyes opened at his sharp command and she stared blankly at the chocolate bar as if she'd never seen one before and then took a reluctant nibble.

Jake removed her sodden coat, which would have struggled to give protection against a light shower in the city, let alone heavy snow in the mountains.

'Don't take my coat off.' She mumbled her protest and tried to stop him but he'd already dropped it on the ground and was dragging extra layers from his rucksack.

'You need to put these on. You need dry clothes. Put on this fleece and then this waterproof shell.'

She stared at the clothes he dropped onto her lap and he gave a sigh and picked them up, deciding that he was going to have to dress her himself. So he pulled the fleece over her head and then manoeuvred her arms through the sleeves, then did the same thing again with another layer and finally zipped her into his spare coat.

It was like dressing a doll. She was limp and unresisting and his coat swamped her, but at least it was dry and weatherproof. He wrapped a scarf around her mouth and nose to warm the air she was breathing, running through the options in his head. Helicopter evacuation? Not in this weather. Which meant calling the team out. But it would take them a couple of hours to reach this point and that was two hours during which Miranda could grow even colder.

'All right.' Pleased to see that she'd finished the chocolate bar, he handed her another and reached into his rucksack for the insulated flask that he always carried. 'This is the situation. We basically have two choices. I can contact the mountain rescue team and then put up a shelter and we can lie naked in a sleeping bag together while we wait. That should warm you up.'

Her eyes slid to his and he saw a glimmer of humour. 'Is that an indecent proposal?'

Something in her slightly cynical tone made him smile. She had a sense of humour and that was a good sign. 'Believe it or not, it wasn't. Skin to skin contact is the fastest way of rewarming a casualty.'

Her teeth were chattering as she nibbled reluctantly on the second chocolate bar. 'That's the most original seduction line I've ever heard and, believe me, I've heard a few.' Her voice was weak and rasping. 'And I'm not a casualty.'

He decided not to point out that she was fast becoming one. 'The second choice is that we walk down. But that requires you to get up and move your legs. Are you up to it?'

'Of course.' More alert now, she rubbed the snow out of her eyes with the back of her hand. 'What do you think I am? Pathetic?'

No, hypothermic.

He was relieved to see that she suddenly seemed to be waking up. 'So tell me what you're doing out here on a day like this.' Concern made his voice sharper than he'd intended. 'Do you have a death wish?'

'No. And the day was nothing like this earlier this morning. It was sunny.' Despite the extra layers he'd given her, her teeth were still chattering and her breath clouded the freezing air. 'And I was out for a walk, just like you.'

Jake glanced down at her feet and lifted an eyebrow. '*Not* like me,' he pointed out gently. 'You're wearing trainers.'

Her hands still clutching the chocolate bar, the girl stared down at her feet and gave a wan smile. 'Well, they were all I had. I don't possess walking boots. I thought I'd be all right providing I stuck to the path.'

'Is this the same path that has just disappeared under a layer of snow? And didn't you possess gloves either?' Jake gave a sigh and reached inside his rucksack again. 'If you don't own walking boots then you shouldn't be out on the mountains, especially not at the height of winter. What were you thinking of?'

For a moment those incredible eyes were haunted by ghosts and then she turned her head away. 'Oh, I don't know,' she said huskily. 'This and that. Stuff.'

Stuff?

Something about the set of her profile made him frown and want to question her further but then he reminded himself that hesitation could make the difference between life and death in the mountains. This wasn't the time for polite conversation. 'Finish the chocolate.' He laid a pair of gloves on her lap. 'And then put these on before you develop frostbite in your fingers. Have you any idea what the temperature is today?'

She finished the last of the chocolate and then slowly wriggled her hands into the gloves. 'No, but it certainly isn't the Bahamas, that's for sure. The sun was shining when I left.'

It was a common mistake, Jake reflected. Believing that a cloudless blue sky would last. A significant proportion of the calls to the mountain rescue team were made by people who had underestimated the changeability of the weather. 'You shouldn't be out here on your own in this weather. It's Christmas Day, you should be home with family, eating turkey.' The moment the words left his mouth he wanted to kick himself. Presumably, if that had been an option she would have taken it, and her next words confirmed his suspicion.

'I don't have any family.' She spoke the words calmly,

as if it wasn't that great a problem. 'But you're completely right, of course. Coming out here was a stupid thing to do. It's just that it was beautiful and I needed to think and—'

'And you didn't want to sit in by yourself on Christmas Day. You don't have to explain to me.' He gave a wry smile. 'All around the country at this precise moment in time, people are opening presents they don't want from relatives they haven't seen all year and gaining pounds that they're going to spend the next few months failing to lose.'

'So is that what you're doing up here in the wilderness? Avoiding presents and weight gain?' Her gaze rested on his shoulders and then lifted to his mouth and lingered there for a moment. Then she lifted her eyes to his again and he felt something stir inside him. The urge to kiss her was so powerful that he forced himself to take a step backwards, reminding himself that this wasn't the time or the place.

Or the woman. He didn't know what her problem was, but it was clearly something significant.

'I happen to love it up here in the wilderness.' He watched as she slowly stood up. 'It's my favourite place.'

'Oh.' She hugged her arms around her body to try and stop the shivering. 'Well, lucky for me that you happened to be passing. If you'll just point me in the right direction, I'll make my way home. Sorry to have bothered you and eaten all your chocolate rations. I hope there are plenty more waiting for you back on your Christmas tree.'

He was torn between exasperation and admiration. He knew she was hideously cold and uncomfortable. Every other female he knew would have been moaning, hysterical or both by now. Miranda seemed remarkably calm. *Too calm?*

'This isn't a shopping centre with a hidden exit. Do you have any idea how much danger you're in?'

'Yes, actually,' she said calmly, stamping her feet to clear her trainers of the snow. 'But I assume that panicking isn't going to help. Better to make a plan and get on with it.'

'And that's what you were doing, sitting on the rock, when I found you? Planning?'

'Actually, I was trying to work out which way was up and which way was down.' She squinted through the steady fall of snow. 'I didn't want to move until I was sure and everything seems to have merged. You can't tell the difference between the sky and the ground.'

Jake gave a disbelieving shake of his head. 'It's called a whiteout,' he informed her gently, wondering what would have happened to her if he hadn't chosen to take this particular path. 'One of the most dangerous weather conditions that exists in the mountains.'

'I've never seen one before.' She stretched out a hand and caught some of the thick snowflakes as they landed. 'Gosh.'

'Gosh? *Gosh?*' Shaking his head with exasperation, Jake lifted the flask. 'Here—drink some of this.' He poured the creamy liquid into the cup and handed it to her.

'What is it? I don't drink alcohol.'

'And I don't give alcohol to victims of hypothermia. It would kill them.'

She lifted her chin and her dark eyes flashed with anger. 'I'm *not* a victim.' Her tone was chilly. 'Don't ever call me a victim.'

He found himself wondering why that one word seemed to trouble her more than her immediate situation. 'You will be a victim if we don't warm you up soon. It's hot chocolate. It will give you energy and warm you up.' He pushed the flask into her gloved hands. 'Stop talking and drink.'

'Hot chocolate? You keep pulling amazing things out of your bag.' Her teeth were chattering again as she clutched the mug. 'Clothes and now hot drinks. Who are you, Father Christmas?'

'A well-equipped climber,' he said pointedly, and she stared into the mug without enthusiasm.

'We can't all afford fancy equipment.'

'It isn't about fancy equipment! It's about safety. And if you don't have the right equipment, you shouldn't be out here.' He heard his voice sharpen and stopped talking. What was the matter with him? He never lectured people. On the contrary, he believed that people had the right to live their lives the way they wanted to live them. But he didn't feel remotely relaxed about Miranda.

What if she did the same thing again and he wasn't around to rescue her?

He shook himself, wondering why he cared so much about someone he'd known for less than an hour.

She sipped the chocolate. 'Oh...' She closed her eyes and gave a low moan of delight. 'That's delicious. I've never tasted anything better in my life.'

Looking at the thickness of her dark lashes and the vulnerability of her soft mouth, Jake felt a thud of lust and almost laughed at himself.

He really needed to get out more. His life was truly in a sorry state if he was lusting after a half-frozen woman whose knowledge of the mountains could have been written on a bootlace.

She drank the chocolate and he pushed the Thermos back into his rucksack and withdrew a rope and harness.

'I'm going to put this on you because your footwear has no grip and the ground is slippery.'

She looked at the rope. 'You're going to lower me down the mountain?'

'We're going to *walk* down the mountain. I'm going to tie

you to me,' he explained patiently. 'That way, if you slip, I catch you.'

'Or I pull you over, too.'

He refrained from pointing out that he had more muscle in one arm than she appeared to have in her entire body. 'That isn't going to happen.'

She took a deep breath and gave him a slightly chilly smile. 'Thanks for the chocolate and the extra layers. I'll be fine now. I can get down by myself. If you give me your address, I'll deliver your things back to you after Christmas.'

He stared at her, unable to believe what he was hearing. 'You'll be fine?'

By rights she should be clinging to him, begging him not to leave her. Instead, she was dismissing him.

'Absolutely fine.' Her eyes were filled with determination. 'I'm warm again now so I don't need any more help, although I'd love to borrow the hat. I'm sorry to have bothered you this much.'

'Bothered me?' He frowned at her, wondering what was going through her head. 'Miranda, you don't have a clue where you are and you don't have any equipment to help you survive in these weather conditions. Just how, precisely, do you plan to get yourself down on your own?'

'If you'd be kind enough to just point me towards the path and tell me when I go left or right, I'll be fine.'

He blinked. She sounded like someone asking for directions in a city. 'The path,' he pointed out gently, 'is currently buried under several centimetres of snow. And it doesn't go left or right—it curves, subtly. Step too far to the left and you'll find yourself at the bottom of the valley faster than you'd planned, step too far to the right and you'll fall into the ravine.'

Her smile faltered slightly. 'I'm sure I'll manage.'

He struggled to keep the sarcasm out of his voice. 'How?'

'Because I'm used to doing things by myself. I'm a survivor,' she said firmly, and there was something in her tone that made Jake look at her searchingly.

Was she trying to convince him or herself?

As intrigued as he was puzzled, he gave a quick shake of his head. One minute she was chatty and then next distracted, far away, as if she had something more important on her mind than survival.

What was the matter with her?

And what was she doing up here on her own on Christmas Day?

Ignoring her attempts to dismiss him, he fastened the rope to the harness on her waist with swift, skilled movements of his hands. 'Do you even know which way is down?'

'No. But it sounds as if I'm going to find it soon enough if I take a wrong step.'

'You're not going to take a wrong step.' He checked the knot on the rope.

'I don't want you to give up your walk to rescue me.'

She was clearly fiercely independent. He rubbed a hand across his face to clear his vision and tried another tack. 'I'd already finished my walk so we're walking in the same direction anyway.'

'Oh. Well, that's different. If you're going that way…' she shrugged '…we might as well walk together. Why do you have all this equipment?'

'Part of my job.'

'Your job?'

Jake gave the rope a gentle tug. He'd decided to keep the rope short so that if she slipped it would reduce the sliding distance. 'I'm in the mountain rescue team. And if we don't both go down now, we'll be calling out the entire team later, which would be extremely embarrassing for me.'

She stared dubiously at the mist and snow. 'All right. I suppose it makes sense to walk together. I can certainly see why they call it a whiteout.'

'Can you walk?'

'Of course.' She looked affronted and stamped her feet as if to prove that they were still working. 'I'm just cold.'

'It's just that most people walking in trainers in this weather end up with a sprained ankle at the very least,' he drawled, securing the top of his rucksack and swinging it back onto his back. 'But if you're intact, we'll get going.'

'How far is it?'

'Don't you know?'

She shook her head. 'I didn't really notice the time. I just walked…'

Something in her voice made him take a closer look at her. *Why* had she just walked? What had occupied her mind so totally that she hadn't noticed the time or the change in the weather?

Telling himself that it was none of his business, Jake checked the rope one more time and then jerked his head in the direction of the path. 'Come on. This way.'

She squinted forward. 'It all looks the same to me. How do you know where the path is supposed to be?'

'Because I know this walk well and I recognise the terrain.'

He walked steadily, matching his pace to hers and keeping a close eye on her.

She was cold, he could see that, but nowhere near as cold as she'd been when he'd found her. They weren't far from the car park now so he wasn't too worried.

He was more worried about the blank, slightly vacant

look in her huge dark eyes. Once they started to walk she sank into silence, her eyes straight ahead, stepping where he told her to step.

He sensed that something was very wrong.

Was it was just the pressures of Christmas Day? Was she avoiding everyone else's happiness?

They reached the car park without mishap and he reached down and detached the rope from her waist.

'We're here.' He glanced around him with a frown. At this level, the mist had lifted sufficiently to improve the visibility but he could only see one car. His. 'Where did you park?'

'Oh.' She blinked and took a deep breath as if waking herself up. 'Over there.'

His gaze followed the direction of her vague gesture but he saw nothing. 'Your car's been stolen.'

It happened, of course, in these isolated car parks.

'No.' She shook her head and gave him a wan smile as she handed back the harness. 'I don't have a car. I have a bike.'

A bike? He stared again and finally saw a rusty, ancient bicycle propped against a tree.

'That's yours?'

'Yes.' She pulled the hat from her head and he frowned.

'What are you doing?'

'Returning your clothes. Thank you so much.'

'Stop. Wait...' He put the hat back on her head, feeling her silky hair brush his fingers. 'You can't get on that bike and cycle—you're frozen.' And he didn't want her to leave. He wanted to get to know her. *He wanted to—*

'I'll warm up when I get back to my—' She broke off and flinched slightly. 'Home. I'll be fine at home.'

Was he imagining things or had her voice changed when she'd said the word 'home'? He was picking up all sorts of signals but so far he wasn't sure what any of them meant.

But he intended to find out.

'What are your plans now? Are you spending the rest of the day with friends?'

She stared at him for a long time and then shook her head slowly. 'No,' she said quietly, 'I'm not. But I'll be fine. I always am.'

Why was someone like her spending the day on her own?

Suddenly he had an urgent desire to know what was wrong—what had brought that haunted look to her face. *And he had an even more urgent desire to drag her into his arms and kiss her until her pale cheeks gained some colour.*

Unable to remember a time when he'd had such a powerful reaction to a woman, Jake closed his hand over her wrist, unwilling to let her go.

'Come on.' Without questioning the impulse, he strode purposefully over to his car with her in tow. Still with one hand around her slender wrist, he opened his boot, slung his gear inside and then opened the passenger door. 'Hop in. I'll get your bike.'

'What do you mean, hop in?' She stared at the car and then at him and he gave a shrug and his most non-threatening smile.

'It's Christmas Day, Miranda, and you and I seem to be the only two people on the planet that don't have someone to spend it with. So I suggest we spend it together. You can warm up at my place and we can sprawl on my sofas and watch endless movies.'

And get to know each other.

Her gaze became as cold as the weather and she tried to pull away from him. 'No, thank you.'

'It wasn't an indecent proposal,' he drawled softly, releasing her immediately. 'Just a friendly one. No hidden agenda.'

Her slender body was tense. Poised. 'Everyone has a hidden agenda.'

'All right—you caught me.' He leaned against his car and smiled. 'I do have a hidden agenda and it's entirely selfish. I don't want to be on my own on Christmas Day. I get morose. That's why I was in the mountains. I saved you so now you need to save me. Keep me company.'

Her eyes met his. And then she looked away and gave a tiny shake of her head, as if she was feeling something that she didn't want to feel. 'This is ridiculous. I don't—'

Suddenly it seemed imperative that he persuade her. *He wasn't going to let her go.* 'Do you have anywhere else you have to be?'

'No.' Her dark eyes clouded and she looked away from him, staring into the distance with a slightly blank expression on her beautiful face. 'I don't.'

'So what's the problem?'

Her eyes lifted to his again, her gaze solemn and considering. 'All right. Just for a few hours.'

Wondering why her answer had lifted his spirits so much, Jake bundled her inside the car and retrieved her bike.

Suddenly he was looking forward to the rest of Christmas Day.

CHAPTER TWO

MIRANDA lay in the hot bath with her eyes closed, feeling the delicious warmth spread back through her frozen limbs.

On the chair at the far side of the huge bathroom lay the neat pile of clothes that the man had given her.

The man...

The knowledge that she hadn't, so far, even asked his name brought a faint smile of derision to her face.

She should probably be worried, but she wasn't.

Strangers didn't frighten her. She knew from experience that hurt and pain most often came from those who were familiar and close to you, not from strangers. When there was a murder, didn't the police start by questioning the family?

No, she wasn't afraid of strangers and she certainly wasn't afraid of the man who had rescued her.

And now, right at this precise moment, she was glad of her impulsive decision to accept his invitation.

It was Christmas Day. *And she hated Christmas Day.* There was no reason at all why she had to hurry back to her miserable, lonely flat.

It was important that she looked after herself.

And it was just for one day.

After that, she'd vanish into the sunset and never see him again. And she had no reason to feel guilty about that because he had been the one who'd insisted that she spend the rest of the day with him because he hated Christmas, too.

She frowned and slid deeper under the water. Why would a man like him hate Christmas Day? She would have thought that women would have been lining up at his door, fighting over who was going to help him hang baubles on his tree.

But she knew better than anyone that life didn't always send you what you deserved. Which was why it was important to make the most of the moment and that was exactly what she was doing right now.

Having justified her actions to herself, she allowed herself to just enjoy the delicious sensation of warmth and hummed softly, luxuriating in the hot, scented water until she felt her eyelids droop. With a determined effort she forced them open again.

Not very sensible to be rescued from a freezing mountain, only to drown in a steaming bath, she thought as she turned off the tap and lifted herself reluctantly from the water. It was the only way to ensure that she stayed awake.

Aware that her rescuer would probably come looking for her if she didn't reappear soon, she reluctantly stood up and reached for the towel he'd left out for her. It was wonderful to feel warm after being so very, very cold. Vowing to buy some books on safety in the mountains before venturing out again, she dried herself and then examined the pile of clothes he'd given her.

She pulled on a pair of fleecy tracksuit bottoms and the jumper and then sat down on the chair and started to laugh. She looked completely ridiculous. If she'd needed a reminder of the differences between their physiques then she had it now. The trousers were at least a foot too long and the sleeves of the jumper hung several inches past the tips of her fingers.

The clothes acted as a wake-up call.

What on earth was she doing here?

She was behaving like Goldilocks, wandering lost in a forest and seeking shelter.

Why exactly had she decided to accept his invitation? She'd been all ready to refuse but there was something about him that had made it impossible to say no.

He'd rescued her when she'd been lost and, in a way, part of her was still lost.

Wiping the steam from the bathroom mirror, she stared at her reflection for a moment. She looked more like Snow White than Goldilocks, with her pale skin and the black rings under her eyes. She wasn't sleeping well and she knew that she had to do something about it. She needed to rest. She needed to think about—

'Miranda?'

The sound of a deep male voice from the other side of the door made her jump and she turned with a start. 'Yes?'

'Are you decent?'

'Oh, yes, I—'

The door opened and he strolled into the room. Her heart missed a beat. He was a man who would always attract the attention of women, and not just because of the athletic power of his physique. He'd changed into a pair of snug-fitting black jeans and a blue jumper almost the exact colour of his eyes. His damp hair suggested that there was obviously another bathroom somewhere in his house.

His gaze lingered on hers for several long seconds and she felt warmth seep into her cheeks. Suddenly her heart pumped harder and a dangerous, liquid heat uncurled deep inside her. Something happened when she looked at him. Something that she'd never felt before.

Then he ran a hand over the back of his neck and his gaze turned from searching to amused. 'Not exactly the same size, are we?'

Her heart still pumping, she pushed the sleeves of his jumper up her arms in an attempt to find her hands. 'They're great. Perfect.'

They covered everything, which was what she wanted. *She wasn't in the mood to offer explanations.*

'Turn the legs up or you'll break your neck on my stairs,' he advised, reaching for a dry towel from the pile and handing it to her. 'Come on. There's a fire in the living room. It's really cosy. You can dry your hair in there.'

She rolled up the legs of the trousers and followed him, unable to resist the temptation to peep as she walked along the landing and down the stairs.

His house was huge, she thought wistfully. Huge and gorgeous. Polished wood floors, soft rugs and huge windows, it succeeded in being stylish and welcoming at the same time.

He intercepted her glance. 'My sister's an interior designer. She can't resist the temptation to manage my living space. It's called interfering.'

'Lucky you.' What wouldn't she have given to have a sibling to interfere in her life?

Pushing away the thought, she followed him into the large living room. More huge windows overlooked the garden and the lawn sloped down to the shore of the lake. The mist had lifted, the snow had stopped and in the distance the fells rose, snowy and breathtakingly beautiful.

A crackling log fire formed the focus of the room and Miranda found herself wanting to sink down onto the thick, opulent rug and purr like a cat.

It was hard to believe that people actually lived like this, she mused as she looked at the exquisite painting above the fire. It all seemed a million miles from her real life.

Then her eyes rested on a photograph on the mantelpiece. There was no mistaking the man in the photo. The same wicked blue eyes, the same cropped dark hair and dangerous smile. And he was rolling in the snow with two laughing children.

She picked it up, the warmth draining from her body, her mouth so dry she could hardly form the words. 'Are they yours? Are you married?' She almost laughed at herself. Of course he was married! Why would a man like him be single?

'They're my nephews—my sister's children. I'm not married.' His eyes narrowed and his gaze was suddenly intent. 'Do you think I'd have invited you back here if I was married with children? Do I look as though I'm married?'

'Appearances can be deceptive.' Hoping that he didn't notice that her hand was shaking, she put the photograph carefully back on the table.

This was ridiculous.

She ought to leave, she thought to herself, suddenly unsettled by the feelings she was having.

But then she thought of the small, freezing bedroom with the bare walls and peeling paintwork that awaited her. She was in no hurry to go home.

If he wasn't married, what harm could it do to stay? She wasn't hurting anyone.

Just for the rest of the day, she promised herself, and then she'd go back to the harsh reality of her life.

She sank down onto the sofa. It was deep and squashy and comfortable and suddenly she just wanted to curl up and sleep. 'This is a lovely room.'

'Thanks. What can I get you to drink?' He stood by the fire, fingers hooked into the pockets of his jeans as he watched her. 'Wine? Champagne?'

'Oh.' She brushed her damp hair away from her face. 'Something non-alcoholic, please. Juice? Tonic?'

'It's Christmas. Don't you fancy anything stronger?'

'No, thanks. I have to cycle home later. I don't want to be drunk in charge of a heap of rust.'

He smiled and handed her a glass. 'So where's home, Miranda? And why were you avoiding Christmas Day?'

'It's just not my favourite time,' she said evasively, and he gave a wry smile of understanding.

'Too much of the media portrayal of happy families?'

'Oh, no. That's all nonsense.'

His blue eyes lingered on hers. 'Is it?'

'Of course.' She curled her legs under her and grinned at him. 'It's an image created by advertisers would have you believe that the perfect family exists, but it doesn't. At least, only on the surface. Underneath, it's all very different.'

'Different in what way?'

'Things are never as they appear on the surface. All families have secrets.' She sipped at her drink. 'Take the family in that yoghurt advert on television.'

He smiled. 'I know the one you mean. Healthy, happy and smiling. Two children and a dog. The sun is shining and there isn't a cloud in the sky.'

'That's the one.' She put her drink down on the small table next to the sofa, laughter in her eyes. 'But do you want to know the truth? The father is probably having an affair with his wife's best friend and the wife doesn't know yet but wouldn't care anyway because she has a secret life as a high-class escort whenever her husband is away on business. It actually suits her that he isn't around much because she doesn't particularly enjoy his company except when they're eating yoghurt in front of a film crew.'

Amusement flickered in his gaze and he tilted his head to one side as he listened. 'And the children?'

She nestled more deeply in the sofa, wondering why he was so easy to talk to. 'The girl has been so damaged by the lack of attention from her parents that she's now shoplifting regularly with her friends and has already started smoking and taking drugs behind the toilets at school, and the little boy is being badly bullied but hasn't told anyone and no one has noticed because they don't show enough interest in each other as individuals.' She stopped and took a breath and he lifted a dark eyebrow in question. The amusement in his eyes had been replaced by speculation.

'And the dog? Looked like a perfectly good-natured Labrador to me. No vices. Are you about to tell me that he's bitten the neighbour and needs a doggy psychiatrist?'

She laughed. 'They've received an official warning from the police because he regularly fouls the pavement and barks so loudly that he wakes the neighbours. So far he hasn't actually bitten anyone but don't think that just because he looks friendly he can't have a bad side. Dogs and people have a way of surprising you.'

'That's right. They do.' He studied her closely. 'Sounds like the family from hell.'

Her smile faded. 'A pretty normal family, actually. I'm just making the point that the picture presented by the media falls short of the real thing. Families are full of imperfections.'

'Is that your experience?'

She realised suddenly that she'd said too much. *Revealed more than she'd intended.* 'It's the truth.'

He swirled the last of his drink around his glass. 'I agree

that families are complicated,' he said slowly, 'and I agree that it's pretty hard to find the right person and make it all work in today's fast-paced, driven, consumer-orientated environment. And I think happiness is probably something different for each person. The important thing is to find someone like-minded and then live your own definition of happiness together.'

She stared at him. 'You really believe that?'

'Why wouldn't I?'

'Because it's a romantic view of relationships.'

'I disagree. I think it's a realistic view.'

'Believing that a family can be truly happy isn't realistic.'

His gaze was searching. 'Clearly you've never met anyone in a good relationship.'

'Neither have you.' She lifted her drink. 'You can't judge a family by watching from the outside. You have to be on the inside to know the truth. You probably have friends who you *think* are happy...'

A slight frown touched his brows and something flickered across his face. 'I have friends who I *know* are happy,' he said softly, and she shook her head.

'*How* do you know? Are you there when the door closes and they're left alone together? Do you know anything about the rows that they have in private?'

'No, but I know a lot about the rows they have in public,' he said dryly, reaching for the bottle and topping up his drink. 'He's Spanish and she's Irish and to call their relationship volatile would probably be to risk accusations of understatement but, believe me, they're happy. It might not work for everyone, but it works for them. And that's what I mean when I say you have to find someone who wants what you want. One person's happy marriage is another person's living hell.'

Miranda felt the cold trickle down her spine. *She knew everything there was to know about hell.*

For a moment she sat in frozen silence and then felt the sofa dip as he sat down next to her.

'Tell me about yourself. Tell me what you're thinking about.'

She shook the shadows away from her mind. 'Nothing.' She'd already said far too much. She smiled at him and handed him her empty glass. 'So—given that you're such a romantic, why aren't you married?'

He pulled a face. 'I'm not sure that I'm particularly romantic. And I don't have a wife because I happen to be picky about who I spend the rest of my life with.' The gleam in his blue eyes made her heart skip and dance and she gave herself a sharp talking-to. It wasn't so long ago she'd fallen for a charming smile and smooth patter. She wasn't about to do it again in a hurry.

He put her empty glass down on the table. 'If you ask me, the biggest problem with relationships is the reality gap.'

'Reality gap?'

'The gap between reality and expectations. People are basically flawed. If you expect families to be perfect then you're doomed to disappointment.'

'Maybe.' She was suddenly very aware of him. 'Do you realise that I haven't even asked your name?'

He smiled. 'It's Jake. Jake Blackwell.'

She nodded. The name fitted the man, she decided, leaning her head back against the sofa. Strong. Masculine. 'Well, Jake Blackwell, I haven't thanked you properly for rescuing me today.'

'It was my pleasure.' His gaze lingered on her face. 'It's good to have company on Christmas Day. But promise me you won't go out in the mountains again without the proper equipment and experienced company.'

She lifted her head. 'I'll do something about the equipment but the company is outside my control. I've only just moved to the area. I don't know anyone.'

'You know me.' His quiet statement hovered in the air between them and there was something in his eyes that made her stomach flip.

She gave herself a mental shake and looked away, determined to ignore all the signals that her body was sending her. Mind over matter. Common sense over chemistry.

'I'm sure you have better things to do than walk with a complete beginner who thinks that a whiteout is something you can achieve with a good washing powder.'

He laughed. 'Not really. Any time you want to walk in the hills, I'll be happy to act as escort.'

'Thank you.' Her voice was husky and she still didn't dare meet his eyes. Neither did she think it worth telling him that, after today, she wouldn't be seeing him again.

How could she?

It just wasn't possible. Her life was already more complicated than she would ever have believed possible and so far she hadn't begun to work out how she was going to unravel it all. And, anyway, he probably wasn't interested in tomorrow either. Hadn't he been honest about the fact that he just didn't want to spend Christmas Day on his own?

'You ought to eat something. I'll go and raid the kitchen and then we can sprawl on the sofa and watch agonisingly awful Christmas television. We can spend the afternoon guessing what's really happening behind the happy families.'

'Sounds good to me.'

He brought out a selection of food and switched on

the television but, in the end, they talked more than they watched and it was dark by the time Miranda glanced at her watch and realised how late it was.

She really ought to be going, she thought reluctantly, but somehow couldn't find the enthusiasm or motivation necessary to move. And was that surprising? All that awaited her was a cold, cheerless bedroom in an equally cheerless flat. But at least it was cheap, which was the important thing. At the moment she just needed to save her money.

Jake had retreated to the kitchen in search of more food and she flicked idly through the channels, stopping at the picture of a sad-looking child. The narrator informed her in low, mournful tones that the little girl was just one of many children waiting for adoption who would be without parents this year.

Miranda felt tears prick her eyes and blinked furiously. What on earth was the matter with her? Then she gave a sigh. She knew *exactly* why she was feeling so emotional, but it didn't make it any easier to cope with!

Strolling back into the room with a plate full of warm mince pies, Jake deposited them on the nearest table and sat down next to her on the sofa. 'You look really sad. What's the matter? Are you crying?'

Horrified at her uncharacteristic lack of control, she summoned up a smile, wishing he hadn't chosen that precise moment to come back into the room. 'Of course I'm not crying. Just a bit tired, I think.' It was a partial truth. 'Just ignore me. I need to go home and go to bed.'

'Not until you've sampled these gorgeous mince pies. And if you think I'm going to let you go home when you're upset, you don't know me. It's still early. There's no hurry.' His expression was concerned. 'I wish you'd tell me what's the matter. Is it the whole Christmas thing?'

'No. I'm just being stupid.' Despite her best efforts, her eyes filled again. She heard him give a soft curse and then she was pulled into his arms.

He was all hard muscle and masculine strength and for a long, indulgent moment she closed her eyes and allowed herself the luxury of leaning on someone. *Just for a moment,* she promised herself. What harm could it do?

Then he released her slightly and slipped his fingers under her chin, tilting her face to look at him. 'You're very beautiful, do you know that?' His voice was low and husky and she felt her heart bang hard against her ribs as she stared into those, blue, blue eyes.

Pull away now, Miranda, a voice said inside her head, but she suddenly found that she couldn't move.

His gaze lingered on hers, dropped to her mouth and then his head lowered.

And he kissed her. Gently at first, his mouth brushing over hers, his gaze holding her trapped. Then he coaxed her lips apart with the tip of his tongue and slid both hands into her hair, holding her head steady while he took the kiss several stages further.

Her eyes drifted shut and suddenly she felt as though she were falling. Her head spun, her body felt suddenly weak and everything inside her was either pounding or fluttering.

Never before, in her entire adult life, had she felt like this.

By the time he finally lifted his head, she couldn't remember why she'd been crying. She couldn't remember anything.

'Oh… You… I should go,' she muttered in a feeble attempt to regain some sort of control.

'Stay,' he breathed, his mouth inches from hers. 'Stay the night with me and we'll spend tomorrow together. You don't need to go.'

Her senses shimmered with awareness and everything

weakened. She didn't want to feel it. She didn't want to feel anything. Feeling meant vulnerability and vulnerability just meant pain. 'Work tomorrow. I have to go...home...' She stumbled over the word because no one in their right mind could really apply that word to a grotty room with damp patches on the walls and a threadbare carpet.

'Tomorrow,' he groaned, bringing his mouth against hers again. 'You can go home tomorrow.'

How had he ever learned to kiss like that? she wondered dreamily as his mouth transported her to a different place entirely. Threadbare carpets and cranky landlords were forgotten as she was enveloped in a sensual cloak of erotic anticipation. Suddenly everything seemed perfect, even though things were about as far from perfect as they could get.

'Upstairs...' Jake murmured, tugging at the jumper, and she suddenly froze and shook her head. She couldn't let him remove the jumper. If he removed the jumper then he'd see—

'No—really, we can't.'

'Why not? You've already said that there's no one at home to worry about you.' His hands were warm on the bare skin of her back and she pulled away quickly.

She almost wanted to laugh at the absurdity of the situation. But at the same time she wanted to cry. *Why did he have to come into her life now, when there was absolutely no room for him?*

'I suppose this is the point where I'm supposed to apologise for rushing you.' His voice was soft. 'But I'm not going to apologise for doing something that felt completely right.'

She bit her lip and waited for the frantic bump of her heart to slow to something approaching normal levels. 'Did I see you bring a mince pie into the room?'

His mouth was still close to hers. 'Are you changing the subject?'

'Yes.' She wished he wouldn't look at her like that. There was a sexy gleam in those wicked blue eyes that made it almost impossible to concentrate. 'I'm hungry.'

He hesitated briefly and then sat back. 'You have a ferocious appetite for a woman,' he drawled, moving away from her and reaching for the plate. 'Anyone would think you haven't eaten for a month.'

She gave an awkward laugh and helped herself from the plate. 'They're good. Did you make them?'

'Don't be ridiculous. I'm a man. I can cook the basics but I draw the line at mince pies. These are courtesy of my sister, who filled my freezer when she was here last.'

'Is that the same sister who is the mother of those children?' She glanced across at the photograph and he nodded.

'Jessica.'

Miranda sighed. What would it be like, she wondered, to have a sister to fill your freezer?

She ate another two and decided that any more would appear greedy so she stopped and snuggled back against the sofa. Suddenly she felt deliciously full and alarmingly drowsy.

'Five minutes,' she murmured, closing her eyes. 'Just five minutes and then I'm going to have to go home.'

And as she finished speaking, she fell asleep.

CHAPTER THREE

THE telephone woke him from a delicious dream of being wrapped in silky dark hair and kissed by a warm, soft mouth.

Cursing softly, still half-asleep, Jake reached out and answered it. 'Yes.'

'Mr Blackwell?'

He recognised the voice of the senior midwife on the obstetric unit and was instantly awake. 'Ruth?' He glanced round his living room and realised that he was alone. *Where was Miranda?* She'd fallen asleep and he'd covered her in blankets and then proceeded to fall asleep next to her. Only there was no sign of her now. And the weak, winter sunlight shining through the windows told him that it was morning.

'Jake—are you still there?'

Trying to ease the ache from his shoulders, he forced himself to concentrate on the phone. 'Yes, I'm here. What's happening?'

Was she using the bathroom?

'I've got a nightmare going on here, that's what's happening. I've just admitted a woman who was hoping for a home birth—fifth baby. But the last one was delivered by Caesarean section.'

Jake struggled to make sense of what she was saying. 'Fifth baby?' His brain was still foggy with sleep and his shoulders ached. He hadn't slept on a sofa since he'd been a student and now he remembered why. 'She doesn't sound like the best candidate for a home birth.'

'Which is presumably why she didn't register with anyone,' Ruth said wearily. 'She was staying with her parents for Christmas and she's just turned up here in labour because her mother-in-law has bullied her into it. Very stroppy. Hates hospitals. Hates doctors. I've managed to persuade her to let me check the foetal heart rate and there's some bradycardia. I'm not very happy about her really and I don't want to call Mr Hilton because I think she's going to be quite difficult to manage and you're good with difficult patients and he's not.'

Merry Christmas, Jake.

He closed his eyes and breathed out heavily. 'All right—what else?'

'You're not going to like the next bit of news.'

'I wasn't crazy about the last bit.' He smothered a yawn. 'Go on.'

'Lucy Knight's waters have broken.'

Lucy Knight? Jake rubbed his eyes with his fingers, trying to wake himself up. The penny dropped. 'Oh, hell—Lucy. She's only thirty-four weeks. When?'

'She called us early this morning.'

'Is she on her way in?'

'She's here already. Mr Hilton was prowling around and wanted to see her, but I said you were coming in today.'

'You're a star.' Having a colleague like Edgar Hilton was of dubious benefit. The man was a revered obstetrician with myriad publications to his name, but he was also renowned for his inability to let a mother labour without interference. It was a subject on which he and Jake disagreed at regular intervals. 'So is she having contractions?' He kept the phone to his ear as he wandered through to the kitchen, listening as the senior midwife outlined the situation. 'And you're sure it's amniotic fluid? OK—well, put her on the monitor and I'll be in as quickly as I can.'

'I feel guilty asking you. You're not supposed to be working today.'

Jake prowled round the kitchen, still holding the phone to his ear. *No sign of Miranda.* 'Don't be ridiculous, Ruth. It's my job.'

When had she left? During the night or early this morning?

'Well, even you're allowed a day off.'

'I had a day off. Christmas Day.' And it had turned out to be better than he'd ever hoped. *Finally, he'd met a woman who fascinated him in every way.* And now she'd vanished. Why had she vanished? He knew that she was interested in him too. Was it because he'd rushed her? Was that why she'd left? Pondering the facts, he reached for a jumper that he'd left over the back of one of the chairs. 'Give me ten minutes to shower and sort myself out here and then I'll be in.'

He replaced the receiver and sprinted upstairs, calling Miranda's name and checking in the bedrooms and the bathrooms. There was no sign of her.

She'd gone.

And he had absolutely no idea where because he hadn't had the sense to take her address. Hadn't seen the need, because he'd had no idea that she was going to perform a vanishing act.

Damn.

And now he had to go into the hospital because he didn't want to leave Lucy Knight to the tender mercies of Edgar Hilton and he didn't like the sound of the woman who'd planned to deliver her fifth baby at home. It promised to be a long and tiring day.

Cursing long and fluently, he showered quickly and then dressed and went to the kitchen to find his car keys.

Her bicycle had gone and there was a note on his windscreen that just said, 'Thank you.'

Thank you for what? Rescuing her? *Kissing her?*

No surname, no phone number, no address. Nothing to tell him where to find her again.

Miranda.

It was only the second time in his life that he'd felt instantly and powerfully drawn to a woman. The first had been Christy, and since then he'd virtually given up hope of finding anyone who interested him on anything other than a physical level.

Until yesterday.

Everything about Miranda had fascinated him. He'd always thought of himself as a man who understood women, but he'd found her complex and unpredictable. She'd shown strength and courage where other women would have panicked, but then she'd shown cynicism way beyond her years where other women would have been dreamily romantic. And what about her family? When he'd found her on the mountain, she'd said that she didn't have any family, but most people had some family somewhere. Had she fallen out with them? He frowned as he read the note again and then crumpled it up and stuffed it into his pocket.

He intended to find out. And he intended to find out why she'd left without leaving him her phone number or address.

She'd felt as strongly as he did, he knew that for sure, so why the secrecy?

What did she have to hide?

What was she afraid of?

Muttering about the complexities of women, Jake drove towards the hospital, mindful of the icy roads.

He was going to track her down, he vowed as he drove through the gates of the hospital and pulled up in a space marked with his name.

Complex she may be, but there'd been a powerful connection between them and he wasn't about to let that go.

He strode onto the labour ward minutes later to be greeted by Ruth, the midwife who had phoned him.

He lifted a hand and tugged gently at the tinsel in her greying hair. 'Is that a new look?'

'It's my Christmas look,' she said primly, lifting a hand to protect the tinsel, 'and I don't welcome any of your usual sarcastic comments. You're lucky I'm even trying to look festive, given what's going on in this place at the moment.'

'Me? Sarcastic?' Jake went through to his office and frowned at the pile of papers on his desk. He'd only had one day off, for goodness' sake. How could so much paperwork have accumulated so quickly? 'So—how's our Lucy?'

'Scared,' Ruth said frankly, handing him a fat set of notes. 'You know what happened last time, although not here, of course, thank goodness. The baby was stillborn and she was utterly devastated. She's afraid the same thing is going to happen.'

Jake lifted his gaze to hers. 'We're not going to let that happen. I probably ought to warn you now that if her waters have broken then my threshold for inducing her is very low.'

'Usually you do expectant management.'

'Usually women don't have Lucy's history. She'll

probably go into labour on her own anyway, but we'll keep a close eye on her. Just as a matter of interest, what's the bed state on SCBU?'

'They've got room,' Ruth said immediately. 'I checked earlier because I knew you'd ask me that question.'

'I'm that predictable?'

'You're that thorough.' Ruth's gaze softened. 'It's why you're such a brilliant obstetrician, Jake. You treat every woman as an individual case, regardless of protocol. And you don't miss anything.'

'Let's hope not. How's your staffing situation?' He knew that the whole hospital had been affected by the flu bug that was going around, and Obstetrics was no exception.

'It's been better but I've got a lovely bank nurse working today. Sweet girl. Smiley and calm. She's going to be with us for a while, hopefully. At least over the holiday period.'

'Good. Jake nodded. 'Lucy needs someone calm.'

'You know that Lucy wants to have a vaginal delivery...'

Jake sighed and dragged his fingers through his hair. 'Yes, I know she does. Obviously it's what we all want. It's the way babies are supposed to be born.'

Ruth grinned at him. 'For an obstetrician, you're a revelation, do you know that?'

'I can't understand why you think I gain any enjoyment from increasing my workload,' Jake drawled, and she gave a little shrug.

'All I'm saying is that it's lovely to work with a senior doctor who is on the same wavelength. And Lucy feels it, too. Just knowing you were coming in calmed her down,' Ruth told him. 'She trusts you.'

Jake gave a wry smile. 'No pressure, then.'

'Your job is one long pressure,' Ruth replied as they walked down the corridor. 'I've put her in Suite 1 because it's more homely and I think she'll find it less stressful than some of the other rooms. She's not bleeding but she's had some funny pains off and on. They've got a bed on the ward if you want to keep her in.'

'Husband with her?'

Ruth nodded. 'Of course. And he's more anxious than she is.'

'Not surprisingly.'

Ruth paused outside the door. 'How was Christmas, by the way?'

For a moment Jake had a vision of a beautiful, mysterious woman with clouds of dark hair and a soft, tempting mouth that tasted as sweet as it looked. 'Christmas was interesting.'

Ruth raised an eyebrow. 'Meaning?'

'Meaning that it was interesting.' Not wanting to elaborate, Jake pushed open the door of the labour suite and stopped dead. Miranda was sitting on the bed, talking to Lucy.

His Miranda.

He blinked and checked that he wasn't hallucinating. Same ebony hair, same pale skin and soft pink mouth.

The mouth that he'd kissed and explored in sensual detail the night before.

For a moment he just stared at her stupidly, trying to work out what she was doing there. To the best of his recollection, he hadn't revealed where he worked or what his job was so she couldn't possibly have followed him.

'This is Miranda Harding.' Ruth's curious expression told him that something of his shock must have shown in his face. 'She's a midwife and she's going to be doing bank work with us for a while.'

Midwife? She was a midwife?

'Hello, Miranda.' Somehow Jake managed to keep any

trace of irony out of his tone and he noted the faint tinge of colour in her cheeks with interest. It was quite obvious that she wasn't pleased to see him.

He gritted his teeth. Well, of course she wasn't pleased to see him. If she'd wanted to see him, presumably she wouldn't have stolen away in the middle of the night without leaving a number.

What exactly was she afraid of?

They were going to have a conversation, he promised himself, sooner rather than later.

'Miranda, this is Mr Blackwell, one of our consultants,' Ruth murmured, her eyes still on Jake's face. Questioning. 'He's going to be looking after Lucy.'

Miranda cleared her throat but it was Lucy who spoke, cutting through the mounting tension in the room.

'Oh, Mr Blackwell, I feel so guilty, dragging you away from your Christmas. It's Boxing Day. You should be at home with your family.'

'Don't feel guilty, Lucy.' Jake was still looking at Miranda. 'I'd finished all the food and that's the important bit.' With a huge effort he turned his attention to his patient, promising himself that he'd deal with Miranda later. 'You were fine when I saw you in clinic last week so when did all this start?'

'Christmas Eve. I did a bit of last-minute shopping with my mum and I had a bit of pain but I didn't really think anything of it. Then, this morning, my waters broke.'

'Plenty of movements from the baby?'

'Oh, yes.' Lucy nodded. 'I've been counting, just like you told me to.'

Jake smiled. He'd been monitoring Lucy right the way through her pregnancy, and he liked her a lot. 'But no pains?'

'Nothing since Christmas Eve.' Lucy frowned. 'We had

a quiet day yesterday, ate too much turkey, you know the sort of thing. Then I had an early night but when I woke up this morning my waters broke all over the bathroom floor. Gushed everywhere. Very embarrassing thing to happen.' She chewed her lip, her eyes huge and anxious. 'It's bad news, isn't it? Is the baby going to come early?'

Jake's gaze was steady. 'Very probably, but we'll try and keep him inside you for as long as possible. The first thing I'm going to do is arrange for you to have a steroid injection. That will help the baby's lungs in the event that he's delivered early.'

'All right.' Lucy's hands were curled into fists in her lap. 'What else?'

'I'm going to run some tests and then I'll decide. You're going to need to stay in, I'm afraid, for now at least.' He turned to Miranda, his expression cool. 'Can you arrange for her to have 12 milligrams of betamethasone IM straight away? And contact the ward and arrange for a bed.'

She avoided looking him in the eye. 'Of course. Could you write the betamethasone on the chart for me?'

Why wouldn't she look at him? It wasn't as if they'd done anything except kiss. Was it really so embarrassing and awkward? He wrote on the drug chart and handed it to her.

'I'm going to keep an eye on you for a while, Lucy. See what happens. If there's no sign of any activity, I might let you go home tomorrow.'

'You're not going to induce me?'

'Not yet.' Jake's tone was both gentle and reassuring. 'If we can hang on another week, it would be better for the baby. Better a week in your tummy than a week in an incubator.'

Lucy gave a brave smile and a nod. 'Yes.'

He heard the catch in her voice and sat down on the edge

of her bed. Her hands were still curled into fists and he took
hold of them gently and uncurled them. 'Relax, Lucy.' His
voice was sympathetic as he rubbed her hands between his
and warmed them. 'I know you're worried but I'm not going
to let you out of my sight until I'm satisfied that all is well.'
He waved a hand around the delivery suite, his gaze sardonic. 'Enjoy the surroundings. Order room service.' He
turned to Miranda who had stood up while he'd been talking to Lucy and now had her back to him. 'I want to do an
ultrasound, please.'

Ruth stepped forward with a smile. 'I'll show you where
we keep the machine, Miranda.'

Jake watched Miranda, wondering why she had her back
to him. Then she slowly turned round and the reason became
immediately clear. His eyes dropped to her waist and he
inhaled sharply.

'Stop looking so shocked,' Ruth laughed, punching him
on the arm in a teasing gesture. 'Midwives are allowed to be
pregnant too, you know. In fact, the mothers love it. Shows
we're capable of understanding what they're going through.
Miranda is six months now. More than capable of doing a
good day's work still.'

Miranda didn't look at him and Jake's mouth tightened.

She was pregnant.

How could she be pregnant? *And how the hell had he not
noticed?*

He was an obstetrician, for goodness' sake. He dealt with
pregnant women on a daily basis. And he'd had a woman
who was six months pregnant in his house and he hadn't
even noticed.

Well done, Jake. Good going. He closed his eyes briefly.
The signs had all been there. The fact that she ate so much,

her extreme tiredness, the fact that she burst into tears for apparently no reason...

But what had she been doing on her own in the mountains on Christmas Day? *And what had she been doing kissing him when she was six months pregnant with another man's baby?*

Angry with himself and even more angry with her, his jaw clenched and his eyes hardened.

He'd thought she was interesting and beautiful and appealing. It turned out she was duplicitous and lacking in morals. No wonder she'd made cynical comments about families. Clearly she had no sense of responsibility.

'Never known you speechless before, Jake,' Ruth teased, walking Miranda to the door. 'We'll just go and get the ultrasound machine while you pull yourself together.'

'Do you think the baby will be all right, Mr Blackwell?'

Aware that Lucy was looking at him expectantly, Jake pulled himself together and stood up.

'We're going to check everything, Lucy,' he assured her, managing a smile despite the turmoil inside him, 'and we're going to keep a very close eye on you. Leave the worrying to me if you can. It's what they pay me for. But I'm afraid you're spending the rest of Boxing Day in here with us.'

'I'd be too scared to go home anyway,' she confessed ruefully.

Miranda came back with the ultrasound machine and Jake resisted the temptation to drag her back into the corridor and demand an immediate explanation for her behaviour. That was going to have to wait until they were alone. But they would be alone, he promised himself, and they were going to talk, whether she liked it or not.

Where had the father of her baby been when she'd been spending Christmas Day at his house? Had they had a row?

The guy must have been worrying himself sick. He knew he would have done if his wife or girlfriend had vanished without any warning.

His eyes slid to her neat little bump and he asked himself again how he could possibly not have noticed that she was six months pregnant. She was so slight.

But when he'd first seen her she'd been wearing a bulky waterproof jacket and then she'd changed straight into his jumper, which had been at least six sizes too large. Large enough to conceal a pregnancy.

Why? *Why would she want to hide something like that?*

Forcing himself to concentrate on his patient, Jake slid the transducer across Lucy's rounded abdomen and studied the picture on the screen. Later, he vowed, he'd get her on her own and find out what was going on.

'OK, everything looks fine with the baby, Lucy, but I want you to stay in for now, if that's all right with you.'

'Whatever you think.'

'I think that if your waters have broken, I want you where I can see you for the rest of the day,' Jake said calmly, reaching for some paper towels and wiping the jelly from her abdomen.

'That's fine by me. I don't want you to go off duty.' Lucy gave a worried smile. 'I want you to sleep here in the room with me tonight!'

Ruth smiled. 'Oh, don't worry about that—the work I've got for him, he'll still be here at New Year, but he certainly won't be sleeping.'

Jake gently covered Lucy with a blanket and stood up. 'Stop worrying,' he said softly, and then turned to Miranda. 'I want her kept on the monitor for the time being and let me know if there's any changes. I'll be back to check on her when I've seen the other lady.'

Miranda nodded and he turned to Ruth. 'Where is she?'

'Room 2.'

Jake could see from the look on Ruth's face that she was expecting the consultation to be difficult, and the moment he walked into the room he knew that she was right. The couple didn't appear to be speaking but the atmosphere crackled with tension.

The husband was hovering helplessly in the background and the woman, Gail, was leaning over a beanbag and her face was pale and sweaty. The moment she saw Jake, her features tensed.

'I need to tell you straight away that I don't want to be here and I certainly don't want any intervention.'

'Of course you don't.' Jake's voice was calm as he walked across to her and pulled up a chair. 'I'm Jake Blackwell, one of the obstetric consultants. I gather you were hoping for a home birth so being in here must be rather a shock for you.'

'I've had three at home and one in hospital.' She glared at him and then winced as another pain gripped her. 'And I don't want to repeat the experience. It's all monitors and machines that beep at you. That isn't what nature intended.'

'I completely agree.'

She stared at him. 'You do?'

'Absolutely. My belief is that nature should be allowed the upper hand, unless she appears to be getting things wrong which, I'm afraid, she sometimes does.' He turned to look at Ruth, his gaze questioning. 'Notes?'

'I've requested them from her hospital,' Ruth murmured. 'I'm going to get someone else to take Lucy to the ward and ask Miranda to come in here. I think she'd be helpful.' She slid out of the room, leaving Jake alone with the couple.

He looked at the CTG trace that Ruth had handed him and studied the pattern. Then he put the trace down on the table and concentrated his attention on Gail, knowing that he was going to have to handle her carefully.

'All right. I think honesty is the best way forward so I'm going to be straight with you.'

She tensed and glared at him with blatant hostility. 'You want to induce me so that you can have this room for the next poor woman—'

'I'm not given to inducing women unless the health of the baby is threatened,' Jake said smoothly, aware that Miranda had just entered the room. 'I've certainly never induced a woman to satisfy a staffing or bed need and I don't intend to start now.'

'I had three babies at home with no problems.' Her voice rose and her husband put a hand on her arm to calm her. 'And then with number four my placenta was low-lying so they had to take me in and I had a Caesarean section. And they were all totally useless! I had an infection and was really ill—'

'Oh, you poor thing.' Miranda hurried across the room. 'I can quite see why you wouldn't want to be here. You must be terribly anxious about it all.'

Jake looked at her and felt a flicker of admiration. She'd seen through the stroppy, angry exterior and seen the anxiety, just as he had.

'You obviously had a less than perfect experience last time,' he said quietly, turning his attention back to Gail, 'and for that I'm sorry. It's always disappointing when childbirth doesn't go as nature intended.'

'It was a nightmare. I shouldn't be here.' Gail glared at her husband. 'And I wouldn't be if your mother hadn't forced the issue.'

'She didn't want you having a baby in her kitchen on Boxing Day, love,' her husband said awkwardly, running a finger around the neck of his jumper as if it was suddenly too tight. Gail tried to struggle to her feet.

'Well, I'm sorry if I'm inconveniencing everybody, but I just want to go home now!'

Miranda slipped an arm around her shoulders. 'Please, Gail, just stay and listen to Mr Blackwell. He'll take a look at you and make some suggestions. We're asking you to listen, that's all. No one's forcing anything on you.'

'I had three babies at home with no problems whatsoever.' Gail's voice rose as she looked at Jake. 'Give me one good reason why I shouldn't have this one at home.'

'Because having had a Caesarean section last time, you'll be at slight risk of the scar opening up,' he said frankly. 'And with your fifth baby you're more likely to have other problems, so it's safer for both of you if you're in an environment where we're geared up to help if necessary.'

'Intervene, you mean.'

Jake picked up the trace and leaned towards Gail. 'Look at this.' He ran his finger over the line on the paper. 'This tells me that your baby's heart rate was a bit slow here—and again here. I want to keep an eye on that.'

'There are always variations in heart rate,' Gail said immediately, her gaze challenging. 'At home they don't monitor it constantly so you don't know about it and you don't worry. And the baby is still fine when it's born.'

'Sometimes that's true.' Jake's voice was quiet. 'But are you willing to take that chance? What I'd like to do, with your permission, is ask Miranda to monitor you for a while so that I can get a better look at what's happening during each contraction.'

'You're just going to drag me into Theatre at the first opportunity and cut me open!'

Jake shook his head. 'If you want to check my records,

I have a very low Caesarean section rate compared to the national average,' he said calmly, 'but I'm not willing to sacrifice a baby to keep that rate low. I can't promise you that I won't perform a Caesarean section if I think it's necessary, but I can promise you that we'll make the decision together. If everything goes well, there's no reason why you can't just quietly deliver your baby here. It's not home, that's true, but it's a comfortable room and we do our best to make it as relaxing as possible.'

Gail stared at him and then at her husband, who looked exhausted, stressed and totally out of his depth.

'Oh, hell, I don't know,' she muttered under her breath, and then her eyes slid to the trace again and she put a protective hand on her abdomen. 'You really think that the baby might be in trouble?'

'I don't know. We need to do some more tests.'

Gail hesitated and then gave a reluctant nod. 'All right. I suppose I'll stay. For now. But I don't want a stream of staff through here, staring at me or practising on me.'

'There won't be a stream of staff. Just me. I'm going to be staying with you,' Miranda assured her, and Gail gave a wan smile.

'I've heard that before. We both know that if my labour happens to run past the end of your shift I'll get someone else,' she said bitterly. 'I had three midwives in total last time I had the misfortune to deliver in hospital.'

'Well, that isn't going to happen this time,' Miranda said softly, putting a hand on her shoulder. 'I can promise you that, whatever happens, I will stay until you've had this baby.'

Gail looked at her and gave a disbelieving laugh. 'It's Boxing Day. You're pregnant yourself and you've got a

family waiting for you. I should think it's bad enough working, let alone running into overtime.'

Miranda's gaze didn't flicker. 'I'm staying until you've
had the baby. Now, if it's all right with you, I want to put you
on the monitor and see what's happening.'

Something in the stiff set of her slim shoulders drew
Jake's gaze but there was nothing in her face to reveal what
she was thinking. Who was her family? Where was the
father of her baby? Suddenly he wished Gail had chosen to
be more direct in her questioning. He might have received
answers to some of the questions buzzing around his head.

'I'll be on the unit if you need me.' He stood up and went
back to his office to catch up on some paperwork, but every
time he thought he was making headway he was interrupted.

He saw another patient for Ruth and then called the ward
to check on Lucy.

When he looked up Miranda was standing in the doorway. Her gaze was wary and it was obvious that she would
have preferred not to seek his help. 'Gail's progressing
slowly. I presume you don't want to accelerate labour with
oxytocin?'

Jake shook his head. 'There's some evidence that it in-
creases the risk of rupture. How's the foetal heart?'

'Showing variable decelerations.' Miranda handed him
a trace. 'Gail's complaining of pains, which might just be
normal labour pain, of course, but I have a bad feeling about
her.'

Never one to dismiss the instincts of a midwife, Jake
looked at her. 'She had a lower transverse incision, which
makes a uterine rupture less likely. And she's only had one
previous Caesarean section.'

Miranda nodded. 'That's all true, I know, but her labour is
slowing down and the baby's heart rate isn't as I would like it

to be. And there's something about this pain she's complaining of that worries me. It just doesn't sound like labour pain.'

Jake dragged his eyes away from the smooth skin of her cheeks and concentrated his attention on the trace. Instantly he saw the problem. 'I'll take another look at her but it certainly isn't going to be easy to persuade her to allow us to intervene in any shape or form. Is she still as defensive as ever?'

'I don't think she means to be defensive. She's just very frightened.'

'There's often more to a person than meets the eye, isn't that right, Miranda?'

She had the grace to blush. 'Perhaps.'

'You and I are going to talk,' he said softly, and she straightened her shoulders.

'There's nothing to talk about.'

'There's plenty to talk about, but it will keep for now. We need to see to Gail.'

CHAPTER FOUR

WHY was it, Miranda wondered as they walked through the labour ward towards Gail's room, that every time she lowered her guard, it backfired?

When she'd made the impulsive decision to go back to Jake's house the day before, it hadn't occurred to her for even a moment that she'd ever see him again, let alone find herself working side by side with him.

And now he'd seen that she was pregnant and had jumped to all the wrong conclusions.

She gave a sigh as she pushed open the door to Gail's room. Well, she could hardly blame him for that, could she? He didn't know anything about her circumstances because she hadn't shared them with him. And she had no intention of sharing them with him.

It had been a mistake to go back to his house with him the day before. A luxury she should never have allowed herself. She'd been naive to think that she could just enjoy the moment and walk away.

She pulled herself back to the present and concentrated on supporting Gail, who was listening to Jake.

'I'm not happy with what I'm seeing,' he said gently. 'The baby's heart rate is slow and I'm worried about your scar.'

Gail stared at him defensively, a sheen of sweat on her brow and her eyes blank with pain. 'The scar will be fine. I've read enough to know that the chances of a uterine rupture are minimal and I'm not having another Caesarean section. I'd rather take the risk.'

'It's true that it isn't common for the uterus to rupture,' Jake agreed, 'but in certain circumstances it can happen. And the risk isn't just to your life, it's to the baby's life.'

Her fear and frustration barely contained, Gail's eyes filled and she looked away from him. 'I should have stayed at home,' she muttered, her voice clogged by the threat of tears. 'I should never have let them bully me into coming in. Everything would have been fine, then.'

'No, Gail. It wouldn't have been fine.' Determined to add her voice to Jake's, Miranda stepped forward and slid an arm round the woman's shoulders. 'I'm a huge advocate of home birth, but this is one baby that never should have been born at home. And I think, deep down, you know that.'

Gail sniffed. 'Where are you going to have your baby?'

'Oh...' Aware of Jake's glance in her direction, Miranda's face flamed. 'I don't know. I've only just moved into the area and I haven't had time to give it much thought yet.'

And she couldn't talk about it in front of Jake. It was too personal. *Too intimate.*

Before she could question her further, Gail pulled a face and placed a hand on her abdomen. 'Ouch! That hurt.'

'Another contraction?'

'It didn't feel like it.' The woman's face was pale and she grimaced again. 'Oh...'

'It could be the scar.' Jake stepped forward. 'I know it's

the last thing you want, but I want to take you into Theatre, Gail. Just to be on the safe side.'

Miranda caught his gaze and knew instinctively that he was starting to share her bad feeling. 'She's only three centimetres dilated,' she reminded him in a soft voice, and he nodded.

'I know. I want her in Theatre.'

'All right.'

Gail stared at him. 'I really don't know—'

'Gail.' His voice was urgent as he sat down on the edge of the bed. 'My job is to deliver a healthy baby from a healthy mother. You're not letting me do that job. I know it's hard for you but I'm asking you to trust me.'

'Well, it's just that I don't—' Gail broke off and gasped, one hand on her abdomen. 'Oh—what *is* that pain?'

'The trace is showing foetal bradycardia,' Miranda murmured, and Jake gave a decisive nod and turned as Ruth walked into the room.

'We need to deliver this baby right now and I want it done under general.'

Jake's swift glance said it all and Ruth hurried off to bleep the anaesthetist and prepare the theatre.

'What's happening?' Gail's eyes were wide with fear now and tears glistened. 'Oh, God, it's all going wrong, isn't it?'

Her husband stepped forward, his face pale and his eyes darting nervously to Jake, seeking reassurance.

'Gail, so far the baby is fine.' Jake's tone remained calm. 'But I think there may be a problem with your uterus. I have a suspicion that's what the pain is. I'm going to have to take you to Theatre. I'm sorry. I know it wasn't in our plans and I know it will be disappointing for you, but there's no other way. I don't want to risk the baby and I know you don't either.'

'I don't want an operation. Not like last time. I'm terrified of epidurals.' Hanging onto control by a thread, the tears spilled over from Gail's eyes and Jake took her hand in both of his, his blue eyes kind.

'I know you're worried,' he said quietly, 'but you have to let me do what has to be done. I need to deliver this baby and I need to do it fast. And we won't do it under epidural. It will be under general. You'll be asleep.'

All animosity forgotten, Gail clutched his hand. 'I'm *so* scared.'

'You wouldn't be human if you weren't, but let me do the worrying.' Jake's voice was firm. 'I need you to trust me, Gail.'

Miranda swallowed at the kindness and confidence in his voice.

She was hopeless at trusting men and yet at this precise moment she'd trust Jake with her life, she thought to herself, and obviously Gail felt the same way because she gave a wan smile and a nod and reluctantly let go of his hand so that he could leave the room and prepare for the delivery.

Gail's husband was white with strain and Ruth guided him gently out of the room and showed him where he could wait.

Miranda stayed with Gail in the anaesthetic room, holding her hand until she was unconscious and mercifully oblivious to everything that was going on around her.

Meanwhile, Jake had changed and scrubbed and was waiting in Theatre.

He glanced up as they pushed Gail into the room.

'Right, folks, let's work fast.' He spoke to the anaesthetist. 'Have we ordered blood?'

'Six units of whole blood and I've requested a full blood

count and coagulation studies. She's got two peripheral lines in and I've bleeped the haematology doctor on call.'

'Tell me when I can start.'

The anaesthetist checked his machines and nodded. 'Her blood pressure is dropping. She's bleeding from somewhere. You were right to bring her to Theatre—you'd better start.'

'Ruth, I want porters ready to fetch that blood and I want the crash trolley in here.' Jake's voice was calm, 'I'm not taking any chances.'

Miranda watched while he swiftly and skilfully opened the abdomen and then made another incision in the fascia.

'Forceps.' Without lifting his gaze from the wound, he held out a hand and the theatre nurse immediately handed him forceps followed by scissors which he used to lengthen the incision and separate the muscles of the abdominal wall. Then he made an opening in the peritoneum and carefully examined the uterus.

'She's bleeding badly and I can't see where from—suction, please.' He held out his hand again and removed the clots. 'Uterine rupture of any degree is extremely rare,' he muttered, 'so why did it have to be on my shift and with a patient who wouldn't let me near her? OK—that's looking better. I can see what I'm doing now. Retractor.'

Miranda watched in fascination. She'd never seen a surgeon as slick and fast as Jake. His concentration was absolute, his fingers moving swiftly as he delivered the baby and the placenta.

She found that she was holding her breath and when the baby suddenly started crying there was a collective sigh of relief, but Jake's gaze didn't shift from the operation site. His responsibility towards the baby had ended with delivery. Now he was concentrating on the mother.

'There's significant blood loss,' he murmured, lifting the

uterus out of the pelvis to determine the extent of the injury. 'Put 20 units of oxytocin in a litre of saline. I want 60 drops a minute until the uterus contracts. Clamp.'

The nurse handed him the instrument he needed and he moved with swift precision, clamping and ligating bleeding vessels and then using figure-of-eight stitches where necessary. Finally he was satisfied that the bleeding had stopped.

Miranda watched in breathless silence as he drained a haematoma that had formed and then examined the area again. 'Her previous Caesarean section was stitched with a single layer of sutures—a way of shortening the time in the operating room but it does increase the risk of uterine rupture. I'll do a double-layer closure this time.' His eyes still on the wound, he held out a gloved hand. 'I'm ready to stitch.'

The scrub nurse handed him the correct suture and he set about repairing the tear. 'More light,' he requested at one point. 'I need to see the ureter. Don't want to be stitching that. Right—clots here. Sponge, please.'

The nurse obliged and Jake carefully removed the clots.

Miranda stepped closer, her curiosity overcoming her reluctance to draw attention to herself. 'Is her bladder OK?' She knew that bladder injury was a very real risk but Jake gave a nod of his head.

'It all looks fine. And no signs of infection so I'm ready to close. The uterus has contracted. Reduce that drip to 20 drops a minute. How's that baby doing?' Finally, once he knew the mother was out of danger, he turned his attention to the paediatrician. 'Give me some good news, Howard.'

The paediatrician smiled. 'Little girl and doing very well indeed.'

'Apgar scores?' Jake's fingers flew as he stitched with equal measures of speed and skill.

'Eight, nine and ten.'

Miranda smiled with relief. The Apgar score measured neonatal heart rate, respirations, tone, colour, and reflexes immediately after delivery. Gail's baby had good scores.

Finally Jake finished and stepped back. 'All right. Well done, everyone. Thank you very much. Ruth, tell the ward to contact me if there are any signs of infection. Day or night, I want them to phone me. Gail has had a rough enough ride. She doesn't need any more problems. And we need to redeem the reputation of the medical profession.'

Everything about him was calm and steady, Miranda observed as she watched him strip off his gloves and walk towards the swing doors. Just like the time he'd rescued her from the mountain. He assessed the situation and just did what needed to be done. Panic and Jake Blackwell clearly didn't go together.

He was an amazing doctor.

But it didn't take a genius to see that he was angry with her.

And who could blame him?

Dreading the inevitable confrontation, she took her time helping Ruth to clear up Theatre and then waited in the recovery room until Gail was well enough to be transferred to the ward.

It was nearing the end of her shift when she finally returned to the labour ward. There was no sign of Jake.

Weak with relief that she was going to be spared a difficult conversation, at least for the time being, Miranda found Ruth. 'Is there anything else you want me to do?'

'Are you joking?' Ruth gave her a smile. 'You've already worked far longer than you should have done, considering it's Boxing Day. I'm sure you have places you want to be. Go home.'

Miranda gave a wan smile. 'I'm fine.' Exhausted would have been a more appropriate word but she'd grown used to tiredness over the last few months. And there was no denying that the money would be very welcome. 'I'll see you tomorrow.'

'Marvellous. Thank you so much for today. You were my present from Father Christmas,' Ruth joked as she checked on the number of delivery packs. 'I was expecting to struggle through Christmas with no staff, and suddenly they called me out of the blue and said that they had a midwife available.'

'I was relieved to get work,' Miranda confessed, running a hand over her bump and pulling a face. 'I thought you might not want me.'

And then she would have been in trouble because she needed every penny she could save. Pretty soon she wouldn't be able to work at all...

'You're fit and healthy. That's all that matters. See you tomorrow.'

Miranda grabbed her jumper and jacket and walked slowly to the set of railings where she'd left her bike. She was so tired, she wanted to cry. Her legs ached, her head throbbed and her eyelids drooped. All she wanted was her bed. At least she'd be too tired to notice the grimness of her surroundings, she thought as she walked across the badly lit car park. She doubted she was even going to find the energy to undress.

She'd just stooped to take the lock off her bike when a smooth male voice came from directly behind her.

'Running away, Miranda?'

Not having expected to see anyone, she gave a cry of alarm and covered her mouth with her hand. 'Oh—you frightened me.'

It was Jake and he was leaning against the railings, watching her, his handsome face cold and unsmiling.

'Why?' His tone was as chilly as the weather. 'Expecting someone else, perhaps? Your husband?'

Tall and broad-shouldered, his blue eyes glittered dangerously in the darkness and he looked nothing like a respectable consultant. *Nothing like the kind, reassuring man she'd seen calming Gail and Lucy earlier.*

The anger in his eyes was unmistakable and her heart gave an uncomfortable lurch.

She hadn't anticipated that he'd be angry when he discovered that she was pregnant, but neither had she anticipated the fact that she'd see him again.

They said that your sins always caught up with you and it seemed as though her sin, although small, was currently biting at her heels.

She should never have gone home with him and she *definitely* shouldn't have kissed him.

She ignored the tension in his jaw and the question in his eyes and tried to turn the conversation to safe ground. 'You were amazing in Theatre.' She'd hoped that reminding him that they were colleagues would be sufficient to encourage him to back off, but his gaze didn't shift from hers.

'I don't want to talk about work, Miranda.' His blue eyes were hard. 'I want to talk about what the hell you were doing, spending the day with me yesterday—*kissing* me—when you're pregnant with another man's baby!'

She didn't even have enough energy to defend herself.

A freezing gust of wind howled across the car park and a few flakes of snow wafted past her face. She was cold, tired and she still had to cycle the two miles home. The last thing she needed was confrontation. And she didn't need to think about a kiss that she'd spent one whole night and day trying to forget.

'Can we talk about this another time?'

'No.' His voice was thin. 'We can't.'

'All right.' She turned to face him, so tired that her own temper started to bubble up. 'For a start, I didn't kiss you— you kissed me.'

'So this is my fault?'

How could she ever have thought he was a nice man? Looming over her now, he looked tough, intimidating and just about as far from nice as it was possible to be.

She was a lousy judge of men, she decided with no small degree of self-derision. Lousy.

'I didn't say it was your fault.'

'Good. Because I may have kissed you but you kissed me right back. What's your excuse? Are you going to blame the atmosphere? Or the alcohol you didn't drink? Where was the father of your baby while you were kissing me?!'

'Damn you, Jake!' Exhaustion and disappointment made her temper break loose. For a moment she'd thought he was different. Special. 'You know absolutely nothing about my life! And one kiss doesn't give you the right to moralise on a subject about which you know nothing!'

She swayed slightly and he swore softly and gripped the tops of her arms with strong hands.

'Look at you, you're exhausted! What are you trying to do to yourself, Miranda? Yesterday you were walking on your own in the middle of nowhere in lousy weather and today you've just worked a ridiculously long shift. You're pregnant. You should be looking after yourself and the baby.'

His words were the final straw. She *was* looking after herself and the baby. *She had to because there was no one else to do it.*

'I'm perfectly aware of my responsibilities towards the baby,' she spat, wriggling her arms out of his grip and glaring at him. 'That's why I turn up at work even though I'm exhausted. Not all of us have the luxury of being able to spend our pregnancy lazing around in bed. And my life is none of your business.'

'You keep making it my business.' He moved towards her, his blue eyes glittering in his handsome face. 'It was my business when you tried to half kill yourself on a mountain yesterday and it was my business when you spent the day with me and kissed me. And it was my business today when you were working on my unit.'

She backed away and wrapped her arms around herself to try and stop the shivering. She was going to have to find another job. *This was never going to work.* Suddenly she just wanted to go home. If the tiny flat that she'd rented could be classed as home. 'Fine. I made a mistake, walking on the mountains without checking the weather, I admit it. And I admit that I should never have gone home with you, but you wouldn't take no for an answer and it seemed harmless enough at the time. Obviously it wasn't, but you know what they say about hindsight.' She turned and pulled her bike away from the railings. 'Now, I need to get home.'

'On that?' He stared at her bike in disbelief and her answering glance was loaded with derision and disillusionment.

'Yes, on this. We're not all the fortunate owners of a Porsche, Mr Blackwell. And now, if you'll excuse me, I expect we'll see each other tomorrow.' Unfortunately. She was tempted to call the agency and ask them to send her somewhere else but she knew that there wasn't anywhere else. This was the only obstetric unit for miles around. And she wasn't in a position to move again. She had to think of the baby now. She had to put down roots—make a home for them both.

A feeling of warmth spread through her and a rush of protectiveness. The same feelings she'd had from the moment she'd discovered she was pregnant. Given the circumstances, she probably should have been appalled, but she'd been thrilled and delighted. *Excited.* Of all the things she regretted in her life, becoming pregnant wasn't one of them.

'That's it?' He reached out and gripped her handlebars so that she couldn't go anywhere. 'That's all the explanation you're prepared to give me?'

The warmth inside her faded. 'What do you want me to say?' She gripped the bike tightly, trying to ignore the insistent throbbing in her head. 'That I'm a slut who kisses men even though she's six months pregnant? There we are—I said it. I behaved badly.' Her tone was flippant and slightly bitter. 'I shouldn't have gone home with you and I shouldn't have kissed you.'

'Then why did you?'

'Because you were pushy and because I—' She broke off, struggling to explain something that she hadn't even managed to explain to herself. Why had she gone home with him? 'It was Christmas Day. I didn't want to be on my own.'

'Why would you have been on your own? Did you have a row with your husband?'

Husband? 'No!' She didn't want him thinking that of her. 'I'm not married.'

'Partner, then.'

Partner? What a joke. 'Mr Blackwell.' She tugged at the bike so that he was forced to let go. 'I think we should just forget the whole thing now. I'm grateful to you for rescuing me and giving me somewhere nice to spend Christmas Day. But it's history. Christmas has a way of doing funny things to people. If you don't believe me, just think about the increase in suicides and all the people who make utter fools of themselves at office parties. We all go a little mad at Christmas. And now I need to go home.' Before her aching, exhausted body gave up the ghost and slithered to the ground.

His mouth was set in a grim line. 'Is he waiting for you?'

Why was he persisting in this line of questioning? 'Does it matter?'

'I want to know what sort of man would let his girlfriend climb alone in the mountains in the middle of winter and then let her vanish for a day and a night without calling the police.'

The same sort of man that didn't care that he'd made a girl pregnant.

Miranda gritted her teeth and gave another shiver. She didn't want to think about him. He wasn't worth it. She and the baby didn't need him. They didn't need anyone. 'My life isn't your business.'

'You made it my business when you forced me to rescue you from a mountain and when you kissed me back.' He was glaring right back at her. 'You can't cycle home in this weather. Why isn't he picking you up?'

'Oh, for goodness' sake, why do you care? Goodnight, Mr Blackwell.' She tried to push past him but his powerful, athletic frame blocked her path and he muttered something under his breath and then lifted her bike.

'Come on, I'll give you a lift home. Your bike can go on the back of my car. It isn't the first time.' He strode across the car park with her bike and she stared after him in a mixture of misery, temper and frustration. *And consternation.*

She didn't *want* him to give her a lift home. She didn't want to give him the chance to question her further or find out anything about her.

'Miranda!' Having fastened her bike, he turned, his glance impatient. 'Get in the car before you freeze.'

Short of bodily wrestling the bike away from him she had very little choice but to stalk across to him and climb into his car. Again. Her mind was working overtime. She needed to find a way out of this situation and she needed to do it fast. There was no way that he could be allowed to drive her home. It would stimulate more questions that she had no intention of answering.

'All right, give me directions.' He slammed the door shut, slid into the driver's seat and started the engine. 'Where do you live?'

'Not far,' she said vaguely. 'Turn right out of here and then take the first road on the left.' She felt several wriggly movements from the baby and put a hand on her stomach with a soft smile. It was as if he or she was reminding her that she shouldn't give away too much.

Jake stared at her for a moment and then his mouth tightened and he reversed out of his space. 'You look pale.'

'Do I?' It was probably the shock, she thought numbly. The shock of seeing him again, mingled with the worry of having to reveal details of her life that she didn't want to reveal. Suddenly she was struck by inspiration. 'Take the second road on the right. That's it. If you drop me here, that's fine.'

He slowed the car. 'Here?'

'Yes.' It wasn't where she lived but he didn't need to know that. 'Thanks.'

He pulled up and removed the bike from his car, glancing at the row of large Victorian houses. 'Is this where you live?'

'Thanks for the lift,' she said quickly, ignoring his question and taking the bike. 'And I'm sorry about yesterday and everything. If it's OK with you, I'd just like us both to forget it ever happened. I'll see you at work, Mr Blackwell. Thanks a lot.'

'Hold on a minute, you can't just—' He was interrupted by his mobile phone and he cursed softly as he reached into his pocket and answered the call.

Silently thanking the hospital for choosing to call at that precise moment, Miranda climbed onto her bike, made sure that he wasn't looking in her direction and then silently pedalled away from him into the darkness.

Fifteen minutes later, in a very different part of town, she let herself into her tiny flat, propped her bike against the wall of the gloomy living room and yanked off her gloves.

Relieved that he obviously hadn't managed to follow her, she locked the door firmly behind her, dragged herself the few steps to the bed and sat down. She eyed the damp patch on the wall with resigned humour.

'It's a good job you're not born yet, hotshot.' She rubbed a hand over her stomach, talking to the baby as she often did. 'At least you can't see where we're living. I promise to do better than this by the time you make an appearance but, in the meantime, at least I'm saving money for us both.'

She pushed away thoughts of Jake's spacious, comforting living room. She wasn't going to think about his fabulous bathroom and she wasn't going to think about the flickering fire or the deep, comfy sofas. And she most definitely wasn't going to think about *that* kiss.

It had been a stupid, wild moment and it wasn't going to be repeated.

She could hardly blame him for being annoyed. He'd judged on appearances, and hadn't she done exactly the same thing herself in the past? Wasn't that why she was in this situation? The facts at his disposal suggested that she'd deceived him and she, of all people, knew exactly how that felt—remembered only too well the sharp, vicious pain of discovering the depth of someone's deception.

Part of her wanted to defend herself, blurt out the whole truth so that he realised just how wrong he was, but what was the point of that? It didn't matter what he thought of her, she reminded himself. In fact, it was probably a good thing that he had a low opinion of her. It would stop him pursuing her further.

She gave a laugh of self-mockery. What man in his right mind would pursue a woman who was six months pregnant? She toed off her shoes and wriggled her aching feet. Not a man like Jake Blackwell, that was for sure. He clearly lived in fairy-tale land. He saw a pregnant woman and assumed she had a caring partner somewhere. *If only...*

For a moment she remembered Jake's skill and kindness with the women on the unit. Then she remembered the warm, tumbling feeling in her tummy when he'd kissed her, and buried her head in the pillow with a groan. *Why* had she kissed him?

It was bad enough having been self-indulgent enough to go back to his house, but to have kissed him was *unforgivably* stupid. And now she was paying the price. Her long-dormant body was well and truly awakened. Her body and brain were disturbingly unsettled. *She wanted things she shouldn't want and could never have.*

She sat up and brushed her hair out of her eyes in a determined gesture. She needed to put Jake out of her mind. Tomorrow at work she'd be brisk and professional and she had no doubt that he would be the same. Now that he knew that she was pregnant, why would he take the trouble to pursue her?

They'd shared a kiss and now he was annoyed because he

felt that she'd deceived him. And that suited her fine because she didn't want his approval. Really, she didn't.

By tomorrow the damage to his ego would have faded and she'd be just another member of staff. And that was what she wanted. Absolutely.

Too tired even to take her clothes off, she flopped back onto the pillow, pulled the duvet over herself and fell into a deep sleep.

CHAPTER FIVE

THE unit was already busy when she arrived the next morning.

'I can't believe the number of women who came in last night,' Ruth muttered as she checked the whiteboard and added another name. 'I'm going to need you in Room 3, Miranda, if that's OK. Daisy Priest. Really nice lady, but it's her first baby and she's a bit nervous. Her waters have broken but she's still only two centimetres dilated so I think you're in for a long one. Mr Hardwick is her consultant, but she's not very likely to need him.'

There was something in Ruth's tone that made Miranda give her a second look, but the older woman had already hurried on to the next topic. From her own point of view, Miranda was relieved that Jake wasn't Daisy's consultant. Not that he was likely to get involved in a normal delivery, but at least it meant that she was guaranteed a day where she didn't have to bump into him. A day to gather herself together after the conflict of the previous day.

'No problem.'

'Call me if you need any help. Oh, by the way...' Ruth

gave a quick frown '…she has a doula called Annie, with her. Nice lady. She's been in here before.'

Miranda nodded, knowing that a doula was someone who accompanies a woman in labour, giving her emotional support during childbirth. "OK. Thanks, Ruth."

'No problem.' Visibly stressed by pressure of work and lack of staff, Ruth hurried off to greet a woman who had just been transferred from the antenatal ward and Miranda walked down the corridor to find Daisy.

She was a woman in her twenties with a mass of curling blonde hair, and she was deep in conversation with an older woman who seemed to ooze calm and serenity.

Miranda introduced herself and Daisy looked at her anxiously.

'I hope you don't mind me bringing Annie, my doula. I know that not many women do, and—'

'That's fine,' Miranda reassured her quickly. 'Actually, where I trained in London, quite a few women used doulas. I think it's lovely for a pregnant woman to have the extra support.'

'It's just that I wanted someone familiar with me,' Daisy explained, 'and my husband Callum is hopeless with anything medical. Useless. He's downstairs in the shop, buying us a stock of magazines, because he couldn't stand witnessing a contraction. How pathetic is that?'

Miranda smiled and picked up Daisy's notes from the table. 'It can be very hard for a man to watch his wife in pain,' she said quietly, 'and I quite understand the need for a familiar and friendly face while you deliver.'

She knew from past experience that doulas were there to 'mother the mother' rather than offer advice on delivery and she had no problems at all with Annie being part of the process.

'I've read everything there is to read and watched every-thing there is to watch,' Daisy told Miranda, and then gave a grin. 'Don't look like that. The one thing that the books warn you about is that labour rarely goes according to plan. Annie keeps telling me that I've got to stay relaxed and go with the flow. I'm glad she's here because, to be perfectly honest, I find Mr Hardwick, the consultant, really scary. He always seems cross.'

Miranda put down the notes she'd been reading. 'I haven't actually met him, but I'm sure he isn't cross. Perhaps just a bit serious. I see you're hoping for a water birth?'

Daisy nodded. 'I love the idea of being in the water. I swam every day in my pregnancy. One of my friends gave birth in water and she loved it. Do you think it's possible?'

'Absolutely, although we won't want you to get into the water too soon or it might slow your labour down. And we might ask you to leave the water for the actual delivery.' Miranda made a mental note to check on the hospital policy for water births.

'That's fine. I don't care about that.' Daisy screwed up her face and gritted her teeth. 'Ouch. That's really starting to hurt.'

'Remember your breathing, Daisy.' Annie put her arm round the younger woman's shoulders. 'Breathe through the contraction.'

Miranda slid a hand over Daisy's abdomen to feel the strength of the contraction and talked quietly to her as she gave a little moan of pain and clenched her fists. Finally she relaxed. 'It's going off now…' She breathed out heav-ily. 'Why did it sound so easy during antenatal class? They made you feel as though you could cope with anything, but the truth is that the pain takes you over.'

'Lots of women say that.' Miranda stood up. 'That was a

pretty strong contraction. You might find the water comforting. Have you considered any other forms of pain relief?'

'I just want to try the water to start with,' Daisy said firmly, glancing at Annie for reassurance. 'I know that I might need something more and if I do then that's fine, but just for now I want to see how I go. I suppose I'm afraid that if I plan something else, I might grab it instead of managing.'

'So...' Miranda sat down on the chair next to the bed and gave a smile. 'Have you painted the nursery?'

Daisy gave a dreamy smile. 'It's perfect. You should see it. Primrose yellow with such pretty curtains...'

They talked and Miranda monitored her, and halfway through the morning she slipped out to talk to Ruth about the hospital policy on water birth.

'She's five centimetres dilated and her contractions are strong and regular now. I think she could go into the water if that's OK with you?'

'No problem,' Ruth said immediately. 'Daisy is a perfect candidate, but none of our consultants like the mothers to deliver in the pool. To be honest, Mr Hardwick doesn't like women to use water at all, but he's had to agree to it because of the pressure from women.'

'What about Mr Blackwell?' Miranda couldn't stop herself asking the question and then kicked herself when Ruth shot her a curious look.

'Jake? Oh he's perfectly relaxed about it. I've never met another doctor quite like him and I've worked with quite a few. He believes that women should labour in whatever way feels best for them. Such a contrast from a couple of his colleagues, who glance at their watches from the moment a woman walks through the door and then start reaching for the forceps.' There was a weariness in Ruth's tone that was hard to miss.

'Because they want to get women out as soon as possible?'

'Partly.' Ruth shrugged. 'And I suppose there's an element of control there. They want the woman safely delivered in as short a time as possible. Some obstetricians are nervous of litigation and are less inclined to take risks than others.'

'And Jake Blackwell isn't?'

Ruth frowned. 'I wouldn't say he takes risks. He's just very relaxed and confident and he puts the mother first. He tries to let women do what they were built to do. He has a very low rate of intervention. I'll tell you this much...' Ruth reached up and rubbed a name off the whiteboard with a scrap of tissue '...if I was having a baby, there's no one I'd rather deliver it. Talking of which, where are you having yours?'

'Oh...' Miranda blushed and placed a hand on her abdomen in a self-conscious gesture. 'I don't know, to be honest. I've only just moved into the area. Here, I presume, given that it's the only unit for miles around.'

'You should register with someone.'

'I know.' Miranda pulled a face. 'It's on my list of things to do. And I wouldn't know who to register with.'

Ruth dropped the tissue in the bin. 'Why don't you ask Jake? He's brilliant. The best, in my opinion. Tom Hunter is good, too, although not quite so approachable. If I were you, I'd go for Jake.'

'No, I couldn't possibly do that!' The words burst out before she could stop them and Ruth gave her a long, searching look.

'All right.' She spoke quietly. 'But you ought to register with someone. Are you carrying your notes?'

Still struggling from the emotional turmoil of imagining the intimacy of Jake delivering her baby, Miranda stared at her. 'What? Oh—yes. Yes, I am. But it's been a very straightforward pregnancy. No problems at all.'

Except for the fact that her life was a total mess. But that probably didn't count, she assured herself. Physically she was fine and that was all health professionals ever cared about.

Ruth was still looking at her. 'Think about it,' she urged. 'As you say, if you're living around here then this is the only unit in the area.'

Miranda nodded. 'I'll do something about it, I promise.'

She and Ruth prepared the water and Annie helped Daisy into the pool.

Instantly the frown on her face faded and her eyes closed. 'Oh—that feels completely fantastic,' she murmured, as she spread her arms out and slid further under the water.

At that moment her husband came into the room, clutching magazines and water. A tall man with glasses and a beard, his tension was obvious as he looked at his wife.

'So how's it going?'

Still with her eyes closed, Daisy smiled. 'Perfect.'

Her husband breathed a sigh of relief and put the magazines down on the table. 'Can I do anything?' It was obvious from his tone that he was hoping that the answer was going to be no and Daisy chuckled.

'Just sit and talk to me for a bit.'

Miranda stayed with Daisy for the whole day, monitoring the baby's heart with the waterproof, handheld Doppler and generally offering support.

Towards the end of her shift she slipped out of the room to give Ruth an update and found her talking to an older man in a suit.

'This is Mr Hardwick,' Ruth said quickly. 'Mr Hardwick, this is Miranda, one of our new midwives. She's looking after Daisy.'

The consultant made a disapproving sound. 'Is she nearing the end of the first stage? I'm going out to dinner tonight and I don't want to be disturbed.'

Miranda bit back the sharp response that flew to the tip of her tongue. 'She's doing very well. She's in the water now and—'

He frowned. 'That will slow her labour down.'

Miranda took a deep breath. 'On the contrary, I've often found that the relaxing effect of the water actually pushes labour forward, providing the mother isn't put into the water too soon. Daisy didn't go in until she was five centimetres dilated and now she's—'

'I want her out of the pool for delivery.' Mr Hardwick's mouth tightened. 'It's impossible to estimate blood loss in 600 litres of water.'

'Of course.' Miranda felt her hackles rise. 'There's nothing to suggest that this will be anything other than a routine, normal delivery. The foetal heart is—'

'Obstetrics is nothing if not unpredictable, young lady,' the consultant interrupted her again, his tone frosty. He then turned to Ruth. 'I'll be in my office for another hour and then I have a car picking me up.'

Without uttering another word, he strode off the labour ward and Ruth sighed.

'Sorry about that. Communication skills aren't his forte.'

'Nice for the mothers,' Miranda said dryly. 'Now I see why Daisy finds him scary.'

'Yes, well, Jake is on tonight so if there are any problems we'll get him to sort her out, quietly and competently, while Mr H. is eating his starter,' Ruth said quickly, picking up a set of notes and making for the door. 'How's she doing, anyway?'

'Fine. I don't anticipate any problems.'

She was to regret those words.

Daisy's labour continued smoothly and as she reached the end of the first stage, Annie and Miranda helped her out of the pool.

Daisy groaned and slumped over a beanbag. 'I'm going to kneel. It's what we agreed would be best and it's what I feel I want to do.'

'Fine. Use any position that feels right.' Opening a delivery pack and quickly snapping on a pair of gloves, Miranda examined the labouring woman. 'I can see the baby's head, Daisy. You're doing so well. It won't be long now.'

Daisy continued to push and the head was delivered but then immediately retracted.

It wasn't something that Miranda had ever seen before but she knew exactly what it meant and felt cold fingers of panic slide down her spine. Without hesitation, she reached out and hit the emergency buzzer behind Daisy's head.

'Daisy, you're doing really well,' she said calmly, 'but the baby's shoulders don't seem to want to be born so we just need a bit of help here.'

And she needed it quickly. There wasn't going to be any time to disturb Mr Hardwick's dinner. They had minutes to deliver the baby.

'I want you to turn all the way over and back onto all fours—Annie and I are going to help you.'

She knew that such a manoeuvre might help dislodge the baby, but in this case nothing happened and seconds later Ruth hurried into the room, closely followed by Jake.

'She's had two contractions with no restitution—Turtle's

sign—and having her on all fours hasn't worked,' Miranda told them quickly.

Without any further questioning, Jake immediately took charge.

'We'll try the McRoberts manoeuvre. I need you on your back, Daisy, and I need you to stop pushing—can we get her onto the bed, please?'

Ruth and Miranda quickly helped Daisy onto the bed and flexed and abducted her legs while Jake washed his hands and pulled on a pair of gloves.

He applied supra-pubic pressure then did something magical with his hands and the baby slithered out, screaming and bawling.

'Little girl, Daisy,' Jake said calmly, clamping the cord and handing the baby to the mother, as relaxed as if it had been a perfectly normal delivery.

It was only then that Miranda realised that she'd been holding her breath. The tension left her in a rush and her knees suddenly felt weak.

As if sensing her state, Jake gave her a gentle smile. 'Everything's fine. Good job, Miranda.'

She swallowed, grateful for the praise but not at all sure that it was justified. He was the one who'd delivered the baby, and with a minimum of fuss and bother. He'd been so calm that it was quite possible that Daisy had no idea of just how serious the situation had been. Suddenly she was swamped by uncertainties and insecurities. What if he hadn't been just down the corridor? What if they'd had to call Mr Hardwick away from his dinner? He never would have arrived on time.

'She's so beautiful,' Daisy breathed, just as the paediatrician hurried into the room.

'Did someone bleep me?'

Jake glanced up briefly. 'Everything's fine here, Howard, but, given that you've made the trip specially, perhaps you'd be good enough to take a look at the baby for us,' he said easily, focusing his attention back on the delivery of the placenta.

Daisy released the baby reluctantly and the paediatrician checked her over and pronounced everything to be fine. An hour later mother and baby were transferred to the ward. It was three hours after Miranda's shift should have ended.

Drained and exhausted and more than a little troubled by the events of the day, she walked slowly towards the changing room and dragged on her coat and scarf.

Wondering how on earth she was going to find the energy to cycle home, she pushed open the door that led to the stairs and then stopped. Jake was standing there, his broad shoulders leaning against the wall, blue eyes narrowed as he watched her.

'I've been waiting for you—you've just worked a ridiculously long day. Again. Are you all right?'

She almost laughed. She was so far from all right that it wasn't true, but she could hardly tell him that, could she? 'I'm fine.'

'You're a liar.'

She lifted a hand and tried to rub away the nagging ache in her forehead. 'If you want a rehash of last night's conversation, I ought to warn you that this isn't a good time. I know you're mad with me, but—'

'I'm not mad with you.'

'Last night you—'

'Last night I was angry, yes,' he admitted, 'but you have to admit that I had a lot to take in. I've had time to think about what you said and you're right, of course. Your life is none of my business but, for some reason that I don't entirely understand, I keep wanting to make it my business.'

'Jake—'

'I'm worried about you.' His voice was firm and masculine and his gaze was disturbingly intent. 'You shouldn't be working these hours when you're six months pregnant. I hope when you get home, he's spoiling you and feeding you decent food.'

Miranda thought of the contents of her fridge and gave a wan smile. 'Of course.'

Something flashed in Jake's eyes and he straightened. 'Come on, then. The least I can do is drop you home again.'

She glanced at him, startled. He hadn't actually dropped her home the night before, but he didn't know that, of course.

Too tired to argue with him, she followed him down to street level and watched in weary silence as he secured her bike to the back of his car.

Without speaking, he took the same route that she'd given him the day before and pulled up in the same street. Then he looked at her with a strange gleam in his eyes.

'Are you going to tell me the truth now?'

'About what?'

'Well, about where you live, for a start.' His tone was pleasant. 'I know it isn't here.'

Her spine straightened. 'I don't know what you mean.'

'Oh, I think you do.' He switched off the engine. 'You don't live here, do you, Miranda?'

She stared at him. 'I—'

'After I finished on the phone last night, I went looking for you. I knocked on every door in this street but no one had ever heard of a midwife called Miranda.' His gaze didn't shift from her face. 'Funny, that, don't you think?'

She swallowed hard. 'Jake, I—'

'So then I started to ask myself why you'd lie about where you lived.' His voice was steady and calm. 'It's obvious that you're involved with someone and that's fine, but I would like to know why you're lying to me. Why not just tell me the truth?'

'I'm not lying. I haven't lied once—'

'We're sitting outside a house where you don't live. What's that if it's not a lie?'

She looked away from him. 'I'm not used to confiding in people.'

'Giving me your address counts as confiding?' His tone was mild and she turned back to look at him.

'All right, you can take me home. But then I want you to leave. I'm not prepared to answer questions and I don't owe you any explanations.'

Jake pulled up outside the dimly lit block of flats and felt a shiver pass through him. In the darkness the whole area was threatening and unsavoury, and he knew from experience that daylight didn't improve it at all.

It was rough and dangerous and left him with one burning question that needed answering.

What on earth was Miranda doing, living in a place like this?

It seemed that the longer he spent with her, the less he knew about her life.

'Thanks for the lift.' She undid her seat belt but his hand closed over hers before she could open the door.

'Not so fast.' Her hand was slender and cold and he felt it tremble slightly under the pressure of his. Suddenly he knew she was hiding something. Something big. 'I'll see you to your door.'

'There's really no need. I can—'

'I'll see you to your door.' His mouth set in a grim line, Jake released her hand, opened his own door and walked round the car to help her out. 'Or are you afraid that your partner is going to give me a black eye?'

He was testing her reaction because he'd come to the conclusion the previous night that she didn't have a partner, and his suspicions were proved correct as she hesitated fractionally and then her slim shoulders sagged.

'I'm on my own.' Her voice was so soft he could barely hear her. 'No one is going to give you a black eye. But I still don't need you to walk me to the door.'

'Indulge me.' In fact, she looked so exhausted he wondered whether he should carry her, but he managed to stand aside as she walked towards the steps and led him up two flights.

'This is where I live.' She took a key out of her pocket. 'Thanks for bringing me home. I'll see you tomorrow.'

She pushed open the door and he caught a brief glimpse of damp patches and threadbare carpet.

It was enough to make up his mind. There was no way he was leaving her here without at least understanding what was going on.

He followed her into the room, resisting her feeble attempts to close the door on him with a gentle push of his shoulders. Once inside, his gaze bordered on the incredulous as he glanced around the gloomy room. 'What are you doing, living in a place like this?' He winced suddenly, aware that his words were insulting, but then he decided that there was absolutely no way that she could possibly think that her living conditions were anything other than awful.

It explained a great deal. It explained why she'd hesitated over using the word 'home'. No one in their right mind would refer to this flat as 'home'.

She lifted her chin. 'It's fine.'

He eyed the huge damp patch on the wall. 'Miranda, it's miserable.'

'I'm saving my money. And now I'd like you to leave, please, because—'

'I'm not going anywhere.' He pushed the door shut behind him and noticed that it made very little difference to the freezing temperature. The place bordered on the uninhabitable.

'Jake—'

'I can't believe you're living here. And I'm not leaving until you tell me why.'

She sighed. 'It's cheap.'

'I can believe it.' His expression was grim as he stared at the carpet. 'Is that the most important factor? Why do you need to save your money? Why isn't he supporting you?'

'Who?'

'The guy who made you pregnant. You might not still be with him, but at the very least he has a responsibility towards his child.' Anger tore through him and suddenly he wanted to plant his fist through the damp, mouldy walls.

Her eyes narrowed dangerously. 'I don't need anyone's support, Jake. I can look after myself.'

'But it's not just you, is it, Miranda?' His eyes dropped to the smooth swell of her stomach. 'It's the baby, too.'

'The baby is fine and, please, don't judge me. You don't know anything about me and you couldn't possible understand.'

'I happen to want to understand. Did he leave you?' He knew that he probably shouldn't be asking but he couldn't help himself. He just knew that he couldn't leave her here like this. 'Is that what happened?'

She dragged off her coat and dropped it on the bed. 'Why do you care?'

He exhaled sharply, forced to admit that it was a reasonable question. And one he was having trouble answering. 'I care. Let's leave it at that.'

For a moment his eyes held hers and then she looked away. 'He was never here. He left as soon as he found out about the baby.'

'Honourable guy.' He couldn't keep the sarcasm out of his voice and wanted to kick himself when he saw the pain in her eyes. 'Damn, I'm sorry.'

'It's fine.' She sounded so tired that he wanted to gather her up and hug her. *Take her away from all this.*

'Miranda—'

'It really doesn't matter. I'll see you tomorrow, Jake. Thanks for the lift.' She walked through to the tiny kitchen. It was so small that she could barely turn in it and he decided that whoever had designed the flat should be made to live in it for a day.

'You think I'm going to leave you here?' He leaned against the doorframe and watched as she put the kettle on and pulled open the fridge—a fridge that was empty except for a box of eggs and one small carton of yoghurt. It was the final straw. 'Go and pack your things.' He said the words quietly and she turned with the yoghurt in her hand, her expression startled.

'Pardon?'

He couldn't blame her for looking surprised. He felt surprised, too. Wondering whether he'd gone mad, he folded his arms across his chest.

'I said, go and pack your things. I'm taking you back to my house.'

She pushed the fridge door shut. 'Don't be ridiculous.'

He tried to lighten the atmosphere. 'Sweetheart, you're the only woman I've ever made that offer to, so think hard before you turn it down.'

The brief flash of laughter in her eyes assured him that she hadn't lost her sense of humour.

'I think you're the one who probably needs to think hard. If it's seduction on your mind, Mr Blackwell, I think you've chosen badly.'

What exactly was on his mind? He had absolutely no idea. He just knew that there was no way he could leave her in this place, any more than he could have left her on the mountain. 'Come with me.'

She sighed and put the yoghurt down. 'Are you always this stubborn?'

'Yes.' He watched her steadily. 'On second thoughts, where's your suitcase? I'll pack for you.'

'Jake—'

'I'm not leaving here without you. It's as simple as that.'

'This is ridiculous.'

He smiled placidly, pleased by his decision. It felt right. 'No. It's just the way it is. Pack, Miranda, or I'll carry you out of here wearing only the clothes you're standing in, and we both know that my clothes are far too big for you.'

The reminder of the last time she'd worn his clothes brought a faint flush to her cheeks and he felt something stir inside him.

Never in his life had a woman posed so many questions. *And never had he so badly wanted to discover the answers.*

'Has anyone ever told you you're a bully?'

'I'm not a bully. I just know what I want and I'm very good at getting it.' In this case he knew what he wanted but he didn't understand why he wanted it. He valued his personal space more than anything else in his life. No matter who he dated, *no matter how hot the relationship,* no woman had ever moved into his house.

'I know what I want, too, and—'

'You're too exhausted to have the first clue what you want.'

She gave a weary smile. 'You might be right about that. I just want to lie down for five minutes.'

He wondered whether he should point out that she looked as though she needed a lot longer than five minutes but decided against it. 'Just pack, Miranda, and in under half an hour you'll be lying in a deep bubble bath with a soft, comfy bed awaiting your arrival.'

Something close to longing flashed into her eyes. 'You make it extremely hard to say no.'

'That's the general idea.'

She walked towards him. Without her shoes she barely reached his shoulders and he stared in fascination at her delicate bone structure and silky, dark hair. She was a woman of contrasts. Who would have thought that underneath that fragile, feminine exterior lurked the strength and determination of a lioness? She was the most independent woman he'd ever met.

She lifted an eyebrow. 'You're blocking my door and I need to pack for an overnight stay.'

Relieved and elated but unable to identify exactly why, Jake decided to get her out of there before she had time to change her mind. 'Pack for longer than that. I'm not bringing you back here until the place has been remodelled. I'm surprised you haven't gone down with some vile disease.'

'I'm tougher than I look.'

'Evidently.' He stood to one side and she wriggled through, her cheeks flushing again as their bodies touched.

Visibly flustered, she walked away from him, grabbed

a bag and stuffed a few things inside. 'I'm ready.' Her eyes flickered with uncertainty. 'I still think this is ridiculous.'

'Not ridiculous.' He took the bag from her and gave her a gentle push towards the front door, eager to get her into his car before she had time to change her mind. 'Sensible. And be careful on those stairs. Don't fall asleep on your way down.'

CHAPTER SIX

FOR the second time in a week, Miranda lay in a deep, warm bath full of bubbles in Jake's gorgeous house.

Deep down she knew that she probably shouldn't be here. She should have put up more of an argument. But Jake wasn't a man to take no easily and she hadn't been able to find the energy to protest.

And who could blame her for that?

What woman in their right mind would chose squalor over luxury, even if it was only for a short time? She was so exhausted that her whole body was shrieking with protest and at that precise moment she wasn't sure that she even had the energy to climb out of the bath. And she felt desperately worried about everything that had happened with Daisy. Had it been her fault? Should she have been able to anticipate the problem that had arisen?

A knock on the door interrupted her thoughts and Jake appeared, carrying two mugs. 'I brought you sustenance.'

Miranda gave a soft gasp of embarrassment and slid further under the bubbles. Why hadn't she remembered to lock the door? 'You can't come in here!'

He pushed the door shut with his shoulder. 'Why not? You're tired. I was worried about you. I wanted to check you hadn't fallen asleep in the bath.' Totally unrepentant, he put the two mugs on top of the laundry basket, then reached for a towel and held it out to her. 'Get out now while you're still awake and you can drink the hot chocolate I made you.'

'Hot chocolate?' With only her face showing through the snowy bubbles, Miranda stared longingly at the mug. 'Is that the same sort of hot chocolate you gave me on the mountain?'

'The very same.' He'd changed out of his suit into a pair of jeans and a soft, casual shirt that had obvious been washed repeatedly. He'd pushed the sleeves up to the elbows to reveal strong forearms dusted with dark hairs. 'Drink it now and by the time you're dressed, dinner will be ready.'

'You've cooked?'

'Not exactly.' He grinned and gave a shrug. 'I had some help from the local pizza company. Full of calories, I know, but you look as though you could do with building up.' His eyes lingered on her face. 'Are you all right? You look worried.'

He was observant, she had to give him that. 'I'm worried that I did all the wrong things with Daisy,' she blurted out suddenly. 'Should I have spotted a problem sooner?'

'Is that why you're frowning?' He sat down on the chair next to the laundry basket. 'The simple answer is, no, it certainly wasn't your fault. Why would you think it was?'

'I've never seen shoulder dystocia before,' she confessed. 'I've heard about it, of course. Who hasn't? But I've never actually seen it. I keep wondering whether I missed some important signs earlier. Perhaps if I'd spotted something, it wouldn't have happened.'

'Don't be too hard on yourself.' His tone was firm. 'A

significant proportion of cases have absolutely no identifiable risk factors. You know that as well I do.'

Miranda was still running through the entire nightmare in her mind. 'Perhaps I should have done something differently when I saw the head retract. I tried left lateral then I tried putting her on all fours and then I moved her through 180 degrees but it didn't work.'

His gaze was steady. 'You did all the right things. And you called for help immediately, which is the most important thing of all.'

'But perhaps I should have tried the McRoberts manoeuvre first, instead of putting her on all fours. Will you explain something to me?' Miranda chewed her lip. 'Doesn't lying her on her back just narrow the pelvic outlet?'

'It corrects sacral lordosis and removes the sacral prominence as an obstruction.'

'So you basically have more space?'

Jake grinned and lifted one of the mugs to his lips. 'That's the theory. Unfortunately not all babies are entirely familiar with the theory.'

'Yes, well, that's my other worry. What if it hadn't worked? What then?' Miranda was thoroughly absorbed. 'You don't think there's value in performing an episiotomy presumably?'

Jake shook his head. 'The baby is impacted under the bony structures of the pelvis and the episiotomy will only deal with soft tissues. Knowing that you'd already had her in left lateral and on all fours, if the McRoberts manoeuvre hadn't worked then I would have tried to deliver the posterior arm, but obviously that isn't without risk.' He leaned forward and handed her the second mug of chocolate. 'Now, stop worrying and drink something. You must be starving. You did well today.'

Grateful for the frothy mountain of bubbles that at least afforded her a reasonable degree of privacy, she sipped the chocolate, warmed by his reassurance. 'I finally met Mr Hardwick.'

'And that was doubtless an uplifting experience.' His soft drawl made her wonder how on earth the two consultants managed to work side by side as colleagues when their approach to obstetrics was so dramatically different. They probably didn't really work together much, she mused.

'He was rude.'

Jake nodded and finished his chocolate. 'Sounds fairly typical. He trained in an age when consultants were considered gods who dealt out instructions that people followed without question. These days we tend to favour discussion with the patient.'

'If you hadn't been in the hospital, what would have happened to that woman?'

'Well, strictly speaking, Hardwick wasn't on call so he didn't have to be there.' Jake suppressed a yawn. 'It all comes down to whether you want to hang around if one of your patients is in. Hardwick tends to keep an eye on his private patients and ignore his less well-heeled clients.'

Miranda frowned. 'That's awful.'

'Is it?' Jake lifted an eyebrow and his gaze was faintly sardonic. 'Would you want him around when your baby is delivered?'

Miranda shuddered. 'Most definitely not.'

'I rest my case. Talking of which, if you haven't chosen an obstetrician yet, you should speak to Tom Hunter. He's brilliant.' Jake glanced at his watch and stood up. 'Pizza delivery imminent. You'd better get dressed, unless you fancy wrestling with mozzarella in the bath.'

She slid further into the water. 'I can't get dressed with you standing there.'

He rolled his eyes. 'Miranda, I'm an obstetrician. I've seen pregnant women before.'

'You haven't seen me.'

His eyes locked with hers and she felt colour seep into her cheeks. It was the warmth of the water that made her body heat, she told herself hastily. Nothing more. She knew better than to fall for any man, let alone a man like Jake. He was single for a reason and she had no intention of becoming another notch on his belt.

She almost laughed at her own thoughts. As if Jake would truly be interested in her! She was six months pregnant with another man's child, for goodness' sake. She didn't exactly fit into the box entitled 'Uncomplicated Relationships'. Not to mention the fact that he probably didn't even find pregnant women attractive…

When he'd said that she was beautiful and had kissed her, it had been on Christmas Day, before he'd found out that she was pregnant. Things were very different now.

Furious with herself for allowing her thoughts to drift down that path, she glared at him. 'Leave me in peace and I'll get out of the bath.'

He took the empty mug from her. 'Fair enough. I'll meet you downstairs in five minutes. Any longer than that and I'm coming back upstairs to find you.'

'Has anyone ever told you that you're controlling?'

He smiled and strolled towards the door. 'Frequently. Blame it on the job. Occasionally I'm required to make instant, unilateral decisions. Sometimes that spills into my personal life.'

She watched him leave, a small, regretful smile on her face. He was an indecently attractive man but it wasn't his just his looks that made her stomach curl. It was his strength and his confidence.

And she shouldn't be noticing or caring. Didn't she ever learn?

Determined not to dwell on his attributes, determined to forget that amazing kiss, she pulled herself reluctantly from the warm, soothing bath and wrapped herself in the fluffy, warm towel.

He heard her come into the room and turned, his eyes lingering on her flushed cheeks and the soft curve of her mouth. Dressed in pyjamas, with her hair secured on top of her head with a clip, she looked impossibly young and vulnerable and he felt something clench deep inside his gut.

Carefully hiding his reaction, he pulled out a chair and waved a hand. 'Sit down. I didn't know what you liked on pizza so I ordered everything.'

She peeped into the box and laughed. 'So I see. As an obstetrician, aren't you supposed to be preaching the sermon of optimum nutrition?'

'A little bit of what you want is good for you and I've decided that what you need most is calories and comfort.' He pushed the box towards her. 'Eat. Do you want a plate?'

Ravenous, she shook her head and reached into the box. 'No point.' She chewed and gave a moan of delight. 'Oh, this is delicious.'

'Good.' He watched the way her small pink tongue sneaked out and licked her lips and suddenly found himself in the grip of a vicious attack of lust. 'So—tell me your life story.'

She stopped chewing. 'Sorry?'

Cursing himself for having disturbed her meal, Jake decided that, having done so, he may as well push on with his questioning. 'I want to know what's happened to the father of your baby. You accused me of jumping to the wrong conclusion and I'm sure that you're right. So give me the facts. That way, I won't do it again.'

'You're very direct, aren't you?'

'I think it's better that way.' He trapped her gaze with his. 'It prevents misunderstandings.'

She gave a slightly cynical laugh. 'Does it?'

'I think so. Who is he, Miranda?'

She hesitated. 'I suppose I owe you an explanation so I'll tell you, and then I don't want to talk about it any more.'

'You don't owe me anything,' he said calmly. 'But I want you to tell me.'

'Why?'

Good question. 'Because you look like someone who needs a friend? So that I can track him down and black his eye for leaving you to struggle like this?'

'I'm not struggling.' She gave him a fierce glare and he fought back a smile, remembering how independent she'd been on the mountain. She clearly had a thing about looking after herself and yet she looked so young with her dark hair still damp from the bath and a slice of pizza in her hand.

Far too young to be a single mother with no support.

'Don't stop eating,' he said quietly. 'You need the food. Tell me who he was, Miranda.'

Ignoring the pizza in her hand, she chewed her lip and stared miserably at the kitchen table. 'Saying it out loud makes it even worse.'

He leaned forward and eased the slice of pizza from between her fingers.

'Eat.' He slid the pizza between her teeth and she gave a wan smile before obediently biting off a piece.

'I met him in a chat room on the internet.'

*What was a beautiful woman like her doing, resorting to
chat rooms on the internet?* 'And?'

She shrugged. 'His name was Peter and he seemed nice.
We chatted about all sorts of things. He liked all the same
things as me—it was uncanny really.' She shook herself.
'Anyway, we spoke on the phone a couple of times and then
we arranged to meet. He told me he was thirty-eight, which
is a bit old, I suppose, but I wasn't worried.'

'So you met?'

'In a pub. He was good company and I...' She flushed.
'And I suppose the truth is that I was so lonely that I didn't
bother asking the questions I should have asked.'

Jake felt more questions surge up inside him. Why was
she lonely? Did she have no friends or family? With a determined effort he limited his question to one. 'What happened?'

'We went on a few dates and then, after about a month, he
confessed that he'd lied to me and that he was actually forty-
eight, not thirty-eight. I was really shocked. Not because of
his age,' she added hastily, 'but just that he'd deceived me.
I couldn't understand why he just hadn't told me the truth
right from the beginning.'

Jake gritted his teeth. 'And why didn't he?'

'He told me that he was afraid I wouldn't want to meet
him if he'd been honest about his age.'

Jake pushed the pizza box towards her. 'Eat another slice
before you tell me the rest.'

'How do you know there's more?'

'Because it's written all over your face.'

She chewed slowly on the pizza and then sucked her fingers. 'We went out for a few more weeks and he persuaded
me...' She blushed. 'I mean, I was obviously willing and—'

His appetite suddenly gone, Jake abandoned his slice of pizza. 'He persuaded you to go to bed with him.'

'Yes.' She sat back in her chair and closed her eyes briefly. 'I really want to tell you that I was madly in love with him but if I'm honest I think I was just incredibly lonely. And maybe that's why I didn't pick up any of the signs. I suppose I didn't want to see them.'

'What sort of signs?'

'He always called me, I was never allowed to call him except on his mobile and that was usually switched off. We only ever met when he suggested it—'

'Because he was married?'

She stared at him, stricken. 'Is it that obvious to you?'

Clearly it hadn't entered her head. 'You're giving me all the facts,' he pointed out gently, 'whereas you were only in possession of half of them and then only what he chose to give you.'

She shook her head. 'You've no idea how many times I've gone over and over it in my head, wondering why I missed the clues. It seems so obvious now, but at the time—'

'Passion can be a powerful emotion.'

'There wasn't that much passion.' A faint colour touched her cheeks. 'In fact, I—' She broke off and he frowned.

'What?'

'Nothing.' She gave him a smile that looked more than a little forced. 'Anyway, the rest is pretty obvious. I discovered I was pregnant. He was completely horrified and suddenly produced a picture of his blonde wife together with four matching children. And that, as they say, is the end of the story.' Her tone was light but he saw the pain in her eyes.

'And how did you feel about being pregnant?'

'At first panicky and very alone.' She let out a long breath and gave a soft smile. 'And then pleased. I know that sounds weird, but I was pleased. It just felt sort of...right. I can't really explain it.'

'He owes you maintenance at the very least.'

'I don't want anything from him.' She sat up in her chair, dignified despite the pyjamas and the damp hair. 'I'm used to managing on my own and that's what I'll do. The only difference is that now there are two of us to look after.'

'So why the Lake District? What about your family?' *Why was she used to managing on her own?*

Shadows flickered across her pretty face. 'I don't have any family,' she said flatly, standing up quickly and helping herself to a glass of water. She kept her back to him. 'I decided to move right away from London so I picked the Lake District because I've had a picture of it in my mind for as long as I can remember. I always loved poetry at school.'

'Poetry?' His own mind was elsewhere, sifting carefully through information. There was something about her answer that didn't seem quite right. Or rather, there was something about the way she'd answered that hadn't felt right. He knew instinctively that she was lying. But why would she lie about family? Had they fallen out because she was pregnant? Was she embarrassed about her family?

'Wordsworth.' She turned to face him, still holding the glass of water. 'He lived here, you must know that.'

'Of course.' He gave her an apologetic smile. 'It's just that I was born here and you tend to take it all for granted after a while.'

'Maybe.' Her tone was wistful. 'Well, anyway, it sounded like an idyllic place. A good place to bring up a child. And not as expensive as London.'

He wanted to know more about what had happened to her family.

It was clear that, if her family were alive, they wanted

nothing to do with her. *Or she wanted nothing to do with them.* Jake tried to imagine sticking a pin in the map and then deciding to build a life in a strange place. Tried to imagine what it would be like to have no roots. 'All right, I can understand you choosing the Lake District, but what made you choose that terrible flat?'

'It was all there was at the time and it was cheap,' she said simply. 'It's just me on my own and when the baby comes I'm not going to be able to work for a while so I don't want to waste any of it now. I'm going to look for something else soon. Somewhere I can move to after the baby is born.'

His eyes narrowed. 'How much are you paying in rent?'

She named a figure that seemed exorbitant for one dark room full of damp patches but he managed not to let his jaw drop. 'Right. Move in with me and you can save even more money.'

'You can't be serious.'

'I'm perfectly serious. Why not?' He waved a hand around the house. 'This place is far too big for me and you'd be much more comfortable here.'

'No.' Her voice cracked and something fierce flashed in her eyes. 'I don't need anyone's help. And I don't depend on anyone.'

She was ferociously independent and he sensed that if he didn't handle the situation with enormous care, she'd be back in her damp flat before he had time to dispose of the empty pizza box. He leaned back in his chair, stretched his legs out and kept his voice calm and steady. 'That's good, because I don't want you to depend on me. I'm just suggesting that you move into one of my spare rooms. You can pay me the same rent you're currently paying your landlord.'

'Absolutely not.' But he'd seen the brief hesitation and took instant advantage.

'Why? You're prepared to pay rent to a total stranger in return for a room.'

'That's different.'

'How is it different?' His voice was gentle and he watched her face for her reaction. 'Is it different because we kissed?'

She put the glass down and looked away from him. It was clear that, given the chance, she would have pretended that it hadn't happened. 'It wasn't a real kiss. It was Christmas Day, we were both lonely and—'

'Attracted to each other?'

Colour seeped into her cheeks. 'You can't possibly be attracted to me.'

'No?' The fact that she hadn't denied her own attraction to him gave him more satisfaction than he would have believed possible. He wondered if he dared risk moving towards her but decided against it. 'Why can't I be attracted to you?'

'I'm six months pregnant.' *With another man's baby.* The words hung in the air, unsaid, and he gave a patient smile.

'And?' His gaze didn't shift from her face. 'None of the books I studied said that pregnancy changes a person. You're still you.'

'A very fat version of me.'

The fact that she suffered from all the usual insecurities suffered by pregnant women made him want to smile. 'You're a midwife. You should know that most men find their wives extremely attractive during pregnancy.'

'I'm not your wife.'

His desire to smile faded. He should have been relieved about that. Instead, he found himself thinking how amazing it would be if she was his wife. He'd have the right to snuggle up with her and kiss the frown away from her beautiful face. 'That's true, but—'

'I'm not anyone's wife and I don't ever intend to be.' The fire was back in her eyes. 'I don't want a family.'

Was this just about the man who'd lied to her or was there something more to her comment?

His eyes slid from her fierce gaze to her softly rounded abdomen. 'I hate to tell you this, sweetheart, but you're about to become a family, whether you like it or not.'

She placed her hand on her stomach in an instinctively defensive gesture. 'That's entirely different. I want this baby, but I don't—'

'There's no such thing as a typical family, Miranda.' He took a gentle nudge at her fears and prejudices. 'Everyone creates something different. Family is a pretty generic word for people living together and trying to make it work in the best way they can.'

'Is that right?' There was a weary cynicism in her eyes that lit the fire of his own anger. He didn't know what had caused the pain. He just knew that it shouldn't be there.

He decided to shift the subject slightly. 'Are you going to carry on giving donations to your crooked landlord or are you going to give me the money instead?'

'You're serious about renting me a room?'

He didn't want to take her money at all, but he knew that there was no other way she'd even consider the possibility. 'Very serious.'

She was silent for a moment, her head tilted to one side, her damp hair sliding out of the confines of the clip and over one shoulder. 'All right.' She said the words slowly, as if she wanted to see how they sounded. 'But I'll move out when the baby arrives.'

'Why would you do that?'

'Because you don't need a screaming infant keeping you awake at night. And because I can't lodge here for ever. I need to find somewhere permanent that I can turn into a home.'

He realised with a stab of shock that he wanted her to make her home here. *With him*.

Startled by his own thoughts, Jake lifted a hand to his forehead and rubbed at the frown lines. This was ridiculous. He'd only known her for a couple of days. The humour of the situation wasn't wasted on him. He'd lost count of the number of women who had dropped hints about moving in with him. He'd developed various strategies for gently but firmly locking his door with the woman on the outside. So why did he suddenly want to lock the door and keep Miranda on the *inside*?

'Fine.' He knew that his thoughts would have her scurrying hard back to her damp-ridden, gloomy flat without a backward look so he kept them to himself. 'Consider this a base until you find something more suitable.'

'It's very generous of you.' She fiddled with her hands, clearly troubled by something. 'I still don't understand why would you do this for me.'

'Does there have to be a reason?'

'Isn't there always?' She gave a cynical laugh. 'I'd be guessing at the sex aspect if it weren't for the fact that I'm six months pregnant.'

'There's a great deal more to my motives than sex.' His gaze was direct. 'OK, I'm not going to lie to you, Miranda, because you've obviously heard enough lies. The truth is, I don't exactly know why I want you to live here. There was something between us from the first moment we met on Christmas Day. When I woke up and found you gone I was frantic—frustrated. Then, when I discovered you at work, I felt light-headed until you stood up and I saw that you were pregnant. I've always had a rule that I never tread on another man's toes, so I was prepared to walk away even though I felt as though something important had been snatched away from me.'

Her dark eyes were huge. *Wary.* 'Jake—'

'Let me finish.' He stood up and walked towards her. 'Then I discovered that you're on your own. That I'm not treading on anyone's toes. And that changes everything, Miranda. Why do I want you to stay here? Because I can't let you go, it's as simple as that. I'm not sure what that means, but I'd like to find out.'

'I'm six months pregnant.'

'That doesn't change the person you are.'

'This is ridiculous, Jake—'

'Is it?' He saw the shock in her eyes and in a way it mirrored his own feelings because normally he backed away from women, didn't pursue them. It was ironic, he reflected, that the first time he was truly interested in a woman she was six months pregnant, fiercely independent and wary of men. With a faint smile of self-mockery he recognised that some of the women he'd dated would view his current situation as nothing more than poetic justice.

She stared at him and the tension in the room rose to agonising levels.

'I—I don't really know what you're saying but I don't want a relationship, Jake. Not with any man. I'm not trying to create a family.'

He smiled. 'As I said, you've got yourself a family, Miranda.'

'Well, it's just going to be me and the baby and that's fine by me.'

Why? he wondered to himself. Was it just because of the baby's father or was there more to it than met the eye? Something to do with her own family.

'You're worn out,' he said softly, deciding that it was best to end the conversation before he did something that might frighten her off. 'Go to bed, Miranda. We can talk tomorrow.'

'But you can't just—'

'Don't complicate the simple,' he advised. 'You're sleeping here tonight. Any more than that we can discuss at another time.'

CHAPTER SEVEN

'I DON'T think you should drive me to work,' Miranda said the next morning as she sipped the cup of tea Jake had made for her and nibbled on a piece of toast.

'Why not?'

'Because people might notice and talk. And that would be embarrassing.'

She'd been awake for most of the night, thinking about what he'd said. *He hadn't wanted to let her go.* Even while most of her was backing off, deafened by alarm bells, a small part of her was shiny with happiness.

'Coming from a woman who rides a heap of rust in public, I find it hard to believe that you care about what people think.' There was laughter in his eyes and she looked away, wishing that his smile wasn't so compelling.

He smiled at everyone, she reminded herself firmly. It was just the kind of man he was. You felt as though the smile was only for you, but it wasn't.

She had to be careful. Very careful. It would be foolish and dangerous to allow herself to dream.

'That's entirely different.' She put her empty mug into the

dishwasher and then turned to face him. 'I'm pregnant, Jake. People will make the same assumptions about me that you did, and I don't want that. I don't want people thinking that I'm dishonest or unfaithful or any of the other things people assume when they see a pregnant woman with a man who isn't her husband.'

He gave a shrug, his expression unconcerned. 'As you told me on Christmas Day, what people see on the outside rarely resembles the inside so what does it matter? Let them gossip.' Evidently indifferent to the views of others, he strolled towards the door and held it open for her. 'Come on or we'll be late.'

She stared at him with mounting frustration. She was so used to taking charge of her own life that she wasn't sure how to deal with Jake.

But she decided that this wasn't worth an argument so she slid into the warmth and comfort of his car and squashed down the uncomfortable feelings bubbling up inside her. This was all wrong, she knew it was. What exactly did he want from her? And what exactly did she want from him?

Nothing, was the short answer to that. There was no way she'd ever consider entering into a serious relationship and a fling wasn't her style.

She had no opportunity to ponder the question further because once they arrived on the labour ward they were so busy that they had no time to discuss anything except the professional.

She felt as though she was on her feet all day and she was more than a little relieved to find Jake lounging by the doorway at the end of her shift, waiting to take her home.

Deciding that this was definitely not the time to argue with him, she slid gratefully into his car, pushing aside the horrible suspicion that people were watching them.

He was right. What did it matter? And why did she care? She, of all people, who knew only too well that outward appearances were entirely deceptive.

He drove her to her old flat and stood while she cleared out the rest of her things. She carried them to his car and then hunted in her pocket for the keys.

'I just need to deliver these back to the landlord.'

'Tell me which flat he lives in. I'll do it.'

'I can—'

'You're tired. Why waste energy walking up the stairs again when all you have to do is point me in the right direction and I'll do it for you?'

'He lives in the flat directly beneath mine, but I need to give him notice and explain to him that—'

'I'll explain,' Jake said, prising the keys from her fingers and heading back towards the building.

She ought to have argued with him, she knew that. It wasn't good to let people do things for you when you could perfectly well do it yourself. But he was right when he said that she was tired.

It was only when he slid back into the car and dropped an envelope into her lap that she realised that she'd actually dozed off for a few minutes.

'What's that?' Muzzy-headed from lack of sleep, she picked up the envelope and gasped as she saw the amount of money inside. 'Where did this come from?'

'Your landlord.' Jake started the engine and glanced over his shoulder before pulling away from the kerb. 'I explained that you were living with me now and he apologised profusely for the state of the property that he's renting to you and immediately returned your deposit and last month's rent as a goodwill gesture.'

'You spoke to the landlord?'

'That's right.' His eyes were fixed on the road. 'Very reasonable chap.'

There was something about the grim set of his mouth that made her wonder and then her gaze dropped and she saw the red mark across his knuckles. 'You hit him! Oh, my God, Jake…'

'He walked into my hand.'

She covered her mouth with her hand, appalled. 'What's come over you?'

'I don't like people who take advantage of other people.' He glanced in her direction, his eyes glittering dangerously. For once there was no trace of humour in his gaze, just grim determination and a hardness that she hadn't seen before. 'Once we'd had a good chat, he saw sense.'

'How dare you interfere?' She was outraged. 'Jake, I didn't ask you to get that money for me!'

He pulled into the drive of his house and switched off the engine. 'The guy is a crook, Miranda.'

'It doesn't give you the right to hit him.' She undid her seat belt with shaking hands. 'I—'

'What's the matter?'

Her heart was banging against her chest. 'You really need to ask me that question? You just beat someone up and—'

'I didn't beat anyone up.' His voice was weary. 'He said some things I didn't like. Things he shouldn't have said. He's a bully, Miranda. A sleazy, nasty bully.'

'You hit him.'

Jake ran a hand through his hair. 'He attacked me, Miranda,' he said quietly. 'Accused me of taking away his business.'

Self-defence? She relaxed slightly and the pounding of her heart slowed. 'He hit you? I'm sorry.' Her voice was little more than a whisper. 'It's all my fault. I shouldn't have let you go in there.'

'Better me than you. Next time choose your landlord with more care.' Without waiting for a response from her, he opened the car door and walked towards the house.

She caught up with him in the kitchen. Looking at his stiff, icy profile, Miranda felt frustration and something else that she couldn't quite identify. A tiny part of her felt warm and cosseted. No man had ever defended her before. Maybe it shouldn't have felt good *but it did.*

He was only trying to help and she'd been rude and churlish. He'd been injured, standing up for her, and all she'd done had been to yell at him.

Suddenly ashamed of herself, she wrapped her arms around her waist and took a deep breath. 'I'm sorry,' she began, and he muttered something under his breath, before turning to her with a smile.

'No, I'm the one who should be sorry. I'm used to women who like to be pampered. You're the most independent person I've ever met. I thought I was doing you a favour.'

'You *were* doing me a favour. I hate that man—he makes my flesh crawl. It's just that I don't want you to feel sorry for me.'

'I don't.' His voice was soft. 'But you're a friend and it's natural to want to help a friend, isn't it?'

Miranda bit her lip. 'I don't know. I suppose if I'm honest, I've never really had a close friend before.'

'Are you joking?' He reached into the fridge for a beer. 'Women always have close friends.'

'Do they?' Miranda pushed away thoughts of her childhood and sat down at the kitchen table. 'I suppose I've always found it hard to be close to people.'

He studied her face for a moment and then smiled. 'Any chance of some first aid for my knuckles?'

She rummaged in his freezer for an icepack and fussed over his hands. 'Does it hurt badly?'

'If I say yes, will you kiss it better?'

She shot him a warning look. 'Be careful or I might damage your other hand.'

As the days passed Miranda felt nothing but pleased that she'd agreed to move in with Jake. In the warmth and comfort of his house, she slept better. In fact, there were several occasions when Jake had to wake her in the mornings.

She knew that, at some point, she was going to have to find somewhere to live once the baby was born, but she was so busy at work that all she wanted to do when she arrived home was collapse in a heap and sleep until her next shift.

And Jake made it easy for her to do that.

He was easy to live with, she discovered, and after that first night he'd kept the conversation friendly but impersonal.

Which was a good thing, she told herself firmly as she slid out of bed on a Saturday morning a month or so after she'd first moved in. She didn't want anything else.

Anticipating a slow, lazy day, she dressed in comfortable clothes and went downstairs to the kitchen to find Jake frying bacon.

'It's a lovely day.' He glanced towards her. 'Fancy a walk?'

After her first, disastrous foray into the mountains, he'd taken her to the mountain rescue base and shown her all the equipment they used in rescues and talked to her about safety. She realised again how fortunate she was that he'd been the one to find her on Christmas Day. Since then he'd found walking gear that fitted her and had insisted on taking her on some gentle hikes.

She slid a hand over her rounded abdomen. 'You fancy delivering a baby in the wild, Mr Blackwell?'

'You know me.' He gave her a wicked grin as he slid crispy bacon onto a plate. 'I love a challenge.'

She stared at the bacon. 'Is that for me? Because I can cook my own breakfast and you don't have to—'

'I don't have to wait on you.' His tone was patient. 'I know that, Miranda, and I'm not waiting on you. I was making breakfast for myself so adding a few extra rashers of bacon seemed like common sense.'

It sounded logical, put like that. 'I'm going to be the size of a small bus.'

'You have no flesh on you whatsoever,' he said dryly, dropping two slices of bread onto her plate and putting a jug of coffee in the centre of the table. 'That bump is all baby. Am I allowed to pour your coffee or does that offend your independent streak?'

'I know you're laughing at me but I won't depend on anyone.'

'You can relax. I don't want you to depend on me. Just for the record, you're cooking dinner tonight.' He poured coffee into two mugs and pushed one across to her. 'There we are. You should put milk in it. You need building up.'

She patted her stomach and there was humour in her eyes. 'You want to have to refashion all your doors just so that I can pass through them?'

'As I said, that bump is all baby.'

'Big baby, then.'

'Does that worry you?' He bit into his own sandwich and she looked at him, thinking, not for the first time, that he was incredibly astute. She saw it over and over again at work and not just among the women he delivered. He noticed when a midwife was slightly off colour, he knew that Delia in the staff restaurant was having trouble with her hip. He didn't miss anything and she really liked that about him.

Men were supposed to be useless at picking up signals and yet Jake seemed to notice everything.

'Honestly? A bit, yes. I suppose all women are apprehensive about delivery.' She picked up the sandwich and nibbled the corners. 'But I'm sure it will be all right. I took your advice and saw Tom Hunter. He's a nice guy.'

'Everything all right?'

'Yes, seems to be. I'm boringly healthy. Low blood pressure, plenty of movements.' She felt a little embarrassed discussing it. 'He didn't anticipate any problems.'

'He's a good obstetrician.' Jake sipped his coffee and grinned. 'Not as outstanding as me, of course, but I couldn't deliver your baby.'

'Why not?'

His eyes locked on hers. 'Because I'm emotionally involved and that isn't a good thing. Obstetricians have to be able to take a step back.'

His words made her insides shift alarmingly. 'Why are you emotionally involved? I'm just your lodger.'

He studied her face for a long moment, his blue eyes revealing nothing of his thoughts. 'If you've finished your breakfast, I think we should go for that walk. Exercise is good for you. If Tom didn't mention that fact then he should have done.'

'Jake—' she couldn't let the subject drop that easily '—we've been living together for a month now and you haven't mentioned—' She broke off and he smiled.

'The fact that there's this amazing chemistry between us?'

She blushed. 'After a month of living with me you've

probably discovered that I'm a long way from being your ideal woman. I'm stubborn and independent and I fall asleep when I'm not working—'

'I'm assuming that the sleep thing will improve once the baby is born, and I happen to like your independent streak.' He stood up. 'Let's leave the clearing-up until later. It's February and you, of all people, know how changeable the weather can be. The sun's shining at the moment so we should make the most of it.'

Aware that he'd changed the subject, she followed him to the door, feeling as though the conversation was only half-finished.

'Jake—'

'Miranda.' He turned to face her, his eyes gentle. 'Are you sure you want to pursue this line of questioning? If you ask me, I'm going to be honest about how I feel and you'll be obliged to tell me that the relationship isn't going anywhere and then I'll argue with you and that will ruin our walk. So let's drop it for now.'

For now?

He was implying that he still had feelings for her, and yet...

She bit her lip, knowing that he was right. Whatever he said, she was going to back off.

'Get your boots on.' Jake pushed them towards her. 'I'll do them up for you.'

'I can do them myself, just about.' She slipped on another thermal layer and pulled on a jumper and then her coat. 'I'm boiling.'

'That's because you're in my house. It's freezing outside. We won't stay out for long and we'll do something flat so that it isn't strenuous.'

'What do you think I am?' She frowned as she fastened

her boots, determined not to show him what a struggle it was. 'Pathetic?'

'No. Seven months pregnant.' He stepped forward, zipped up her jacket and handed her a hat. 'Wear that.'

'I'll get hat hair.'

'Women.' He rolled his eyes and walked towards the door. 'Better hat hair than hypothermia, sweetheart. Wear it.'

He drove to a lake that she hadn't visited before and parked the car. 'We'll just walk around the shore path. Very gentle and easy.'

It was a perfect clear day, crisp and cold but fresh and invigorating. The snow crunched underfoot and Miranda stamped her foot down into virgin snow. 'Don't you just love that?' She couldn't hold back the grin. 'Being the first person to touch the snow?'

'Just as long as the mark is caused by your foot and not your bottom.' He took her arm. 'I know I'll be on the receiving end of a lecture about your independent nature, but hold onto me or you might slip and break something. Perhaps we shouldn't have come.'

She lifted an eyebrow. 'You think I've forgotten how to walk?'

'No. I think the ground is slippery and your weight distribution has shifted.'

'You're just looking for an excuse to touch me.' She was teasing but the look in his eyes made her smile fade.

'I don't need an excuse, Miranda,' he said softly, his eyes burning into hers. 'When I think the time is right, I'm going to touch you and we won't be by a frozen lake when I do it.'

Suddenly she found it difficult to breath. 'Jake—'

'We agreed not to get serious today.' He stroked a hand down her cheek and then turned away, adjusting the rucksack that he always carried on his back. 'Come on, walk. But hold my arm so that you don't slip.'

Feeling slightly weak and shaky, she did as he instructed, her fingers curling into the solid swell of his biceps. She wanted to ask what he meant but she was afraid of stirring up something she wasn't able to handle.

They walked for about half an hour and Jake stopped and pulled out a flask. 'It's cold today. The temperature is dropping. I wouldn't be surprised if we have more snow.'

'Is the lake really frozen?'

'Only around the edges. It's very deceptive. The ice is extremely thin. Last year we had to rescue two children who thought it would be fun to skate and fell in.'

'Oh, my goodness.' Miranda took the hot drink from him gratefully. 'How did you get them out?'

'We balanced logs on the ice and used the ropes from our climbing gear.' They drank and talked and then Jake stuffed the flask back in his backpack. 'Have you finished? We probably ought to be making a move.'

'Let's go a bit further before we turn back. It's so lovely to be outdoors.'

His blue eyes gleamed. 'Can this possibly be the same girl who was wearing trainers and not much else when I met her on Christmas Day? I thought you were a city girl.'

'Not any more.' She shook her head and glanced around her wistfully. 'I never want to go near a city again. The baby and I are going to live here happily ever after.'

'That sounds lonely.'

Aware of his searching gaze, she blushed slightly. 'I don't think so. As you once said to me, families come in many different guises.'

'I meant, lonely for you.' He stepped closer to her. 'Aren't you a little young to be dismissing the male species from your life?'

It was impossible to look away and her heart fluttered and skipped at the look in his eyes. 'I'm trying to keep my life simple.'

'Is that right?' Somehow his head had moved nearer to hers and now his mouth hovered, tantalisingly close. She stared up at him, hypnotised by the slightly slumberous look in his eyes. His jaw was rough with stubble and he looked more handsome than any man had a right to look, and her body's reaction was as intense as it was instant.

Her legs wobbled, her insides tumbled and swirled and that was before he even touched her. Perhaps he knew the effect he was having on her because the last thing she saw before his mouth came down on hers and her eyes drifted closed was lazy amusement in those wicked blue eyes.

Then he kissed her and she slipped into his kiss as easily as she had that first time, on Christmas Day.

No wonder she hadn't been able to resist him, she thought dizzily. His mouth was warm and skilled, his kiss slow and so erotically seductive that all the power drained out of her legs. Unable to stand without support, she clutched at his jacket and felt his arms slide around her as he pulled her against him.

Lost in a mysterious world of sensation that she'd never before discovered, it was only after he'd reluctantly released her that she realised his mobile phone was ringing.

Swearing fluently under his breath, Jake kept one arm around her and used the other to dig deep in his pocket for his phone. 'Yes?' His response was less than enthusiastic and she could understand why. She was ready to strangle the person who'd interrupted them. Or perhaps she should be grateful, she said to herself as she eased herself away from the pressure of his arm, taking advantage of the fact that all his attention was now on the phone. It seemed that it was all too easy to give in to Jake's charms. No matter how hard her lesson, she seemed to have no willpower where he was concerned.

'Problem, I'm afraid.' Jake snapped the phone shut and dropped it into his pocket, his eyes narrowed as he stared down the path ahead of them.

'You're not on call. Mr Hardwick is supposed to be covering this weekend.'

'It isn't a baby. It's a woman who's slipped by the lake and broken her ankle.'

'Which lake?'

Jake was squinting into the distance. 'This lake. You and I are the advance party, sweetheart.'

'You want me to help you with a mountain rescue?' It was hard to keep the irony out of her voice and he turned to her, his eyes gleaming with appreciation.

'Actually, we've always thought that an extremely pregnant woman would be an asset to the team.' He trailed a finger down her cheek in an affectionate gesture that had her heart racing. 'We're not up a mountain and I don't need you to do any rescuing, but I do have to go and help and I'm not prepared to leave you here or let you walk back to the car on your own.'

Wondering what it was about him that had such a powerful effect on her, she adopted a frosty tone. 'You think I'm helpless?'

'No, I think you're very pregnant and this walk probably wasn't a sensible idea, but it becomes even less so if you go back on your own. What if something happens, Miranda?' He frowned. 'It isn't about independence, it's about common sense.'

She thought for a moment and nodded. 'All right. I'm not going to argue with you.'

'You're not?'

'No. What do you want me to do?'

'She dialled 999 a few minutes ago and the leader of the mountain rescue team thinks that she's not far from here. If he's right then we should be able to stretcher her down the valley and meet the ambulance at the road.'

'I only see one problem with that.'

He started walking along the path. 'What's that?'

'We don't have a stretcher. Or do you carry one in your magic bag, along with the hot chocolate?'

He laughed. 'My colleagues will be bringing the stretcher, the ambulance will wait at the end of the path and our job is to administer first aid and make sure she's comfortable.'

'They're going to walk along here, carrying a stretcher?'

'It breaks into pieces.'

'Oh, yes, I remember now. You showed me one that evening you took me around the mountain rescue centre.'

They walked for another fifteen minutes and then Jake waved a hand. 'There she is. I see her. By that tree.'

'She looks all huddled up.' Miranda frowned. 'I hope she's all right.'

'Let's find out, shall we?'

They reached the woman and she gave a wan smile. 'I didn't think anyone else would be stupid enough to walk along here in this weather, but I see I was wrong.'

'I'm Jake Blackwell, I'm from the mountain rescue team.' Jake dropped down so that he could examine her ankle. 'I'm going to make you comfortable and then we're going to get you out of here. Some of my colleagues are coming with a stretcher and we'll carry you back to the ambulance. What's your name?'

'Verity. Verity Williams. This is so embarrassing.' The woman closed her eyes briefly. 'I've always scoffed at people who need the services of the mountain rescue team—always thought they were frivolous or badly equipped.'

Miranda shot a guilty look at Jake, who winked at her.

'It can happen to the best of us, Verity. Now, if you don't mind, I'm just going to take a look at the damage.' His tone reassuring, he undid the laces of her boot and Miranda caught hold of the woman's hand and encouraged her to squeeze.

'Oh, that's agony!' Verity's face drained of colour and she gasped in pain as Jake carefully eased the boot off her foot.

Miranda pulled a face. She could see instantly that Verity's foot was badly swollen and discoloured. Was it broken? And what, she wondered, was Jake going to do about that out here in the middle of nowhere?

'Does it hurt here?' Jake was examining the ankle carefully and the woman gasped again.

'Yes. It's just a sprain, I'm sure, not a break.' She winced and tried to wriggle into a more comfortable position while Jake dug his mobile phone out of his pocket and opened the top of his rucksack.

He pulled out a pad, a coiled rope and a knife and set about making a splint, his movements slick and confident.

'Miranda, can you just check her pedal pulse? The foot looks a reasonable colour and she has sensation and movement so I'm assuming her circulation isn't impaired, but I want to check.' The phone tucked under his ear, he started talking to the person on the other end, giving a report on the woman's condition and a description of their whereabouts, while he cut the pad and fashioned a splint.

Miranda removed her glove and checked the pulse in the woman's foot, feeling the delicate throb under her fingertips with relief. 'She has a good pulse,' she told Jake as he snapped the phone shut and finished splinting the leg.

'Right.' Jake secured the splint and glanced at his watch. 'I think they'll be along with that stretcher in another fifteen minutes, Verity, so hang in there.'

'Fifteen minutes?' Miranda gaped at him. 'It's taken us almost an hour to get to this point.'

'The mountain rescue team aren't in the advanced stages of pregnancy,' he reminded her, rocking back on his heels and pushing his hand back into his rucksack.

Verity's face brightened. 'You're about to have a baby? Oh, you lucky things. How wonderful for you.'

Miranda frowned. 'Well, actually, the baby isn't—'

'We're thrilled,' Jake said firmly, pulling out an extra layer and slipping it around Verity's shoulders. 'Best thing that could have happened.'

Confused as to why he would let the woman continue with her misunderstanding, Miranda opened her mouth to correct him and gave a gasp of shock as Jake leaned forward and kissed her. 'I'm plucking up courage to ask her to marry me,' he murmured, 'but I have a feeling she's going to turn me down so I keep postponing the moment.'

Marry him?

Miranda was speechless and Verity gave a sigh.

'You don't want to marry him?' She turned to look at Miranda who managed a weak smile.

'I haven't known him that long.' Realising how that sounded, Miranda felt a rush of embarrassment. What would Verity think of her? *She could hardly explain that she couldn't marry him because she was pregnant with another man's baby, could she?*

'I knew my husband for about five minutes before I realised that he was the one.' Verity sighed. 'When it's right, there's just no point in waiting.'

Jake smiled. 'My point exactly.'

Miranda looked at him, trying to read his mind. Was he serious? Why did something that seemed so complicated to her seem so simple to everyone else?

Still reeling from his words, she tried to concentrate as Jake engaged Verity in conversation about marriage, babies and life generally, but her mind kept wandering back to his surprise announcement.

Did he really want to marry her?

And then she glanced across at him, saw the way he was taking Verity's mind off the pain with an animated discussion on the risks of a certain climbing technique and she suddenly realised that he'd just been trying to distract Verity.

Her spirits slumped and she gave an irritated frown, totally unable to understand her own reaction. She didn't want to marry him. She didn't want to marry anyone. So why did the realisation that his proposal had been nothing more than distraction therapy leave her feeling so flat?

'Here come the cavalry.' Rising to his feet in an athletic movement, Jake gave Verity a quick smile. 'We'll soon have you back to civilisation.'

'What a pity.' Verity glanced round her with a sigh. 'I love it here. This view is vastly preferably to the view from my office window, but there you are. Can't always have what you want in life.'

'Why not? I always think that what you want is worth fighting for.' Jake's gaze lingered on Miranda for a brief moment and then he turned his attention to his colleagues who arrived carrying the stretcher and other equipment.

After that it all happened so quickly and smoothly that Miranda could do little except watch in amazement.

With the efficiency of a team clearly used to working together, they assembled the stretcher and in no time at all they were ready to carry her Verity along the path towards the ambulance.

'I'm not going to be able to keep up with you,' Miranda told Verity, 'so I'll say goodbye now. I hope your ankle doesn't take long to heal.'

'And I hope you agree to marry your young man!' Verity smiled her thanks at Jake. 'Men like him don't come along very often. You should snap him up.'

'I agree. She definitely should.' Ignoring the curious glances of the rest of the team, Jake strolled back to collect his gear, leaving his colleagues to set off down the path.

Miranda stood still, chewing her lip, a frown on her face. 'Don't you mind that they're all gossiping now?'

'Why would I mind?'

'You let her think that the baby is yours and that you want to marry me. Just how far are you prepared to go in the name of distraction?'

'It wasn't about distraction.' He swung his rucksack onto his back. 'I'm crazy about you, Miranda, and the baby is part of you. You've got to stop thinking that your pregnancy makes any difference to the way I feel about you.'

The way he felt about her?

She felt suddenly light-headed. *He was crazy about her?* She felt a flicker of happiness and excitement that she ruthlessly squashed. 'You might think you don't mind about the baby, but that's before reality sets in.'

His eyes were amused. 'You think I don't know about babies?'

'You know about *delivering* babies, Jake. Delivering them isn't the same as living with them.' Especially when that baby wasn't his.

'I have nieces and nephews. I'm a very hands-on uncle and godfather.'

'And you return home to your perfect, peaceful house at night. It isn't the same thing at all!'

He took her arm and tucked it through his as they walked back down the path towards the car. 'I'm not precious about my house, Miranda. A house is a home, not a showpiece, despite what my sister may think.'

'Do you have any idea what children would do to your cream sofa?'

'Actually, yes,' he said in a lazy, masculine drawl. 'My godson, Ben, is always spilling drinks. My sofa has been the lucky recipient on at least three occasions.'

She sighed. 'You've got an answer for everything.'

'If you're telling me that I'm persistent, yes, I am. But I'm also patient.' The amusement in his eyes faded. 'I don't want you to feel under pressure. I'm willing to wait for you to make the first move.'

They were back at the car and she'd never felt so confused in her life. 'I'm not going to make the first move.'

He unlocked the car with a smile, his expression unperturbed. 'Then we're in for a frustrating few months, angel. Good job there are plenty of frozen lakes for me to jump into.'

He kept his word about not making the first move and for the next two weeks they worked together, ate dinner together, chatted about everything. But he didn't kiss her. And she didn't kiss him.

What was the point, when she knew it wasn't going anywhere?

No matter how great the attraction, she wasn't willing to

subject herself to more trauma when it ended, and she knew it would end.

So she gritted her teeth and ignored the rush of excitement she felt whenever he walked into a room and she forced herself not to stare at him when they ate a meal together and not once did she reach for him even though her hands were burning to touch him.

Jake himself worked punishing hours, sometimes spending whole nights at the hospital, returning home briefly just to shower and shave before returning to do his ward round. His commitment to his patients was absolute and his skill and patience with the mothers astonished her. And she learned a great deal from him and found her confidence growing. He taught her to trust her instincts and not doubt herself.

Just how far she'd come was brought home to her when a young woman was admitted to the labour ward with flu-like symptoms.

Miranda helped her into one of the side rooms and quickly glanced at the letter from the GP. Clearly he'd spoken to one of the obstetric registrars, who had then arranged for admission.

'I've never had a headache like this,' the woman groaned softly as she curled up on the bed and covered her face with her arms. 'I feel totally hideous—you have no idea.'

'I'm going to phone the doctor to tell him you're here and then I'm going to make you more comfortable,' Miranda told her gently, frowning slightly as she touched the woman's forehead. She was burning hot and the expression in her eyes was slightly glazed.

Feeling very uneasy and unwilling to leave the woman on her own, Miranda was about to hit the buzzer when Jake's SHO, Belinda Morris, walked into the room.

'Hi, there. I spoke to the GP about Cathy,' she said cheerfully, walking over to the bed and giving the woman a sympathetic look. 'I'm Dr Morris. You poor thing. Flu is rotten at any time, but even more so when you're pregnant. Life can be very unfair.'

Clearly the junior doctor wasn't in the least alarmed by Cathy's condition and Miranda forced herself to relax, telling herself that she was just being hypersensitive. It was just because of that one case of shoulder dystocia, she told herself. She'd been imagining emergencies with every patient since then.

While Dr Morris carried out an examination, Miranda checked Cathy's temperature and found it to be extremely high.

'No surprises there, then,' Dr Morris said briskly, when Miranda showed her the reading.

Still telling herself that she was being over-anxious, Miranda slipped off Cathy's top and frowned. 'How long have you had this rash, Cathy?'

Cathy lay with her eyes closed. Her breathing was shallow and her cheeks were flushed. 'Don't know,' she murmured finally. 'Nothing there this morning.'

'Viral rashes are very common with flu,' Belinda said briskly, pushing her stethoscope back in her pocket. 'They resolve over time. Nothing to worry about.'

Miranda wished she felt equally confident. Suddenly her anxiety refused to be suppressed. 'I think we should call Mr Blackwell.'

'He's in a meeting at the moment. We'll just keep her in for the time being, monitor the baby and see how she goes.' Belinda walked towards the door with a confident and slightly superior smile. 'I'll let Jake know that she's here. Call me if anything changes.'

The door closed behind her and Miranda looked at the rash again. Viruses often cause a rash, she repeated to herself. Viruses often cause a rash. On impulse she picked up a glass from the side of the bed and pressed it against the woman's skin. The rash didn't blanch.

Without hesitation, Miranda hit the emergency button and seconds later Ruth came running in.

Her anxiety levels soaring, Miranda checked Cathy's temperature again, her hands shaking slightly. 'Call Mr Blackwell. Call him now.' She hesitated briefly. 'And we need to give her intravenous penicillin right away.'

Ruth looked at her and then the rash. 'Right. I'll arrange it.' Without argument or discussion, she left the room and was back moments later accompanied by Jake.

Miranda had never been so relieved to see anyone. Calmed by his presence, she turned back to her patient. 'When did you start to feel ill, Cathy?'

'Last night.' Cathy moved her arms and opened her eyes. 'I can see two of you,' she murmured drowsily. 'Is that normal?'

Jake strode over to the bedside. He was dressed in a beautifully cut suit that emphasised the width of his shoulders and the strength of his physique. He looked serious and businesslike and the usual humour was missing from his blue eyes. It was obvious that he'd come straight from a difficult meeting and Miranda felt a flash of insecurity.

What if she'd bothered him for no reason? What if she was wrong?

She came straight to the point. 'Cathy was sent in by her GP with flu-like symptoms but she has a rash on her torso and I think we should probably give her penicillin right away.' She didn't want to mention the word 'meningitis' because she didn't want to frighten the patient and she didn't want to waste time taking Jake out of the room to brief him on her fears.

Jake took one look at Cathy and reached into his pocket for a tourniquet. 'Have you got the penicillin there?' His voice calm, he held out a hand for the syringe which Ruth handed him and quickly checked the ampoule. 'Great. We're just going to give you an injection of some antibiotic, Cathy, and then we're going to take some blood and get you transferred somewhere more comfortable. Are you allergic to penicillin?'

Eyes closed, Cathy shook her head slowly and Jake injected the penicillin just as Belinda came back into the room.

'Oh, Jake, I didn't know you were out of your meeting. I was going to tell you about Cathy when you—'

'I want you to take blood cultures and then start an infusion.' Discarding the empty syringe, Jake rose to his feet, his handsome face serious. 'I'm going to talk to ITU.'

'ITU?' Belinda frowned. 'But I—'

'Cultures.' Jake's tone was cool. 'Ruth—get me Geoff Masters on the phone, please. He's the consultant in Communicable Disease Control. I need to tell him what's happening.'

After that things moved swiftly. Cathy was transferred to ITU and Jake continued to liaise with other consultants over her management.

'He's been up on ITU for hours,' Ruth told Miranda later as they changed to go home. 'No one has ever seen a case of meningitis in a pregnant woman before so they're all huddled around, discussing the best way to treat her.'

'Is she worse?'

'No. Better, apparently. Thanks to the brilliance of a certain midwife on the labour ward—Jake's words, by the way, not mine.' Ruth wriggled into a thick jumper and reached for her coat. 'He hauled Dr Morris over the coals. Wanted to know why she hadn't called him the second she set eyes on the patient.'

Miranda grabbed her bag out of her locker. 'Maybe she was afraid of getting him out of a meeting.'

Ruth gave her a pointed look. 'You weren't.'

'I think that case of shoulder dystocia has made me jumpy. I see emergencies everywhere.'

'Well, that's fortunate for young Cathy, then, but I think you're dismissing what you've done rather lightly. Jake is asking questions as to why the GP didn't give her penicillin.'

'Well, to be fair, meningitis wouldn't be the first thing you think of in a pregnant woman with a temperature and a rash,' Miranda murmured, and Ruth stopped and looked at her.

'You thought of it.'

'And thank goodness for that.' Jake's deep drawl came from the doorway and both Ruth and Miranda turned in surprise.

'You're not supposed to come in here,' Ruth scolded. 'This is the midwives' changing room. It could be full of naked women.'

Jake smiled placidly. 'I keep hoping.'

'How is she?'

'Better.' Jake's blue eyes were warm as he turned to look at Miranda. 'And it's undoubtedly thanks to you. If you hadn't insisted on calling me and having the penicillin ready, it might have been a different story.'

'I was afraid I might be wasting your time.'

'I suspect you might have just saved two lives so any time you feel the inclination to bother me, please, do so.'

'I'm just so relieved she's all right.'

'Well, she's not totally out of the woods, but she's

definitely responding to antibiotics and all the scans and blood tests suggest that the baby is all right, although we won't know for sure until it's delivered.'

Ruth put her coat on. 'If it's been confirmed as meningitis, shouldn't Miranda take Rifampicin or something?'

Jake shook his head. 'We've talked about that. For healthcare professionals it's really only recommended if you've given mouth-to-mouth or similar. Given Miranda is pregnant, I'd be reluctant to give her anything, and Geoff Masters agrees.'

'I wasn't with her for that long,' Miranda said reasonably. 'She was transferred almost immediately. All I really did was take her temperature.'

Jake nodded. 'The risk is minuscule.' He glanced at his watch. 'I've told them to call me if there's any change. Let's go home.'

Aware that Ruth was looking at her with a quizzical expression on her face, Miranda sighed. 'Jake's very generously letting me a room in his house, just until I find somewhere suitable.'

'Good.' Ruth beamed at both of them, swept up her bag and walked towards the door. 'I'm off, then. Need to feed my husband and recharge my batteries, ready for another exciting day in the office tomorrow. I feel we're in desperate need of a run of normal deliveries, just so that we can all remind ourselves that sometimes it can all go swimmingly well, without any of this drama and tension.'

Miranda and Jake walked towards the car. 'You must be knackered.' He unlocked the car door and held it open while she slid inside.

'I am tired.'

'Quick supper and early bed.' He drove home quickly, a slight frown on his face as he concentrated on the road.

Sneaking a glance at his strong profile, Miranda wondered what he was thinking. Was he worrying about Cathy?

'What on earth made you even think of meningitis? It obviously didn't cross the minds of the GP or my SHO.'

'I've seen a similar rash before. In a child when I was doing a paediatric module.'

'Lucky for Cathy.' He turned the car into his drive and pulled up outside the house. 'You go and have a bath. I'll knock something up for supper.'

'I'm cooking tonight.' Miranda undid her seat belt and wriggled out of the car. Her bump was starting to feel larger by the day.

'No way.'

'Jake, you don't have to wait on me. I want to cook. It's my turn. Why don't you have a bath? By the time you've finished, I'll have it ready.'

He opened his mouth to argue and then clearly saw something in her eyes that made him change his mind because he smiled. 'Good. Fine. In that case, I'll go for a quick run. I haven't done any exercise for days. It clears my head and removes the stress.'

'There's snow on the ground.'

'It muffles the sound of my bones creaking,' he drawled, humour gleaming in his blue eyes. 'Short run, quick shower then supper. All right with you?'

Miranda took a quick shower herself and changed then wandered into the beautiful, spacious kitchen.

She ran a hand over the smooth work surface, her expression wistful. Who could dislike cooking in surroundings like these?

Pulling herself together, she opened the fridge, pulled out some chicken and vegetables and started chopping.

By the time Jake came back from his run she had garlic and ginger sizzling in a pan and all the ingredients prepared.

'Smells delicious. ' He sniffed the contents of the pan and smiled. 'Stir-fry?'

'Is that all right with you? It's just that it's quick and—'

'It's perfect. I'll be back down in three minutes if I skip a shave.'

She tossed chicken in the hot oil, added water to the noodles and was just assembling everything when he appeared in the doorway, dark hair still damp from the shower. Her heart lurched and her insides shifted alarmingly. Suddenly she wished he'd taken the extra few minutes to shave. Why did the stubble make him more attractive? Was it because he looked less like a respectable consultant and more…dangerous?

She permitted herself a wry smile. All men were dangerous. She knew that better than anyone. Giving herself a sharp talking-to, she rescued the plates that she had warming in the oven and lifted the pan from the heat.

'Sit down, it's ready.'

'I have to confess that I love it when you cook.' He leaned forward and gave an appreciative sniff. 'You're very creative in the kitchen.'

'I love your kitchen.' She served a generous portion onto his plate and then took a smaller helping herself. 'What about you?'

'I don't think it's one of my more obvious talents, but I manage.'

'Did your mother teach you the basics?'

'Are you joking?' He picked up his fork with a grin. 'My mother doesn't let anyone into her kitchen. My sister took pity on me after spending a weekend. Or, I suppose, if I'm honest, she took pity on herself. She was fed up with eating my idea of food. How did you learn? Did your mother teach you to cook?'

Her hand froze on the fork. It was a perfectly reasonable question. Hadn't she just asked him exactly the same one? 'No.' She couldn't keep the stiffness out of her tone. 'No, she didn't. I taught myself.'

His gaze lingered on her face for a moment and then he turned his attention back to his plate. 'You've always said that you don't have any family. What happened?'

She put her fork down, her appetite suddenly gone. 'I suppose I do have family.' She almost choked on the word and wondered why she didn't just lie. 'It's just that we're not in touch any more.'

'And you don't want to talk about it.' His tone was gentle, his blue eyes suddenly intent as he studied the tension in her face. 'All right, we'll talk about something else. Are you sleeping better now?'

She gave a faint smile. 'Hard not to in that amazing bed.'

'Another one of my sister's purchases. She always said that since she was my most frequent guest, she was going to buy herself a comfortable bed to sleep in.'

'You mentioned a niece and nephews, so she's obviously married.'

'Oh, yes. To an architect. They worked together on a project, that's how they met.' Jake leaned forward and helped himself to more food. 'And now I have two cheeky nephews and a baby niece.'

Envy sliced through her and she gave a puzzled frown. Why envy? She never envied families. She knew that they were rarely what they seemed. 'Do they live far away?'

'Far enough.' He leaned forward, picked up her fork and handed it to her. 'Eat, or I'll have to force-feed you.'

'I'm not that hungry.'

'Eat.'

Feeling thoroughly unsettled and not really understanding why, Miranda speared a thin strip of chicken and nibbled it. 'Why do you say far enough? You're obviously close to her.'

'We're twins,' Jake confessed. 'So, yes, we're close. A bit too close sometimes. She's inclined to meddle in my life.'

'Like decorating your house?'

'That sort of meddling I can live with.' He picked up his glass. 'What I don't like is her interference in my love life. She's always inviting me to dinner and introducing me to yet another of her recently divorced, unattached friends.'

Miranda couldn't help smiling. 'It's pretty hard to meet people. That sounds as good a way as any.'

'That's because you don't know my sister.' Jake suppressed a yawn and pushed his chair away from the table. 'Let's just say that her idea of my ideal woman and my idea of my ideal woman don't exactly coincide.'

'What's your ideal woman?' The moment she asked the question she wished she hadn't. His blue eyes lifted to hers and didn't shift.

'I'm looking at her.'

She gave a soft gasp and looked away. 'Jake…'

'I know what you're going to say next so I'll save you the breath and that way you can concentrate on clearing the food on your plate. You're going to say that I've only known you a short time, you're going to remind me that you're pregnant, just in case I'd forgotten, and then you're going to say that you're not interested in men because relationships always go wrong.'

It was so close to what she would have said that she gaped at him. 'Are you a mind-reader?'

'No, but I think I probably understand women better than most men.' He put his glass down on the table and leaned forward, his eyes still on her face. 'I have a twin sister and on top of that I spend every day talking to women at a time when they're at their most emotionally vulnerable. I have a pretty good idea what all your arguments will be, although I don't understand all your reasons because you don't trust me enough to tell me about your family. I'm hoping that, in time, that will change.'

She stared at him, stunned by what he was saying. 'I've told you about Peter.'

'Yes. But there's more and that's fine.' His tone was conversational, as if they were discussing nothing more serious than the weather. 'I'm willing to wait until you're ready to tell me.'

She was his ideal woman?

'Jake—'

'I'm not expecting a response to what I just said.' He stood up and flicked on the kettle. 'You asked me about my ideal woman and I told you.'

'But that's ridiculous.' Her voice was hoarse. 'Why would you be interested in me? What could I possibly have that you want?'

He turned to face her, dark lashes partially shielding the expression in his eyes. 'You don't have a very high opinion of yourself, do you, sweetheart?'

'I just don't see why a man like you would be interested in a woman like me. It doesn't make sense.'

'A man like me?' He raised an eyebrow in question. 'What sort of woman should a man like me be interested in, Miranda? Tell me. I'm intrigued to know.'

She took a deep breath. 'You're clever and good-looking, you don't need me to tell you that. You must have hopeful women trailing after you in droves. You certainly don't need someone as—' She broke off and hesitated. 'Complicated. You don't need someone as complicated as me.'

'You've worked with me for long enough to know that I thrive on complicated. I find routine and predictability unspeakably boring.' He smiled. 'Finish your dinner, Miranda, and stop worrying.'

She ignored her food. 'I need you to know that nothing is going to happen between us. Not ever. I just don't—'

'It's already happened and you know it.' His voice level, he spooned coffee into a cafetiere and picked up the kettle. 'There's a connection between us that we cannot possibly deny, but I understand that this is a big thing for you. So we'll just live with it for a bit and see where our relationship goes. I'm a patient man.'

'Patience has nothing to do with it and our relationship isn't going anywhere!' There was a note of panic in her voice. Why wasn't he listening to her? 'And what do you mean, it's a big thing for me? Given that you're in your thirties and single, it would seem a reasonable guess that a relationship is a big thing for you, too.'

With a sigh he leaned forward and removed the redundant fork from her numb fingers. 'It's big, yes. Of course it is. But I'm not scared of commitment. And I'm only single because I'm very, very choosy.'

'Have you ever been in love?' The question flew from her lips before she could stop it, and he paused for a moment.

'Yes.' His voice was quiet. 'Once.'

'What happened?'

His hesitation was fractional. 'Before I could say anything to her, she fell in love with another man. Chances are it wouldn't have made a difference if I'd spoken up earlier, but I made a promise to myself that if I ever met another woman who affected me as much as she did, I was going to tell her straight away.' He stabbed some food onto the fork and held it to her mouth. 'Eat, sweetheart. The baby needs it even if you don't.'

Why did the moment seem so impossibly intimate? The words he'd just spoken? Or the look in his sexy blue eyes or the fact that he was feeding her with her own fork? Whichever, she felt warm colour touch her cheekbones.

If he was choosy, why had he chosen her when she surely possessed none of the attributes that he was likely to look for in a prospective partner? She wanted to ask about the other woman. The woman he'd been in love with. But she was all too aware that she was probing into his life while revealing nothing about her own.

Why did she want to know about him?

Why was she interested?

Confused and unsettled, she took the fork from his hand and finished the food on her plate, knowing that he was right that she needed to eat. The fact that she didn't feel hungry was irrelevant.

It didn't matter that he was patient, she told herself as she chewed listlessly. And it didn't matter that he thrived on complications. It didn't even matter that he'd been honest and told her how he felt. Their relationship wasn't going anywhere. All right, so there was chemistry there, she'd be a fool to deny it. But chemistry didn't make a firm foundation for a relationship. Nothing did.

There was no way she'd risk ever exposing her child to a relationship that would inevitably go wrong.

Not even with a man as seductively attractive as Jake Blackwell.

CHAPTER EIGHT

WHY did he always fall in love with unobtainable women?

Working his way through a busy antenatal clinic the next morning, Jake found his attention wandering back to the previous evening.

Of all the women he'd ever met, he'd never encountered one as complex and wary as Miranda. How could a woman be both spirited and fiercely independent and yet touchingly vulnerable at the same time? What had happened in her past to score such deep wounds through her confidence? What had created that determined independence? Genetic make-up or the influence of family?

There was obviously something in her past, something that she refused to reveal. It was impossible to move forward, to counter her fears and anxieties, when he didn't understand the cause. He was determined to find out more about her. Determined to give her the confidence to open up and confide in him.

Patience, he reminded himself as he checked a set of blood results that one of the midwives had handed him. Patience. Hopefully, given time, she'd be able to trust him. In the meantime, he was going to make sure that they spent as much time together as possible.

Given that they were working and living together, it proved gratifyingly easy.

He was called up to the labour ward later that afternoon to see Paula Webb, a woman who had been on the ward for two days following premature rupture of membranes.

'I started having contractions an hour ago. You said you thought that would happen. But I'm only thirty-five weeks, Mr Blackwell,' she muttered, and Jake gave her shoulder a squeeze.

'It's going to be fine, Paula. The baby's heart rate is doing exactly what we like it to do. Try not to worry. I've told you before, that's my job.'

'But it's too early.' Paula screwed up her face as another contraction took hold. 'Is he going to end up in an incubator?'

'I can't promise that he won't,' Jake said honestly, 'but in all likelihood he'll be fine.'

'I really want to have a normal delivery.'

'And that's exactly what we want.' Jake glanced at Miranda, who was looking after Paula. 'She's six centimetres now. There's no reason why she should have any problems but I'm around if you need me.'

Paula looked at him anxiously. 'What time are you going off duty?'

Jake smiled at her. 'When you've had your baby. I'll see you later.'

He walked out of the room and Paula gazed after him. 'He is such a lovely man. One of my friends had Mr Hardwick and she didn't see him once, not once in her entire pregnancy, but I've seen Mr Blackwell almost every time and now he says he won't even go home until I've had the baby.'

'He's an excellent obstetrician.' Miranda sat with Paula and monitored her contractions for the rest of the afternoon, and by five o'clock she was fully dilated and pushing.

Miranda hit the buzzer to ask for some help and then opened a delivery pack just as Ruth and Jake walked into the room.

'Everything all right here?' Jake glanced at the foetal heart rate and gave a satisfied nod. 'That looks good. How are you doing, Paula? Tired?'

'Determined.' Paula screwed up her face and pushed again. 'You're not going to use those forceps on me or do a Caesarean section.'

'Glad to hear it,' Jake's tone was mild. 'I'm essentially lazy by nature, so I have no intention of doing any of those things unless strictly necessary.'

'I can see the head, Paula,' Miranda said. 'One more push and I think we're there.'

Jake looked at Ruth. 'Call the paediatrician. Just in case.' He spoke softly so that Paula couldn't hear, and Miranda knew that he was still slightly concerned about the baby. He was a man who didn't take any chances and she liked that.

The paediatrician arrived just as the shoulder was delivered and the baby slithered into Miranda's waiting hands.

Immediately the baby howled with indignation and Miranda placed him gently in Paula's waiting arms.

'Your son, Paula,' she said huskily, and Paula's eyes filled with tears.

'Oh, he's so beautiful…' She turned her head against her husband's shoulder and he held her as she started to sob.

'I love you, Mike.'

'I love you, too, babe. We're a proper family now.' Her husband's voice was choked and Miranda swallowed down the lump in her throat.

What was the matter with her? She wasn't usually so emotional. It was impossible to watch Paula and her husband and not wonder what it must be like to have that sort of love and support from someone.

Fortunately the delivery was far from over and she concentrated on the placenta and then on making Paula comfortable, blocking out the emotional scenes in the delivery room.

She was still holding herself firmly in check when she walked to the car with Jake.

'That was such a nice delivery. I'm so glad it went smoothly for Paula.'

'Me, too.'

'They're a lovely family.'

'Yes.'

He glanced towards her. 'No cynical comment? Aren't you going to tell me that he's probably having an affair with someone else and she's really pleased because she hates him anyway?'

'No.' She interrupted him and looked away, unaware of the soft brush of snow on her cheeks. 'No, I'm not going to tell you that. I think Paula's lucky. I'm glad nothing went wrong. I was worried it might. You knew it would be all right, didn't you?'

He shrugged. 'No one can ever be certain, of course, but, yes, I had a good feeling.'

'How? Why?' She looked at him helplessly, wishing she had his antennae. 'You just seem to know when something is about to go wrong and you're always there to sort it out before things reach crisis point.'

He pressed the button on his keys and unlocked the doors. 'That's not instinct, that's experience.'

'But don't you ever panic?' She slid into the car and

huddled her coat more closely around herself, suddenly feeling the cold. 'Things can go wrong in the blink of an eye in obstetrics but I've never seen you anything but calm.'

'Do I panic?' He started the engine and frowned thoughtfully. 'No. To be honest, I don't. I just see a problem and try and solve it.'

'You don't worry about the responsibility? Litigation?' Her teeth were chattering and she wished the car would warm up. 'These days everyone is trying to sue everyone.'

Jake laughed and reversed out of his parking space. 'Fortunately the UK isn't as bad as the US. In America they actually have groups of lawyers dedicated to suing us obstetricians for malpractice. Delightful.'

'How do you cope with the pressure?'

'I stay up to date, I listen to mothers and midwives, I don't ignore small warning signs because they invariably mean something and, having done all that, I relax. If you worry too much, you cease to be effective. Put my coat on. You're shivering.'

He noticed everything, she thought as she reached into the back seat for his coat and snuggled underneath it. 'Pregnant women are supposed to be hot all the time. I'm frozen.'

'Probably something to do with the fact that we had two inches of snow last night and you haven't eaten since lunchtime.' He turned the heat up in the car and took a sharp corner carefully, his hands steady on the wheel. 'You must be starving. Or, at least, I hope you are because you're about to be presented with a mountain of food.'

'We're going out?'

'I'm too tired to cook and I'm sick of pizza.' He suppressed a yawn. 'I'm taking you to dinner with some friends of mine. Christy is a wonderful cook. All we have to do is sit there and eat.'

She was horrified. 'But I can't just turn up to dinner! I don't know them and—'

'I know them.'

'But who are you going to say I am? How are you going to introduce me?'

He slowed the car as he drove down a narrow lane and into a huge driveway. 'A friend? My lodger? How would you like me to introduce you?' He switched off the engine, gave her a maddeningly placid smile and then climbed out of the car.

She followed him with a million questions on her lips, none of which she was able to ask because instantly the door opened and a beautiful red-headed woman stood there, smiling.

'I hope you're hungry because I've over-catered.'

'Those are the words I've been fantasising about all day. No lunch—big appetite. Hello, my angel, how are you?' Jake leaned forward and kissed the woman warmly. Miranda stopped dead, suddenly feeling all sorts of things that she didn't want to feel.

Who was the red-headed woman?

And why did she feel such a powerful urge to know?

Jake was perfectly entitled to have a girlfriend.

She was still trying to rationalise her thoughts when a handsome, dark-haired man appeared behind the woman. 'Unhand my wife, Blackwell.'

His wife?

The tension left Miranda and she had a wonderful evening. The conversation was lively and the food excellent. After tucking into salmon in a creamy herb sauce, Miranda helped clear the plates and was immediately trapped by Christy in the kitchen.

'So—where did you meet Jake?'

Miranda put the plates down on the table. 'We're working together,' she said carefully, deciding not to reveal the story of their Christmas Day meeting.

'That's nice.'

'I'm just his lodger. We're friends, nothing more,' Miranda said hastily, and Christy shot her a searching look as she pulled open the fridge door and removed a large fruit salad.

'Am I allowed to ask about the baby or is it a taboo subject?' Balancing the dish on one hand, Christy opened a drawer and rummaged for a large spoon with the other. 'If it's a tactless question, ignore me.'

'It's not tactless.' Miranda rubbed a hand over her abdomen. 'I'm seven months pregnant but I'm not with the father any more. It was a short relationship and he turned out to be married. I didn't know that until afterwards.' Somehow it was important to her that Christy knew the truth.

'Ouch. You poor thing.' Christy's voice was soft. 'That must be difficult for you. Still, at least you have Jake now.'

'Oh, no!' Miranda looked at her, startled. 'I don't have Jake. It isn't like that at all. He just—'

'He just can't take his eyes off you,' Christy finished with a womanly smile. 'I've never seen Jake so smitten and I've known him for a long time. I'm thrilled. Alessandro and I have been waiting for him to meet someone special.'

'I'm just his lodger.'

Christy's smile widened. 'To the best of my knowledge, Jake doesn't have any financial problems, so his reasons for wanting you to share his house must amount to more than a boost to his income.'

'He's been very kind to me, that's true, but—'

'You're the first woman he's ever brought to dinner here so that says a lot.' Juggling fruit salad and bowls, Christy walked back towards the kitchen door where she paused. 'Jake's had plenty of girlfriends but hardly any serious relationships. I just want you to know that. Be kind to him.'

Be kind to him?

And suddenly, without a shadow of a doubt, Miranda knew that Christy was the woman Jake had been in love with.

When? He didn't seem like the type to chase after a married woman.

Her own mind suddenly full of questions, she followed Christy back to the table and Jake looked up.

'You were a long time. Everything OK?'

'Fine.' Miranda managed a smile and Christy dished out fruit salad.

'My fault. I was delving into all her secrets. Woman's prerogative.'

Jake's gaze was thoughtful but he didn't pursue the subject until they were safely back in the car.

'I'm sorry if Christy upset you. It didn't occur to me that she'd ask you questions about your pregnancy, but perhaps it was inevitable.'

'She didn't upset me. She's really nice.'

'And Alessandro?'

Miranda thought about the dark-haired, brooding A and E consultant who had challenged his wife on so many points. 'A bit intimidating,' she said honestly.

'Most women find him irresistible.' Jake's tone was dry. 'Mediterranean heritage and all that.'

'She was the one, wasn't she?' Miranda couldn't not ask the question. 'Christy was the woman you were in love with.'

'What makes you say that?'

'Just something she said when we were in the kitchen.

Something about her caring about you.' She frowned slightly and Jake gave a smile.

'I should hope that she does care about me. That's what friends are supposed to do and, yes, Christy is the woman I was in love with, but it was a long time ago.'

'Does she know?'

'Yes.' Jake's voice was calm. 'Funnily enough, I told her just before Christmas.'

'This Christmas?'

'That's right. She and Alessandro were going through a bad patch. I wanted to remind her that what they had was special. Worth fighting for. I gave her up because I could see that they were perfect together. They still are.'

'You really believe in perfection? Isn't that rather romantic and idealistic? If you expect perfection then any relationship is doomed to fall apart.'

'I didn't say I believed in perfection, I said that they were perfect together. *Not* the same thing. In fact, I would say that it's their imperfections that make them so perfect.'

Miranda laughed. 'Now you've lost me.'

'Well, they both have fiery tempers and they tend to communicate by flinging plates at each other and a great deal of hand-waving and raised voices. Hardly perfect. But they understand each other. They love each other. It works for them.'

She stared at him. 'Ever considered being a marriage guidance counsellor?'

'No. Far too depressing. A large number of people who marry do so for all the wrong reasons. Those marriages cannot possibly be saved and then they're faced with all sorts of nasty, uncomfortable decisions, like whether they should stay together for the sake of the children, that sort of thing.'

'Why did Christy and Alessandro separate?'

Jake was silent for a moment. 'They didn't really. It was a classic case of miscommunication. I suppose they lost their way for a while. It happens all too easily. It's why it's so important to share things with your partner.' He glanced towards her. 'What do you think makes a relationship work?'

'I don't know many relationships that *have* worked so I'm not a good person to ask.' She looked out of the window and recognised the road. 'Oh—we're very near to my old flat. Can we just stop for a second so that I can drop my spare set of keys with the landlord?'

'Can't we just post them?'

'It will only take a minute—I'll just pop them through his letter-box.'

Jake took the necessary detour and pulled up outside the unwelcoming block of flats. 'Give me the keys—I'll do it. I don't want you anywhere near that place.'

'We'll go together. Look what happened last time you went on your own.' Miranda undid her seat belt. 'Someone needs to keep an eye on you. If he happens to be there, I don't want him hitting you again.'

His eyes gleamed with humour. 'What are you, my bodyguard?'

'Absolutely. Pregnant bodyguards are all the rage, haven't you heard?'

As it turned out, the landlord's flat was in darkness and they posted the keys through the door without mishap. They were just returning to the car when Miranda stopped dead.

'What was that?'

'What was what?' Jake gave a shiver and pulled his coat around him. 'It's freezing, Miranda. Get in the car, quickly.'

Miranda frowned and glanced around her. 'I heard something—a weird sound. I'm not sure what it was.'

'Probably the sound of my teeth chattering.' Jake grabbed her arm and tried to guide her towards the car but she shrugged him off.

'Wait. Listen…' She strained her ears and thought she heard a faint mewing sound. 'There. I heard it again.'

'Me, too—a cat, definitely a cat.'

Unconvinced, she turned in the direction of the sound. 'I don't know. It didn't sound much like a cat.'

'Miranda, for goodness' sake, it must be below freezing tonight and you're—'

'Wait there just for a minute.' Without giving him time to argue, she hurried back towards the building and into the stairwell. Lying on the ground was a pile of abandoned plastic shopping bags. There was no sign of a cat.

Miranda glanced around her, searching for the animal that had made the noise, but there was nothing. No sound and no movement. Presuming that whatever creature had made the noise had now found refuge somewhere warm, she turned to walk back to Jake when she heard the sound again.

This time there was no mistaking the sound and she ran back towards the plastic bags with a cry of horror. 'Oh, no! Jake—come quickly.'

'Miranda, I've told you that we need to—' He broke off as he saw what she was holding. 'Oh, my God.' His voice hoarse with disbelief, he dropped to his knees beside her. 'Is she breathing?'

Choked with horror, Miranda cuddled the tiny baby against her. 'Yes, but she's blue with cold. Oh, Jake, some-one's just left her here.'

'And quite recently, too, by the looks of it.' Jake's expression was grim as he glanced around them. 'She can't be more than a few minutes old.'

'We need to look for the mother.'

'We need to get that baby to hospital,' Jake said immediately, standing up and punching a series of numbers into his mobile phone. 'Put her inside your clothes, Miranda, next to your skin. Then go and sit in my car. I'll turn the heater up.'

Her hands shaking, Miranda did as he instructed, tucking the tiny baby against her chest and then closing her cardigan and her coat around her. 'She's freezing, Jake.'

'I've rung Special Care—they'll have a cot ready if we take her straight there.'

Miranda glanced back over her shoulder towards the darkness of the stairwell. 'But the mother—'

'The baby has to be the priority. Once she's safely in the hands of the paediatricians, we'll worry about the mother.' Jake slid the car into gear and drove quickly but carefully towards the hospital.

In no time at all the baby was in an incubator, surrounded by skilled staff all assessing her condition and speculating on her identity.

Miranda and Jake retreated to the tiny staffroom and were in the process of warming themselves up with hot coffee when the police arrived to take statements.

Jake spoke to them and then the consultant paediatrician walked into the room. 'She's very cold and dehydrated. It's a miracle you found her when you did. Any longer and she would have died of hypothermia without any doubt at all.'

The policeman frowned. 'She wasn't wrapped up at all?'

Miranda shook her head. 'Just inside plastic bags.'

'On a night like this?' The man's mouth tightened with disapproval. 'What must the mother have been thinking?'

Miranda put her coffee down on the table. 'I don't suppose she was thinking at all,' she said quietly, her voice shaking slightly. 'I expect she was too busy panicking.'

'Miranda's right.' Jake rubbed a hand over the back of

his neck, his eyes tired. 'Whoever the mother is, she was obviously terrified and completely alone. I'm guessing that we're talking about a teenager and she needs help, possibly urgently. We must try and find her.'

The policeman blinked and then cleared his throat. 'Of course, yes. You're right. We'll arrange for house-to-house enquiries and we'll contact the news stations and broadcast an appeal.'

The paediatrician looked at Miranda. 'The nurses wondered if you wanted to give her a name.'

'Me?'

'Yes. You found her.'

'Oh...' Miranda thought for a moment and then gave a faint smile. 'Bonnie. She's such a pretty little thing.'

'Bonnie, it is.' The policeman scribbled on his pad. 'I'll be in touch. If there's any change in the baby, give us a call.'

He left the room and Miranda turned to Jake, her expression urgent.

'We have to try and find her. The mother, I mean.'

His eyes met hers. 'Miranda, the police are going to do house-to-house enquiries and—'

'And the police have absolutely no idea what it's like to be a terrified teenager.' She glanced towards the paediatrician. 'Bonnie's in good hands now. We can't do any more here.'

Jake's eyes slid to her abdomen. 'It's late, you're tired—'

'I couldn't possibly sleep knowing that a poor teenager is out there somewhere, terrified and possibly bleeding.' Her hands clenched into fists and Jake's eyes rested on her face.

'You don't know it's a teenager.'

She knew he was wondering why her reaction was so extreme but she didn't care. And she certainly didn't intend to offer an explanation. 'Jake!'

'All right.' He muttered something else under his breath

and ran a hand through his hair. 'We'll go back to the flats
and have a look around. But just for an hour. After that we're
going home.'

Two police cars were parked outside the flats and Jake
pulled up behind them while Miranda turned up her collar
and wrapped her scarf round her neck.

'Do you have a torch?'

'Glove compartment.'

Miranda reached inside and tucked the torch in her
pocket. 'Come on. Let's go.' She climbed out of the car and
walked away from the flats, the beam of light from the torch
flickering in front of her.

'Go where, exactly?' Fastening the buttons of his coat,
Jake strode after her. 'Don't you think we should start by
looking around the flats?'

'That's what the police are doing and I just don't think
that's where she's going to be.'

'Why not? That was where she left the baby.'

'Because she wanted it to be found! But that doesn't
mean that *she* wants to be found. Think about it, Jake! If
she wanted her pregnancy to be made public then she would
have turned up at an antenatal clinic. It's far more likely
that she's avoiding people. Maybe she lives there, maybe her
parents live there, but at the moment I think she's huddled
in an alleyway somewhere, trying to work out what to do,'
Miranda reasoned as she crossed the road and walked away
from the flats. 'I don't believe she's in the flats.'

'You've missed your vocation.' Jake watched her with
fascination as he kept pace. 'Have you been watching crime
programmes in your spare time?'

'I don't have any spare time. I have work time and sleep
time.' Miranda stopped dead, her frown slightly impatient
as she tried to focus her mind. She looked around her,

searching for inspiration, trying to think like a frightened teenager. 'What would you do, Jake? Think. You leave your baby somewhere where you know it's going to be found because you want it to be found.'

'Do you?' Jake scratched his head, trying to follow her train of thought. 'Miranda, perhaps we should leave this to the police. They have—'

'The park.' Miranda grabbed his arm and hurried along the road. 'I bet she's in the park.'

'This place has a park?' Jake glanced around him doubtfully and Miranda looked at him impatiently.

'It's where all the teenagers hang out. I've seen them.' She was half running now, her torch winking in the darkness. She pushed open the gate and paused.

Jake peered into the soupy darkness. 'She's not here.'

'You don't know that.' Miranda let the gate go and walked further into the park. 'This is just the play area for the little ones. Further in are bushes and trees. That's where the teenagers hang out. It's where they go to smoke.'

'How do you know all this?'

But before she could answer, Jake grabbed her arm. 'Over there.' He kept his voice low and pointed. 'To the right. Do you see it?'

Miranda followed the direction of his gaze and nodded. 'It's a person. Sitting on the ground. Oh, Jake, I'm sure that's her—'

'It might be nothing. Just a drunk. Miranda, you stay here and I'll go and see who it is.'

'No way. How is she going to react to being approached by a six-foot-two man she doesn't know?' Miranda shrugged him off and hurried across to the figure. 'Hello?' She swung the torch and the light suddenly illuminated a blotched, miserable face.

'G-go away.' The girl's voice was weak. 'I wanna be on my own.'

Miranda immediately dropped the torch and went down on her knees. 'I'm from the hospital. A midwife. We found a baby near here. Was it yours, sweetheart?'

Perhaps it was the endearment or just the relief of being found, but the girl started to sob quietly and the sound had a desperate quality that tore holes in Miranda's heart.

'Don't cry.' She slid her arms round the girl and held her. 'Please, don't cry. We're going to help you. I promise we'll help you.'

'I didn't know what was happening!' The girl choked and sobbed, her words at times almost unintelligible as she talked. 'It hurt. It hurt so much and now the police are there.' The girl hiccoughed and wiped her nose on her sleeve. 'And I know the baby's dead and I'll go to prison. I killed her.'

'You won't go to prison. And she isn't dead. You haven't killed anyone.'

The girl was so distressed that she wasn't listening. 'She came out all blue and messy and I knew she was dead so I left her on the bags. I didn't know what else to do.'

'She isn't dead. Babies sometimes look a bit funny when they're born, that's all,' Miranda soothed, still holding the girl. 'She's beautiful and she's safely in hospital and that's exactly where you should go now. There are people there who will help you.'

Jake crouched down next to her and the girl shrank away, noticing him for the first time.

'Is he a cop?'

'No, he's a doctor. What's your name?'

The girl sniffed. 'Angie. Is the baby really OK?' Her voice was small and she sounded very, very young. 'I didn't want anything to happen to it. I was terrified when I thought it was dead.'

'She— The baby's a little girl. Angie,' Miranda's voice was gentle. 'Come to hospital with us now and we can make sure you're all right. Then someone will come and talk to you about the baby and you can decide what you want to do.'

'I can't keep her.' There was a note of panic in Angie's voice and Miranda hugged her.

'You're not in a fit state to make big decisions like that at the moment. You need help and I'm going to see that you get it. How old are you?'

'Sixteen.' Angie scrubbed at her face with the back of her hand. 'And I don't want to go to hospital. They'd tell my dad.'

'And would that be such a bad thing?'

'I dunno.' Angie sniffed again. 'I wanted to tell my mum but I was too scared. But now I just want to talk to her. I don't even care if she shouts at me. Will you ring her for me if I give you the number?'

'Let's get you to hospital,' Miranda said firmly, 'and once we know that you're fine, we'll help you with everything else.'

CHAPTER NINE

THE police were informed and Miranda stayed with Jake while he examined Angie and then waited until her parents arrived.

'Don't leave me,' Angie begged in a terrified voice, gripping Miranda's hand so tightly that she was given no choice in the matter. Not that she would have left.

Despite Jake's constant reminders that it was really late, that she was tired and should go home, she sat by Angie and talked to her, soothing and reassuring, unable to leave until she was sure that the young girl had someone with her who would care for her and offer the support she so badly needed.

The young teenager had calmed down and was sitting quietly when the door opened and a midwife came in, accompanied by Angie's mother.

Her hair was tangled and she'd obviously been woken from sleep and had dragged on the first clothes that came to hand. But there was no missing the worry in her eyes when she saw her daughter.

'Ange?'

Miranda felt a lump in her throat. What did the future

hold for both of them? How would they manage? What would happen to Bonnie, currently lying in her cot, unaware that her whole future lay in the balance?

'Mum?' Angie's voice shook and she sounded like a very young girl. Nothing like the mother of a child. 'I'm really, really sorry…'

'I don't believe this! What have you been doing?' Her mother covered her mouth with her hand and Angie's face crumpled.

'I'm sorry,' she sobbed, 'I'm so, *so* sorry. Please, don't be angry. Please, don't yell. I didn't mean it to happen. I didn't know it would happen.' Her sobs were so pitiful that Miranda felt her own eyes fill with tears and she held the shaking girl, ready to defend her if necessary.

But it wasn't necessary.

Her mother crossed the room in a flash, tears pouring down her cheeks as she went to her daughter.

'There…' Her voice was choked. 'Don't cry, pet. Mummy's here and everything is going to be all right. We'll sort everything out. You should have told me. You should have told me, you silly thing.'

Angie sobbed and sobbed, her face blotched and swollen with crying. 'I didn't know how. I thought you'd be so mad with me. Dad's going to kill me.' She clung to her mother who shook her head slowly.

'Your dad's not going to kill anyone. He's just worried about you, love. We all are. I wish you'd told us. How did I not notice?' She glanced at Miranda with helpless confusion on her face, still visibly shocked by the circumstances. 'I thought she was putting on some weight so I've been encouraging her to eat a bit less, but it just never occurred to me…'

'You probably weren't looking for it,' Miranda said quietly, and the older woman gave a weary smile.

'Being a parent is the hardest thing in the world.' She stroked her daughter's hair with a gentle hand and instinctively Miranda knew what she was thinking. That her daughter was now a parent, too.

Angie sniffed. 'I don't know what to do, Mum.'

'What do you want to do, love? Whatever you choose, we'll support you.'

Miranda felt warmth and admiration spread through her. Lucky Angie, she thought to herself. Her mother wasn't trying to take over or dictate. She was trying to help her daughter make grown-up decisions by herself.

'I want to keep her.' Angie looked at her mother uncertainly. 'That's stupid, isn't it? I haven't even seen her yet but I know I want to keep her. When I thought she was dead I couldn't stop crying and now I know she's alive—'

'Why is it stupid?' Her mother straightened her shoulders. 'She's our flesh and blood. There'll be enough willing helpers, that's for sure. Of course we're going to keep her. She's family.'

It was two o'clock by the time Jake managed to persuade Miranda to leave, and he was worried by how drained and exhausted she looked.

'Are you all right? You haven't said a word since we left the hospital.' Knowing that she hadn't eaten since lunchtime, Jake made a mug of hot chocolate because he knew she loved it. 'Drink this and then go to bed. I've already agreed with Ruth that you're having tomorrow off. And just to make sure that you don't lift a finger, I'm having tomorrow off, too. After tonight's events, I think we both deserve it.'

'OK.' She didn't seem to be listening to him. And she didn't touch the hot chocolate—just stared into the mug and watched a skin form on the milk.

Deciding that sleep was the priority, he gently eased the mug from her hands and pulled her to her feet.

'You need to go to bed.' He led her up the stairs, opened her bedroom door and gently nudged her inside. 'You did brilliantly with Angie, by the way. She's going to be all right now.'

'Is she? What about the baby?'

He frowned. 'The baby is doing well, Miranda. Thanks to the fact that you discovered her so quickly, she's going to be fine.'

'But what sort of life will she have?' Miranda turned to look at him and her dark eyes were huge and sad. 'Goodnight, Jake.' She closed the door, leaving him on the outside battling with a powerful inclination to go back inside and drag her into his arms.

He stared at the closed door, trying to work out what was going on in her mind.

What had she meant by that comment about the baby?

He ran a hand over the back of his neck, trying to decide what to do. She was tired, he reasoned, and pregnant women were always more emotional when they were tired.

The best thing was for her to have a good night's sleep.

They could talk in the morning.

He strolled into his bedroom and glanced at the clock with a humourless laugh. It was already morning.

He went to bed and woke suddenly to darkness and the sound of noises coming from the kitchen.

Miranda?

Tugging on his jeans, he padded downstairs.

She was sitting at the table with her head in her hands.

Her dark hair flopped forward, hiding her face from his view, but he knew from the movement of her shoulders that she was crying. He swore softly under his breath and went straight to her, dragging out the chair next to her and sitting down.

'Miranda?' He put a hand on her shoulder and gave it a gentle shake. 'Sweetheart, what's wrong?'

For a long moment she didn't answer and then she lifted her head and the pain in her eyes shocked him.

'I just k-keep thinking about B-Bonnie.' She hiccoughed and he frowned slightly as he stroked her shoulders gently.

'Bonnie? But she's fine, angel. Doing really well. Thanks to you.'

Miranda shook her head and tears spilled down her cheeks. 'She's *not* fine. She has a mother too young to look after her and no father. What is her life going to be like?' She scrubbed the palm of her hand over her cheek and he frowned, helpless to know what to say.

'Angie seemed like a really nice girl and her mother was—'

'Angie is nothing more than a child, Jake!' She interrupted him, her voice fierce and her eyes glistening with more tears. 'A child! She should be playing with her friends, doing exams and dreaming about her future, instead of which she's going to be living the life of an adult. Do you have any idea what it's like, being a mother at the age of sixteen?' Her voice shook. 'Having a baby is daunting at any age but at sixteen it's nothing short of terrifying. So much responsibility when you're nothing more than a child yourself. And your whole life is suddenly violently rearranged. You can't do any of the things you should be doing. Instead of studying, you're changing nappies. Instead of going out with friends, you're pushing a pram. So you become isolated and lonely and no one really understands because all the teenagers you know are studying or partying and all the mothers you know are in their thirties, married with other children. No one is like you.' She broke off, her chest rising and falling, and he studied her face and wondered.

Even for an extremely tired, pregnant woman, her reaction was a little too emotional. 'We're not talking about Angie and Bonnie any more, are we?' He reached across the table and grabbed the box of tissues that was stacked on top of a pile of unopened post.

She took the tissue he offered her, blew her nose and then looked away. 'Ignore me—it's been a long and stressful night. I should probably go back to bed.' Her nose was blocked up, her dark lashes were damp from crying and he just wanted to cuddle her.

'You're never going to sleep in this state. You need to get it off your chest and then perhaps you'll be able to relax. Talk to me, Miranda. Tell me what's on your mind.' He hesitated and then decided to take a risk. 'I'm wondering why you care so much and I'm wondering why you know so much about it. Did it happen to you? Were you that mother you described so eloquently?'

'The mother?' She stared at the table and then at him. 'I wasn't the mother, Jake. I was the baby.'

His was silent for a moment, his eyes fixed on her pale face. 'You're—'

'My mother had me at sixteen. I was the baby.'

It made sense, of course. The reason she'd been so desperate to find Bonnie's mother. The way she'd understood Angie's situation. 'You were abandoned?'

Miranda reached for a tissue and blew her nose hard. 'I was luckier than Bonnie. My mother put me in a box covered in towels. Apparently I was in quite a good condition when I was found. She even wrote a note.'

Something twisted inside him but he fought the impulse to drag her into his arms. He knew that, right now, she needed to talk. 'And they traced your mother?'

She nodded. 'Oh, yes. It was all very embarrassing for my grandparents. Treasured only daughter suddenly going off the rails. They'd had such high hopes for her. She was top in her class and very pretty. The world was out there, just waiting for her to conquer it. Only she made a mistake and I came along.' She was silent for a moment, thoughtful. Then she gave a bright smile that was entirely false. 'But they did the right thing. They took me in and brought me up. I lived with them until my mum married Keith.'

'Was he your father?'

'No. Mum never said who my father was. Maybe she didn't know. Have you any idea how that feels?' She looked at him, her expression strangely blank. 'Sometimes I look in the mirror and I search for him. I think to myself, Are those his eyes? Do I have his mouth? Having no idea where you came from is a strange feeling.'

'But your mum did get married.'

'Oh, yes, she did very well for herself. Keith was a barrister. Great job. Public figure. Very well respected. On the outside, we looked like the perfect family.' The bitterness in her tone was unmistakable and Jake looked at her, a feeling of foreboding building inside him.

'And on the inside? Tell me about your stepfather.'

'I think he loved my mum. Or at least, his version of love.' She yanked another tissue out of the box and blew her nose again. 'Unfortunately he didn't feel the same way about me. I suppose I was a constant reminder of my mum's mistake.

The one ugly blot on the otherwise perfect canvas of her life. Everything I did was wrong. He had a hideous temper.'

Jake felt his shoulders tense. 'How terrible. Are you saying he shouted at you? Or did he...?'

'Hit me? Was that what you wanted to ask?' She finished his unspoken question and gave a wan smile. 'Oh, yes. Often. But funnily enough that didn't upset me as much as his contempt. He so obviously couldn't stand the sight of me and that really, really hurt.'

'Didn't anyone know?'

'I didn't want to tell my friends, if that's what you mean. And none of them would have believed me anyway. They all thought I was so lucky.' She blew her nose again. 'Big house. Fancy holidays. Keith was capable of putting on a very impressive act when he had to but he was always so unpredictable I didn't dare take anyone home in case he lost his temper. So gradually I became isolated. They thought I was a snob who didn't want to mix with them. I didn't know how to make myself popular.' She twisted the tissue. 'And I suppose, if I'm honest, I didn't think I was very likeable. Keith had a way of making you feel pretty rotten about yourself.'

Jake let out a long breath and ran a hand over his face. The thought of how she must have suffered made his blood heat to dangerous levels. 'So that's why you were so appalled when I hit your landlord.'

She gave a wan smile. 'I suppose so. I'm not great with violence of any sort.'

Jake struggled to control his shock. She didn't need him to be shocked, she needed him to be supportive. 'Couldn't your mother do anything?'

'My mother didn't want to do anything to wreck her new-found respectability. She was moving in circles that she'd

considered totally out of her reach. I mean, imagine it...'
She suddenly sounded older than her years. 'She left school
at sixteen, pregnant, and here she was, married to a rich
barrister. Quite an achievement, and my mother was very
achievement-focused. All she really cared about was how it
looked to other people. Marrying Keith was a way of wiping
out the mistakes of her past.'

'She condoned his behaviour?'

'She said he was a very busy man with a stressful job and
I ought to try not to annoy him.'

Jake gritted his teeth. 'You didn't tell anyone else? Your
teachers? Your GP?'

'My GP was his squash partner.' Miranda shook her head.
'No. I just tried not to annoy him. The trouble was, I annoyed him by just being me. So I learned to make myself
as invisible as possible and I became very self-reliant.' She
gave a tiny shrug. 'It's history now. Please, don't think I
spend all day, every day thinking about it. It's over. It was
over a long time ago and I refuse to be a victim.'

'But clearly you don't see them any more.'

She shook her head. 'I left home as soon as I could and
they didn't try and stop me. It's affected me, of course it has.
I suppose a psychologist would say that's why I got involved
with Peter. Searching for a father figure.' She gave a smile
of wry self-mockery. 'Ironic, really. In his own way he was
about as good a father figure as Keith. In my head I've in-
vented this mythical dad.'

'And what's he like?'

At first she looked surprised by the question and then she
gave a little shrug. 'Ridiculously perfect. He adores his children so much that he's prepared to put them first and he actually enjoys spending time with them. He delights in their
achievements and he wants to shield them from all harm.'

She sat back in her chair, her expression shifting from tense to dreamy. 'And when I imagine him, he has this look in his eyes. Love, I suppose.' She sounded so wistful that Jake felt an ache building deep inside him. Obviously she'd never known the deep, unconditional love of a parent.

'So what would a psychologist say about your relationship with me?'

'We don't have a relationship.'

'No?' It gave him some satisfaction to see her drop the tissue. Her hand stilled.

'Jake, I—'

'I'm glad you told me because now I understand why you keep backing away. You don't believe that I'll be able to love your baby the way I love you. You don't believe I can love unconditionally.'

'You don't love me. Please, stop saying that.' She covered her face with her hands. 'You can't possibly love me.'

'Why not? Because your stepfather didn't love you? Because your mother didn't stand up for you? That doesn't make you unlovable, sweetheart, it just makes you unlucky. But luck can change and it's time yours did.'

Her hands dropped and she turned to look at him. 'Jake...'

Unable to help himself, he brought his mouth down on hers. Her lips, impossibly soft and sweet, parted under the insistent pressure of his. He felt the hot burn of arousal scorch his body but held himself back, not wanting to rush her, aware that she was still deeply upset and extremely vulnerable. If he'd stopped to think then he probably would have admitted to himself that it wasn't the best time to kiss her, but somehow thinking seemed impossible. He slid a hand into her silky hair and kept the kiss gentle and exploratory. He tasted hesitation and fear. Sensed her reluctance.

And then she slid her arms round his neck and kissed him back, her tongue touching his.

The kiss was mindless, endless, and then she pulled back slightly, her dark eyes clouded.

'We shouldn't be doing this.'

He stroked a hand over the smoothness of her cheek. 'If you can give me one good reason why we should stop, I'll give it my full consideration.'

'I'm pregnant.'

'That's not a reason. You'll have to do better than that.' His lips brushed against hers and he felt her shiver of response.

'My New Year's resolution was to stop believing in romance.' Her voice was breathy and feminine and slid over his nerve endings, increasing his arousal several notches.

'New Year was weeks ago.' He nibbled at her lower lip. 'It's time you broke your resolution.'

'Jake…' She groaned his name against his mouth and he felt aching, tearing claws of lust drag through his loins. He couldn't remember feeling this desperate since he'd been a teenager and suddenly he felt his control slipping.

'Come upstairs with me, Miranda.' He stroked her hair away from her face and kissed her again. 'Now.'

'Yes.' She rose to her feet and he scooped her up into his arms, ignoring her soft gasp of surprise and protest.

'Put me down! You'll slip a disc or something. I weigh a ton.'

'You don't weigh anything,' Jake growled as he carried up the stairs to his bedroom. The curtains were open and moonlight shone through the windows, casting a gentle light over the room. 'You should be heavier than this. You definitely need to eat more. I'm going to devote tomorrow to feeding you.'

Her arms tightened around his neck as he laid her in the centre of the bed. 'What about tonight?'

'That's devoted to something else entirely.' He came down next to her and brought his mouth down on hers, forcing himself to take it slowly. Part of him wanted to strip her naked and take her fast but he knew that she deserved so much more than that. She deserved to be well and truly loved. So he kept his mouth gentle and his hands slow.

He felt her body shift under his, felt the urgency of her own response and removed her top in a smooth movement. Her breasts were perfectly rounded and he lowered his head with a groan of masculine appreciation.

'You're so beautiful.'

'I'm so fat.'

Even though he was aching and throbbing with need, her tiny plea for reassurance was so entirely feminine that it made him smile. 'Sweetheart—do I need to tell you how much I want you?'

She lifted a hand to his face and there was uncertainty in her eyes. 'Do you?'

'Can't you tell? I wanted you from the first moment I saw you sitting by that frozen lake. You looked at me and I was lost.' He moved his body so that she could be left in no doubt as to his own state of arousal and dragged the tips of his fingers over her nipple.

She arched towards him, her mouth damp from his kisses, her dark hair tumbled around her shoulders. She was all woman and her beauty drove all words from his head.

He didn't know how to tell her how he felt.

He only knew how to show her, so he lowered his head and his mouth touched first one breast, then the other. Then his tongue flickered out and he licked and teased before sucking her into the warmth of his mouth. He heard her soft gasp, felt her hands slide into his hair and grip.

He felt her body shift restlessly, felt the stroke of her leg against his, urging him on, but he discovered that he was no longer in a hurry. Who, in their right mind, would want to rush something so impossibly perfect?

He ignored her soft whimper and her searching hands and took his time, removing the rest of her clothes and his and then sliding his mouth down her silken skin, lingering on the curve of her abdomen before moving lower still to discover the heart of her.

He heard her faint gasp of protest turn to a moan of ecstasy as extended his voyage of discovery and pushed the boundaries of intimacy.

'Jake, please…' His name was a sob on her lips. 'Please…'

He knew what she wanted—*knew what she was asking for*—but he wanted more from her, wantcd to push her to the very edge of sanity, and he used his fingers and mouth to do exactly that, his own arousal heightened by her cries and the fierce reaction of her body as he pushed her through clouds of sexual excitement to a powerful climax that rocked her whole body.

Only when the violent spasms finally ceased did he slide up the bed and roll onto his back. He was so aroused he thought he might explode, and he lay for a moment, trying to focus on something other than Miranda. Trying to regain some semblance of control.

And she was silent, too, eyes closed, her lashes dark against her pale cheeks.

'Miranda?' Worried about the lengthy silence, he turned his head towards her. 'Are you all right?'

'I'm not sure.' And then her eyes opened and she gave a slow, satisfied smile. Her gaze fixed on his, she slid a leg over him and then sat up, her cheeks flushed and her dark hair falling forward. 'Is it OK to do this?'

There was a purposeful, seductive gleam in her dark eyes that he found intensely arousing. Dimly aware that she'd asked him a serious question, Jake sucked in a breath and forced himself to think like an obstetrician. 'It's fine,' he groaned. 'I'll be gentle, I promise. Sweetheart, have I told you that you're incredible? And beautiful?'

Despite the intimacy of their position, her smile was shy. 'Do you need glasses?'

'No, I need *you*.' He slid his hands over her hips, positioned her carefully and felt the silken heat of her womanhood tease the tip of his arousal. Afraid that he might explode within seconds of entering her, he slowed the pace, controlling her movements, refusing to allow her the satisfaction she so clearly craved.

'Jake—I need to...' Her breathing shallow, she pushed his hands away impatiently and sank onto him, taking him deep inside her, destroying his plans to take her gently and carefully.

Heat exploded through his sensitised body and he gave a harsh groan and opened his mouth to tell her to slow down, but she lowered her head and kissed him, her delicate tongue coaxing his into a dance every bit as intimate as the rest of their encounter.

Struggling to find his customary control, Jake tried to hold her hips but she grabbed his wrists and anchored them above his head, moving with a slow erotic rhythm that reduced his world to nothing but sensation.

Dimly he knew that this wasn't how he'd intended it to happen. He'd intended to orchestrate the whole thing but somehow she'd taken the initiative.

Reluctantly her mouth left his and she sat up, her hair

sliding over her bare shoulders as she moved over him with the smooth grace of a dancer. The heat in his loins reached intolerable levels and he tried to warn her that she really, really needed to slow down, but the only sound that came from his mouth was a hoarse groan of encouragement. Aware of her own soft cry of release, he felt her body spasm around his and he exploded inside her with propulsive force, driven past the point at which he might have been able to regain his slippery hold on control.

She woke to find him watching her.

'Good morning.' His voice was husky and deep and he leaned forward to deliver a lingering kiss to her mouth. 'You slept well. I'm pleased. How are you feeling?'

Unsettled by the look in his eyes, she rolled onto her back. 'Fine.' Shy? Embarrassed? She thought of all the things she'd told him, *the things they'd done…*

'Fine? Miranda, do not, for one moment, think that you're going to be allowed to pretend that last night didn't happen.'

'I know it happened.' How could she not, when the memories were still so clear in her head?

'And do you also know that I love you?' He spoke softly and then raised himself up on one arm and looked down at her with a gentle smile. 'You're beautiful and good and I want you to be my wife. And, just in case you think I say those words to all the girls, you ought to know that I've never said that to anyone in my life before now.'

His wife?

Her stomach dropped and she looked into those sexy blue eyes and wished that her life wasn't filled with mountains to conquer. No matter how much she loved him, and she did love him, she'd never be able to say yes. She owed it to the baby to refuse him.

'No, Jake.'

'It isn't difficult, Miranda. All you have to do is say you love me, too, and I know you do.'

He was so confident, she thought enviously. Not arrogant, just very sure of himself.

'I care about you,' she said finally, her voice slow and still slightly husky from sleep. 'Of course I do. You've been an amazing friend to me, Jake.'

If she confessed that she loved him, there was no way he'd take no for an answer.

'Friend?' One dark brow lifted as he studied her face. 'Last night had absolutely nothing to do with friendship, Miranda.'

'Last night should never have happened. I was tired and emotional. I told you things that I've never shared with anyone and I probably shouldn't have said it to you but…' She tried to look away from him but he caught her chin in gentle fingers so that she was forced to look at him.

'Are you saying that I took advantage of you?'

'No.' She shook her head. 'I'm saying that I needed comfort and you—' She broke off and he sighed.

'Miranda, last night wasn't about comfort. Comfort was the box of tissues and the hug I gave you in the kitchen. Comfort was the hot chocolate that you didn't drink before you went to bed. What we shared last night had nothing whatsoever to do with comfort. It was hot sex and you know it.'

Memories heated her body and she closed her eyes tightly, trying to block it out and return to reality. *The reality of her life.* 'For goodness' sake, Jake—'

'Stop right there.' He put his fingers over her mouth. 'If this is this is the part where you remind me that you're pregnant, I don't want to hear it. I haven't forgotten that fact, angel. I love the fact that you're pregnant and I'm waiting for you to say that you'll marry me so that I can spend the next few weeks getting used to the idea of finally being a father. I'm aiming to be that ridiculously perfect dad that you've always dreamed about. I'm ready to adopt the baby as my own. I'm ready to love it as my own, if you'll let me.'

Miranda lay there, staring temptation in the face. She loved him, she knew that without a doubt. She loved him for the man he was. But nothing changed the fact that she was having another man's child.

And she, better than anyone, understood the implications of that.

'It would always come between us,' she whispered, 'if not now, then later. He or she might be naughty and you'd be fed up.'

His mouth tightened and she saw a flash of anger in his eyes. 'Let's get one thing straight right now—I'm not your stepfather and I never will be. Neither am I the man who fathered your baby, which I'm actually glad about because he doesn't sound like much of a human being. I love you, Miranda, and I love the baby, too, because it's part of you. And that love is unconditional. Family life isn't always smooth and doesn't come with guarantees, I know that. And all children are naughty sometimes, that's what childhood is all about. And I'm sure that sometimes I *will* get fed up because I'm human just like you, but I'm never going to regret being a father to the baby, I'm not going to bail out, if that's what worries you, and I'm not going to hit anyone. Unless someone threatens a member of my family, that isn't my style.'

She knew from the dangerous gleam in his eyes that he was thinking about her landlord and something shifted inside her. *He'd defended her.*

'I know it seems simple to you, but I can't risk it, Jake.'

She squeezed her eyes tightly shut, unable to watch the pain in his eyes. She told herself that she was doing them both a favour. She was saving three people from greater hurt. 'We should never have done what we did last night because now our relationship is awkward. I'll move out. I should have found somewhere long ago but it was so comfortable here and...' And she'd loved being with Jake. She left the words unspoken and rose out of bed, determined to make it to the bathroom before she made a fool of herself.

She seemed to spend her entire life crying at the moment, she reflected as she bolted the door behind her and sank down onto the edge of the bath.

She was doing the right thing, she knew she was.

But if she was doing the right thing, why did it feel so hard?

CHAPTER TEN

OVER the next week or two, the weather grew colder still and Miranda found it impossible to feel anything but tired and miserable.

She thought she'd be relieved to give up work but once she did she found that she missed the friendship of her colleagues on the labour ward. She felt as though she'd made lifetime friends. For the first time in her life she felt as though she was home.

But home was becoming a touchy subject.

She couldn't carry on living with Jake so she'd been desperately scouring the local paper for flats. She'd found one that would have been all right, but the landlord had said that it wasn't available until the spring and she couldn't wait that long. She needed somewhere now.

At this rate she was going to be living with Jake when the baby arrived, she thought as she trawled through the paper once again for possibilities.

Not that he made things awkward. On the contrary, he was extremely kind to her but somehow that just made it worse.

She was drinking coffee and summoning up the energy to go and see a small flat a mile away from Jake's house when there was a knock on the door.

She opened it to find Christy standing there with a basket in her hand.

'I'm playing Little Red Riding Hood,' she said cheerfully, handing Miranda the basket and walking past her into the house. 'I was baking with my daughter Katy this morning and we thought you might like some. I remember what it was like when I was almost due. I was starving hungry but I couldn't summon up the energy to cook anything. There's bread, scones, some cheese from the deli and some chutney we made last summer from the apples in our garden.'

Miranda carried the basket through to the kitchen. 'That's really kind of you.'

'Not that kind.' Christy shrugged off her coat and dropped it over the chair. 'I actually had an ulterior motive for coming here. Can I put the kettle on?'

'Help yourself.' Miranda put the basket on the table and looked at her warily. 'What's your ulterior motive?'

For a moment Christy didn't answer and her back was towards Miranda so it was impossible to read her face. She filled the kettle and then she turned. 'I'm worried about Jake.'

'You're worried about him?' Miranda felt a vicious stab of fear. 'Why? What's happened?'

Christy frowned. '*You've* happened. He's in love with you and I gather it isn't reciprocated. He's thoroughly miserable. Crotchety and short-tempered, thoroughly unlike our easy-going Jake. '

Miranda bit her lip. 'I know he thinks he's in love with me, but—'

'If you're suggesting that Jake doesn't know his own

mind, maybe you don't understand him as well as you think you do. I could help you out there.' Christy dipped her hand into the basket and helped herself to one of her own scones. 'Jake knows exactly what he wants in life and he's never wrong. He doesn't change his mind about things. He knew almost from day one that he wanted to be an obstetrician and he was right. It's the perfect specialty for him. And it's the same with women. He doesn't fall in love easily.'

'He was in love with you.'

'Yes.' Christy's voice was calm as she split the scone with a knife and spread each half with butter. 'I think he was, for a short while. And that's one of the biggest compliments I've ever been paid because Jake doesn't fall in love easily so when he does, it's a really big thing. And he's in love with you.'

'Maybe he is.' Miranda sat down on the nearest chair. 'But I'm having another man's baby.'

'I know about that.' Christy put half the scone on a plate and pushed it towards her. 'Eat. Jake's worried that you're not eating enough so I said I'd take charge of your calorie intake between now and delivery.'

Miranda smiled. 'No one has ever fussed over me before the way he does.'

'No?' Christy's eyes were gentle. 'Then make the most of it. Grab it while you can. He wants the baby, Miranda. He wants the baby as much as he wants you, can't you believe that?'

'I believe that he thinks that's the case.' Miranda stared at the scone on her plate. 'But people don't know how they're going to react. The baby isn't his. Nothing can ever change that.'

'And he doesn't want to. Jake is the most balanced, level-headed guy you could ever hope to meet. Have you ever seen him panic?'

'No. No I haven't. He's always Mr Super Cool.'

Christy nodded. 'He's a guy who knows who he is and knows what he wants. And he wants you and the baby. Think about it. Think about what you might be turning down.'

'What if, two years from now, he's tired of having a lively toddler around the house?'

Christy looked at her for a long moment and then stood up, a sad smile on her face. 'If you have to ask me that question, you obviously don't know Jake at all,' she said softly as she picked up her coat. 'He's a good man. A hell of a catch, frankly. You should remember that. Of all the women he's ever dated, you're the one he wants. Wow. Be flattered. And now I need to get going because it's snowing again and Alessandro worries about me when the roads are bad. Don't get up. You look tired. Eat your scone and I'll see myself out.'

Miranda sat in the kitchen, staring out of the window as the snow fell and darkness closed in. Jake had phoned earlier to say that he was going down to A and E to deal with an emergency and he was likely to be very late. And she missed him. Even in such a short time she'd become used to the life they'd led. She'd enjoyed their routine of working together and living together. Now it was just the living and soon it wouldn't even be that because she intended to move into a new flat in the next two weeks.

Outside the wind whistled around the house and she couldn't stop thinking about everything that Christy had said about Jake. Phrases kept running through her head.

'A hell of a catch.'

'You're the one he wants.'

And he was the one she wanted, too.

And suddenly she knew that Christy was right. Jake was nothing like her father and nothing like Peter. He was strong and sexy, kind and tough, all at the same time. And she was crazy about him.

And Christy was right—he did know what he wanted out of life.

And he wanted her and the baby, so why was she turning down the chance of happiness when she was madly in love with him? When she knew he'd make a wonderful partner?

A slow warmth spread through her and she smiled. She was going to talk to him. As soon as he came home from work. She was going to tell him that she'd changed her mind. That she wanted him to adopt the baby. *That she wanted them to be a family.*

Wanting to look her best, she washed and dried her hair, changed into a loose, comfortable dress and made herself a drink.

But there was still no sign of Jake. And she was desperate to talk to him. Suddenly it seemed imperative that he know how she felt.

Feeling jumpy and restless, she stood up and paced around the kitchen and then moved into the living room. She was standing there, staring at the photograph of Jake rolling in the snow with his two nephews, when the first pain hit her.

She gave a cry of shock and clutched at her abdomen, winded by the pain and unable to move. Gradually it eased and she inched her way towards the sofa, trying to talk rationally to herself.

She wasn't due for another month. These were just more Braxton-Hicks' contractions, signs that her body was preparing for labour. She'd felt them before, although never with such severity. The pain would fade and then everything would be fine.

It took less than two minutes for her to realise that everything was far from fine. Less than two minutes for another pain to tear through her body, this time so severe that she was unable to breathe or cry out. She dropped to her knees, closed her eyes and forced herself not to panic.

She was fairly sure that she was in labour.

Fairly sure?

If she hadn't been so frightened, she would have laughed. She was a midwife, for goodness' sake. And she didn't even know whether she was in labour.

Phone.

She needed to get to the phone.

Trying to be calm and rational, she waited for the pain to fade and then staggered over to Jake's phone, only to discover that the line was dead.

Realising that she was going to have to do this on her own, she grabbed some cushions from the sofa and settled herself on the floor to await the next pain.

It would be all right, she told herself, rubbing a hand over her stomach and feeling the tightening against her hand. This time when the pain came she was ready for it and she closed her eyes and breathed the way she'd taught countless pregnant women to breathe in the antenatal classes she'd run.

The pain thundered through her, relentless in its intensity, and she suddenly knew why women were encouraged to have someone with them when they gave birth. You needed someone on the outside. You needed someone who was one step removed from what was happening. You needed love and support—

'Miranda?'

Her eyes flew open and she saw Jake standing in the doorway. His dark hair was dusted with snow and a long coat emphasised his powerful physique. A rush of cold air blew into the room before he closed the door firmly.

'Labour...' she gasped, and then closed her eyes and tried to concentrate on her breathing as another pain hit.

'How far apart?' He was on his knees beside her, his hands freezing as they slid over her abdomen, feeling the contraction. 'When did it start?'

She had to wait for the pain to fade before she could speak. 'Not long ago. And hardly any time apart. I think it's coming, Jake. I know it's a month early, but I'm definitely in labour.'

'You should have called me.'

'Phone not working.' She closed her eyes as she felt another pain hit and then swell to almost unbearable levels before fading back again. But this time she wasn't on her own. This time she felt a strong arm round her shoulders as Jake held her and praised her.

The moment the pain had passed he reached for the phone and then cursed softly and slammed it down again. 'The line must be dead and I've got no signal on my mobile.'

She looked at him with fear in her eyes. 'Jake...'

'Don't worry about it.' He shrugged his broad shoulders out of his coat. 'How do you feel about a home birth?'

'Nervous?'

'That's not very flattering.' He teased her as he stripped off his jumper and pushed up his sleeves. 'I'm an obstetrician. This is my territory.'

'No, it isn't.' She closed her eyes and shifted her position, ready for the next pain. 'You deal with complications. This is supposed to be a normal birth. You obstetricians don't know anything about normal births.'

'Well, I'm sure I'll struggle through and if it all seems a bit bewilderingly normal, I'll just have to turn it round and deliver it as a breech.'

Despite the pain, she managed a laugh. 'You're mad, do you know that?'

'Relax, Miranda. Everything is going to be fine.' He stroked her hair away from her face with a gentle hand and then switched into consultant mode. 'Another contraction?' He took her hand and eased her into a better position, talking to her gently until the wave of pain receded. Then he tried both phones again and shook his head. 'Nothing. Miranda, I think I'd better examine you. I need to know how many centimetres dilated you are. If this baby is about to arrive, I need to boil kettles and do all the other useless and pointless things they do in the movies.'

It was impossible to panic in the face of his humour and confidence.

'You can't examine me, it's too embarrassing. Oh, Jake...' She screwed up her face and sobbed with pain. 'Is it supposed to feel like this? It's agony.' Another pain hit and she was hit by a wave of nausea. 'I feel sick...'

He reached for a decorative ceramic bowl and placed it in front of her. 'Don't worry about it, just keep breathing.' His voice was calm and steady. 'Miranda, I think you're in transition.'

He was behaving like a cool professional while all she wanted was for him to hug her and tell her that he loved her. But she'd sent him away, hadn't she? She'd told him that she didn't want him in her life.

She grabbed his hand and closed her eyes. 'I'm scared—' She broke off as another pain hit her and he waited for it to pass and then gently disengaged himself and stood up.

'Where are you going?' There was a distinct note of panic in her voice and he gave her a reassuring smile.

'For some reason unknown to me, I have a sterile cord clamp in my car so I'm going to fetch that and then I'm going to wash my hands. I think I'm about to deliver a baby.'

She closed her eyes with a groan of denial. 'I can't believe this is happening.' Then she gave a gasp. 'Jake! I want to push. Oh—I can feel the head.'

'Don't push until I've washed my hands.' He strode out of the room but was back moments later with an armful of towels and sheets.

'I *can* feel the head, Jake.' She grabbed his hand again, 'I'm scared.'

'There's nothing to be scared about. Miranda, I just need to take a look and see what's happening.' His voice was gentle and calm and suddenly she wasn't embarrassed any more, she was just worried.

It wasn't supposed to be like this.

'It's far too quick! Don't let anything happen to the baby. What if the cord is round the neck? What if there's something wrong with the foetal heart and we don't even know because I'm not on a monitor?' The words came out in a rush and she broke off as another pain hit and the desire to push was so intense that she could do nothing except follow the instructions of her body.

'The head's coming now, Miranda. Stop pushing. Stop pushing, angel. Pant, that's right… Good girl. Everything's fine.'

She closed her eyes tightly and tried to get her breath back but then another pain swamped her and her body pushed the baby out and into Jake's waiting arms. The baby howled angrily and Miranda sat back with a rush of relief.

'Is the baby all right?' She felt completely shocked by the

speed and violence of it all. If Jake hadn't been there, she didn't know what she would have done.

'Not a baby. A little girl, and she seems absolutely fine.' Jake's voice was strangely flat. 'She's beautiful. Well done.'

He placed the baby carefully in her arms and she stared down at the tiny, perfect features with wonder in her eyes. The howls turned to whimpers as the baby nuzzled Miranda's breast.

'Good idea.' Brisk and businesslike, Jake settled himself into a more comfortable position. 'Feed her, Miranda, if you can. I don't have any drugs with me. Nothing to help your uterus contract so we're going to have to do this the way that nature intended as well. Physiological third stage. Feed her. It will help your uterus contract.'

Some women opted to have a physiological third stage, but Miranda knew that the risks of bleeding were greater and understood why Jake was now paying her more attention than ever. He was worried that she might bleed and he had no access to a telephone.

He was a doctor doing his job.

And he didn't seem at all interested in the baby.

She undid the buttons of her maternity dress and gently lifted the baby to her breast. With remarkably little encouragement, the baby latched onto her nipple and sucked happily. Miranda breathed a sigh of relief but suddenly the happiness of the birth mingled with despair. She wanted to say something, want to speak, but none of the words in her head felt right.

Seemingly oblivious to her emotional state, Jake slid a hand over her abdomen, checking her uterus. 'Everything feels fine.'

And everything was fine. The placenta came away easily and Jake breathed a sigh of relief.

'I don't know what you midwives complain about.' He dragged a forearm over his forehead and gave a lopsided smile. 'Piece of cake. I'm just going to wash my hands and find another heater to put in here. This room isn't warm enough for her.'

He vanished for a moment and the returned with two heaters, a drink for Miranda and the phone in his hand.

'The phone's working again. I want you to go into hospital, Miranda. She looks fine to me and you look fine, too, but it was all a bit quick for my liking and the roads are so bad that we wouldn't be able to get you to hospital in a hurry if it suddenly became necessary.'

Miranda frowned. 'Do I have to?'

'Just for tonight. Oh, by the way, there was a message on the machine. Someone about a flat. The landlord told you it wasn't available until the spring but apparently the tenants have found somewhere else and are moving today, so it's yours whenever you want it.'

She waited for him to say something about not wanting her to leave but he said nothing at all, just finished clearing up, fetched her a few things that he knew she'd need and made a few notes to give to the ambulance crew.

And he still didn't look at the baby.

Which meant only one thing as far as she was concerned. He wasn't interested in her, Miranda thought miserably, holding back the tears that threatened.

It was late the following afternoon when Jake walked up to the side room. In his arms were a teddy bear and a huge bunch of flowers.

This, he decided as he put a hand on the door and steeled himself to open it, was going to be one of the hardest five minutes of his life.

He was going to deliver the flowers, say all the things he was expected to say and then just get out as fast as he could, hopefully before he made a complete and utter fool of himself.

Taking a deep breath, he pushed open the door and walked into the room, a smile pinned on his face. The smile faded instantly when he saw that the room was empty.

And then he heard a faint gurgle coming from the cot by the bed and he realised that the room wasn't empty at all. The baby was in the cot. But there was no sign of Miranda.

Wondering why he was intent on torturing himself, he stepped over to the cot and stared down.

The baby lay with her eyes closed, her tiny mouth moving in her sleep.

Jake felt his heart twist. 'Hi, there.' His voice was soft as he reached down and touched her cheek. 'It's nice to meet you properly.'

Miranda paused in the doorway of her bathroom, her eyes on Jake.

He obviously didn't realise she was in the room and he was talking to the baby. *Touching her.*

'I didn't get a good look at you yesterday,' he was saying softly, a gentle look in his eyes as he leaned over the cot. 'I was too busy worrying about your mum.'

Miranda frowned. He'd been worried about her? He certainly hadn't seemed worried.

The baby gurgled sleepily and Jake smiled. 'You're going to make your mum very happy. Which is a good thing, because it's what she deserves.'

'Jake?' Miranda stepped into the room and he turned to face her, his eyes suddenly wary.

'I didn't know you were there.'

'I was using the bathroom.' She looked at him. 'I—I heard what you said. I didn't know you were worried about me.'

He gave a faint smile. 'You were eavesdropping on a private conversation.'

'Why were you worried? You're a brilliant obstetrician and I've never known you worry about anyone before.'

He stared at her for a long moment and then he gave a humourless laugh. 'I've never been called on to deliver the baby of the woman I love before. Believe me, it's entirely different. Objectivity flies out of the window. I was scared to death.'

Her heart fluttered in her chest. 'The woman you love?'

He shook his head and gave a weary smile. 'I can't argue this with you again, Miranda.' He handed her the flowers and put the teddy bear down on the bed. 'These are for you. I know you'll be coming home later, but everyone needs flowers when they're in hospital. And now I ought to go. I have a clinic and—'

'The clinic can wait.' She clutched the flowers against her chest, her breathing unsteady. 'You haven't told me that you love me since that night we made love. And yesterday, when the baby was born, you hardly looked at her. I assumed that I'd ruined everything. That you'd changed your mind. About her and about me.'

He was silent for a moment and then he ran a hand over the back of his neck, visibly tense. 'Does it really make any difference how I feel, Miranda?'

'Actually, yes, it does.' Her voice cracked and she found herself hoping that the baby wouldn't wake up for a few minutes. There were things that she needed to say, things that were so difficult for her she couldn't risk being interrupted.

But Jake spoke first. 'All right. I wasn't going to say this now. Giving birth is an emotional time for a woman and I wanted to give you some space, but I may as well be honest. You're right when you said that I didn't look at the baby. I didn't. And the reason for that was that I didn't dare. I knew that if I looked at her, all attempts at being one step removed and functioning as an obstetrician would fly out of the window. You gave birth very quickly, Miranda.' His tone was quiet and serious. 'No end of things could have gone wrong and I wanted to make sure that they didn't. I couldn't afford the distraction.'

'And that's why you seemed so detached? Uninterested?'

He walked across to the window and stared out across the hospital car park. 'I wasn't uninterested.'

'What then?'

'It was self-protection.' He turned. 'Because if I'd looked at the baby then I would have fallen in love with her and I can't afford to do that. It's bad enough losing you, without losing her as well.'

'Losing me?'

'You're moving out and you're taking the baby with you. And I don't know how to stop you. I don't know how to prove to you that I love you and I don't know how to prove to you that I love your daughter.'

'I thought it was too late. I thought you'd changed your mind.' Miranda closed her eyes and allowed the happiness to flood through her. 'All night I lay awake, fantasising about you saying those words.'

He frowned. 'Why would you have to fantasise when you knew how I felt?'

'Because I thought you'd changed your mind. You were so cool and detached when you delivered her, I thought that reality had finally hit home. It seemed as though you couldn't wait to get the pair of us out of your house and into hospital.'

'In a way I couldn't,' he confessed. 'I didn't want to put more pressure on you at that particular moment when all your attention should have been on your new baby. And you'd already made it clear how you felt.'

'No.' She shook her head. 'That isn't true. I told you about my fears. I told myself that I had to protect the baby at all costs. What I didn't tell you was that I love you, too. I knew it weeks ago, but I knew if I admitted it you'd never take no for an answer.'

He stilled. 'But if you loved me, why would you want me to take no for an answer?'

'Because I have a responsibility towards my daughter. I'm responsible for her happiness. I thought that promise meant never marrying anyone.' She put the flowers down carefully. 'But then I realised that my daughter's happiness might involve giving her an amazing father. You. I was ready to tell you last night but then I went into labour.'

For a moment he just stood there, staring at her, and then he muttered something under his breath, crossed the room and hauled her into his arms.

'I can't believe you're saying those words,' he groaned against her neck. 'I've been planning my next move with the precision of a military campaign. I've been planning ways to persuade you to trust me enough to marry me.'

'You don't need a military campaign. I trust you, Jake.' She slid her arms round his neck. 'I love you.'

'And I love you.' He lowered his mouth to hers and kissed her long and hard. Then he lifted his head and stroked her hair away from her face. 'How could you possibly think my feelings had changed?'

'I pushed you away—I assumed you'd given up.'

He gave a slow smile. 'I don't give up easily, sweetheart. You should know that about me by now.' He studied her face for a long moment and his smile faded. 'It's important that you understand that. No matter what happens, nothing is going to stop me loving you and the baby. Nothing.'

'You've no idea how it feels to hear you say that.'

'Well, you'd better get used to it because I'm going to be saying it all the time. And what about you?' He hugged her closer. 'As a matter of interest, what changed your mind?'

'I didn't exactly change my mind. I knew I loved you. The only thing that changed was that I decided to tell you. Last night Christy came to see me and after she left I sat in the dark and did a lot of thinking.'

He gave a short laugh. 'That explains the mess in my kitchen. I wondered where the scones came from.'

'She told me a few things. Things that I already knew. Things I was allowing myself to ignore because of Keith.'

'What things?'

'That you're a good man. That you were fully aware of the responsibility you'd be taking on, that if you said you wanted the baby, too, you meant it…'

He frowned and his gaze turned to the cot where the baby lay sleeping. 'It doesn't feel like a responsibility, Miranda. It feels like a gift.'

At that moment the baby woke up and started to whimper. Miranda smiled at Jake. 'Go on, then—if you're going to be her father, you'd better start getting to know her.'

'Have you thought of a name? I can't keep calling her "the baby".'

Miranda brushed her hair out of her eyes. 'Can we call her Hope?'

'Hope Blackwell.' Jake said it slowly and then nodded. 'Hope. Sounds good. What made you think of it?'

She hesitated. 'It's what you've given me. When we met on Christmas Day I was in the depths of despair. I was cold, lost and completely alone,' she said softly, 'and then you appeared out of the mist. And from then on, no matter how many times I tried to push you away, you were always by my side. And that made everything better. I'd grown up believing that happy families were an illusion, but you've convinced me that I'm wrong.'

He smiled and lifted the baby out of the cot. 'So are you giving me Hope or am I giving you Hope?'

'Both.' She watched him. Watched the tender way he held the baby. How could she have doubted him? Feeling ridiculously happy, she sat down in the chair and prepared to feed the baby. 'I'd better ring that man and tell him I no longer want the flat.'

'No need.' Jake placed the baby carefully in her arms. 'I've already done it.'

'You have?' Her eyes widened. 'Why?'

'Because there was no way I was letting you move out! I was buying myself more time.'

She shook her head in amazement. 'You're manipulative, do you know that? Some might even call you arrogant.'

'The word is constant.' He leaned forward and kissed her. 'I'm in love, Miranda. And seeing the baby just doubled my determination to marry you. Two for the price of one. My girls. I love you.'

'And I love you, too.'

* * * * *

Read on for a sneak preview of Sarah's next book
Summer Kisses
coming summer 2012

THEY were all staring.

He could feel them staring even though he stood with his back to them, his legs braced against the slight roll of the ferry, his eyes fixed firmly on the ragged coastline of the approaching island.

The whispers and speculation had started from the moment he'd ridden his motorbike onto the ferry. *From the moment he'd removed his helmet and allowed them to see his face.*

Some of the passengers were tourists, using the ferry as a means to spend a few days or weeks on the wild Scottish island of Glenmore, but many were locals, taking advantage of their only transport link with the mainland.

And the locals knew him. Even after an absence of twelve years, they recognised him.

They remembered him for all the same reasons that he remembered them.

Their faces were filed away in his subconscious; deep scars on his soul.

He probably should have greeted them; islanders were sociable people and a smile and a 'hello' might have begun to bridge the gulf that stretched between them. But his firm mouth didn't shift and the chill in his ice blue eyes didn't thaw.

And that was the root of the problem, he brooded silently as he studied the deadly rocks that had protected this part of the coastline for centuries. He wasn't sociable. He didn't care what they thought of him. He'd never been interested in courting the good opinion of others and he'd never considered himself an islander, even though he'd been born on Glenmore and had spent the first eighteen years of his life trapped within the confines of its rocky shores.

He had no wish to exchange small talk or make friends. Neither did he intend to explain his presence. They'd find out what he was doing here soon enough. It was inevitable. But, for now, he dismissed their shocked glances as inconsequential and enjoyed his last moments of self-imposed isolation.

The first drops of rain sent the other passengers scuttling inside for protection but he didn't move. Instead he stood still, staring bleakly at the ragged shores of the island, just visible through the rain-lashed mist. The land was steeped in lore and legend, with a long, bloody history of Viking invasion.

Locals believed that the island had a soul and a personality. They believed that the unpredictable weather was Glenmore expressing her many moods.

He glanced up at the angry sky with a cynical smile. If that was the case then today she was definitely menopausal.

Or maybe, like the islanders, she'd seen his return and was crying.

The island loomed out of the mist and he stared ahead, seeing dark memories waiting on the shore. *Memories of wild teenage years; of anger and defiance.* His past was a stormy canvas of rules broken, boundaries exploded, vices explored, girls seduced—*far too many girls seduced*—and all against an atmosphere of intense disapproval from the locals who'd thought his parents should have had more control.

Remembering the vicious, violent atmosphere of his home, he gave a humourless laugh. His father hadn't been capable of controlling himself, let alone him. After his mother had left, he'd spent as little time in the house as possible.

The rain was falling heavily as the ferry docked and he

turned up the collar of his leather jacket and moved purposefully towards his motorbike.

He could have replaced his helmet and assured himself a degree of privacy from the hostile stares, but instead he paused for a moment, the wicked streak inside him making sure that they had more than enough time to take one more good look at his face. He didn't want there to be any doubt in their minds. He wanted them to know that he was back.

Let them stare and speculate. It would save him the bother of announcing his return.

With a smooth, athletic movement, he settled his powerful body onto the motorbike and caught the eye of the ferryman, acknowledging his disbelieving stare with a slight inclination of his head. He knew exactly what old Jim was thinking—*that the morning ferry had brought trouble to Glenmore*. And news of trouble spread fast on this island. As if to confirm his instincts, he caught a few words from the crush of people preparing to leave the ferry. *Arrogant, wild, unstable, volatile, handsome as the devil...*

He pushed the helmet down onto his head with his gloved hands. Luckily for him, plenty of women were attracted to arrogant, wild, unstable, volatile men, or his life would have been considerably more boring than it had been.

From behind the privacy of his helmet, he smiled, knowing exactly what would happen next. The rumours would spread like ripples in a pond. Within minutes, news of his arrival would have spread across the island. Ferryman to fisherman, fisherman to shopkeeper, shopkeeper to customer—it would take no time at all for the entire population of the island to be informed of the latest news—that Conner MacNeil had come in on the morning ferry.

The Bad Boy was back on the Island.

© Sarah Morgan 2008

Have Your Say

You've just finished your book.
So what did you think?

We'd love to hear your thoughts on our
'Have your say' online panel
www.millsandboon.co.uk/haveyoursay

- 🌹 Easy to use
- 🌹 Short questionnaire
- 🌹 Chance to win Mills & Boon®
  goodies

Visit us Online

Tell us what you thought of this book now at
www.millsandboon.co.uk/haveyoursay